The

Shields whipped [...]
space with us pronto- [...]
every man we could [...]
clear before we swung into Earth's shadow. Weightlessness
is an unbelievable advantage in handling freight.

Once the freight was all out and snapped to our cargo
line I sent the men back by the same line, then I told
Shields to send over the passenger and cast off.

This little guy came out the ship's air lock, and hooked
on to the ship's line. Handling himself like he was used to
space, he set his feet and dived, straight along the
stretched line, his snap hook running free.

Besides the usual cargo lock we had three GE
Kwikloks.

A Kwiklok is an Iron Maiden without spikes; it fits a
man in a suit, leaving just a few pints of air to scavenge,
and cycles automatically. A big time saver in changing
shifts. I passed through the middlesized one; Tiny, of
course, used the big one. Without hesitation the new man
pulled himself into the small one.

We went into Tiny's office. Tiny strapped down, and
pushed his helmet back. "Well, McNye," he said to the
new man, "Glad to have you with us."

The new radio tech opened his helmet. I heard a low,
pleasant voice answer, "Thank you."

I stared and didn't say anything. From where I was I
could see that the radio tech was wearing a hair ribbon.

—from "Delilah and the Space-Rigger"

**Baen Books by
Robert A. Heinlein**

Assignment in Eternity
Beyond This Horizon
Between Planets
Farmer in the Sky
Farnham's Freehold
The Green Hills of Earth
The Green Hills of Earth & The Menace from Earth
(omnibus)
The Man Who Sold the Moon
The Menace from Earth
Orphans of the Sky
Revolt in 2100 & Methuselah's Children
Expanded Universe
The Rolling Stones
The Puppet Masters
Sixth Column (forthcoming)
Starman Jones (forthcoming)
Star Beast (forthcoming)

THE GREEN HILLS OF EARTH

THE MENACE FROM EARTH

ROBERT A. HEINLEIN

THE GREEN HILLS OF EARTH
AND THE MENACE FROM EARTH

The Green Hills of Earth copyright © 1951 by Robert A. Heinlein; *The Menace from Earth* copyright © 1959 by Robert A. Heinlein. Copyright © 2003 by the Robert A. and Virginia Heinlein Prize Trust. Introduction copyright © 2010 by William A. Patterson; Afterword copyright © 2010 by Robert Buettner.

A Baen Book

Baen Publishing Enterprises
P.O. Box 1403
Riverdale, NY 10471
www.baen.com

ISBN: 978-1-4391-3436-8

Cover art by Bob Eggleton

First Baen paperback printing, May 2011

Distributed by Simon & Schuster
1230 Avenue of the Americas
New York, NY 10020

Library of Congress Cataloging-in-Publication Data:
2009050677

Printed in the United States of America

10 9 8 7 6 5 4 3 2 1

Contents

Acknowledgment
The phrase *The Green Hills of Earth*
derives from a story by C. L. Moore
(Mrs. Henry Kuttner), and is used here
by her gracious permission
R. A. H.

Futures, Histories

by William H. Patterson, Jr.

The large-scale tapestry effect of a historical trend-line extrapolated into the future startled and delighted John W. Campbell, Jr., when Heinlein mentioned it in passing in 1940—and then startled, delighted, and even awed science fiction readers when Campbell published an expanded version of the Future History chart in May 1941. No one knew the concept of a Future! History! had been missing from science fiction until, suddenly, there it was.

Heinlein's Future History came together by accident, indirectly, and built on the work of predecessors. He mentioned Galsworthy's Forsyte Saga—and did not mention but was clearly influenced by James Branch Cabell's part-fantasy, part-realistic social satires of the Biography of the Life of Manuel.

The germ of Heinlein's own tapestry of the future, though, was the backstory he had created for his first novel, *For Us, the Living*, in 1938. Set in the twenty-first century, it gave its-history-our-future, and Heinlein used the backbone of that history-of-the-future to generate an entirely new line of stories. In the spring of 1939, Heinlein began assembling ideas for a try at writing for pulp and included incidents from that fictional history (along with some new-age ideas and even some shaggy dog stories). "Life-Line," the first story he sold, was not taken from that history-of-the-future, but his second story, "Misfit," was. The next six stories he wrote were not—and failed to sell.

A pattern was beginning to emerge.

By August 1939 Heinlein began to work up a novella he had started in the spring. "Vine and Fig Tree" was very much in the *For us, the Living* history-to-come—how the United States recovers from a religious dictatorship. He wanted to interconnect the various stories as he wrote them, mentioning names and incidents from one story in others. But there was so much accumulated detail that he found himself having to sift through his entire pile of notes whenever he wanted to drop such a reference. He thought of the method Sinclair Lewis said he used to organize his own interconnected stories and novels of the fictional city of Zenith in the equally fictional midwestern state of Winnemac: a wall chart.

"So I took an old navigation chart, about 3 x 4 feet," Heinlein related for his colleagues in the Science Fiction Writers of America *Bulletin* in 1975, "turned it over, made the time scale vertical, then set up five columns: stories, characters, technical data, sociological, remarks."

He transferred his notes to the chart, and when he was done he could see at a glance (always providing he could read his handwriting) just how everything related to everything else at the time of his story. The chart stayed on the wall by Heinlein's typewriter, "and was usually messy as I never took the chart down to add to it—just reached over and scrawled on it."

Casually, on his first trip to New York as a new-minted pulp writer, Heinlein mentioned the chart to Campbell, who thereafter nagged him to publish it—which he did in the May 1941 issue of *Astounding* (along with "Universe" and "Blowups Happen" in the same issue).

After World War II, Heinlein worked his stories for the prestige popular magazines into the Future History, and they defined the "middle years" of the progression, published by Shasta Press as the second volume of the Future History, *The Green Hills of Earth and Other Stories*. But *Destination Moon* and the *Post* stories made Heinlein a public figure, and his genre audience became an ever-shrinking proportion of his readership, finally vanishing altogether in the statistics of his last books, issued in million-copy pressings.

But the Future History would not go away, and one story in particular remained on Heinlein's "do-soon" agenda for twenty years. He might have written "Da Capo" for the Shasta Future History series in the early 1950s, but the restrictive contract Shasta wanted for "The Man Who Sold the Moon" turned out so expensive to Heinlein that he gave up the idea of writing any more of the novellas that would have filled the gaps in the Future History (the volume that became *The Green Hills of Earth and Other Stories,* for example, was originally conceived as *The Sound of His Wings*—the story of Nehemiah

Scudder's theocracy that would have preceded "If This Goes On—" The same volume was to have another freshly-written novella, "Fire Down Below," the story of a colonial revolution in Antarctica.

"Da Capo" would have been a very different story if written in the 1950s than it became in 1973 as the concluding section of Heinlein's most complex and ambitious book to date, *Time Enough for Love*.

But Heinlein was to become more ambitious yet in the 1980s. *The Number of the Beast* (1980) finds Lazarus Long and his Boon dock/Tellus Tertius family grown in scope to take in a war in the Cosmic All, across all the universes of all the fictions that could be—and all the realities that could be. The Future History was now one thread in the Multiverse, code-named Timeline: Leslie LeCroix (after the first man to set foot on the Moon. Our consensus reality was code-named Timeline: Neil Armstrong).

Although a few readers were disappointed by Heinlein's drawing together of all his writing into a single, coherent schema, he was simply acting out a basic literary drive: after all, what is T.S. Eliot's "order of literature"—one of the seminal critical insights of the twentieth century—if not an attempt to draw all literature of all times and languages into a single, coherent schema?

Heinlein's World as Myth allows us to see the related-ness to the Future History of all the stories of *The Menace From Earth*, not merely the title story (one of Heinlein's most engaging vignettes of life in an exciting time for the human race). "Columbus Was a Dope," we understand, and "Sky Lift" are happening somewhere else in the

Multiverse, somewhere quite close by the Future History. Other stories—"Water Is for Washing" and "Year of the Jackpot"—take place in universes further away—and possibly up a different space-time axis.

But never mind! *The Circle of Ouroboros* patrols all these universes and many more. And the *Time Corps* retrieves from all those times little treasures of story-teller's art, returning always to the home base Heinlein authored for himself: TIMELINE: LESLIE LECROIX.

THE GREEN HILLS OF EARTH

OF EARTH

THE MENACE FROM EARTH

The
Green Hills
of Earth

To My Parents

THE HEINLEIN TIMELINE

DATES	STORIES	CHARACTERS	TECHNICAL

A.D.

STORIES:

Life Line
"Let There Be Light"
(Word Edgewise)
The Roads Must Roll
Blowups Happen
The Man Who Sold the Moon

Delilah & the Space Rigger
Space Jockey
Requiem
The Long Watch
Gentlemen Be Seated
The Black Pits of Luna—
It's Great To Be Back
"—We Also Walk Dogs"
Searchlight

— 2000 —

Ordeal in Space
The Green Hills of Earth
(Fire Down Below)
Logic of Empire
The Menace From Earth
(The Sound Of His Wings)
(Eclipse)
(The Stone Pillow)
"If This Goes On—"
Coventry

— 2100 —

Misfit
Universe (prologue only)
Methuselah's Children
Universe
Commonsense
(Da Capo)

CHARACTERS:

Pinero
Martin +Douglas
Blekinsop
Wingate
Sam Jones
Satchel
Rhysling
Gaines
Nehemiah Scudder
Harper
Erickson
King
Lentz
Harriman
McIntyre
Cummings
Lazarus Long
Novak
Master Peter
Zeb Jones
John Lyle
Ford
Magelene
MacKinnon
"Fader" Randall
Persephone
The "Doctor"
Libby
McCoy
Rhodes
Doyle

TECHNICAL:

Douglas-Martin sun-power screens
Mechanized roads
Commercial rocket travel
Helicopter
Interplanetary Travel
Hiatus
Developments in psychometrics and psychodynamics
resumed
Limited Use of telepathy
Growth of submolar mechanics, atomic cont., artificial radioactives—Uranium 235—Static submolar engineering (parastatics)

DATA	SOCIOLOGY	REMARKS
Transatlantic rocket flight Antipodes rocket service	THE "CRAZY YEARS" Srike of '76 The "FALSE DAWN" First Rocket to the Moon	Considerable technical advance during this period, accompinied by a gradual deterioration of mores, orientation and social institutions, terminating in mass psychoses in the sixth decade, and the Interregnum.
	Luna City Founded Space Precautionary Act Harriman's Lunar Corporations PERIOD OF IMPERIAL EXPLORATION Revolution in Little America Interplanetary exploration and exploitation American—Australasian anschluss	The Interregnum was followed by a period of reconstruction in which the Voorhis financial proposals gave a temporary economic stability and chance for reorientation. This was ended by the opening of new frontiers and a return to nineteenth century economy. Three revolutions ended the period of planetary imperialism: Antarctica, U.S., and Venus. Space travel ceased until 2072.
Bacteriophage		Little research and only minor technical advances during this period. Extreme puritanism.
The Travel Unit and the Fighting Unit Commercial stereoptics Booster guns Synthetic foods Weather control Wave mechanics The "Barrier"	Rise of religious fanaticism The "New Crusade" Rebellion and independence of Venusian colonists Religious dictatorship in U.S. THE FIRST HUMAN CIVILIZATION	Certain aspects of psychodynamics and psychometrics, mass psychology and social control developed by the priest class. Re-establishment of civil liberty. Renaissance of scientific research. Resumption of space travel. Luna city refounded. Science of social relations, based on the negative statements of semantics. Rigor of epistemology. The Covenant.
Atomic "tailoring" Elements 98—416 Parastatic engineering Rigor of colloids Symbiotic research Longevity		Beginning of the consolidation of the Solar System First attempt at interstellar exploration Civil disorder, followed by the end of human adolescence, and the beginning of first mature culture.

Delilah and the Space-Rigger

SURE, we had trouble building Space Station One—but the trouble was people.

Not that building a station twenty-two thousand three hundred miles out in space is a breeze. It was an engineering feat bigger than the Panama Canal or the Pyramids—or even the Susquehanna Power Pile. But "Tiny" Larsen built her—and a job Tiny tackles gets built.

I first saw Tiny playing guard on a semi-pro team, working his way through Oppenheimer Tech. He worked summers for me thereafter till he graduated. He stayed in construction and eventually I went to work for him.

Tiny wouldn't touch a job unless he was satisfied with the engineering. The Station had jobs designed into it that called for six-armed monkeys instead of grown men in space suits. Tiny spotted such boners; not a ton of material went into the sky until the specs and drawings suited him.

But it was people that gave us the headaches. We had a sprinkling of married men, but the rest were wild kids,

7

attracted by high pay and adventure. Some were busted spacemen. Some were specialists, like electricians and instrument men. About half were deep-sea divers, used to working in pressure suits. There were sandhogs and riggers and welders and shipfitters and two circus acrobats.

We fired four of them for being drunk on the job; Tiny had to break one stiff's arm before he would stay fired. What worried us was where did they get it? Turned out a shipfitter had rigged a heatless still, using the vacuum around us. He was making vodka from potatoes swiped from the commissary. I hated to let him go, but he was too smart.

Since we were falling free in a 24-hour circular orbit, with everything weightless and floating, you'd think that shooting craps was impossible. But a radioman named Peters figured a dodge to substitute steel dice and a magnetic field. He also eliminated the element of chance, so we fired him.

We planned to ship him back in the next supply ship, the R. S. *Half Moon.* I was in Tiny's office when she blasted to match our orbit. Tiny swam to the view port. "Send for Peters, Dad," he said, "and give him the old heave ho. Who's his relief?"

"Party named G. Brooks McNye," I told him.

A line came snaking over from the ship. Tiny said, "I don't believe she's matched." He buzzed the radio shack for the ship's motion relative to the Station. The answer didn't please him and he told them to call the *Half Moon.*

Tiny waited until the TV screen showed the rocket ship's C.O. "Good morning, Captain. Why have you placed a line on us?"

"For cargo, naturally. Get your hopheads over here. I want to blast off before we enter the shadow." The Station spent about an hour and a quarter each day passing through Earth's shadow; we worked two eleven-hour shifts and skipped the dark period, to avoid rigging lights and heating suits.

Tiny shook his head. "Not until you've matched course and speed with us."

"I *am* matched!"

"Not to specification, by my instruments."

"Have a heart, Tiny! I'm short on maneuvering fuel. If I juggle this entire ship to make a minor correction on a few lousy tons of cargo, I'll be so late I'll have to put down on a secondary field. I may even have to make a dead-stick landing." In those days all ships had landing wings.

"Look, Captain," Tiny said sharply, "the only purpose of your lift was to match orbits for those same few lousy tons. I don't care if you land in Little America on a pogo stick. The first load here was placed with loving care in the proper orbit and I'm making every other load match. Get that covered wagon into the groove."

"Very well, Superintendent!" Captain Shields said stiffly.

"Don't be sore, Don," Tiny said softly. "By the way, you've got a passenger for me?"

"Oh, yes, so I have!" Shields' face broke out in a grin.

"Well, keep him aboard until we unload. Maybe we can beat the shadow yet."

"Fine, fine! After all, why should I add to your troubles?"

The skipper switched off, leaving my boss looking puzzled.

We didn't have time to wonder at his words. Shields whipped his ship around on gyros, blasted a second or two, and put her dead in space with us pronto—and used very little fuel, despite his bellyaching. I grabbed every man we could spare and managed to get the cargo clear before we swung into Earth's shadow. Weightlessness is an unbelievable advantage in handling freight; we gutted the *Half Moon*—by hand, mind you—in fifty-four minutes.

The stuff was oxygen tanks, loaded, and aluminum mirrors to shield them, panels of outer skin—sandwich stuff of titanium alloy sheet with foamed glass filling—and cases of jato units to spin the living quarters. Once it was all out and snapped to our cargo line I sent the men back by the same line—I won't let a man work outside without a line no matter how space happy he figures he is. Then I told Shields to send over the passenger and cast off.

This little guy came out the ship's air lock, and hooked on to the ship's line. Handling himself like he was used to space, he set his feet and dived, straight along the stretched line, his snap hook running free. I hurried back and motioned him to follow me. Tiny, the new man, and I reached the air locks together.

Besides the usual cargo lock we had three G. E. Kwikloks.

A Kwiklok is an Iron Maiden without spikes; it fits a man in a suit, leaving just a few pints of air to scavenge, and cycles automatically. A big time saver in changing shifts. I passed through the middlesized one; Tiny, of course, used the big one. Without hesitation the new man pulled himself into the small one.

We went into Tiny's office. Tiny strapped down, and

pushed his helmet back. "Well, McNye," he said. "Glad to have you with us."

The new radio tech opened his helmet. I heard a low, pleasant voice answer, "Thank you."

I stared and didn't say anything. From where I was I could see that the radio tech was wearing a hair ribbon.

I thought Tiny would explode. He didn't need to see the hair ribbon; with the helmet up it was clear that the new "man" was as female as Venus de Milo. Tiny sputtered, then he was unstrapped and diving for the view port. "Dad!" he yelled. "Get the radio shack. Stop that ship!"

But the *Half Moon* was already a ball of fire in the distance, Tiny looked dazed. "Dad," he said, "who else knows about this?"

"Nobody, so far as I know."

He thought a bit. "We've got to keep her out of sight. That's it—we keep her locked up and out of sight until the next ship matches in." He didn't look at her.

"What in the world are you talking about?" McNye's voice was higher and no longer pleasant.

Tiny glared. "You, that's what. What are you—a stowaway?"

"Don't be silly! I'm G. B. McNye, electronics engineer. Don't you have my papers?"

Tiny turned to me. "Dad, this is your fault. How in Chr—pardon me, Miss. How did you let them send you a woman? Didn't you even read the advance report on her?"

"Me?" I said. "Now see here, you big squarehead! Those forms don't show sex; the Fair Employment

Commission won't allow it except where it's pertinent to the job."

"You're telling *me* it's not pertinent to the job *here?*"

"Not by job classification it ain't. There's lots of female radio and radar men, back Earthside."

"This isn't Earthside." He had something. He was thinking of those two-legged wolves swarming over the job outside. And G. B. McNye was pretty. Maybe eight months of no women at all affected my judgment, but she would pass.

"I've even heard of female rocket pilots," I added, for spite.

"I don't care if you've heard of female archangels; I'll have no women here!"

"Just a minute!" If I was riled, *she* was plain sore. "You're the construction superintendent, are you not?"

"Yes," Tiny admitted.

"Very well, then, how do *you* know what sex I am?"

"Are you trying to deny that you are a woman?"

"Hardly! I'm proud of it. But officially you don't know what sex G. Brooks McNye is. That's why I use 'G' instead of Gloria. I don't ask favors."

Tiny grunted. "You won't get any. I don't know how you sneaked in, but get this, McNye, or Gloria, or whatever—you're fired. You go back on the next ship. Meanwhile we'll try to keep the men from knowing we've got a woman aboard."

I could see her count ten. "May I speak," she said finally, "or does your Captain Bligh act extend to that, too?"

"Say your say."

"I didn't sneak in. I am on the permanent staff of the

Station, Chief Communications Engineer. I took this vacancy myself to get to know the equipment while it was being installed. I'll live here eventually; I see no reason not to start now."

Tiny waved it away. "There'll be men and women both here—some day. Even kids. Right now it's stag and it'll stay that way."

"We'll see. Anyhow, you can't fire me; radio personnel don't work for you." She had a point; communicators and some other specialists were lent to the contractors, Five Companies, Incorporated, by Harriman Enterprises.

Tiny snorted. "Maybe I can't fire you; I can send you home. 'Requisitioned personnel must be satisfactory to the contractor.'—meaning me. Paragraph Seven, clause M; I wrote that clause myself."

"Then you know that if requisitioned personnel are refused without cause the contractor bears the replacement cost."

"I'll risk paying your fare home, but I won't have you here."

"You are most unreasonable!"

"Perhaps, but I'll decide what's good for the job. I'd rather have a dope peddler than have a woman sniffing around my boys!"

She gasped. Tiny knew he had said too much; he added, "Sorry, Miss. But that's it. You'll stay under cover until I can get rid of you."

Before she could speak I cut in. "Tiny—look behind you!"

Staring in the port was one of the riggers, his eyes bugged out. Three or four more floated up and joined him.

Then Tiny zoomed up to the port and they scattered like minnows. He scared them almost out of their suits; I thought he was going to shove his fists through the quartz.

He came back looking whipped. "Miss," he said, pointing, "wait in my room." When she was gone he added, "Dad, what'll we do?"

I said, "I thought you had made up your mind, Tiny."

"I have," he answered peevishly. "Ask the Chief Inspector to come in, will you?"

That showed how far gone he was. The inspection gang belonged to Harriman Enterprises, not to us, and Tiny rated them mere nuisances. Besides, Tiny was an Oppenheimer graduate; Dalrymple was from M.I.T.

He came in, brash and cheerful. "Good morning, Superintendent. Morning, Mr. Witherspoon. What can I do for you?"

Glumly, Tiny told the story. Dalrymple looked smug. "She's right, old man. You can send her back and even specify a male relief. But I can hardly endorse 'for proper cause' now, can I?"

"Damnation. Dalrymple, we can't have a woman around here!"

"A moot point. Not covered by contract, y'know."

"If your office hadn't sent us a crooked gambler as her predecessor I wouldn't be in this jam!"

"There, there! Remember the old blood pressure. Suppose we leave the endorsement open and arbitrate the cost. That's fair, eh?"

"I suppose so. Thanks."

"Not at all. But consider this: when you rushed Peters off before interviewing the newcomer, you cut yourself down to one operator. Hammond can't stand watch twenty-four hours a day."

"He can sleep in the shack. The alarm will wake him."

"I can't accept that. The home office and ships' frequencies must be guarded at all times. Harriman Enterprises has supplied a qualified operator; I am afraid you must use her for the time being."

Tiny will always cooperate with the inevitable; he said quietly, "Dad, she'll take first shift. Better put the married men on that shift."

Then he called her in. "Go to the radio shack and start makee-learnee, so that Hammond can go off watch soon. Mind what he tells you. He's a good man."

"I know," she said briskly. "I trained him."

Tiny bit his lip. The C.I. said, "The Superintendent doesn't bother with trivia—I'm Robert Dalrymple, Chief Inspector. He probably didn't introduce his assistant either—Mr. Witherspoon."

"Call me Dad," I said.

She smiled and said, "Howdy, Dad." I felt warm clear through. She went on to Dalrymple, "Odd that we haven't met before."

Tiny butted in. "McNye, you'll sleep in my room—"

She raised her eyebrows; he went on angrily, "Oh, I'll get my stuff out—at once. And get this: keep the door locked, off shift."

"You're darn tootin' I will!" Tiny blushed.

I was too busy to see much of Miss Gloria. There was cargo to stow, the new tanks to install and shield. That left the most worrisome task of all: putting spin on the living quarters. Even the optimists didn't expect much interplanetary traffic for some years; nevertheless Harriman Enterprises wanted to get some activities moved in and paying rent against their enormous investment.

I.T.&T. had leased space for a microwave relay station—several million a year from television alone. The Weather Bureau was itching to set up its hemispheric integrating station; Palomar Observatory had a concession (Harriman Enterprises donated that space); the Security Council had some hush-hush project; Fermi Physical Labs and Kettering Institute each had space—a dozen tenants wanted to move in now, or sooner, even if we never completed accommodations for tourists and travelers.

There were time bonuses in it for Five Companies, Incorporated—and their help. So we were in a hurry to get spin on the quarters.

People who have never been out have trouble getting through their heads—at least I had—that there is no feeling of weight, no up and down, in a free orbit in space. There's Earth, round and beautiful, only twenty-odd thousand miles away, close enough to brush your sleeve. You know it's pulling you towards it. Yet you feel no weight, absolutely none. You float.

Floating is fine for some types of work, but when it's time to eat, or play cards, or bathe, it's good to feel weight on your feet. Your dinner stays quiet and you feel more natural.

You've seen pictures of the Station—a huge cylinder, like a bass drum, with ships' nose pockets dimpling its sides. Imagine a snare drum, spinning around inside the bass drum; that's the living quarters, with centrifugal force pinch-hitting for gravity. We could have spun the whole Station but you can't berth a ship against a whirling dervish.

So we built a spinning part for creature comfort and an outer, stationary part for docking, tanks, storerooms, and the like. You pass from one to the other at the hub. When Miss Gloria joined us the inner part was closed in and pressurized, but the rest was a skeleton of girders.

Mighty pretty though, a great network of shiny struts and ties against black sky and stars—titanium alloy 1403, light, strong, and non-corrodable. The Station is flimsy compared with a ship, since it doesn't have to take blastoff stresses. That meant we didn't dare put on spin by violent means—which is where jato units come in.

"Jato"—Jet Assisted Take-Off—rocket units invented to give airplanes a boost. Now we use them wherever a controlled push is needed, say to get a truck out of the mud on a dam job. We mounted four thousand of them around the frame of the living quarters, each one placed just so. They were wired up and ready to fire when Tiny came to me looking worried. "Dad," he said, "let's drop everything and finish compartment D-113."

"Okay," I said. D-113 was in the non-spin part.

"Rig an air lock and stock it with two weeks supplies."

"That'll change your mass distribution for spin," I suggested.

"I'll refigure it next dark period. Then we'll shift jatos."

When Dalrymple heard about it he came charging around. It meant a delay in making rental space available. "What's the idea?"

Tiny stared at him. They had been cooler than ordinary lately; Dalrymple had been finding excuses to seek out Miss Gloria. He had to pass through Tiny's office to reach her temporary room, and Tiny had finally told him to get out and stay out. "The idea," Tiny said slowly, "is to have a pup tent in case the house burns."

"What do you mean?"

"Suppose we fire up the jatos and the structure cracks? Want to hang around in a space suit until a ship happens by?"

"That's silly. The stresses have been calculated."

"That's what the man said when the bridge fell. We'll do it my way."

Dalrymple stormed off.

Tiny's efforts to keep Gloria fenced up were sort of pitiful. In the first place, the radio tech's biggest job was repairing suit walkie-talkies, done on watch. A rash of such troubles broke out—on her shift. I made some shift transfers and docked a few for costs, too; it's not proper maintenance when a man deliberately busts his aerial.

There were other symptoms. It became stylish to shave. Men started wearing shirts around quarters and bathing increased to where I thought I would have to rig another water still.

Came the shift when D-113 was ready and the jatos readjusted. I don't mind saying I was nervous. All hands were ordered out of the quarters and into suits. They perched around the girders and waited.

Men in space suits all look alike; we used numbers and colored armbands. Supervisors had two antennas, one for a gang frequency, one for the supervisors' circuit. With

Tiny and me the second antenna hooked back through the radio shack and to all the gang frequencies—a broadcast.

The supervisors had reported their men clear of the fireworks and I was about to give Tiny the word, when this figure came climbing through the girders, inside the danger zone. No safety line. No armband. One antenna.

Miss Gloria, of course. Tiny hauled her out of the blast zone, and anchored her with his own safety line. I heard his voice, harsh in my helmet: "Who do you think you are? A sidewalk superintendent?"

And her voice: "What do you expect me to do? Go park on a star?"

"I told you to stay away from the job. If you can't obey orders, I'll lock you up."

I reached him, switched off my radio and touched helmets. "Boss! Boss!" I said. "You're broadcasting!"

"Oh—" he says, switches off, and touches helmets with her. We could still hear her; she didn't switch off. "Why, you big baboon, I came outside because you sent a search party to clear everybody out," and, "How would I know about a safety line rule? You've kept me penned up." And finally. "We'll see!"

I dragged him away and he told the boss electrician to go ahead. Then we forgot the row for we were looking at the prettiest fireworks ever seen, a giant St. Catherine's wheel, rockets blasting all over it. Utterly soundless, out there in space—but beautiful beyond compare.

The blasts died away and there was the living quarters, spinning true as a flywheel—Tiny and I both let out sighs of relief. We all went back inside then to see what weight tasted like.

It tasted funny. I went through the shaft and started down the ladders, feeling myself gain weight as I neared the rim. I felt seasick, like the first time I experienced no weight. I could hardly walk and my calves cramped.

We inspected throughout, then went to the office and sat down. It felt good, just right for comfort, one-third gravity at the rim. Tiny rubbed his chair arms and grinned, "Beats being penned up in D-l13."

"Speaking of being penned up," Miss Gloria said, walking in, "may I have a word with you, Mr. Larsen?"

"Uh? Why, certainly. Matter of fact, I wanted to see you. I owe you an apology, Miss McNye. I was—"

"Forget it," she cut in. "You were on edge. But I want to know this: how long are you going to keep up this nonsense of trying to chaperone me?"

He studied her. "Not long. Just till your relief arrives."

"So? Who is the shop steward around here?"

"A shipfitter named McAndrews. But you can't use him. You're a staff member."

"Not in the job I'm filling. I am going to talk to him. You're discriminating against me, and in my off time at that."

"Perhaps, but you will find I have the authority. Legally I'm a ship's captain, while on this job. A captain in space has wide discriminatory powers."

"Then you should use them with discrimination!"

He grinned. "Isn't that what you just said I was doing?"

We didn't hear from the shop steward, but Miss Gloria started doing as she pleased. She showed up at the movies, next off shift, with Dalrymple. Tiny left in the middle—good show, too; *Lysistrata Goes to Town,* relayed up from New York.

As she was coming back alone he stopped her, having seen to it that I was present. "Umm—Miss McNye . . ."

"Yes?"

"I think you should know, uh, well . . . Chief Inspector Dalrymple is a married man."

"Are you suggesting that my conduct has been improper?"

"No but—"

"Then mind your own business!" Before he could answer she added, "It might interest you that he told me about your four children."

Tiny sputtered. "Why . . . why, I'm not even married!"

"So? That makes it worse, doesn't it?" She swept out.

Tiny quit trying to keep her in her room, but told her to notify him whenever she left it. It kept him busy riding herd on her. I refrained from suggesting that he get Dalrymple to spell him.

But I was surprised when he told me to put through the order dismissing her. I had been pretty sure he was going to drop it.

"What's the charge?" I asked.

"Insubordination!"

I kept mum. He said, "Well, she won't take orders."

"She does her work okay. You give her orders you wouldn't give to one of the men—and that a man wouldn't take."

"You disagree with my orders?"

"That's not the point. You can't prove the charge, Tiny."

"Well, charge her with being female! I can prove *that*."

I didn't say anything. "Dad," he added wheedlingly, "you know how to write it. 'No personal animus against Miss McNye, but it is felt that as a matter of policy, and so forth and so on.'"

I wrote it and gave it to Hammond privately. Radio techs are sworn to secrecy but it didn't surprise me when I was stopped by O'Connor, one of our best metalsmiths. "Look, Dad, is it true that the Old Man is getting rid of Brooksie?"

"Brooksie?"

"Brooksie McNye—says to call her Brooks. Is it true?"

I admitted it, then went on, wondering if I should have lied.

It takes four hours, about, for a ship to lift from Earth. The shift before the *Pole Star* was due, with Miss Gloria's relief, the timekeeper brought me two separation slips. Two men were nothing; we averaged more each ship. An hour later he reached me by supervisors' circuit, and asked me to come to the time office. I was out on the rim, inspecting a weld job; I said no. "*Please*, Mr. Witherspoon," he begged, "you've *got* to." When one of the boys doesn't call me "Dad," it means something. I went.

There was a queue like mail call outside his door; I went in and he shut the door on them. He handed me a double handful of separation slips. "What in the great depths of night is this?" I asked.

"There's dozens more I ain't had time to write up yet."

None of the slips had any reason given—just "own choice."

"Look, Jimmie—what goes on here?"

"Can't you dope it out, Dad? Shucks, I'm turning in one, too."

I told him my guess and he admitted it. So I took the slips, called Tiny and told him for the love of Heaven to come to his office.

Tiny chewed his lip considerable. "But, Dad, they *can't* strike. It's a non-strike contract with bonds from every union concerned."

"It's no strike, Tiny. You can't stop a man from quitting."

"They'll pay their own fares back, so help me!"

"Guess again. Most of 'em have worked long enough for the free ride."

"We'll have to hire others quick, or we'll miss our date."

"Worse than that, Tiny—we won't finish. By next dark period you won't even have a maintenance crew."

"I've never had a gang of men quit me. I'll talk to them."

"No good, Tiny. You're up against something too strong for you."

"*You're* against me, Dad?"

"I'm never against you, Tiny."

He said, "Dad, you think I'm pig-headed, but I'm *right*. You can't have one woman among several hundred men. It drives 'em nutty."

I didn't say it affected him the same way; I said, "Is that bad?"

"Of course. I can't let the job be ruined to humor one woman."

"Tiny, have you looked at the progress charts lately?"

"I've hardly had time to—what about them?"

I knew why he hadn't had time. "You'll have trouble proving Miss Gloria interfered with the job. We're ahead of schedule."

"We *are?*"

While he was studying the charts I put an arm around his shoulder. "Look, son," I said, "sex has been around our planet a long time. Earthside, they never get away from it, yet some pretty big jobs get built anyhow. Maybe we'll just have to learn to live with it here, too. Matter of fact, you had the answer a minute ago."

"I did? I sure didn't know it."

"You said, 'You can't have *one* woman among several hundred men.' Get me?"

"Huh? No, I don't. Wait a minute! Maybe I do."

"Ever tried jiu jitsu? Sometimes you win by relaxing."

"Yes. Yes!"

"When you can't beat 'em, you jine 'em."

He buzzed the radio shack. "Have Hammond relieve you, McNye, and come to my office."

He did it handsomely, stood up and made a speech— he'd been wrong, taken him a long time to see it, hoped there were no hard feelings, etc. He was instructing the home office to see how many jobs could be filled at once with female help. "Don't forget married couples," I put in mildly, "and better ask for some older women, too."

"I'll do that," Tiny agreed. "Have I missed anything, Dad?"

"Guess not. We'll have to rig quarters, but there's time."

"Okay. I'm telling them to hold the *Pole Star,* Gloria, so they can send us a few this trip."

"That's fine!" She looked really happy.

He chewed his lip. "I've a feeling I've missed something. Hmm—I've got it. Dad, tell them to send up a chaplain for the Station, as soon as possible. Under the new policy we may need one anytime." I thought so, too.

Space Jockey

JUST as they were leaving the telephone called his name. "Don't answer it," she pleaded. "We'll miss the curtain."

"Who is it?" he called out. The viewplate lighted; he recognized Olga Pierce, and behind her the Colorado Springs office of Trans-Lunar Transit.

"Calling Mr. Pemberton. Calling—Oh, it's you, Jake. You're on. Flight 27, Supra-New York to Space Terminal. I'll have a copter pick you up in twenty minutes."

"How come?" he protested. "I'm fourth down on the call board."

"You *were* fourth down. Now you are standby pilot to Hicks—and he just got a psycho down-check."

"Hicks got psychoed? That's silly!"

"Happens to the best, chum. Be ready. 'Bye now."

His wife was twisting sixteen dollars worth of lace handkerchief to a shapeless mass. "Jake, this is ridiculous. For three months I haven't seen enough of you to know what you look like."

27

"Sorry, kid. Take Helen to the show."

"Oh, Jake, I don't care about the show; I wanted to get you where they couldn't reach you for once."

"They would have called me at the theater."

"Oh, no! I wiped out the record you'd left."

"Phyllis! Are you trying to get me fired?"

"Don't look at me that way." She waited, hoping that he would speak, regretting the side issue, and wondering how to tell him that her own fretfulness was caused, not by disappointment, but by gnawing worry for his safety every time he went out into space.

She went on desperately, "You don't have to take this flight, darling; you've been on Earth less than the time limit. Please, Jake!"

He was peeling off his tux. "I've told you a thousand times: a pilot doesn't get a regular run by playing space-lawyer with the rule book. Wiping out my follow-up message—why did you do it, Phyllis? Trying to ground me?"

"No, darling, but I thought just this once—"

"When they offer me a flight I take it." He walked stiffly out of the room.

He came back ten minutes later, dressed for space and apparently in good humor; he was whistling: "—the caller called Casey at ha' past four; he kissed his—" He broke off when he saw her face, and set his mouth, "Where's my coverall?"

"I'll get it. Let me fix you something to eat."

"You know I can't take high acceleration on a full stomach. And why lose thirty bucks to lift another pound?"

Dressed as he was, in shorts, singlet, sandals, and pocket belt, he was already good for about minus-fifty pounds in weight bonus; she started to tell him the weight penalty on a sandwich and a cup of coffee did not matter to them, but it was just one more possible cause for misunderstanding.

Neither of them said much until the taxicab clumped on the roof. He kissed her goodbye and told her not to come outside. She obeyed—until she heard the helicopter take off. Then she climbed to the roof and watched it out of sight.

The traveling-public gripes at the lack of direct Earth-to-Moon service, but it takes three types of rocket ships and two space-station changes to make a fiddling quarter-million-mile jump for a good reason: Money.

The Commerce Commission has set the charges for the present three-stage lift from here to the Moon at thirty dollars a pound. Would direct service be cheaper?—a ship designed to blast off from Earth, make an airless landing on the Moon, return and make an atmosphere landing, would be so cluttered up with heavy special equipment used only once in the trip that it could not show a profit at a thousand dollars a pound! Imagine combining a ferry boat, a subway train, and an express elevator—

So Trans-Lunar uses rockets braced for catapulting, and winged for landing on return to Earth to make the terrific lift from Earth to our satellite station Supra-New York. The long middle lap, from there to where Space Terminal circles the Moon, calls for comfort—but no landing gear. The *Flying Dutchman* and the *Philip Nolan* never land; they were even assembled in space, and they resemble winged rockets like the *Skysprite* and the *Firefly* as little as a Pullman train resembles a parachute.

The *Moonbat* and the *Gremlin* are good only for the jump from Space Terminal down to Luna . . . no wings, cocoon-like acceleration-and-crash hammocks, fractional controls on their enormous jets.

The change-over points would not have to be more than air-conditioned tanks. Of course Space Terminal is quite a city, what with the Mars and Venus traffic, but even today Supra-New York is still rather primitive, hardly more than a fueling point and a restaurant-waiting room. It has only been the past five years that it has even been equipped to offer the comfort of one-gravity centrifuge service to passengers with queasy stomachs.

Pemberton weighed in at the spaceport office, then hurried over to where the *Skysprite* stood cradled in the catapult. He shucked off his coverall, shivered as he handed it to the gateman, and ducked inside. He went to his acceleration hammock and went to sleep; the lift to Supra-New York was not his worry—his job was deep space.

He woke at the surge of the catapult and the nerve-tingling rush up the face of Pikes Peak. When the *Skysprite* went into free flight, flung straight up above the Peak, Pemberton held his breath; if the rocket jets failed to fire, the ground-to-space pilot must try to wrestle her into a glide and bring her down, on her wings.

The rockets roared on time; Jake went back to sleep.

When the *Skysprite* locked in with Supra-New York, Pemberton went to the station's stellar navigation room. He was pleased to find Shorty Weinstein, the computer, on duty. Jake trusted Shorty's computations—a good thing when your ship, your passengers, and your own skin depend thereon. Pemberton had to be a better than average mathematician himself in order to be a pilot; his own limited talent made him appreciate the genius of those who computed the orbits.

"Hot Pilot Pemberton, the Scourge of the Spaceways—Hi!" Weinstein handed him a sheet of paper.

Jake looked at it, then looked amazed. "Hey, Shorty—you've made a mistake."

"Huh? Impossible. Mabel can't make mistakes." Weinstein gestured at the giant astrogation computer filling the far wall.

"*You* made a mistake. You gave me an easy fix—'Vega, Antares, Regulus.' You make things easy for the pilot and your guild'll chuck you out." Weinstein looked sheepish but pleased. "I see I don't blast off for seventeen hours. I could have taken the morning freight." Jake's thoughts went back to Phyllis.

"UN canceled the morning trip."

"Oh—" Jake shut up, for he knew Weinstein knew as little as he did. Perhaps the flight would have passed too close to an A-bomb rocket, circling the globe like a policeman. The General Staff of the Security Council did not give out information about the top secrets guarding the peace of the planet.

Pemberton shrugged. "Well, if I'm asleep, call me three hours minus."

"Right. Your tape will be ready."

While he slept, the *Flying Dutchman* nosed gently into her slip, sealed her airlocks to the Station, discharged passengers and freight from Luna City. When he woke, her holds were filling, her fuel replenished, and passengers boarding. He stopped by the post office radio desk, looking for a letter from Phyllis. Finding none, he told himself that she would have sent it to Terminal. He went on into the restaurant, bought the facsimile *Herald-Tribune,* and settled down grimly to enjoy the comics and his breakfast.

A man sat down opposite him and proceeded to plague him with silly questions about rocketry, topping it by misinterpreting the insignia embroidered on Pemberton's singlet and miscalling him "Captain." Jake hurried through breakfast to escape him, then picked up the tape from his automatic pilot, and went aboard the *Flying Dutchman.*

After reporting to the Captain he went to the control room, floating and pulling himself along by the handgrips. He buckled himself into the pilot's chair and started his check off.

Captain Kelly drifted in and took the other chair as Pemberton was finishing his checking runs on the ballistic tracker. "Have a Camel, Jake."

"I'll take a rain check." He continued; Kelly watched him with a slight frown. Like captains and pilots on Mark Twain's Mississippi—and for the same reasons—a spaceship captain bosses his ship, his crew, his cargo, and his passengers, but the pilot is the final, legal, and unquestioned boss of how the ship is handled from blast-off to the end of the trip. A captain may turn down a given pilot—nothing more. Kelly fingered a slip of paper tucked in his pouch and turned over in his mind the words with which the Company psychiatrist on duty had handed it to him.

"I'm giving this pilot clearance, Captain, but you need not accept it."

"Pemberton's a good man. What's wrong?"

The psychiatrist thought over what he had observed while posing as a silly tourist bothering a stranger at breakfast. "He's a little more anti-social than his past record shows. Something on his mind. Whatever it is, he can tolerate it for the present. We'll keep an eye on him."

Kelly had answered, "Will you come along with him as pilot?"

"If you wish."

"Don't bother—I'll take him. No need to lift a dead-head."

Pemberton fed Weinstein's tape into the robot-pilot, then turned to Kelly. "Control ready, sir."

"Blast when ready, Pilot." Kelly felt relieved when he heard himself make the irrevocable decision.

Pemberton signaled the Station to cast loose. The great ship was nudged out by an expanding pneumatic ram until she swam in space a thousand feet away, secured by a single line. He then turned the ship to its blast-off direction by causing a flywheel, mounted on gymbals at the ship's center of gravity, to spin rapidly. The ship spun slowly in the opposite direction, by grace of Newton's Third Law of Motion.

Guided by the tape, the robot-pilot tilted prisms of the pilot's periscope so that Vega, Antares, and Regulus would shine as one image when the ship was headed right; Pemberton nursed the ship to that heading . . . fussily; a mistake of one minute of arc here meant two hundred miles at destination.

When the three images made a pinpoint, he stopped the flywheels and locked in the gyros. He then checked the heading of his ship by direct observation of each of the stars, just as a salt-water skipper uses a sextant, but with incomparably more accurate instruments. This told him nothing about the correctness of the course Weinstein had ordered—he had to take that as Gospel—but it assured him that the robot and its tape were behaving as planned. Satisfied, he cast off the last line.

Seven minutes to go—Pemberton flipped the switch permitting the robot-pilot to blast away when its clock told it to. He waited, hands poised over the manual controls, ready to take over if the robot failed, and felt the old, inescapable sick excitement building up inside him.

Even as adrenalin poured into him, stretching his time sense, throbbing in his ears, his mind kept turning back to Phyllis.

He admitted she had a kick coming—spacemen shouldn't marry. Not that she'd starve if he messed up a landing, but a gal doesn't want insurance; she wants a husband—minus six minutes.

If he got a regular run she could live in Space Terminal. No good—idle women at Space Terminal went bad. Oh, Phyllis wouldn't become a tramp or a rum bum; she'd just go bats.

Five minutes more—he didn't care much for Space Terminal himself. Nor for space! "The Romance of Interplanetary Travel"—it looked well in print, but he knew what it was: A job. Monotony. No scenery. Bursts of work, tedious waits. No home life.

Why didn't he get an honest job and stay home nights?

He knew! Because he was a space jockey and too old to change.

What chance has a thirty-year-old married man, used to important money, to change his racket? (Four minutes.) He'd look good trying to sell helicopters on commission, now, wouldn't he?

Maybe he could buy a piece of irrigated land and— Be your age, chum! You know as much about farming as a cow knows about cube root! No, he had made his bed when he picked rockets during his training hitch. If he had bucked for the electronics branch, or taken a GI scholarship—too late now. Straight from the service into Harriman's Lunar Exploitations, hopping ore on Luna. That had torn it.

"How's it going, Doc?" Kelly's voice was edgy.

"Minus two minutes some seconds." Damnation— Kelly knew better than to talk to the pilot on minus time.

He caught a last look through the periscope. Antares seemed to have drifted. He unclutched the gyro, tilted and spun the flywheel, braking it savagely to a stop a moment later. The image was again a pinpoint. He could not have explained what he did: it was virtuosity, exact juggling, beyond textbook and classroom.

Twenty seconds . . . across the chronometer's face beads of light trickled the seconds away while he tensed, ready to fire by hand, or even to disconnect and refuse the trip if his judgment told him to. A too-cautious decision might cause Lloyds' to cancel his bond; a reckless decision could cost his license or even his life—and others.

But he was not thinking of underwriters and licenses,

nor even of lives. In truth he was not thinking at all; he was feeling, feeling his ship, as if his nerve ends extended into every part of her. Five seconds . . . the safety disconnects clicked out. Four seconds . . . three seconds . . . two seconds . . . one?

He was stabbing at the hand-fire button when the roar hit him.

Kelly relaxed to the pseudo-gravity of the blast and watched.

Pemberton was soberly busy, scanning dials, noting time, checking his progress by radar bounced off Supra-New York. Weinstein's figures, robot-pilot, the ship itself, all were clicking together.

Minutes later, the critical instant neared when the robot should cut the jets. Pemberton poised a finger over the hand cut-off, while splitting his attention among radarscope, accelerometer, periscope, and chronometer. One instant they were roaring along on the jets; the next split second the ship was in free orbit, plunging silently toward the Moon. So perfectly matched were human and robot that Pemberton himself did not know which had cut the power.

He glanced again at the board, then unbuckled. "How about that cigarette, Captain? And you can let your passengers unstrap."

No co-pilot is needed in space and most pilots would rather share a toothbrush than a control room. The pilot works about an hour at blast off, about the same before contact, and loafs during free flight, save for routine checks and corrections. Pemberton prepared to spend one hundred and four hours eating, reading, writing letters, and sleeping—especially sleeping.

When the alarm woke him, he checked the ship's position, then wrote to his wife. "Phyllis my dear," he began, "I don't blame you for being upset at missing your night out. I was disappointed, too. But bear with me, darling, I should be on a regular run before long. In less than ten years I'll be up for retirement and we'll have a chance to catch up on bridge and golf and things like that. I know it's pretty hard to—"

The voice circuit cut in. "Oh, Jake—put on your company face. I'm bringing a visitor to the control room."

"No visitors in the control room, Captain."

"Now, Jake. This lunkhead has a letter from Old Man Harriman himself. 'Every possible courtesy—' and so forth."

Pemberton thought quickly. He could refuse—but there was no sense in offending the big boss. "Okay, Captain. Make it short."

The visitor was a man, jovial, oversize—Jake figured him for an eighty pound weight penalty. Behind him a thirteen-year-old male counterpart came zipping through the door and lunged for the control console. Pemberton snagged him by the arm and forced himself to speak pleasantly. "Just hang on to that bracket, youngster. I don't want you to bump your head."

"Leggo me! Pop—make him let go."

Kelly cut in. "I think he had best hang on, Judge."

"Umm, uh—very well. Do as the Captain says, Junior."

"Aw, gee, Pop!"

"Judge Schacht, this is First Pilot Pemberton," Kelly said rapidly. "He'll show you around."

"Glad to know you, Pilot. Kind of you, and all that."

"What would you like to see, Judge?" Jake said carefully.

"Oh, this and that. It's for the boy—his first trip. I'm an old spacehound myself—probably more hours than half your crew." He laughed. Pemberton did not.

"There's not much to see in free flight."

"Quite all right. We'll just make ourselves at home— eh, Captain?"

"I wanna sit in the control seat," Schacht Junior announced. Pemberton winced. Kelly said urgently, "Jake, would you mind outlining the control system for the boy? Then we'll go."

"He doesn't have to show me anything. I know all about it. I'm a Junior Rocketeer of America—see my button?" The boy shoved himself toward the control desk.

Pemberton grabbed him, steered him into the pilot's chair, and strapped him in. He then flipped the board's disconnect.

"Whatcha doing?"

"I cut off power to the controls so I could explain them."

"Aintcha gonna fire the jets?"

"No." Jake started a rapid description of the use and purpose of each button, dial, switch, meter, gimmick, and scope.

Junior squirmed. "How about meteors?" he demanded.

"Oh, that—maybe one collision in half a million Earth-Moon trips. Meteors are scarce."

"So what? Say you hit the jackpot? You're in the soup."

"Not at all. The anti-collision radar guards all directions five hundred miles out. If anything holds a steady bearing for three seconds, a direct hook-up starts the jets. First a warning gong so that everybody can grab something solid, then one second later—*Boom!*—We get out of there fast."

"Sounds corny to me. Lookee, I'll show you how Commodore Cartwright did it in *The Comet Busters*—"

"Don't touch those controls !"

"You don't own this ship. My pop says—"

"Oh, Jake!" Hearing his name, Pemberton twisted, fish-like, to face Kelly.

"Jake, Judge Schacht would like to know—" From the corner of his eye Jake saw the boy reach for the board. He turned, started to shout—acceleration caught him, while the jets roared in his ear.

An old spacehand can usually recover, catlike, in an unexpected change from weightlessness to acceleration. But Jake had been grabbing for the boy, instead of for anchorage. He fell back and down, twisted to try to avoid Schacht, banged his head on the frame of the open air-tight door below, and fetched up on the next deck, out cold.

Kelly was shaking him. "You all right, Jake?"

He sat up. "Yeah. Sure." He became aware of the thunder, the shivering deckplates. "The jets! Cut the power!"

He shoved Kelly aside and swarmed up into the control room, jabbed at the cut-off button. In sudden ringing silence, they were again weightless.

Jake turned, unstrapped Schacht Junior, and hustled him to Kelly. "Captain, please remove this menace from my control room."

"Leggo! Pop—he's gonna hurt me!"

The elder Schacht bristled at once. "What's the meaning of this? Let go of my son!"

"Your precious son cut in the jets."

"Junior—did you do that?"

The boy shifted his eyes. "No, Pop. It . . . it was a meteor."

Schacht looked puzzled. Pemberton snorted. "I had just told him how the radar-guard can blast to miss a meteor. He's lying."

Schacht ran through the process he called "making up his mind," then answered, "Junior never lies. Shame on you, a grown man, to try to put the blame on a helpless boy. I shall report you, sir. Come, Junior."

Jake grabbed his arm. "Captain, I want those controls photographed for fingerprints before this man leaves the room. It was not a meteor; the controls were dead, until this boy switched them on. Furthermore the anti-collision circuit sounds an alarm."

Schacht looked wary. "This is ridiculous. I simply objected to the slur on my son's character. No harm has been done."

"No harm, eh? How about broken arms—or necks? And wasted fuel, with more to waste before we're back in the groove. Do you know, Mister 'Old Spacehound,' just how precious a little fuel will be when we try to match orbits with Space Terminal—if we haven't got it? We may have to dump cargo to save the ship, cargo at $60,000 a

ton on freight charges alone. Finger prints will show the
Commerce Commission whom to nick for it."

When they were alone again Kelly asked anxiously, "You
won't really have to jettison? You've got a maneuvering
reserve."

"Maybe we can't even get to Terminal. How long did
she blast?"

Kelly scratched his head. "I was woozy myself."

"We'll open the accelerograph and take a look."

Kelly brightened. "Oh, sure! If the brat didn't waste
too much, then we just swing ship and blast back the same
length of time."

Jake shook his head. "You forgot the changed mass-
ratio."

"Oh . . . oh, yes!" Kelly looked embarrassed. Mass-
ratio . . . under power, the ship lost the weight of fuel
burned. The thrust remained constant; the mass it pushed
shrank. Getting back to proper position, course, and
speed became a complicated problem in the calculus of
ballistics. "But you can do it, can't you?"

"I'll have to. But I sure wish I had Weinstein here."
Kelly left to see about his passengers; Jake got to work. He
checked his situation by astronomical observation and by
radar. Radar gave him all three factors quickly but with
limited accuracy. Sights taken of Sun, Moon, and Earth
gave him position, but told nothing of course and speed,
at that time—nor could he afford to wait to take a second
group of sights for the purpose.

Dead reckoning gave him an estimated situation, by
adding Weinstein's predictions to the calculated effect of

young Schacht's meddling. This checked fairly well with the radar and visual observations, but still he had no notion of whether or not he could get back in the groove and reach his destination; it was now necessary to calculate what it would take and whether or not the remaining fuel would be enough to brake his speed and match orbits.

In space, it does no good to reach your journey's end if you flash on past at miles per second, or even crawling along at a few hundred miles per hour. To catch an egg on a plate—don't bump!

He started doggedly to work to compute how to do it using the least fuel, but his little Marchant electronic calculator was no match for the tons of IBM computer at Supra-New York, nor was he Weinstein. Three hours later he had an answer of sorts. He called Kelly. "Captain? You can start by jettisoning Schacht & Son."

"I'd like to. No way out, Jake?"

"I can't promise to get your ship in safely without dumping. Better dump now, before we blast. It's cheaper."

Kelly hesitated; he would as cheerfully lose a leg. "Give me time to pick out what to dump."

"Okay." Pemberton returned sadly to his figures, hoping to find a saving mistake, then thought better of it. He called the radio room. "Get me Weinstein at Supra-New York."

"Out of normal range."

"I know that. This is the Pilot. Safety priority—urgent. Get a tight beam on them and nurse it."

"Uh . . . aye aye, sir. I'll try."

Weinstein was doubtful. "Cripes, Jake, I can't pilot you."

"Dammit, you can work problems for me!"

"What good is seven-place accuracy with bum data?"

"Sure, sure. But you know what instruments I've got; you know about how well I can handle them. Get me a better answer."

"I'll try." Weinstein called back four hours later. "Jake? Here's the dope: You planned to blast back to match your predicted speed, then made side corrections for position. Orthodox but uneconomical. Instead I had Mabel solve for it as one maneuver."

"Good!"

"Not so fast. It saves fuel but not enough. You can't possibly get back in your old groove and then match Terminal without dumping."

Pemberton let it sink in, then said, "I'll tell Kelly."

"Wait a minute, Jake. Try this. Start from scratch."

"Huh?"

"Treat it as a brand-new problem. Forget about the orbit on your tape. With your present course, speed, and position, compute the cheapest orbit to match with Terminal's. Pick a new groove."

Pemberton felt foolish. "I never thought of that."

"Of course not. With the ship's little one-lung calculator it'd take you three weeks to solve it. You set to record?"

"Sure."

"Here's your data." Weinstein started calling it off.

When they had checked it, Jake said, "That'll get me there?"

"Maybe. *If* the data you gave me is up to your limit of accuracy; *if* you can follow instructions as exactly as a robot, *if* you can blast off and make contact so precisely that you don't need side corrections, then you might squeeze home. Maybe. Good luck, anyhow." The wavering reception muffled their goodbyes.

Jake signaled Kelly. "Don't jettison, Captain. Have your passengers strap down. Stand by to blast. Minus fourteen minutes."

"Very well, Pilot."

The new departure made and checked, he again had time to spare. He took out his unfinished letter, read it, then tore it up.

"Dearest Phyllis," he started again, "I've been doing some hard thinking this trip and have decided that I've just been stubborn. What am I doing way out here? I like my home. I like to see my wife.

"Why should I risk my neck and your peace of mind to herd junk through the sky? Why hang around a telephone waiting to chaperone fatheads to the Moon—numbskulls who couldn't pilot a rowboat and should have stayed at home in the first place?

"Money, of course. I've been afraid to risk a change. I won't find another job that will pay half as well, but, if you are game, I'll ground myself and we'll start over. All my love,

"Jake"

He put it away and went to sleep, to dream that an entire troop of Junior Rocketeers had been quartered in his control room.

The close-up view of the Moon is second only to the space-side view of the Earth as a tourist attraction;

nevertheless Pemberton insisted that all passengers strap down during the swing around to Terminal. With precious little fuel for the matching maneuver, he refused to hobble his movements to please sightseers.

Around the bulge of the Moon, Terminal came into sight—by radar only, for the ship was tail foremost. After each short braking blast Pemberton caught a new radar fix, then compared his approach with a curve he had plotted from Weinstein's figures—with one eye on the time, another on the 'scope, a third on the plot, and a fourth on his fuel gauges.

"Well, Jake?" Kelly fretted. "Do we make it?"

"How should I know? You be ready to dump." They had agreed on liquid oxygen as the cargo to dump, since it could be let to boil out through the outer valves, without handling.

"Don't say it, Jake."

"Damn it—I won't if I don't have to." He was fingering his controls again; the blast chopped off his words. When it stopped, the radio maneuvering circuit was calling him.

"*Flying Dutchman*, Pilot speaking," Jake shouted back.

"Terminal Control—Supra reports you short on fuel."

"Right."

"Don't approach. Match speeds outside us. We'll send a transfer ship to refuel you and pick up passengers."

"I think I can make it."

"Don't try it. Wait for refueling."

"Quit telling me how to pilot my ship!" Pemberton switched off the circuit, then stared at the board, whistling morosely. Kelly filled in the words in his mind: *"Casey* said to the fireman, 'Boy, you better jump, cause two locomotives are agoing to bump!'"

"You going in the slip anyhow, Jake?"

"Mmm—no, blast it. I can't take a chance of caving in the side of Terminal, not with passengers aboard. But I'm not going to match speeds fifty miles outside and wait for a piggyback."

He aimed for a near miss just outside Terminal's orbit, conning by instinct, for Weinstein's figures meant nothing by now. His aim was good; he did not have to waste his hoarded fuel on last minute side corrections to keep from hitting Terminal. When at last he was sure of sliding safely on past if unchecked, he braked once more. Then, as he started to cut off the power, the jets coughed, sputtered, and quit.

The *Flying Dutchman* floated in space, five hundred yards outside Terminal, speeds matched.

Jake switched on the radio. "Terminal—stand by for my line. I'll warp her in."

He had filed his report, showered, and was headed for the post office to radiostat his letter, when the bullhorn summoned him to the Commodore-Pilot's office. Oh, oh, he told himself, Schacht has kicked the Brass—I wonder just how much stock that bliffy owns? And there's that other matter—getting snotty with Control.

He reported stiffly. "First Pilot Pemberton, sir."

Commodore Soames looked up. "Pemberton—oh, yes. You hold two ratings, space-to-space and airless-landing."

Let's not stall around, Jake told himself. Aloud he

said, "I have no excuses for anything this last trip. If the Commodore does not approve the way I run my control room, he may have my resignation."

"What are you talking about?"

"I, well—don't you have a passenger complaint on me?"

"Oh, that!" Soames brushed it aside. "Yes, he's been here. But I have Kelly's report, too—and your chief jetman's, and a special from Supra-New York. That was crack piloting, Pemberton."

"You mean there's no beef from the Company?"

"When have I failed to back up my pilots? You were perfectly right; I would have stuffed him out the air lock. Let's get down to business: You're on the space-to-space board, but I want to send a special to Luna City. Will you take it, as a favor to me?"

Pemberton hesitated; Soames went on, "That oxygen you saved is for the Cosmic Research Project. They blew the seals on the north tunnel and lost tons of the stuff. The work is stopped—about $130,000 a day in overhead, wages, and penalties. The *Gremlin* is here, but no pilot until the *Moonbat* gets in—except you. Well?"

"But I—look, Commodore, you can't risk people's necks on a jet landing of mine. I'm rusty; I need a refresher and a checkout."

"No passengers, no crew, no captain—your neck alone."

"I'll take her."

Twenty-eight minutes later, with the ugly, powerful hull of the *Gremlin* around him, he blasted away. One strong shove to kill her orbital speed and let her fall toward the Moon, then no more worries until it came time to "ride 'er down on her tail."

He felt good—until he hauled out two letters, the one he had failed to send, and one from Phyllis, delivered at Terminal.

The letter from Phyllis was affectionate—and superficial. She did not mention his sudden departure; she ignored his profession completely. The letter was a model of correctness, but it worried him.

He tore up both letters and started another. It said, in part: "—never said so outright, but you resent my job.

"I have to work to support us. You've got a job, too. It's an old, old job that women have been doing a long time—crossing the plains in covered wagons, waiting for ships to come back from China, or waiting around a mine head after an explosion—kiss him goodbye with a smile, take care of him at home.

"You married a spaceman, so part of your job is to accept my job cheerfully. I think you can do it, when you realize it. I hope so, for the way things have been going won't do for either of us.

> Believe me, I love you.
> Jake"

He brooded on it until time to bend the ship down for his approach. From twenty miles altitude down to one mile he let the robot brake her, then shifted to manual while still falling slowly. A perfect airless-landing would be the reverse of the take-off of a war rocket—free fall, then one long blast of the jets, ending with the ship stopped dead as she touched the ground. In practice a pilot must feel his way down, not too slowly; a ship could burn all the fuel this side of Venus fighting gravity too long.

Forty seconds later, falling a little more than 140 miles per hour, he picked up in his periscopes the thousand-foot static towers. At 300 feet he blasted five gravities for more than a second, cut it, and caught her with a one-sixth gravity, Moon-normal blast. Slowly he eased this off, feeling happy.

The *Gremlin* hovered, her bright jet splashing the soil of the Moon, then settled with dignity to land without a jar.

The ground crew took over; a sealed runabout jeeped Pemberton to the tunnel entrance. Inside Luna City, he found himself paged before he finished filing his report. When he took the call, Soames smiled at him from the viewplate. "I saw that landing from the field pick-up, Pemberton. You don't need a refresher course."

Jake blushed. "Thank you, sir."

"Unless you are dead set on space-to-space, I can use you on the regular Luna City run. Quarters here or Luna City? Want it?"

He heard himself saying, "Luna City. I'll take it."

He tore up his third letter as he walked into Luna City post office. At the telephone desk he spoke to a blonde in a blue moonsuit. "Get me Mrs. Jake Pemberton, Suburb six-four-oh-three, Dodge City, Kansas, please."

She looked him over. "You pilots sure spend money."

"Sometimes phone calls are cheap. Hurry it, will you?"

✿ ✿ ✿

Phyllis was trying to phrase the letter she felt she should have written before. It was easier to say in writing that she was not complaining of loneliness nor lack of fun, but that she could not stand the strain of worrying about his safety. But then she found herself quite unable to state the logical conclusion. Was she prepared to face giving him up entirely if he would not give up space? She truly did not know . . . the phone call was a welcome interruption.

The viewplate stayed blank. "Long distance," came a thin voice. "Luna City calling."

Fear jerked at her heart. "Phyllis Pemberton speaking."

An interminable delay—she knew it took nearly three seconds for radio waves to make the Earth-Moon round trip, but she did not remember it and it would not have reassured her. All she could see was a broken home, herself a widow, and Jake, beloved Jake, dead in space.

"Mrs. Jake Pemberton?"

"Yes, yes! Go ahead." Another wait—had she sent him away in a bad temper, reckless, his judgment affected? Had he died out there, remembering only that she fussed at him for leaving her to go to work? Had she failed him when he needed her? She knew that her Jake could not be tied to apron strings; men—grown-up men, not mammas' boys—had to break away from mother's apron strings. Then why had she tried to tie him to hers?—she had known better; her own mother had warned her not to try it.

She prayed.

Then another voice, one that weakened her knees with relief: "That you, honey?"

"Yes, darling, yes! What are you doing on the Moon?"

"It's a long story. At a dollar a second it will keep. What I want to know is—are you willing to come to Luna City?"

It was Jake's turn to suffer from the inevitable lag in reply.

He wondered if Phyllis were stalling, unable to make up her mind. At last he heard her say, "Of course, darling. When do I leave?"

"When—say, don't you even want to know *why*?"

She started to say that it did not matter, then said, "Yes, tell me." The lag was still present but neither of them cared. He told her the news, then added, "Run over to the Springs and get Olga Pierce to straighten out the red tape for you. Need my help to pack?"

She thought rapidly. Had he meant to come back anyhow, he would not have asked. "No. I can manage."

"Good girl. I'll radiostat you a long letter about what to bring and so forth. I love you. 'Bye now!"

"Oh, I love you, too. Goodbye, darling."

Pemberton came out of the booth whistling. Good girl, Phyllis. Staunch. He wondered why he had ever doubted her.

The Long Watch

"Nine ships blasted off from Moon Base. Once in space, eight of them formed a globe around the smallest. They held this formation all the way to Earth.

"The small ship displayed the insignia of an admiral—yet there was no living thing of any sort in her. She was not even a passenger ship, but a drone, a robot ship intended for radioactive cargo. This trip she carried nothing but a lead coffin and a Geiger counter that was never quiet."

—from the editorial *After Ten Years*, film 38, 17 June 2009, Archives of the *N. Y. Times*

JOHNNY DAHLQUIST blew smoke at the Geiger counter. He grinned wryly and tried it again. His whole body was radioactive by now. Even his breath, the smoke from his cigarette, could make the Geiger counter scream.

How long had he been here? Time doesn't mean much on the Moon. Two days? Three? A week? He let his mind run back: the last clearly marked time in his mind was when the Executive Officer had sent for him, right after breakfast—

"Lieutenant Dahlquist, reporting to the Executive Officer."

Colonel Towers looked up. "Ah, John Ezra. Sit down, Johnny. Cigarette?"

Johnny sat down, mystified but flattered. He admired Colonel Towers, for his brilliance, his ability to dominate, and for his battle record. Johnny had no battle record; he had been commissioned on completing his doctor's degree in nuclear physics and was now junior bomb officer of Moon Base.

The Colonel wanted to talk politics; Johnny was puzzled. Finally Towers had come to the point; it was not safe (so he said) to leave control of the world in political hands; power must be held by a scientifically selected group. In short—the Patrol.

Johnny was startled rather than shocked. As an abstract idea, Towers' notion sounded plausible. The League of Nations had folded up; what would keep the United Nations from breaking up, too, and thus lead to another World War. "And you know how bad such a war would be, Johnny."

Johnny agreed. Towers said he was glad that Johnny

got the point. The senior bomb officer could handle the work, but it was better to have both specialists.

Johnny sat up with a jerk. "You are going to *do* something about it?" He had thought the Exec was just talking.

Towers smiled. "We're not politicians; we don't just talk. We act."

Johnny whistled. "When does this start?"

Towers flipped a switch. Johnny was startled to hear his own voice, then identified the recorded conversation as having taken place in the junior officers' messroom. A political argument he remembered, which he had walked out on . . . a good thing, too! But being spied on annoyed him.

Towers switched it off. "We *have* acted," he said. "We know who is safe and who isn't. Take Kelly—" He waved at the loud-speaker. "Kelly is politically unreliable. You noticed he wasn't at breakfast?"

"Huh? I thought he was on watch."

"Kelly's watch-standing days are over. Oh, relax; he isn't hurt."

Johnny thought this over. "Which list am I on?" he asked. "Safe or unsafe?"

"Your name has a question mark after it. But I have said all along that you could be depended on." He grinned engagingly. "You won't make a liar of me, Johnny?"

Dahlquist didn't answer; Towers said sharply, "Come now—what do you think of it? Speak up."

"Well, if you ask me, you've bitten off more than you can chew. While it's true that Moon Base controls the Earth, Moon Base itself is a sitting duck for a ship. One bomb—*blooie!*"

Towers picked up a message form and handed it over; it read: I HAVE YOUR CLEAN LAUNDRY—ZACK. "That means every bomb in the *Trygve Lie* has been put out of commission. I have reports from every ship we need worry about." He stood up. "Think it over and see me after lunch. Major Morgan needs your help right away to change control frequencies on the bombs."

"The control frequencies?"

"Naturally. We don't want the bombs jammed before they reach their targets."

"What? You said the idea was to *prevent* war."

Towers brushed it aside. "There won't be a war—just a psychological demonstration, an unimportant town or two. A little bloodletting to save an all-out war. Simple arithmetic."

He put a hand on Johnny's shoulder. "You aren't squeamish, or you wouldn't be a bomb officer. Think of it as a surgical operation. And think of your family."

Johnny Dahlquist had been thinking of his family. "Please, sir, I want to see the Commanding Officer."

Towers frowned. "The Commodore is not available. As you know, I speak for him. See me again—after lunch."

The Commodore was decidedly not available; the Commodore was dead. But Johnny did not know that.

Dahlquist walked back to the messroom, bought cigarettes, sat down and had a smoke. He got up, crushed out the butt, and headed for the Base's west airlock. There he got into his space suit and went to the lockmaster. "Open her up, Smitty."

The marine looked surprised. "Can't let anyone out

on the surface without word from Colonel Towers, sir. Hadn't you heard?"

"Oh, yes! Give me your order book." Dahlquist took it, wrote a pass for himself, and signed it "by direction of Colonel Towers." He added, "Better call the Executive Officer and check it."

The lockmaster read it and stuck the book in his pocket. "Oh, no, Lieutenant. Your word's good."

"Hate to disturb the Executive Officer, eh? Don't blame you." He stepped in, closed the inner door, and waited for the air to be sucked out.

Out on the Moon's surface he blinked at the light and hurried to the track-rocket terminus; a car was waiting. He squeezed in, pulled down the hood, and punched the starting button. The rocket car flung itself at the hills, dived through and came out on a plain studded with projectile rockets, like candles on a cake. Quickly it dived into a second tunnel through more hills. There was a stomach-wrenching deceleration and the car stopped at the underground atom-bomb armory.

As Dahlquist climbed out he switched on his walkie-talkie. The space-suited guard at the entrance came to port-arms. Dahlquist said, "Morning, Lopez," and walked by him to the airlock. He pulled it open.

The guard motioned him back. "Hey! Nobody goes in without the Executive Officer's say-so." He shifted his gun, fumbled in his pouch and got out a paper. "Read it, Lieutenant."

Dahlquist waved it away. "I drafted that order myself. *You* read it; you've misinterpreted it."

"I don't see how, Lieutenant."

Dahlquist snatched the paper, glanced at it, then pointed to a line. "See? '—except persons specifically designated by the Executive Officer.' That's the bomb officers, Major Morgan and me."

The guard looked worried. Dahlquist said, "Damn it, look up 'specifically designated'—it's under '*Bomb Room, Security, Procedure for,*' in your standing orders. Don't tell me you left them in the barracks!"

"Oh, no, sir! I've got 'em." The guard reached into his pouch. Dahlquist gave him back the sheet; the guard took it, hesitated, then leaned his weapon against his hip, shifted the paper to his left hand, and dug into his pouch with his right.

Dahlquist grabbed the gun, shoved it between the guard's legs, and jerked. He threw the weapon away and ducked into the airlock. As he slammed the door he saw the guard struggling to his feet and reaching for his side arm. He dogged the outer door shut and felt a tingle in his fingers as a slug struck the door.

He flung himself at the inner door, jerked the spill lever, rushed back to the outer door and hung his weight on the handle. At once he could feel it stir. The guard was lifting up; the lieutenant was pulling down, with only his low Moon weight to anchor him. Slowly the handle raised before his eyes.

Air from the bomb room rushed into the lock through the spill valve. Dahlquist felt his space suit settle on his body as the pressure in the lock began to equal the pressure in the suit. He quit straining and let the guard raise the handle. It did not matter; thirteen tons of air pressure now held the door closed.

He latched open the inner door to the bomb room, so that it could not swing shut. As long as it was open, the airlock could not operate; no one could enter.

Before him in the room, one for each projectile rocket, were the atom bombs, spaced in rows far enough apart to defeat any faint possibility of spontaneous chain reaction. They were the deadliest things in the known universe, but they were his babies. He had placed himself between them and anyone who would misuse them.

But, now that he was here, he had no plan to use his temporary advantage.

The speaker on the wall sputtered into life. "Hey! Lieutenant! What goes on here? You gone crazy?" Dahlquist did not answer. Let Lopez stay confused—it would take him that much longer to make up his mind what to do. And Johnny Dahlquist needed as many minutes as he could squeeze. Lopez went on protesting. Finally he shut up.

Johnny had followed a blind urge not to let the bombs—his bombs!—be used for "demonstrations on unimportant towns." But what to do next? Well, Towers couldn't get through the lock. Johnny would sit tight until hell froze over.

Don't kid yourself, John Ezra! Towers could get in. Some high explosive against the outer door—then the air would whoosh out, our boy Johnny would drown in blood from his burst lungs—and the bombs would be sitting there, unhurt. They were built to stand the jump from Moon to Earth; vacuum would not hurt them at all.

He decided to stay in his space suit; explosive decompression didn't appeal to him. Come to think about it, death from old age was his choice.

Or they could drill a hole, let out the air, and open the door without wrecking the lock. Or Towers might even have a new airlock built outside the old. Not likely, Johnny thought; a *coup d'etat* depended on speed. Towers was almost sure to take the quickest way—blasting. And Lopez was probably calling the Base right now. Fifteen minutes for Towers to suit up and get here, maybe a short dicker—then *whoosh!* the party is over.

Fifteen minutes—

In fifteen minutes the bombs might fall back into the hands of the conspirators; in fifteen minutes he must make the bombs unusable.

An atom bomb is just two or more pieces of fissionable metal, such as plutonium. Separated, they are no more explosive than a pound of butter; slapped together, they explode. The complications lie in the gadgets and circuits and gun used to slap them together in the exact way and at the exact time and place required.

These circuits, the bomb's "brain," are easily destroyed—but the bomb itself is hard to destroy because of its very simplicity. Johnny decided to smash the "brains"—and quickly!

The only tools at hand were simple ones used in handling the bombs. Aside from a Geiger counter, the speaker on the walkie-talkie circuit, a television rig to the base, and the bombs themselves, the room was bare. A bomb to be worked on was taken elsewhere—not through fear of explosion, but to reduce radiation exposure for personnel. The radioactive material in a bomb is buried in a "tamper"—in these bombs, gold. Gold stops alpha, beta, and much of the deadly gamma radiation but not neutrons.

The slippery, poisonous neutrons which plutonium gives off had to escape, or a chain reaction—explosion!—would result. The room was bathed in an invisible, almost undetectable rain of neutrons. The place was unhealthy; regulations called for staying in it as short a time as possible.

The Geiger counter clicked off the "background" radiation, cosmic rays, the trace of radioactivity in the Moon's crust, and secondary radioactivity set up all through the room by neutrons. Free neutrons have the nasty trait of infecting what they strike, making it radioactive, whether it be concrete wall or human body. In time the room would have to be abandoned.

Dahlquist twisted a knob on the Geiger counter; the instrument stopped clicking. He had used a suppressor circuit to cut out noise of "background" radiation at the level then present. It reminded him uncomfortably of the danger of staying here. He took out the radiation exposure film all radiation personnel carry; it was a direct-response type and had been fresh when he arrived. The most sensitive end was faintly darkened already. Half way down the film a red line crossed it. Theoretically, if the wearer was exposed to enough radioactivity in a week to darken the film to that line, he was, as Johnny reminded himself, a "dead duck."

Off came the cumbersome space suit; what he needed was speed. Do the job and surrender—better to be a prisoner than to linger in a place as "hot" as this.

He grabbed a ball hammer from the tool rack and got busy, pausing only to switch off the television pick-up. The first bomb bothered him. He started to smash the cover plate of the "brain," then stopped, filled with reluctance. All his life he had prized fine apparatus.

He nerved himself and swung; glass tinkled, metal creaked. His mood changed; he began to feel a shameful pleasure in destruction. He pushed on with enthusiasm, swinging, smashing, destroying!

So intent was he that he did not at first hear his name called.

"Dahlquist! Answer me! Are you there?"

He wiped sweat and looked at the TV screen. Towers' perturbed features stared out.

Johnny was shocked to find that he had wrecked only six bombs. Was he going to be caught before he could finish? Oh, no! He *had* to finish. Stall, son, stall! "Yes, Colonel? You called me?"

"I certainly did! What's the meaning of this?"

"I'm sorry, Colonel."

Towers' expression relaxed a little. "Turn on your pick-up, Johnny, I can't see you. What was that noise?"

"The pick-up is on," Johnny lied. "It must be out of order. That noise—uh, to tell the truth, Colonel, I was fixing things so that nobody could get in here."

Towers hesitated, then said firmly, "I'm going to assume that you are sick and send you to the Medical Officer. But I want you to come out of there, right away. That's an order, Johnny."

Johnny answered slowly. "I can't just yet, Colonel. I came here to make up my mind and I haven't quite made it up. You said to see you after lunch."

"I meant you to stay in your quarters."

"Yes, sir. But I thought I ought to stand watch on the bombs, in case I decided you were wrong."

"It's not for you to decide, Johnny. I'm your superior officer. You are sworn to obey me."

"Yes, sir." This was wasting time; the old fox might have a squad on the way now. "But I swore to keep the peace, too. Could you come out here and talk it over with me? I don't want to do the wrong thing."

Towers smiled. "A good idea, Johnny. You wait there. I'm sure you'll see the light." He switched off.

"There," said Johnny. "I hope you're convinced that I'm a half-wit—you slimy mistake!" He picked up the hammer, ready to use the minutes gained.

He stopped almost at once; it dawned on him that wrecking the "brains" was not enough. There were no spare "brains," but there was a well-stocked electronics shop. Morgan could jury-rig control circuits for bombs. Why, he could himself—not a neat job, but one that would work. Damnation! He would have to wreck the bombs themselves—and in the next ten minutes.

But a bomb was solid chunks of metal, encased in a heavy tamper, all tied in with a big steel gun. It couldn't be done—not in ten minutes.

Damn!

Of course, there was one way. He knew the control circuits; he also knew how to beat them. Take this bomb: if he took out the safety bar, unhooked the proximity circuit, shorted the delay circuit, and cut in the arming circuit by hand—then unscrewed *that* and reached in *there*, he could, with just a long, stiff wire, set the bomb off.

Blowing the other bombs and the valley itself to Kingdom Come.

Also Johnny Dahlquist. That was the rub.

All this time he was doing what he had thought out, up to the step of actually setting off the bomb. Ready to go, the bomb seemed to threaten, as if crouching to spring. He stood up, sweating.

He wondered if he had the courage. He did not want to funk—and hoped that he would. He dug into his jacket and took out a picture of Edith and the baby. "Honeychile," he said, "if I get out of this, I'll never even try to beat a red light." He kissed the picture and put it back. There was nothing to do but wait.

What was keeping Towers? Johnny wanted to make sure that Towers was in blast range. What a joke on the jerk! Me—sitting here, ready to throw the switch on him. The idea tickled him; it led to a better: why blow himself up—alive?

There was another way to rig it—a "dead man" control. Jigger up some way so that the last step, the one that set off the bomb, would not happen as long as he kept his hand on a switch or a lever or something. Then, if they blew open the door, or shot him, or anything—up goes the balloon!

Better still, if he could hold them off with the threat of it, sooner or later help would come—Johnny was sure that most of the Patrol was not in this stinking conspiracy—and then: Johnny comes marching home! What a reunion! He'd resign and get a teaching job; he'd stood his watch.

All the while, he was working. Electrical? No, too little time. Make it a simple mechanical linkage. He had it doped out but had hardly begun to build it when the loud-speaker called him. "Johnny?"

"That you, Colonel?" His hands kept busy.

"Let me in."

"Well, now, Colonel, that wasn't in the agreement." Where in blue blazes was something to use as a long lever?

"I'll come in alone, Johnny, I give you my word. We'll talk face to face."

His word! "We can talk over the speaker, Colonel." Hey, that was it—a yardstick, hanging on the tool rack.

"Johnny, I'm warning you. Let me in, or I'll blow the door off."

A wire—he needed a wire, fairly long and stiff. He tore the antenna from his suit. "You wouldn't do that, Colonel. It would ruin the bombs."

"Vacuum won't hurt the bombs. Quit stalling."

"Better check with Major Morgan. Vacuum won't hurt them; explosive decompression would wreck every circuit." The Colonel was not a bomb specialist; he shut up for several minutes. Johnny went on working.

"Dahlquist," Towers resumed, "that was a clumsy lie. I checked with Morgan. You have sixty seconds to get into your suit, if you aren't already. I'm going to blast the door."

"No, you won't," said Johnny. "Ever hear of a 'dead man' switch?" Now for a counterweight—and a sling.

"Eh? What do you mean?"

"I've rigged number seventeen to set off by hand. But I put in a gimmick. It won't blow while I hang on to a strap I've got in my hand. But if anything happens to me—*up she goes!* You are about fifty feet from the blast center. Think it over."

There was a short silence. "I don't believe you."

"No? Ask Morgan. He'll believe me. He can inspect it, over the TV pick-up." Johnny lashed the belt of his space suit to the end of the yardstick.

"You said the pick-up was out of order."

"So I lied. This time I'll prove it. Have Morgan call me."

Presently Major Morgan's face appeared. "Lieutenant Dahlquist?"

"Hi, Stinky. Wait a sec." With great care Dahlquist made one last connection while holding down the end of the yardstick. Still careful, he shifted his grip to the belt, sat down on the floor, stretched an arm and switched on the TV pick-up. "Can you see me, Stinky?"

"I can see you," Morgan answered stiffly. "What is this nonsense?"

"A little surprise I whipped up." He explained it—what circuits he had cut out, what ones had been shorted, just how the jury-rigged mechanical sequence fitted in.

Morgan nodded. "But you're bluffing, Dahlquist, I feel sure that you haven't disconnected the 'K' circuit. You don't have the guts to blow yourself up."

Johnny chuckled. "I sure haven't. But that's the beauty of it. It can't go off, *so long as I am alive.* If your greasy boss, ex-Colonel Towers, blasts the door, then I'm dead and the bomb goes off. It won't matter to me, but it will to him. Better tell him." He switched off.

Towers came on over the speaker shortly. "Dahlquist?"

"I hear you."

"There's no need to throw away your life. Come out and you will be retired on full pay. You can go home to your family. That's a promise."

Johnny got mad. "You keep my family out of this!"

"Think of them, man."

"Shut up. Get back to your hole. I feel a need to scratch and this whole shebang might just explode in your lap."

Johnny sat up with a start. He had dozed, his hand hadn't let go the sling, but he had the shakes when he thought about it.

Maybe he should disarm the bomb and depend on their not daring to dig him out? But Towers' neck was already in hock for treason; Towers might risk it. If he did and the bomb were disarmed, Johnny would be dead and Towers would have the bombs. No, he had gone this far; he wouldn't let his baby girl grow up in a dictatorship just to catch some sleep.

He heard the Geiger counter clicking and remembered having used the suppressor circuit. The radioactivity in the room must be increasing, perhaps from scattering the "brain" circuits—the circuits were sure to be infected; they had lived too long too close to plutonium. He dug out his film.

The dark area was spreading toward the red line.

He put it back and said, "Pal, better break this deadlock or you are going to shine like a watch dial." It was a figure of speech; infected animal tissue does not glow—it simply dies, slowly.

The TV screen lit up; Towers' face appeared. "Dahlquist? I want to talk to you."

"Go fly a kite."

"Let's admit you have us inconvenienced."

"Inconvenienced, hell—I've got you stopped."

"For the moment. I'm arranging to get more bombs—"

"Liar."

"—but you are slowing us up. I have a proposition."

"Not interested."

"Wait. When this is over I will be chief of the world government. If you cooperate, even now, I will make you my administrative head."

Johnny told him what to do with it. Towers said, "Don't be stupid. What do you gain by dying?"

Johnny grunted. "Towers, what a prime stinker you are. You spoke of my family. I'd rather see them dead than living under a two-bit Napoleon like you. Now go away— I've got some thinking to do."

Towers switched off.

Johnny got out his film again. It seemed no darker but it reminded him forcibly that time was running out. He was hungry and thirsty—and he could not stay awake forever. It took four days to get a ship up from Earth; he could not expect rescue any sooner. And he wouldn't last four days—once the darkening spread past the red line he was a goner.

His only chance was to wreck the bombs beyond repair, and get out—before that film got much darker.

He thought about ways, then got busy. He hung a weight on the sling, tied a line to it. If Towers blasted the door, he hoped to jerk the rig loose before he died.

There was a simple, though arduous, way to wreck the bombs beyond any capacity of Moon Base to repair them. The heart of each was two hemispheres of plutonium, their flat surface polished smooth to permit perfect contact when slapped together. Anything less would prevent the chain reaction on which atomic explosion depended.

Johnny started taking apart one of the bombs.

He had to bash off four lugs, then break the glass envelope around the inner assembly. Aside from that the bomb came apart easily. At last he had in front of him two gleaming, mirror-perfect half globes.

A blow with the hammer—and one was no longer perfect. Another blow and the second cracked like glass; he had tapped its crystalline structure just right.

Hours later, dead tired, he went back to the armed bomb. Forcing himself to steady down, with extreme care he disarmed it. Shortly its silvery hemispheres too were useless. There was no longer a usable bomb in the room— but huge fortunes in the most valuable, most poisonous, and most deadly metal in the known world were spread around the floor.

Johnny looked at the deadly stuff. "Into your suit and out of here, son," he said aloud. "I wonder what Towers will say?"

He walked toward the rack, intending to hang up the hammer. As he passed, the Geiger counter chattered wildly.

Plutonium hardly affects a Geiger counter; secondary infection from plutonium does. Johnny looked at the hammer, then held it closer to the Geiger counter. The counter screamed.

Johnny tossed it hastily away and started back toward his suit.

As he passed the counter it chattered again. He stopped short.

He pushed one hand close to the counter. Its clicking picked up to a steady roar. Without moving he reached into his pocket and took out his exposure film.

It was dead black from end to end.

Plutonium taken into the body moves quickly to bone marrow. Nothing can be done; the victim is finished. Neutrons from it smash through the body, ionizing tissue, transmuting atoms into radioactive isotopes, destroying and killing. The fatal dose is unbelievably small; a mass a tenth the size of a grain of table salt is more than enough—a dose small enough to enter through the tiniest scratch. During the historic "Manhattan Project" immediate high amputation was considered the only possible first-aid measure.

Johnny knew all this but it no longer disturbed him. He sat on the floor, smoking a hoarded cigarette, and thinking. The events of his long watch were running through his mind.

He blew a puff of smoke at the Geiger counter and smiled without humor to hear it chatter more loudly. By now even his breath was "hot"—carbon-14, he supposed, exhaled from his blood stream as carbon dioxide. It did not matter.

There was no longer any point in surrendering, nor would he give Towers the satisfaction—he would finish out this watch right here. Besides, by keeping up the bluff that one bomb was ready to blow, he could stop them from capturing the raw material from which bombs were made. That might be important in the long run.

He accepted, without surprise, the fact that he was not unhappy. There was a sweetness about having no further worries of any sort. He did not hurt, he was not uncomfortable, he was no longer even hungry. Physically he still felt fine and his mind was at peace. He was dead—he knew that he was dead; yet for a time he was able to walk and breathe and see and feel.

He was not even lonesome. He was not alone; there were comrades with him—the boy with his finger in the dike, Colonel Bowie, too ill to move but insisting that he be carried across the line, the dying Captain of the *Chesapeake* still with deathless challenge on his lips, Rodger Young peering into the gloom. They gathered about him in the dusky bomb room.

And of course there was Edith. She was the only one he was aware of. Johnny wished that he could see her face more clearly. Was she angry? Or proud and happy?

Proud though unhappy—he could see her better now and even feel her hand. He held very still.

Presently his cigarette burned down to his fingers. He took a final puff, blew it at the Geiger counter, and put it out. It was his last. He gathered several butts and fashioned a roll-your-own with a bit of paper found in a pocket. He lit it carefully and settled back to wait for Edith to show up again. He was very happy.

✿ ✿ ✿

He was still propped against the bomb case, the last of his salvaged cigarettes cold at his side, when the speaker called out again. "Johnny? Hey, Johnny! Can you hear me? This is Kelly. It's all over. The *Lafayette* landed and Towers blew his brains out. Johnny? *Answer me.*"

When they opened the outer door, the first man in carried a Geiger counter in front of him on the end of a long pole. He stopped at the threshold and backed out hastily. "Hey, chief!" he called. "Better get some handling equipment—uh, and a lead coffin, too."

"Four days it took the little ship and her escort to reach Earth. Four days while all of Earth's people awaited her arrival. For ninety-eight hours all commercial programs were off television; instead there was an endless dirge—the Dead March *from* Saul, *the* Valhalla *theme,* Going Home, *the Patrol's own* Landing Orbit.

"The nine ships landed at Chicago Port. A drone tractor removed the casket from the small ship; the ship was then refueled and blasted off in an escape trajectory, thrown away into outer space, never again to be used for a lesser purpose.

"The tractor progressed to the Illinois town where Lieutenant Dahlquist had been born, while the dirge continued. There it placed the casket on a pedestal, inside a barrier marking the distance of safe approach. Space marines, arms reversed and heads bowed, stood guard around it; the crowds stayed outside this circle. And still the dirge continued.

"When enough time had passed, long, long after the

heaped flowers had withered, the lead casket was enclosed in marble, just as you see it today."

Gentlemen, Be Seated

IT TAKES both agoraphobes and claustrophobes to colonize the Moon. Or make it agoraphiles and claustrophiles, for the men who go out into space had better not have phobias. If anything on a planet, in a planet, or in the empty reaches around the planets can frighten a man, he should stick to Mother Earth. A man who would make his living away from *terra firma* must be willing to be shut up in a cramped spaceship, knowing that it may become his coffin, and yet he must be undismayed by the wide-open spaces of space itself. Spacemen—men who *work* in space, pilots and jetmen and astrogators and such—are men who like a few million miles of elbow room.

On the other hand the Moon colonists need to be the sort who feel cozy burrowing around underground like so many pesky moles.

On my second trip to Luna City I went over to Richardson Observatory both to see the Big Eye and to

75

pick up a story to pay for my vacation. I flashed my Journalists' Guild card, sweet-talked a bit, and ended with the paymaster showing me around. We went out the north tunnel, which was then being bored to the site of the projected coronascope.

It was a dull trip—climb on a scooter, ride down a completely featureless tunnel, climb off and go through an airlock, get on another scooter and do it all over again. Mr. Knowles filled in with sales talk. "This is temporary," he explained. "When we get the second tunnel dug, we'll cross-connect, take out the airlocks, put a northbound slidewalk in this one, a southbound slidewalk in the other one, and you'll make the trip in less than three minutes. Just like Luna City—or Manhattan."

"Why not take out the airlocks now?" I asked, as we entered another airlock—about the seventh. "So far, the pressure is the same on each side of each lock."

Knowles looked at me quizzically. "You wouldn't take advantage of a peculiarity of this planet just to work up a sensational feature story?"

I was irked. "Look here," I told him. "I'm as reliable as the next word-mechanic, but if something is not kosher about this project let's go back right now and forget it. I won't hold still for censorship."

"Take it easy, Jack," he said mildly—it was the first time he had used my first name; I noted it and discounted it. "Nobody's going to censor you. We're glad to cooperate with you fellows, but the Moon's had too much bad publicity now—publicity it didn't deserve."

I didn't say anything.

"Every engineering job has its own hazards," he insisted,

"and its advantages, too. Our men don't get malaria and they don't have to watch out for rattlesnakes. I can show you figures that prove it's safer to be a sandhog in the Moon than it is to be a file clerk in Des Moines—all things considered. For example, we rarely have any broken bones in the Moon; the gravity is so low—while that Des Moines file clerk takes his life in his hands every time he steps in or out of his bathtub."

"Okay, okay," I interrupted, "so the place is safe. What's the catch?"

"It *is* safe. Not company figures, mind you, nor Luna City Chamber of Commerce, but Lloyd's of London."

"So you keep unnecessary airlocks. Why?"

He hesitated before he answered, "Quakes."

Quakes. Earthquakes—moonquakes, I mean. I glanced at the curving walls sliding past and I wished I were in Des Moines. Nobody wants to be buried alive, but to have it happen in the Moon—why, you wouldn't stand a chance. No matter how quick they got to you, your lungs would be ruptured. No air.

"They don't happen very often," Knowles went on, "but we have to be prepared. Remember, the Earth is eighty times the mass of the Moon, so the tidal stresses here are eighty times as great as the Moon's effect on Earth tides."

"Come again," I said. "There isn't any water on the Moon. How can there be tides?"

"You don't have to have water to have tidal stresses. Don't worry about it; just accept it. What you get is unbalanced stresses. They can causes quakes."

I nodded. "I see. Since everything in the Moon has to

be sealed airtight, you've got to watch out for quakes. These airlocks are to confine your losses." I started visualizing myself as one of the losses.

"Yes and no. The airlocks would limit an accident all right, if there was one—which there won't be—this place is *safe*. Primarily they let us work on a section of the tunnel at no pressure without disturbing the rest of it. But they are more than that; each one is a temporary expansion joint. You can tie a compact structure together and let it ride out a quake, but a thing as long as this tunnel has to give, or it will spring a leak. A flexible seal is hard to accomplish in the Moon."

"What's wrong with rubber?" I demanded. I was feeling jumpy enough to be argumentative. "I've got a ground-car back home with two hundred thousand miles on it, yet I've never touched the tires since they were sealed up in Detroit."

Knowles sighed. "I should have brought one of the engineers along, Jack. The volatiles that keep rubbers soft tend to boil away in vacuum and the stuff gets stiff. Same for the flexible plastics. When you expose them to low temperature as well they get brittle as eggshells."

The scooter stopped as Knowles was speaking and we got off just in time to meet half a dozen men coming out of the next airlock. They were wearing spacesuits, or, more properly, pressure suits, for they had hose connections instead of oxygen bottles, and no sun visors. Their helmets were thrown back and each man had his head pushed through the opened zipper in the front of his suit, giving him a curiously two-headed look. Knowles called out, "Hey, Konski!"

One of the men turned around. He must have been six feet two and fat for his size. I guessed him at three hundred pounds, earthside. "It's Mr. Knowles," he said happily. "Don't tell me I've gotten a raise."

"You're making too much money now, Fatso. Shake hands with Jack Arnold. Jack, this is Fatso Konski—the best sandhog in four planets."

"Only four?" inquired Konski. He slid his right arm out of his suit and stuck his bare hand into mine. I said I was glad to meet him and tried to get my hand back before he mangled it.

"Jack Arnold wants to see how you seal these tunnels," Knowles went on. "Come along with us."

Konski stared at the overhead. "Well, now that you mention it, Mr. Knowles, I've just finished my shift."

Knowles said, "Fatso, you're a money grubber and inhospitable as well. Okay—time-and-a-half." Konski turned and started unsealing the airlock.

The tunnel beyond looked much the same as the section we had left except that there were no scooter tracks and the lights were temporary, rigged on extensions. A couple of hundred feet away the tunnel was blocked by a bulkhead with a circular door in it. The fat man followed my glance. "That's the movable lock," he explained. "No air beyond it. We excavate just ahead of it."

"Can I see where you've been digging?"

"Not without we go back and get you a suit."

I shook my head. There were perhaps a dozen bladder-like objects in the tunnel, the size and shape of toy balloons. They seemed to displace exactly their own weight of air; they floated without displaying much tendency to rise or settle. Konski batted one out of his way and answered me before I could ask. "This piece of tunnel was pressurized today," he told me. "These tag-alongs search out stray leaks. They're sticky inside. They get sucked up against a leak, break, and the goo gets sucked in, freezes and seals the leak."

"Is that a permanent repair?" I wanted to know.

"Are you kidding? It just shows the follow-up man where to weld."

"Show him a flexible joint," Knowles directed.

"Coming up." We paused half-way down the tunnel and Konski pointed to a ring segment that ran completely around the tubular tunnel. "We put in a flex joint every hundred feet. It's glass cloth, gasketed onto the two steel sections it joins. Gives the tunnel a certain amount of springiness."

"Glass cloth? To make an airtight seal?" I objected.

"The cloth doesn't seal; it's for strength. You got ten layers of cloth, with a silicone grease spread between the layers. It gradually goes bad, from the outside in, but it'll hold five years or more before you have to put on another coat."

I asked Konski how he liked his job, thinking I might get some story. He shrugged. "It's all right. Nothing to it. Only one atmosphere of pressure. Now you take when I was working under the Hudson—"

"And getting paid a tenth of what you get here," put in Knowles.

"Mr. Knowles, you grieve me," Konski protested. "It ain't the money; it's the art of the matter. Take Venus. They pay as well on Venus and a man has to be on his toes.

The muck is so loose you have to freeze it. It takes real caisson men to work there. Half of these punks here are just miners; a case of the bends would scare 'em silly."

"Tell him why you left Venus, Fatso."

Konski expressed dignity. "Shall we examine the movable shield, gentlemen?" he asked.

We puttered around a while longer and I was ready to go back. There wasn't much to see, and the more I saw of the place the less I liked it. Konski was undogging the door of the airlock leading back when something happened.

I was down on my hands and knees and the place was pitch dark. Maybe I screamed—I don't know. There was a ringing in my ears. I tried to get up and then stayed where I was. It was the darkest dark I ever saw, complete blackness. I thought I was blind.

A torchlight beam cut through it, picked me out, and then moved on. "What was it?" I shouted. "What happened? Was it a quake?"

"Stop yelling," Konski's voice answered me casually. "That was no quake, it was some sort of explosion. Mr. Knowles—you all right?"

"I guess so." He gasped for breath. "What happened?"

"Dunno. Let's look around a bit." Konski stood up and poked his beam around the tunnel, whistling softly. His light was the sort that has to be pumped; it flickered.

"Looks tight, but I hear—Oh, oh! sister!" His beam was focused on a part of the flexible joint, near the floor.

The "tag-along" balloons were gathering at this spot. Three were already there; others were drifting in slowly. As we watched, one of them burst and collapsed in a sticky mass that marked the leak.

The hole sucked up the burst balloon and began to hiss. Another rolled onto the spot, joggled about a bit, then it, too, burst. It took a little longer this time for the leak to absorb and swallow the gummy mass.

Konski passed me the light. "Keep pumping it, kid." He shrugged his right arm out of the suit and placed his bare hand over the spot where, at that moment, a third bladder burst.

"How about it, Fats?" Mr. Knowles demanded.

"Couldn't say. Feels like a hole as big as my thumb. Sucks like the devil."

"How could you get a hole like that?"

"Search me. Poked through from the outside, maybe."

"You got the leak checked?"

"I think so. Go back and check the gauge. Jack, give him the light."

Knowles trotted back to the airlock. Presently he sang out, "Pressure steady!"

"Can you read the vernier?" Konski called to him.

"Sure. Steady by the vernier."

"How much we lose?"

"Not more than a pound or two. What was the pressure before?"

"Earth-normal."

"Lost a pound four tenths, then."

"Not bad. Keep on going, Mr. Knowles. There's a tool kit just beyond the lock in the next section. Bring me back a number three patch, or bigger."

"Right." We heard the door open and clang shut, and we were again in total darkness. I must have made some sound for Konski told me to keep my chin up.

Presently we heard the door, and the blessed light shone out again. "Got it?" said Konski.

"No, Fatso, No . . ." Knowles' voice was shaking. "There's no air on the other side. The other door wouldn't open."

"Jammed, maybe?"

"No. I checked the manometer. There's no pressure in the next section."

Konski whistled again. "Looks like we'll wait till they come for us. In that case—Keep the light on me, Mr. Knowles. Jack, help me out of this suit."

"What are you planning to do?"

"If I can't get a patch, I got to make one, Mr. Knowles. This suit is the only thing around." I started to help him—a clumsy job since he had to keep his hand on the leak.

"You can stuff my shirt in the hole," Knowles suggested.

"I'd as soon bail water with a fork. It's got to be the suit; there's nothing else around that will hold the pressure." When he was free of the suit, he had me smooth out a portion of the back, then, as he snatched his hand away, I slapped the suit down over the leak. Konski promptly sat on it. "There," he said happily, "we've got it corked. Nothing to do but wait."

I started to ask him why he hadn't just sat down on the leak while wearing the suit; then I realized that the seat of the suit was corrugated with insulation—he needed a smooth piece to seal on to the sticky stuff left by the balloons.

"Let me see your hand," Knowles demanded.

"It's nothing much." But Knowles examined it anyway.

I looked at it and got a little sick. He had a mark like a stigma on the palm, a bloody, oozing wound. Knowles made a compress of his handkerchief and then used mine to tie it in place.

"Thank you, gentlemen," Konski told us, then added, "We've got time to kill. How about a little pinochle?"

"With your cards?" asked Knowles.

"Why, Mr. Knowles! Well—never mind. It isn't right for paymasters to gamble anyhow. Speaking of paymasters, you realize this is pressure work now, Mr. Knowles?"

"For a pound and four tenths differential?"

"I'm sure the union would take that view—in the circumstances."

"Suppose *I* sit on the leak?"

"But the rate applies to helpers, too."

"Okay, miser—triple-time it is."

"That's more like your own sweet nature, Mr. Knowles. I hope it's a nice long wait."

"How long a wait do you think it will be, Fatso?"

"Well, it shouldn't take them more than an hour, even if they have to come all the way from Richardson."

"Hmm . . . what makes you think they will be looking for us?"

"Huh? Doesn't your office know where you are?"

"I'm afraid not. I told them I wouldn't be back today."

Konski thought about it. "I didn't drop my time card. They'll know I'm still inside."

"Sure they will—tomorrow, when your card doesn't show up at my office."

"There's that lunkhead on the gate. He'll know he's got three extra inside."

"Provided he remembers to tell his relief. And provided he wasn't caught in it, too."

"Yes, I guess so," Konski said thoughtfully. "Jack—better quit pumping that light. You just use up more oxygen."

We sat there in the darkness for quite a long time, speculating about what had happened. Konski was sure it was an explosion; Knowles said that it put him in mind of a time when he had seen a freight rocket crash on take off. When the talk started to die out, Konski told some stories. I tried to tell one, but I was so nervous—so *afraid*, I should say—that I couldn't remember the snapper. I wanted to scream.

After a long silence Konski said, "Jack, give us the light again. I got something figured out."

"What is it?" Knowles asked.

"If we had a patch, you could put on my suit and go for help."

"There's no oxygen for the suit."

"That's why I mentioned you. You're the smallest—there'll be enough air in the suit itself to take you through the next section."

"Well—okay. What are you going to use for a patch?"

"I'm sitting on it."

"Huh?"

"This big broad, round thing I'm sitting on. I'll take my pants off. If I push one of my hams against that hole, I'll guarantee you it'll be sealed tight."

"But—No, Fats, it won't do. Look what happened to your hand. You'd hemorrhage through your skin and bleed to death before I could get back."

"I'll give you two to one I wouldn't—for fifty, say."

"If I win, how do I collect?"

"You're a cute one, Mr. Knowles. But look—I've got two or three inches of fat padding me. I won't bleed much—a strawberry mark, no more."

Knowles shook his head. "It's not necessary. If we keep quiet, there's air enough here for several days."

"It's not the air, Mr. Knowles. Noticed it's getting chilly?"

I had noticed, but hadn't thought about it. In my misery and funk being cold didn't seem anything more than appropriate. Now I thought about it. When we lost the power line, we lost the heaters, too. It would keep getting colder and colder . . . and colder.

Mr. Knowles saw it, too. "Okay, Fats. Let's get on with it."

I sat on the suit while Konski got ready. After he got his pants off he snagged one of the tag-alongs, burst it, and smeared the sticky insides on his right buttock. Then he turned to me. "Okay, kid—up off the nest." We made the swap-over fast, without losing much air, though the leak hissed angrily. "Comfortable as an easy chair, folks." He grinned.

Knowles hurried into the suit and left, taking the light with him. We were in darkness again.

After a while, I heard Konski's voice. "There a game we can play in the dark, Jack. You play chess?"

"Why, yes—play at it, that is."

"A good game. Used to play it in the decompression chamber when I was working under the Hudson. What do you say to twenty on a side, just to make it fun?"

"Uh? Well, all right." He could have made it a thousand; I didn't care.

"Fine. King's pawn to king three."

"Uh—king's pawn to king's four."

"Conventional, aren't you? Puts me in mind of a girl I knew in Hoboken—" What he told about her had nothing to do with chess, although it did prove she was conventional, in a manner of speaking. "King's bishop to queen's bishop four. Remind me to tell you about her sister, too. Seems she hadn't always been a redhead, but she wanted people to think so. So she—sorry. Go ahead with your move."

I tried to think but my head was spinning. "Queen's pawn to queen three."

"Queen to king's bishop three. Anyhow, she—" He went on in great detail. It wasn't new and I doubt if it ever happened to him, but it cheered me up. I actually smiled, there in the dark. "It's your move," he added.

"Oh." I couldn't remember the board. I decided to get ready to castle, always fairly safe in the early game. "Queen's knight to queen's bishop three."

"Queen advances to capture your king's bishop's pawn—checkmate. You owe me twenty, Jack."

"Huh? Why that can't be!"

"Want to run over the moves?" He checked them off.

I managed to visualize them, then said, "Why, I'll be a dirty name! You hooked me with a fool's mate!"

He chuckled. "You should have kept your eye on my queen instead of on the redhead."

I laughed out loud. "Know any more stories?"

"Sure." He told another. But when I urged him to go on, he said, "I think I'll just rest a little while, Jack."

I got up. "You all right, Fats?" He didn't answer; I felt my way over to him in the dark. His face was cold and he didn't speak when I touched him. I could hear his heart faintly when I pressed an ear to his chest, but his hands and feet were like ice.

I had to pull him loose; he was frozen to the spot. I could feel the ice, though I knew it must be blood. I started to try to revive him by rubbing him, but the hissing of the leak brought me up short. I tore off my own trousers, had a panicky time before I found the exact spot in the dark, and sat down on it, with my right buttock pressed firmly against the opening.

It grabbed me like a suction cup, icy cold. Then it was fire spreading through my flesh. After a time I couldn't feel anything at all, except a dull ache and coldness.

There was a light someplace. It flickered on, then went out again. I heard a door clang. I started to shout.

"Knowles!" I screamed. "Mr. Knowles!"

The light flickered on again. "Coming, Jack—"

I started to blubber. "Oh, you made it! You made it."

"I didn't make it, Jack. I couldn't reach the next section. When I got back to the lock I passed out." He stopped to wheeze. "There's a crater—" The light flickered off and fell clanging to the floor. "Help me, Jack," he said querulously. "Can't you see I need help? I tried to—"

I heard him stumble and fall. I called to him, but he didn't answer.

I tried to get up, but I was stuck fast, a cork in a bottle . . .

※ ※ ※

I came to, lying face down—with a clean sheet under me.

"Feeling better?" someone asked. It was Knowles, standing by my bed, dressed in a bathrobe.

"You're dead," I told him.

"Not a bit." He grinned. "They got to us in time."

"What happened?" I stared at him, still not believing my eyes.

"Just like we thought—a crashed rocket. An unmanned mail rocket got out of control and hit the tunnel."

"Where's Fats?"

"Hi!"

I twisted my head around; it was Konski, face down like myself.

"You owe me twenty," he said cheerfully.

"I owe you—" I found I was dripping tears for no good reason. "Okay, I owe you twenty. But you'll have to come to Des Moines to collect it."

The Black Pits of Luna

THE morning after we got to the Moon we went over to Rutherford. Dad and Mr. Latham—Mr. Latham is the man from the Harriman Trust that Dad came to Luna City to see—Dad and Mr. Latham had to go anyhow, on business. I got Dad to promise I could go along because it looked like just about my only chance to get out on the surface of the Moon. Luna City is all right, I guess, but I defy you to tell a corridor in Luna City from the sublevels in New York—except that you're light on your feet, of course.

When Dad came into our hotel suite to say we were ready to leave, I was down on the floor, playing mumblety-peg with my kid brother. Mother was lying down and had asked me to keep the runt quiet. She had been dropsick all the way out from Earth and I guess she didn't feel very good. The runt had been fiddling with the lights, switching them from "dusk" to "desert suntan" and back again. I collared him and sat him down on the floor.

Of course, I don't play mumblety-peg any more, but, on the Moon, it's a right good game. The knife practically floats and you can do all kinds of things with it. We made up a lot of new rules.

Dad said, "Switch in plans, my dear. We're leaving for Rutherford right away. Let's pull ourselves together."

Mother said, "Oh, mercy me—I don't think I'm up to it. You and Dickie run along. Baby Darling and I will just spend a quiet day right here."

Baby Darling is the runt.

I could have told her it was the wrong approach. He nearly put my eye out with the knife and said, "Who? What? I'm going too. Let's go!"

Mother said, "Oh, now, Baby Darling—don't cause Mother Dear any trouble. We'll go to the movies, just you and I."

The runt is seven years younger than I am, but don't call him "Baby Darling" if you want to get anything out of him. He started to bawl. "You said I could go!" he yelled.

"No, Baby Darling. I haven't mentioned it to you. I—"

"Daddy said I could go!"

"Richard, did you tell Baby he could go?"

"Why, no, my dear, not that I recall. Perhaps I—"

The kid cut in fast. "You said I could go anywhere Dickie went. You promised me you promised me you promised me." Sometimes you have to hand it to the runt; he had them jawing about who told him what in nothing flat. Anyhow, this is how, twenty minutes later, the four of us were up at the rocket port with Mr. Latham and climbing into the shuttle for Rutherford.

✿ ✿ ✿

The trip only takes about ten minutes and you don't see much, just a glimpse of the Earth while the rocket is still near Luna City and then not even that, since the atom plants where we were going are all on the back side of the Moon, of course. There were maybe a dozen tourists along and most of them were dropsick as soon as we went into free flight. So was Mother. Some people never will get used to rockets.

But Mother was all right as soon as we grounded and were inside again. Rutherford isn't like Luna City; instead of extending a tube out to the ship, they send a pressurized car out to latch on to the airlock of the rocket, then you jeep back about a mile to the entrance to underground. I liked that and so did the runt. Dad had to go off on business with Mr. Latham, leaving Mother and me and the runt to join up with the party of tourists for the trip through the laboratories.

It was all right but nothing to get excited about. So far as I can see, one atomics plant looks about like another; Rutherford could just as well have been the main plant outside Chicago. I mean to say everything that is anything is out of sight, covered up, shielded. All you get to see are some dials and instrument boards and people watching them. Remote control stuff, like Oak Ridge. The guide tells you about the experiments going on and they show you some movies—that's all.

I liked our guide. He looked like Tom Jeremy in *The Space Troopers*. I asked him if he was a spaceman and he looked at me kind of funny and said, no, that he was just a Colonial Services ranger. Then he asked me where I went to school and if I belonged to the Scouts. He said he was scoutmaster of Troop One, Rutherford City, Moonbat Patrol.

I found out there was just the one patrol—not many scouts on the Moon, I suppose.

Dad and Mr. Latham joined us just as we finished the tour while Mr. Perrin—that's our guide—was announcing the trip outside. "The conducted tour of Rutherford," he said, talking as if it were a transcription, "includes a trip by spacesuit out on the surface of the Moon, without extra charge, to see the Devil's Graveyard and the site of the Great Disaster of 1984. The trip is optional. There is nothing particularly dangerous about it and we've never had anyone hurt, but the Commission requires that you sign a separate release for your own safety if you choose to make this trip. The trip takes about one hour. Those preferring to remain behind will find movies and refreshments in the coffee shop."

Dad was rubbing his hands together. "This is for me," he announced. "Mr. Latham, I'm glad we got back in time. I wouldn't have missed this for the world."

"You'll enjoy it," Mr. Latham agreed, "and so will you, Mrs. Logan. I'm tempted to come along myself."

"Why don't you?" Dad asked.

"No, I want to have the papers ready for you and the Director to sign when you get back and before you leave for Luna City."

"Why knock yourself out?" Dad urged him. "If a man's word is no good, his signed contract is no better. You can mail the stuff to me at New York."

Mr. Latham shook his head. "No, really—I've been

out on the surface dozens of times. But I'll come along
and help you into your spacesuits."

Mother said, "Oh dear," she didn't think she'd better
go; she wasn't sure she could stand the thought of being
shut up in a spacesuit and besides glaring sunlight always
gave her a headache.

Dad said, "Don't be silly, my dear; it's the chance of a
lifetime," and Mr. Latham told her that the filters on the
helmets kept the light from being glaring. Mother always
objects and then gives in. I suppose women just don't have
any force of character. Like the night before—earth-night,
I mean, Luna City time—she had bought a fancy moonsuit to wear to dinner in the Earth-View room at the hotel,
then she got cold feet. She complained to Dad that she
was too plump to dare to dress like that.

Well, she did show an awful lot of skin. Dad said,
"Nonsense, my dear. You look ravishing." So she wore it
and had a swell time, especially when a pilot tried to pick
her up.

It was like that this time. She came along. We went
into the outfitting room and I looked around while Mr.
Perrin was getting them all herded in and having the
releases signed. There was the door to the airlock to the
surface at the far end, with a bull's-eye window in it and
another one like it in the door beyond. You could peek
through and see the surface of the Moon beyond, looking
hot and bright and sort of improbable, in spite of the
amber glass in the windows. And there was a double row
of spacesuits hanging up, looking like empty men. I
snooped around until Mr. Perrin got around to our party.

"We can arrange to leave the youngster in the care of

the hostess in the coffee shop," he was telling Mother. He reached down and tousled the runt's hair. The runt tried to bite him and he snatched his hand away in a hurry.

"Thank you, Mr. Perkins," Mother said, "I suppose that's best—though perhaps I had better stay behind with him."

"'Perrin' is the name," Mr. Perrin said mildly. "It won't be necessary. The hostess will take good care of him."

Why do adults talk in front of kids as if they couldn't understand English? They should have just shoved him into the coffee shop. By now the runt knew he was being railroaded. He looked around belligerently. "I go, too," he said loudly. "You promised me."

"Now Baby Darling," Mother tried to stop him. "Mother Dear didn't tell you—" But she was just whistling to herself; the runt turned on the sound effects.

"You said I could go where Dickie went; you promised me when I was sick. You promised me you promised me—" and on and on, his voice getting higher and louder all the time.

Mr. Perrin looked embarrassed. Mother said, "Richard, you'll just have to deal with your child. After all, you were the one who promised him."

"Me, dear?" Dad looked surprised. "Anyway, I don't see anything so complicated about it. Suppose we did promise him that he could do what Dickie does—we'll simply take him along; that's all."

Mr. Perrin cleared his throat. "I'm afraid not. I can outfit your older son with a woman's suit; he's tall for his age. But we just don't make any provision for small children."

Well, we were all tangled up in a mess in no time at all. The runt can always get Mother to running in circles. Mother has the same effect on Dad. He gets red in the face and starts laying down the law to me. It's sort of a chain reaction, with me on the end and nobody to pass it along to. They came out with a very simple solution—I was to stay behind and take care of Baby Darling brat!

"But, Dad, you said—" I started in.

"Never mind!" he cut in. "I won't have this family disrupted in a public squabble. You heard what your mother said."

I was desperate. "Look, Dad," I said, keeping my voice low, "if I go back to Earth without once having put on a spacesuit and set foot on the surface, you'll just have to find another school to send me to. I won't go back to Lawrenceville; I'd be the joke of the whole place."

"We'll settle that when we get home."

"But, Dad, you promised me specifically—"

"That'll be enough out of you, young man. The matter is closed."

Mr. Latham had been standing near by, taking it in but keeping his mouth shut. At this point he cocked an eyebrow at Dad and said very quietly, "Well, R.J.—I thought your word was your bond?"

I wasn't supposed to hear it and nobody else did—a good thing, too, for it doesn't do to let Dad know that you know that he's wrong; it just makes him worse. I changed the subject in a hurry. "Look, Dad, maybe we all can go out. How about that suit over there?" I pointed at a rack that was inside a railing with a locked gate on it. The rack had a couple of dozen suits on it and at the far end, almost out of sight, was a small suit—the boots on it hardly came down to the waist of the suit next to it.

"Huh?" Dad brightened up. "Why, just the thing! Mr. Perrin! Oh, Mr. Perrin—here a minute! I thought you didn't have any small suits, but here's one that I think will fit."

Dad was fiddling at the latch of the railing gate. Mr. Perrin stopped him. "We can't use that suit, sir."

"Uh? Why not?"

"All the suits inside the railing are private property, not for rent."

"What? Nonsense—Rutherford is a public enterprise. I want that suit for my child."

"Well, you can't have it."

"I'll speak to the Director."

"I'm afraid you'll have to. That suit was specially built for his daughter."

And that's just what they did. Mr. Latham got the Director on the line, Dad talked to him, then the Director talked to Mr. Perrin, then he talked to Dad again. The Director didn't mind lending the suit, not to Dad, anyway, but he wouldn't order Mr. Perrin to take a below-age child outside.

Mr. Perrin was feeling stubborn and I don't blame him, but Dad soothed his feathers down and presently we were all climbing into our suits and getting pressure checks and checking our oxygen supply and switching on our walkie-talkies. Mr. Perrin was calling the roll by radio and reminding us that we were all on the same circuit, so we had better let him do most of the talking and not to make casual remarks or none of us would be able to hear.

Then we were in the airlock and he was warning us to stick close together and not try to see how fast we could run or how high we could jump. My heart was knocking around in my chest.

The outer door of the lock opened and we filed out on the face of the Moon. It was just as wonderful as I dreamed it would be, I guess, but I was so excited that I hardly knew it at the time. The glare of the sun was the brightest thing I ever saw and the shadows so inky black you could hardly see into them. You couldn't hear anything but voices over your radio and you could reach down and switch off that.

The pumice was soft and kicked up around our feet like smoke, settling slowly, falling in slow motion. Nothing else moved. It was the *deadest* place you can imagine.

We stayed on a path, keeping close together for company, except twice when I had to take out after the runt when he found out he could jump twenty feet. I wanted to smack him, but did you ever try to smack anybody wearing a spacesuit? It's no use.

Mr. Perrin told us to halt presently and started his talk. "You are now in the Devil's Graveyard. The twin spires behind you are five thousand feet above the floor of the plain and have never been scaled. The spires, or monuments, have been named for apocryphal or mythological characters because of the fancied resemblance of this fantastic scene to a giant cemetery. Beelzebub, Thor, Siva, Cain, Set—" He pointed around us. "Lunologists are not agreed as to the origin of the strange shapes. Some claim to see indications of the action of air and water as well as volcanic action. If so, these spires must have been standing for an unthinkably long period, for today, as you see, the Moon—" It was the same sort of stuff you can read any month in *Spaceways Magazine,* only we were seeing it and that makes a difference, let me tell you.

The spires reminded me a bit of the rocks below the lodge in the Garden of the Gods in Colorado Springs when we went there last summer, only these spires were lots bigger and, instead of blue sky, there was just blackness and hard, sharp stars overhead. Spooky.

Another ranger had come with us, with a camera. Mr. Perrin tried to say something else, but the runt had started yapping away and I had to switch off his radio before anybody could hear anything. I kept it switched off until Mr. Perrin finished talking.

He wanted us to line up for a picture with the spires and the black sky behind us for a background. "Push your faces forward in your helmets so that your features will show. Everybody look pretty. There!" he added as the other guy snapped the shot. "Prints will be ready when you return, at ten dollars a copy."

I thought it over. I certainly needed one for my room at school and I wanted one to give to—anyhow, I needed another one. I had eighteen bucks left from my birthday money; I could sweet-talk Mother for the balance. So I ordered two of them.

We climbed a long rise and suddenly we were staring out across the crater, the disaster crater, all that was left of the first laboratory. It stretched away from us, twenty miles across, with the floor covered with shiny, bubbly green glass instead of pumice. There was a monument. I read it:

HERE ABOUT YOU
ARE THE MORTAL REMAINS OF
Kurt Schaeffer
Maurice Feinstein
Thomas Dooley
Hazel Hayakawa
G. Washington Slappey
Sam Houston Adams
WHO DIED FOR THE TRUTH
THAT MAKES MEN FREE
On the Eleventh Day of August 1984

I felt sort of funny and backed away and went to listen to Mr. Perrin. Dad and some of the other men were asking him questions. "They don't know exactly," he was saying. "Nothing was left. Now we telemeter all the data back to Luna City, as it comes off the instruments, but that was before the line-of-sight relays were set up."

"What would have happened," some man asked, "if this blast had gone off on Earth?"

"I'd hate to try to tell you—but that's why they put the lab here, back of the Moon." He glanced at his watch. "Time to leave, everybody." They were milling around, heading back down toward the path, when Mother screamed.

"Baby! Where's Baby Darling?"

I was startled but I wasn't scared, not yet. The runt is always running around, first here and then there, but he doesn't go far away, because he always wants to have somebody to yap to.

My father had one arm around Mother; he signalled

to me with the other. "Dick," he snapped, his voice sharp in my earphones, "what have you done with your brother?"

"Me?" I said. "Don't look at me—the last I saw Mother had him by the hand, walking up the hill here."

"Don't stall around, Dick. Mother sat down to rest when we got here and sent him to you."

"Well, if she did, he never showed up." At that, Mother started to scream in earnest. Everybody had been listening, of course—they had to; there was just the one radio circuit. Mr. Perrin stepped up and switched off Mother's talkie, making a sudden silence.

"Take care of your wife, Mr. Logan," he ordered, then added, "When did you see your child last?"

Dad couldn't help him any; when they tried switching Mother back into the hook-up, they switched her right off again. She couldn't help and she deafened us. Mr. Perrin addressed the rest of us. "Has anyone seen the small child we had with us? Don't answer unless you have something to contribute. Did anyone see him wander away?"

Nobody had. I figured he probably ducked out when everybody was looking at the crater and had their backs to him. I told Mr. Perrin so. "Seems likely," he agreed. "Attention, everybody! I'm going to search for the child. Stay right where you are. Don't move away from this spot. I won't be gone more than ten minutes."

"Why don't we all go?" somebody wanted to know. "Because," said Mr. Perrin, "right now I've only got one lost. I don't want to make it a dozen." Then he left, taking big easy lopes that covered fifty feet at a step.

Dad started to take out after him, then thought better of it, for Mother suddenly keeled over, collapsing at the knees and floating gently to the ground. Everybody started talking at once. Some idiot wanted to take her helmet off, but Dad isn't crazy. I switched off my radio so I could hear myself think and started looking around, not leaving the crowd but standing up on the lip of the crater and trying to see as much as I could.

I was looking back the way we had come; there was no sense in looking at the crater—if he had been in there he would have shown up like a fly on a plate.

Outside the crater was different; you could have hidden a regiment within a block of us, rocks standing up every which way, boulders big as houses with blow holes all through them, spires, gulleys—it was a mess. I could see Mr. Perrin every now and then, casting around like a dog after a rabbit, and making plenty of time. He was practically flying. When he came to a big boulder he would jump right over it, leveling off face down at the top of his jump, so he could see better.

Then he was heading back toward us and I switched my radio back on. There was still a lot of talk. Somebody was saying, "We've got to find him before sundown," and somebody else answered, "Don't be silly; the sun won't be down for a week. It's his air supply, I tell you. These suits are only good for four hours." The first voice said, "Oh!" then added softly, "like a fish out of water—" It was then I got scared.

A woman's voice, sounding kind of choked, said, "The poor, poor darling! We've got to find him before he suffocates," and my father's voice cut in sharply, "Shut up talking that way!" I could hear somebody sobbing. It might have been Mother.

Mr. Perrin was almost up to us and he cut in, "Silence, everybody! I've got to call the base," and he added urgently, "Perrin, calling airlock control; Perrin, calling airlock control!"

A woman's voice answered, "Come in, Perrin." He told her what was wrong and added, "Send out Smythe to take this party back in; I'm staying. I want every ranger who's around and get me volunteers from among any of the experienced Moon hands. Send out a radio direction-finder by the first ones to leave."

We didn't wait long, for they came swarming toward us like grasshoppers. They must have been running forty or fifty miles an hour. It would have been something to see, if I hadn't been so sick at my stomach.

Dad put up an argument about going back, but Mr. Perrin shut him up. "If you hadn't been so confounded set on having your own way, we wouldn't be in a mess. If you had kept track of your kid, he wouldn't be lost. I've got kids of my own; I don't let 'em go out on the face of the Moon when they're too young to take care of themselves. You go on back—I can't be burdened by taking care of you, too."

I think Dad might even have gotten in a fight with him if Mother hadn't gotten faint again. We went on back with the party.

The next couple of hours were pretty awful. They let us sit just outside the control room where we could hear Mr. Perrin directing the search, over the loudspeaker. I thought at first that they would snag the runt as soon as they started using the radio direction-finder—pick up his power hum, maybe, even if he didn't say anything—but no such luck; they didn't get anything with it. And the searchers didn't find anything either.

A thing that made it worse was that Mother and Dad didn't even try to blame me. Mother was crying quietly and Dad was consoling her, when he looked over at me with an odd expression. I guess he didn't really see me at all, but I thought he was thinking that if I hadn't insisted on going out on the surface this wouldn't have happened. I said, "Don't go looking at me, Dad. Nobody told me to keep an eye on him. I thought he was with Mother."

Dad just shook his head without answering. He was looking tired and sort of shrunk up. But Mother, instead of laying in to me and yelling, stopped her crying and managed to smile. "Come here, Dickie," she said, and put her other arm around me. "Nobody blames you, Dickie. Whatever happens, you weren't at fault. Remember that, Dickie."

So I let her kiss me and then sat with them for a while, but I felt worse than before. I kept thinking about the runt, somewhere out there, and his oxygen running out. Maybe it wasn't my fault, but I could have prevented it and I knew it. I shouldn't have depended on Mother to look out for him; she's no good at that sort of thing. She's the kind of person that would mislay her head if it wasn't knotted on tight—the ornamental sort. Mother's *good*, you understand, but she's not practical.

She would take it pretty hard if the runt didn't come back. And so would Dad—and so would I. The runt is an awful nuisance, but it was going to seem strange not to have him around underfoot. I got to thinking about that remark, "Like a fish out of water." I accidentally busted an aquarium once; I remember yet how they looked. Not pretty. If the runt was going to die like that—

I shut myself up and decided I just had to figure out some way to help find him.

After a while I had myself convinced that I *could* find him if they would just let me help look. But they wouldn't of course.

Dr. Evans the Director showed up again—he'd met us when we first came in—and asked if there was anything he could do for us and how was Mrs. Logan feeling? "You know I wouldn't have had this happen for the world," he added. "We're doing all we can. I'm having some ore-detectors shot over from Luna City. We might be able to spot the child by the metal in his suit."

Mother asked how about bloodhounds and Dr. Evans didn't even laugh at her. Dad suggested helicopters, then corrected himself and made it rockets. Dr. Evans pointed out that it was impossible to examine the ground closely from a rocket.

I got him aside presently and braced him to let me join the hunt. He was polite but unimpressed, so I insisted. "What makes you think you can find him?" he asked me. "We've got the most experienced Moon men available out there now. I'm afraid, son, that you would get yourself lost or hurt if you tried to keep up with them. In this country, if you once lose sight of landmarks, you can get hopelessly lost."

"But look, Doctor," I told him, "I know the runt—I mean my kid brother, better than anyone else in the world. I won't get lost—I mean I will get lost but just the way he did. You can send somebody to follow me."

He thought about it. "It's worth trying," he said suddenly. "I'll go with you. Let's suit up."

We made a fast trip out, taking thirty-foot strides—the best I could manage even with Dr. Evans hanging on to my belt to keep me from stumbling. Mr. Perrin was expecting us. He seemed dubious about my scheme. "Maybe the old 'lost mule' dodge will work," he admitted, "but I'll keep the regular search going just the same. Here, Shorty, take this flashlight. You'll need it in the shadows."

I stood on the edge of the crater and tried to imagine I was the runt, feeling bored and maybe a little bit griped at the lack of attention. What would I do next?

I went skipping down the slope, not going anywhere in particular, the way the runt would have done. Then I stopped and looked back, to see if Mother and Daddy and Dickie had noticed me. I was being followed all right; Dr. Evans and Mr. Perrin were close behind me. I pretended that no one was looking and went on. I was pretty close to the first rock outcroppings by now and I ducked behind the first one I came to. It wasn't high enough to hide me but it would have covered the runt. It felt like what he would do; he loved to play hide-and-go-seek—it made him the center of attention.

I thought about it. When the runt played that game, his notion of hiding was always to crawl *under* something, a bed, or a sofa, or an automobile, or even under the sink. I looked around. There were a lot of good places; the rocks were filled with blowholes and overhangs. I started working them over. It seemed hopeless; there must have been a hundred such places right around close.

Mr. Perrin came up to me as I was crawling out of the fourth tight spot. "The men have shined flashlights around in every one of these places," he told me. "I don't think it's much use, Shorty."

"Okay," I said, but I kept at it. I knew I could get at spots a grown man couldn't reach; I just hoped the runt hadn't picked a spot I couldn't reach.

It went on and on and I was getting cold and stiff and terribly tired. The direct sunlight is hot on the Moon, but the second you get in the shade, it's cold. Down inside those rocks it never got warm at all. The suits they gave us tourists are well enough insulated, but the extra insulation is in the gloves and the boots and the seats of the pants—and I had been spending most of my time down on my stomach, wiggling into tight places.

I was so numb I could hardly move and my whole front felt icy. Besides, it gave me one more thing to worry about—how about the runt? Was he cold, too?

If it hadn't been for thinking how those fish looked and how, maybe, the runt would be frozen stiff before I could get to him, I would have quit. I was about beat. Besides, it's rather scary down inside those holes—you don't know what you'll come to next.

Dr. Evans took me by the arm as I came out of one of them, and touched his helmet to mine, so that I got his voice directly. "Might as well give up, son. You're knocking yourself out and you haven't covered an acre." I pulled away from him.

The next place was a little overhang, not a foot off the ground. I flashed a light into it. It was empty and didn't seem to go anywhere. Then I saw there was a turn in it. I got down flat and wiggled in. The turn opened out a little and dropped off. I didn't think it was worthwhile to go any deeper as the runt wouldn't have crawled very far in the dark, but I scrunched ahead a little farther and flashed the light down.

I saw a boot sticking out.

That's about all there is to it. I nearly bashed in my helmet getting out of there, but I was dragging the runt after me. He was limp as a cat and his face was funny. Mr. Perrin and Dr. Evans were all over me as I came out, pounding me on the back and shouting. "Is he *dead*, Mr. Perrin?" I asked, when I could get my breath. "He looks awful bad."

Mr. Perrin looked him over. "No . . . I can see a pulse in his throat. Shock and exposure, but this suit was specially built—we'll get him back fast." He picked the runt up in his arms and I took out after him.

Ten minutes later the runt was wrapped in blankets and drinking hot cocoa. I had some, too. Everybody was talking at once and Mother was crying again, but she looked normal and Dad had filled out.

He tried to write out a check for Mr. Perrin, but he brushed it off. "I don't need any reward; your boy found him. You can do me just one favor—"

"Yes?" Dad was all honey.

"Stay off the Moon. You don't belong here; you're not the pioneer type."

Dad took it. "I've already promised my wife that," he said without batting an eye. "You needn't worry."

I followed Mr. Perrin as he left and said to him

privately, "Mr. Perrin—I just wanted to tell you that I'll be back, if you don't mind."

He shook hands with me and said, "I know you will, Shorty."

"It's Great to Be Back"

"HURRY up, Allan!" Home—back to Earth again! Her heart was pounding.

"Just a second." She fidgeted while her husband checked over a bare apartment. Earth-Moon freight rates made it silly to ship their belongings; except for the bag he carried, they had converted everything to cash. Satisfied, he joined her at the lift; they went on up to the administration level and there to a door marked: LUNA CITY COMMUNITY ASSOCIATION—*Anna Stone, Service Manager.*

Miss Stone accepted their apartment keys grimly. "Mr. and Mrs. MacRae. So you're actually leaving us?"

Josephine bristled. "Think we'd change our minds?"

The manager shrugged. "No. I knew nearly three years ago that you would go back—from your complaints."

"From my comp—Miss Stone, I've been as patient about the incredible inconveniences of this, this pressurized rabbit warren as anyone. I don't blame you personally, but—"

111

"Take it easy, Jo!" her husband cautioned her.

Josephine flushed. "Sorry, Miss Stone."

"Never mind. We just see things differently. I was here when Luna City was three air-sealed Quonset huts connected by tunnels you crawled through, on your knees." She stuck out a square hand. "I hope you enjoy being groundhogs again, I honestly do. Hot jets, good luck, and a safe landing."

Back in the lift, Josephine sputtered. "'Groundhogs' indeed! Just because we prefer our native planet, where a person can draw a breath of fresh air—"

"You use the term," Allan pointed out.

"But I use it about people who've never been off Terra."

"We've both said more than once that we wished we had had sense enough never to have left Earth. We're groundhogs at heart, Jo."

"Yes, but—Oh, Allan, you're being obnoxious. This is the happiest day of my life. Aren't you glad to be going home? Aren't you?"

"Of course I am. It'll be great to be back. Horseback riding. Skiing."

"And opera. Real, live grand opera. Allan, we've simply got to have a week or two in Manhattan before we go to the country."

"I thought you wanted to feel rain on your face."

"I want that, too. I want it all at once and I can't wait. Oh, darling, it's like getting out of jail." She clung to him.

He unwound her as the lift stopped. "Don't blubber."

"Allan, you're a beast," she said dreamily. "I'm so happy."

They stopped again, in bankers' row. The clerk in the

National City Bank office had their transfer of account ready. "Going home, eh? Just sign there, and your print. I envy you. Hunting, fishing."

"Surf bathing is more my style. And sailing."

"I," said Jo, "simply want to see green trees and blue sky."

The clerk nodded. "I know what you mean. It's long ago and far away. Well, have fun. Are you taking three months or six?"

"We're not coming back," Allan stated flatly. "Three years of living like a fish in an aquarium is enough."

"So?" The clerk shoved the papers toward him and added without expression, "Well—hot jets."

"Thanks." They went on up to the subsurface level and took the crosstown slidewalk out to the rocket port. The slidewalk tunnel broke the surface at one point, becoming a pressurized shed; a view window on the west looked out on the surface of the Moon—and, beyond the hills, the Earth.

The sight of it, great and green and bountiful, against the black lunar sky and harsh, unwinking stars, brought quick tears to Jo's eyes. Home—that lovely planet was hers! Allan looked at it more casually, noting the Greenwich. The sunrise line had just touched South America—must be about eight-twenty; better hurry.

They stepped off the slidewalk into the arms of some of their friends, waiting to see them off. "Hey—where have you lugs been? The *Gremlin* blasts off in seven minutes."

"But we aren't going in it," MacRae answered. "No, siree."

"What? Not going? Did you change your minds?"

Josephine laughed. "Pay no attention to him, Jack. We're going in the express instead; we swapped reservations. So we've got twenty minutes yet."

"Well! A couple of rich tourists, eh?"

"Oh, the extra fare isn't so much and I didn't want to make two changes and spend a week in space when we could be home in two days." She rubbed her bare middle significantly.

"She can't take free flight, Jack," her husband explained.

"Well, neither can I—I was sick the whole trip out. Still, I don't think you'll be sick, Jo; you're used to Moon weight now."

"Maybe," she agreed, "but there is a lot of difference between one-sixth gravity and no gravity."

Jack Crail's wife cut in. "Josephine MacRae, are you going to risk your life in an atomic-powered ship?"

"Why not, darling? You work in an atomics laboratory."

"Hummph! In the laboratory we take precautions. The Commerce Commission should never have licensed the expresses. I may be old-fashioned, but I'll go back the way I came, via Terminal and Supra-New York, in good old reliable fuel-rockets."

"Don't try to scare her, Emma," Crail objected. "They've worked the bugs out of those ships."

"Not to my satisfaction. I—"

"Never mind," Allan interrupted her. "The matter is settled, and we've still got to get over to the express launching site. Good-by, everybody! Thanks for the send-off. It's been grand knowing you. If you come back to God's country, look us up."

"Good-by, kids!" "Good-by, Jo—good-by, Allan," "Give my regards to Broadway!" "So long—be sure to write." "Good-by." "Aloha—hot jets!" They showed their tickets, entered the air lock, and climbed into the pressurized shuttle between Leyport proper and the express launching site. "Hang on, folks," the shuttle operator called back over his shoulder; Jo and Allan hurriedly settled into the cushions. The lock opened; the tunnel ahead was airless. Five minutes later they were climbing out twenty miles away, beyond the hills that shielded the lid of Luna City from the radioactive splash of the express ships.

In the *Sparrowhawk* they shared a compartment with a missionary family. The Reverend Doctor Simmons felt obliged to explain why he was traveling in luxury. "It's for the child," he told them, as his wife strapped the baby girl into a small acceleration couch rigged stretcher-fashion between her parents' couches. "Since she's never been in space, we daren't take a chance of her being sick for days on end." They all strapped down at the warning siren. Jo felt her heart begin to pound. At last . . . at long last!

The jets took hold, mashing them into the cushions. Jo had not known she could feel so heavy. This was worse, much worse, than the trip out. The baby cried as long as acceleration lasted, in wordless terror and discomfort.

After an interminable time they were suddenly weightless, as the ship went into free flight. When the terrible binding weight was free of her chest, Jo's heart felt as light as her body. Allan threw off his upper strap and sat up. "How do you feel, kid?"

"Oh, I feel fine!" Jo unstrapped and faced him. Then she hiccoughed. "That is, I think I do."

Five minutes later she was not in doubt; she merely wished to die. Allan swam out of the compartment and located the ship's surgeon, who gave her an injection. Allan waited until she had succumbed to the drug, then left for the lounge to try his own cure for spacesickness—Mothersill's Seasick Remedy washed down with champagne. Presently he had to admit that these two sovereign remedies did not work for him—or perhaps he should not have mixed them.

Little Gloria Simmons was not spacesick. She thought being weightless was fun, and went bouncing off floorplate, overhead, and bulkhead like a dimpled balloon. Jo feebly considered strangling the child, if she floated within reach—but it was too much effort.

Deceleration, logy as it made them feel, was welcome relief after nausea—except to little Gloria. She cried again, in fear and hurt, while her mother tried to explain. Her father prayed.

After a long, long time came a slight jar and the sound of the siren. Jo managed to raise her head. "What's the matter? Is there an accident?"

"I don't think so. I think we've landed."

"We can't have! We're still braking—I'm heavy as lead." Allan grinned feebly. "So am I. Earth gravity—remember?"

The baby continued to cry.

They said good-by to the missionary family, as Mrs. Simmons decided to wait for a stewardess from the skyport. The MacRaes staggered out of the ship, supporting each other. "It can't be just the gravity," Jo protested, her feet caught in invisible quicksand. "I've taken Earth-normal acceleration in the centrifuge at the 'Y', back home—I mean back in Luna City. We're weak from spacesickness."

Allan steadied himself. "That's it. We haven't eaten anything for two days."

"Allan—didn't you eat anything either?"

"No. Not *permanently*, so to speak. Are you hungry?"

"Starving."

"How about dinner at Kean's Chophouse?"

"Wonderful. Oh, Allan, we're back!" Her tears started again.

They glimpsed the Simmons' once more, after chuting down the Hudson Valley and into Grand Central Station. While they were waiting at the tube dock for their bag, Jo saw the Reverend Doctor climb heavily out of the next tube capsule, carrying his daughter and followed by his wife. He set the child down carefully. Gloria stood for a moment, trembling on her pudgy legs, then collapsed to the dock. She lay there, crying thinly.

A spaceman—pilot, by his uniform—stopped and looked pityingly at the child. "Born in the Moon?" he asked.

"Why yes, she was, sir." Simmons' courtesy transcended his troubles.

"Pick her up and carry her. She'll have to learn to walk all over again." The spaceman shook his head sadly and glided away. Simmons looked still more troubled, then sat down on the dock beside his child, careless of the dirt.

Jo felt too weak to help. She looked around for Allan, but he was busy; their bag had arrived. It was placed at his feet and he started to pick it up, and then felt suddenly silly. It seemed nailed to the dock. He knew what was in it, rolls of microfilm and colorfilm, a few souvenirs, toilet articles, various irreplaceables—fifty pounds of mass. It *couldn't* weigh what it seemed to.

But it did. He had forgotten what fifty pounds weigh on Earth.

"Porter, mister?" The speaker was grey-haired and thin, but he scooped up the bag quite casually. Allan called out, "Come along, Jo," and followed him, feeling foolish. The porter slowed to match Allan's labored steps.

"Just down from the Moon?" he asked.

"Why, yes."

"Got a reservation?"

"No."

"You stick with me. I've got a friend on the desk at the Commodore." He led them to the Concourse slidewalk and thence to the hotel.

They were too weary to dine out; Allan had dinner sent to their room. Afterward, Jo fell asleep in a hot tub and he had trouble getting her out—she liked the support the water gave her. But he persuaded her that a rubber-foam mattress was nearly as good. They got to sleep very early.

She woke up, struggling, about four in the morning. "Allan. Allan!"

"Huh? What's the matter?" His hand fumbled at the light switch.

"Uh . . . nothing I guess. I dreamed I was back in the

ship. The jets had run away with her. Allan, what makes it so stuffy in here? I've got a splitting headache."

"Huh? It can't be stuffy. This joint is air-conditioned." He sniffed the air. "I've got a headache, too," he admitted.

"Well, do something. Open a window."

He stumbled out of bed, shivered when the outer air hit him, and hurried back under the covers. He was wondering whether he could get to sleep with the roar of the city pouring in through the window when his wife spoke again. "Allan?"

"Yes. What is it?"

"Honey, I'm *cold*. May I crawl in with you?"

"Sure."

The sunlight streamed in the window, warm and mellow.

When it touched his eyes, he woke and found his wife awake beside him. She sighed and snuggled. "Oh, darling, look! Blue sky—we're *home*. I'd forgotten how lovely it is."

"It's great to be back, all right. How do you feel?"

"Much better. How are you?"

"Okay, I guess." He pushed off the covers .

Jo squealed and jerked them back. "Don't do that!"

"Huh?"

"Mamma's great big boy is going to climb out and close that window while mamma stays here under the covers."

"Well—all right." He could walk more easily than the night before—but it was good to get back into bed. Once there, he faced the telephone and shouted at it, "Service!"

"Order, please," it answered in a sweet contralto.

"Orange juice and coffee for two—extra coffee—six eggs, scrambled medium, and whole-wheat toast. And send up a *Times,* and the *Saturday Evening Post.*"

"Ten minutes."

"Thank you." The delivery cupboard buzzed while he was shaving. He answered it and served Jo breakfast in bed. Breakfast over, he laid down his newspaper and said, "Can you pull your nose out of that magazine?"

"Glad to. The darn thing is too big and heavy to hold."

"Why don't you have the stat edition mailed to you from Luna City? Wouldn't cost more than eight or nine times as much."

"Don't be silly. What's on your mind?"

"How about climbing out of that frowsty little nest and going with me to shop for clothes?"

"Unh-uh. No, I am not going outdoors in a moonsuit."

"'Fraid of being stared at? Getting prudish in your old age?"

"No, me lord, I simply refuse to expose myself to the outer air in six ounces of nylon and a pair of sandals. I want some warm clothes first." She squirmed further down under the covers.

"The Perfect Pioneer Woman. Going to have fitters sent up?"

"We can't afford that. Look—you're going anyway. Buy me just any old rag so long as it's warm."

MacRae looked stubborn. "I've tried shopping for you before."

"Just this once—please. Run over to Saks and pick out a street dress in a blue wool jersey, size ten. And a pair of nylons."

"Well—all right."

"That's a lamb. I won't be loafing. I've a list as long as your arm of people I've promised to call up, look up, have lunch with."

He attended to his own shopping first; his sensible shorts and singlet seemed as warm as a straw hat in a snow storm. It was not really cold and was quite balmy in the sun, but it seemed cold to a man used to a never-failing seventy-two degrees. He tried to stay underground, or stuck to the roofed-over section of Fifth Avenue.

He suspected that the salesmen had outfitted him in clothes that made him look like a yokel. But they were warm. They were also heavy; they added to the pain across his chest and made him walk even more unsteadily. He wondered how long it would be before he got his ground-legs.

A motherly saleswoman took care of Jo's order and sold him a warm cape for her as well. He headed back, stumbling under his packages, and trying futilely to flag a ground-taxi. Everyone seemed in such a hurry! Once he was nearly knocked down by a teen-aged boy who said, "Watch it, Gramps!" and rushed off, before he could answer.

He got back, aching all over and thinking about a hot bath. He did not get it; Jo had a visitor. "Mrs. Appleby, my husband—Allan, this is Emma Crail's mother."

"Oh, how do you do, Doctor—or should it be 'Professor'?"

"Mister—"

"—when I heard you were in town I just couldn't wait to hear all about my poor darling. How is she? Is she thin?

Does she look well? These modern girls—I've told her time and again that she must get out of doors—I walk in the Park every day and look at me. She sent me a picture— I have it here somewhere; at least I think I have—and she doesn't look a bit well, undernourished. Those synthetic foods—"

"She doesn't eat synthetic foods, Mrs. Appleby."

"—must be quite impossible, I'm sure, not to mention the taste. What were you saying?"

"Your daughter doesn't live on synthetic foods," Allan repeated. "Fresh fruits and vegetables are one thing we have almost too much of in Luna City. The air-conditioning plant, you know."

"That's just what I was saying. I confess I don't see just how you get food out of air-conditioning machinery on the Moon—"

"*In* the Moon, Mrs. Appleby."

"—but it can't be healthy. Our air-conditioner at home is always breaking down and making the most horrible smells—simply unbearable, my dears—you'd think they could build a simple little thing like an air-conditioner so that—though of course if you expect them to manufacture synthetic foods as well—"

"Mrs. Appleby—"

"Yes, Doctor? What were you saying? Don't let me—"

"Mrs. Appleby," MacRae said desperately, "the air-conditioning plant in Luna City is a hydroponic farm, tanks of growing plants, green things. The plants take the carbon dioxide out of the air and put oxygen back in."

"But—Are you quite sure, Doctor? I'm sure Emma said—"

"Quite sure."

"Well . . . I don't pretend to understand these things, I'm the artistic type. Poor Herbert often said—Herbert was Emma's father; simply wrapped up in his engineering though I always saw to it that he heard good music and saw the reviews of the best books. Emma takes after her father, I'm afraid I do wish she would give up that silly work she is in. Hardly the sort of work for a woman, do you think, Mrs. MacRae? All those atoms and neuters and things floating around in the air. I read all about it in the *Science Made Simple* column in the—"

"She's quite good at it and she seems to like it."

"Well, yes, I suppose. That's the important thing, to be happy at what you are doing no matter how silly it is. But I worry about the child—buried away from civilization, no one of her own sort to talk to, no theaters, no cultural life, no society—"

"Luna City has stereo transcriptions of every successful Broadway play." Jo's voice had a slight edge.

"Oh! Really? But it's not just going to the theater, my dear; it's the society of gentlefolk. Now when I was a girl, my parents—"

Allan butted in, loudly. "One o'clock. Have you had lunch, my dear?"

Mrs. Appleby sat up with a jerk. "Oh, heavenly days! I simply must fly. My dress designer—such a tyrant, but a genius; I must give you her address. It's been charming, my dears, and I can't thank you too much for telling me all about my poor darling. I do wish she would be sensible like you two; she knows I'm always ready to make a home for her—and her husband, for that matter. Now do come and see me, often. I love to talk to people who've been on the Moon—"

"In the Moon."

"It makes me feel closer to my darling. Good-by, then."

With the door locked behind her, Jo said, "Allan, I need a drink."

"I'll join you."

Jo cut her shopping short; it was too tiring. By four o'clock they were driving in Central Park, enjoying fall scenery to the lazy clop-clop of horse's hoofs. The helicopters, the pigeons, the streak in the sky where the Antipodes rocket had passed, made a scene idyllic in beauty and serenity. Jo swallowed a lump in her throat and whispered, "Allan, isn't it beautiful?"

"Sure is. It's great to be back. Say, did you notice they've torn up 42nd Street again?"

Back in their room, Jo collapsed on her bed, while Allan took off his shoes. He sat, rubbing his feet, and remarked, "I'm going barefooted all evening. Golly, how my feet hurt!"

"So do mine. But we're going to your father's, my sweet."

"Huh? Oh, damn, I forgot. Jo, whatever possessed you? Call him up and postpone it. We're still half dead from the trip."

"But, Allan, he's invited a lot of your friends."

"Balls of fire and cold mush! I haven't any real friends in New York. Make it next week."

"'Next week' . . . h'm'm . . . look, Allan, let's go out to the country right away." Jo's parents had left her a tiny place in Connecticut, a worn-out farm.

"I thought you wanted a couple of weeks of plays and music first. Why the sudden change?"

"I'll show you." She went to the window, open since noon. "Look at that window sill." She drew their initials in the grime. "Allan, this city is *filthy*."

"You can't expect ten million people not to kick up dust."

"But we're breathing that stuff into our lungs. What's happened to the smog-control laws?"

"That's not smog; that's normal city dirt."

"Luna City was never like this. I could wear a white outfit there till I got tired of it. One wouldn't last a day here."

"Manhattan doesn't have a roof—and precipitrons in every air duct."

"Well, it should have. I either freeze or suffocate."

"I thought you were anxious to feel rain on your face?"

"Don't be tiresome. I want it out in the clean, green country."

"Okay. I want to start my book anyhow. I'll call your real estate agent."

"I called him this morning. We can move in anytime; he started fixing up the place when he got my letter."

It was a stand-up supper at his father's home, though Jo sat down at once and let food be fetched. Allan wanted to sit down, but his status as guest of honor forced him to stay on his aching feet. His father buttonholed him at the buffet. "Here, son, try this goose liver. It ought to go well after a diet of green cheese."

Allan agreed that it was good.

"See here, son, you really ought to tell these folks about your trip."

"No speeches, Dad. Let 'em read the *National Geographic*."

"Nonsense!" He turned around. "Quiet, everybody! Allan is going to tell us how the Lunatics live."

Allan bit his lip. To be sure, the citizens of Luna City used the term to each other, but it did not sound the same here. "Well, really, I haven't anything to say. Go on and eat."

"You talk and we'll eat." "Tell us about Looney City." "Did you see the Man-in-the-Moon?" "Go on, Allan, what's it like to live on the Moon?"

"Not 'on the Moon'—*in* the moon."

"What's the difference?"

"Why, none, I guess." He hesitated; there was really no way to explain why the Moon colonists emphasized that they lived under the surface of the satellite planet— but it irritated him the way "Frisco" irritates a San Franciscan. "'In the Moon' is the way we say it. We don't spend much time on the surface, except for the staff at Richardson Observatory, and the prospectors, and so forth. The living quarters are underground, naturally."

"Why 'naturally'? Afraid of meteors?"

"No more than you are afraid of lightning. We go underground for insulation against heat and cold and as support for pressure sealing. Both are cheaper and easier underground. The soil is easy to work and the interstices act like vacuum in a thermos bottle. It is vacuum."

"But Mr. MacRae," a serious-looking lady inquired, "doesn't it hurt your ears to live under pressure?"

Allan fanned the air. "It's the same pressure here— fifteen pounds."

She looked puzzled, then said, "Yes, I suppose so, but it is a little hard to imagine. I think it would terrify me to be sealed up in a cave. Suppose you had a blow-out?"

"Holding fifteen pounds pressure is no problem; engineers work in thousands of pounds per square inch. Anyhow, Luna City is compartmented like a ship. It's safe enough. The Dutch live behind dikes; down in Mississippi they have levees. Subways, ocean liners, aircraft—they're all artificial ways of living. Luna City seems strange just because it's far away."

She shivered. "It scares me,"

A pretentious little man pushed his way forward. "Mr. MaeRae—granted that it is nice for science and all that, why should taxpayers' money be wasted on a colony on the Moon?"

"You seem to have answered yourself," Allan told him slowly.

"Then how do you justify it? Tell me that, sir."

"It isn't necessary to justify it; the Lunar colony has paid for itself several times over. The Lunar corporations are all paying propositions. Artemis Mines, Spaceways, Spaceways Provisioning Corporation, Diana Recreations, Electronics Research Company, Lunar Biological Labs, not to mention all of Rutherford—look 'em up. I'll admit the Cosmic Research Project nicks the taxpayer a little, since it's a joint enterprise of the Harriman Foundation and the government."

"Then you admit it. It's the principle of the thing."

Allan's feet were hurting him very badly indeed. "What principle? Historically, research has always paid off." He turned his back and looked for some more goose liver.

A man touched him on the arm; Allan recognized an old schoolmate. "Allan, old boy, congratulations on the way you ticked off old Beetle. He's been needing it—I think he's some sort of a radical."

Allan grinned. "I shouldn't have lost my temper."

"A good job you did. Say, Allan, I'm going to take a couple of out-of-town buyers around to the hot spots tomorrow night. Come along."

"Thanks a lot, but we're going out in the country."

"Oh, you can't afford to miss this party. After all, you've been buried on the Moon; you owe yourself some relaxation after that deadly monotony."

Allan felt his cheeks getting warm. "Thanks just the same, but—ever seen the Earth View Room in Hotel Moon Haven?"

"No. Plan to take the trip when I've made my pile, of course."

"Well, there's a night club for you. Ever see a dancer leap thirty feet into the air and do slow rolls on the way down? Ever try a lunacy cocktail? Ever see a juggler work in low gravity?" Jo caught his eye across the room. "Er . . . excuse me, old man. My wife wants me." He turned away, then flung back over his shoulder, "Moon Haven itself isn't just a spaceman's dive, by the way—it's recommended by the Duncan Hines Association."

Jo was very pale. "Darling, you've got to get me out of here. I'm suffocating. I'm really ill."

"Suits." They made their excuses.

Jo woke up with a stuffy cold, so they took a cab directly to her country place. There were low-lying clouds under them, but the weather was fine above. The sunshine and the drowsy beat of the rotors regained for them the joy of homecoming.

Allan broke the lazy revery. "Here's a funny thing, Jo. You couldn't hire me to go back to the Moon—but last night I found myself defending the Loonies every time I opened my mouth."

She nodded. "I know. Honest to Heaven, Allan, some people act as if the Earth were flat. Some of them don't really believe in anything, and some of them are so matter-of-fact that you know they don't really understand—and I don't know which sort annoys me the more."

It was foggy when they landed, but the house was clean, the agent had laid a fire and had stocked the refrigerator. They were sipping hot punch and baking the weariness out of their bones within ten minutes after the copter grounded. "This," said Allan, stretching, "is all right. It really is great to be back."

"Uh-huh. All except the highway." A new express-and-freight superhighway now ran not fifty yards from the house. They could hear the big diesels growling as they struck the grade.

"Forget the highway. Turn your back and you stare straight into the woods."

They regained their ground-legs well enough to enjoy

short walks in the woods; they were favored with a long, warm Indian summer; the cleaning woman was efficient and taciturn. Allan worked on the results of three years research preparatory to starting his book. Jo helped him with the statistical work, got reacquainted with the delights of cooking, dreamed, and rested.

It was the day of the first frost that the toilet stopped up.

The village plumber was persuaded to show up the next day. Meanwhile they resorted to a homely little building, left over from another era and still standing out beyond the wood pile. It was spider-infested and entirely too well ventilated.

The plumber was not encouraging. "New septic tank. New sile pipe. Pay you to get new fixtures at the same time. Fifteen, sixteen hundred dollars. Have to do some calculating."

"That's all right," Allan told him. "Can you start today?"

The man laughed. "I can see plainly, Mister, that you don't know what it is to get materials and labor these days. Next spring—soon as the frost is out of the ground."

"That's impossible, man. Never mind the cost. Get it done."

The native shrugged. "Sorry not to oblige you. Good day."

When he left, Jo exploded. "Allan, he doesn't want to help us."

"Well—maybe. I'll try to get someone from Norwalk, or even from the city. You can't trudge through the snow out to that Iron Maiden all winter."

"I hope not."

"You must not. You've already had one cold." He stared morosely at the fire. "I suppose I brought it on by my misplaced sense of humor."

"How?"

"Well, you know how we've been subjected to steady kidding ever since it got noised around that we were colonials. I haven't minded much, but some of it rankled. You remember I went into the village by myself last Saturday?"

"Yes. What happened?"

"They started in on me in the barbershop. I let it ride at first, then the worm turned. I started talking about the Moon, sheer double-talk—corny old stuff like the vacuum worms and the petrified air. It was some time before they realized I was ribbing them—and when they did, nobody laughed. Our friend the rustic sanitary engineer was one of the group. I'm sorry."

"Don't be." She kissed him. "If I have to tramp through the snow, it will cheer me that you gave them back some of their sass."

The plumber from Norwalk was more helpful, but rain, and then sleet, slowed down the work. They both caught colds. On the ninth miserable day Allan was working at his desk when he heard Jo come in the back door, returning from a shopping trip. He turned back to his work, then presently became aware that she had not come in to say "hello." He went to investigate.

He found her collapsed on a kitchen chair, crying quietly.

"Darling," he said urgently, "honey baby, whatever is the matter?"

She looked up. "I didn't bead to led you doe."

"Blow your nose. Then wipe your eyes. What do you mean, 'you didn't mean to let me know.' What happened?"

She let it out, punctuated with her handkerchief. First, the grocer had said he had no cleansing tissues; then, when she pointed to them, had stated that they were "sold." Finally, he had mentioned "bringing outside labor into town and taking the bread out of the mouths of honest folk."

Jo had blown up and had rehashed the incident of Allan and the barbershop wits. The grocer had simply grown more stiff. "'Lady,' he said to me, 'I don't know whether you and your husband have been to the Moon or not, and I don't care. I don't take much stock in such things. In any case, I don't need your trade.' Oh, Allan, I'm so unhappy."

"Not as unhappy as he's going to be! Where's my hat?"

"Allan! You're not leaving this house. I won't have you fighting."

"I won't have him bullying you."

"He won't again. Oh my dear, I've tried so hard, but I can't stay here any longer. It's not just the villagers; it's the cold and the cockroaches and always having a runny nose. I'm tired out and my feet hurt all the time." She started to cry again.

"There, there! We'll leave, honey. We'll go to Florida. I'll finish my book while you lie in the sun."

"Oh, I don't want to go to Florida. *I want to go home!*"

"Huh? You mean—back to Luna City?"

"Yes. Oh, dearest, I know you don't want to, but I can't stand it any longer. It's not just the dirt and the cold and the comic-strip plumbing—it's not being understood. It wasn't any better in New York. These groundhogs don't know *anything*."

He grinned at her. "Keep sending, kid; I'm on your frequency."

"Allan!"

He nodded. "I found out I was a Loony at heart quite a while ago—but I was afraid to tell you. My feet hurt, too—and I'm damn sick of being treated like a freak. I've tried to be tolerant, but I can't stand groundhogs. I miss the folks in dear old Luna. They're civilized."

She nodded. "I guess it's prejudice, but I feel the same way."

"It's *not* prejudice. Let's be honest. What does it take to get to Luna City?"

"A ticket."

"Smarty pants. I don't mean as a tourist; I mean to get a job there. You know the answer: Intelligence. It costs a lot to send a man to the Moon and more to keep him there. To pay off, he has to be worth a lot. High I.Q., good compatibility index, superior education—everything that makes a person pleasant and easy and interesting to have around. We've been spoiled; the ordinary human cussedness that groundhogs take for granted, we now find intolerable, because Loonies *are* different. The fact that Luna City is the most comfortable environment man ever built for himself is beside the point—it's the people who count. Let's go home."

He went to the telephone—an old-fashioned,

speech-only rig—and called the Foundation's New York office. While he was waiting, truncheon-like "receiver" to his ear, she said, "Suppose they won't have us?"

"That's what worries me." They knew that the Lunar companies rarely rehired personnel who had once quit; the physical examination was reputed to be much harder the second time.

"Hello . . . hello. Foundation? May I speak to the recruiting office? . . . hello—I *can't* turn on my view plate; this instrument is a hangover from the dark ages. This is Allan MacRae, physical chemist, contract number 1340729. And my wife, Josephine MacRae, 1340730. We want to sign up again. I said we wanted to sign up again . . . okay, I'll wait."

"Pray, darling, pray!"

"I'm praying—How's that! My appointment's still vacant? Fine, fine! How about my wife?" He listened with a worried look; Jo held her breath. Then he cupped the speaker. "Hey, Jo—your job's filled. They want to know if you'll take an interim job as a junior accountant?"

"Tell 'em 'yes!'"

"That'll be fine. When can we take our exams? That's fine, thanks. Good-by." He hung up and turned to his wife. "Physical and psycho as soon as we like; professional exams waived."

"What are we waiting for?"

"Nothing." He dialed the Norwalk Copter Service. "Can you run us into Manhattan? Well, good grief, don't you have radar? All right, all right, g'-by!" He snorted. "Cabs all grounded by the weather. I'll call New York and try to get a modern cab."

Ninety minutes later they landed on top of Harriman Tower.

The psychologist was very cordial. "Might as well get this over before you have your chests thumped. Sit down. Tell me about yourselves." He drew them out, nodding from time to time. "I see. Did you ever get the plumbing repaired?"

"Well, it was being fixed."

"I can sympathize with your foot trouble, Mrs. MacRae; my arches always bother me here. That's your real reason, isn't it?"

"Oh, no!"

"Now, Mrs. MacRae—"

"Really it's not—truly. I want people to talk to who know what I mean. All that's really wrong with me is that I'm homesick for my own sort. I want to go home—and I've got to have this job to get there. I'll steady down, I know I will."

The doctor looked grave. "How about you, Mr. MacRae?"

"Well—it's about the same story. I've been trying to write a book, but I can't work. I'm homesick. I want to go back."

Feldman suddenly smiled. "It won't be too difficult."

"You mean we're in? If we pass the physical?"

"Never mind the physical—your discharge examinations are recent enough. Of course you'll have to go out to Arizona for reconditioning and quarantine. You're probably wondering why it seems so easy when it is supposed to be so hard. It's really simple: We don't want people lured back by the high pay. We do want people who will be happy and as permanent as possible—in short, we want people who think of Luna City as 'home.' Now that you're 'Moonstruck,' we want you back." He stood up and shoved out his hand.

Back in the Commodore that night, Jo was struck by a thought. "Allan—do you suppose we could get our own apartment back?"

"Why, I don't know. We could send old lady Stone a radio."

"Call her up instead, Allan. We can afford it."

"All right! I will!"

It took about ten minutes to get the circuit through. Miss Stone's face looked a trifle less grim when she recognized them.

"Miss Stone, we're coming home!"

There was the usual three-second lag, then—"Yes, I know. It came over the tape about twenty minutes ago."

"Oh. Say, Miss Stone, is our old apartment vacant?" They waited.

"I've held it; I knew you'd come back—after a bit. Welcome home, Loonies."

When the screen cleared, Jo said, "What did she mean, Allan?"

"Looks like we're in, kid. Members of the Lodge."

"I guess so—oh, Allan, look!" She had stepped to the window; scudding clouds had just uncovered the Moon. It was three days old and *Mare Fecunditatis*—the roll of hair at the back of the Lady-in-the-Moon's head—was cleared by the Sunrise line. Near the righthand edge of that great, dark "sea" was a tiny spot, visible only to their inner eyes—Luna City.

The crescent hung, serene and silvery, over the tall buildings. "Darling, isn't it beautiful?"

"Certainly is. It'll be great to be back. Don't get your nose all runny."

"–We Also Walk Dogs"

"GENERAL Services—Miss Cormet speaking!" She addressed the view screen with just the right balance between warm hospitable friendliness and impersonal efficiency. The screen flickered momentarily, then built up a stereo-picture of a dowager, fat and fretful, overdressed and underexercised.

"Oh, my dear," said the image. "I'm *so* upset. I wonder if you *can* help me."

"I'm sure we can," Miss Cormet purred as she quickly estimated the cost of the woman's gown and jewels (if real—she made a mental reservation) and decided that here was a client that could be profitable. "Now tell me your trouble. Your name first, if you please." She touched a button on the horseshoe desk which enclosed her, a button marked CREDIT DEPARTMENT.

"But it's all so *involved*," the image insisted. "Peter *would* go and break his hip." Miss Cormet immediately pressed the button marked MEDICAL. "I've *told* him that polo is dangerous. You've no idea, my dear, how a mother suffers. And just at this time, too. It's *so* inconvenient—"

"You wish us to attend him? Where is he now?"

"Attend him? Why, how silly! The Memorial Hospital will do that. We've endowed them enough, I'm sure. It's my dinner party I'm worried about. The Principessa will be so annoyed."

The answer light from the Credit Department was blinking angrily. Miss Cormet headed her off. "Oh, I see. We'll arrange it for you. Now, your name, please, and your address and present location."

"But don't you *know* my name?"

"One might guess," Miss Cormet diplomatically evaded, "but General Services always respects the privacy of its clients."

"Oh, yes, of course. How considerate. I am Mrs. Peter van Hogbein Johnson." Miss Cormet controlled her reaction. No need to consult the Credit Department for this one. But its transparency flashed at once, rating AAA—unlimited. "But I don't see what you can *do,*" Mrs. Johnson continued. "I can't be two places at once."

"General Services likes difficult assignments," Miss Cormet assured her. "Now—if you will let me have the details . . . "

She wheedled and nudged the woman into giving a fairly coherent story. Her son, Peter III, a slightly shopworn Peter Pan, whose features were familiar to Grace Cormet through years of stereogravure, dressed in every conceivable costume affected by the richly idle in their pastimes, had been so thoughtless as to pick the afternoon before his mother's most important social function to bung himself up—seriously. Furthermore, he had been so thoughtless as to do so half a continent away from his mater.

Miss Cormet gathered that Mrs. Johnson's technique for keeping her son safely under thumb required that she rush to his bedside at once, and, incidentally, to select his nurses. But her dinner party that evening represented the culmination of months of careful maneuvering. What was she to *do*?

Miss Cormet reflected to herself that the prosperity of General Services and her own very substantial income was based largely on the stupidity, lack of resourcefulness, and laziness of persons like this silly parasite, as she explained that General Services would see that her party was a smooth, social success while arranging for a portable full-length stereo screen to be installed in her drawing room in order that she might greet her guests and make her explanations while hurrying to her son's side. Miss Cormet would see that a most adept social manager was placed in charge, one whose own position in society was irreproachable and whose connection with General Services was known to no one. With proper handling the disaster could be turned into a social triumph, enhancing Mrs. Johnson's reputation as a clever hostess and as a devoted mother.

"A sky car will be at your door in twenty minutes," she added, as she cut in the circuit marked TRANSPORTATION, "to take you to the rocket port. One of our young men will be with it to get additional details from you on the way to the port. A compartment for yourself and a berth for your maid will be reserved on the 16:45 rocket for Newark. You may rest easy now. General Services will do your worrying."

"Oh, thank you, my dear. You've been such a help. You've no idea of the *responsibilities* a person in my position has."

Miss Cormet cluck-clucked in professional sympathy while deciding that this particular old girl was good for still more fees. "You *do* look exhausted, madame," she said anxiously. "Should I not have a masseuse accompany you on the trip? Is your health at all delicate? Perhaps a physician would be still better."

"How thoughtful you are!"

"I'll send both," Miss Cormet decided, and switched off, with a faint regret that she had not suggested a specially chartered rocket. Special service, not listed in the master price schedule, was supplied on a cost-plus basis. In cases like this "plus" meant all the traffic would bear.

She switched to EXECUTIVE; an alert-eyed young man filled the screen. "Stand by for transcript, Steve," she said. "Special service, triple-A. I've started the immediate service."

His eyebrows lifted. "Triple-A—bonuses?"

"Undoubtedly. Give this old battleaxe the works—smoothly. And look—the client's son is laid up in a hospital. Check on his nurses. If any one of them has even a shred of sex-appeal, fire her out and put a zombie in."

"Gotcha, kid. Start the transcript."

She cleared her screen again; the "available-for-service" light in her booth turned automatically to green, then almost at once turned red again and a new figure built up in her screen.

No stupid waster this. Grace Cormet saw a well-kempt man in his middle forties, flat-waisted, shrewd-eyed, hard but urbane. The cape of his formal morning clothes was thrown back with careful casualness. "General Services," she said. "Miss Cormet speaking."

"Ah, Miss Cormet," he began, "I wish to see your chief."

"Chief of switchboard?"

"No, I wish to see the President of General Services."

"Will you tell me what it is you wish? Perhaps I can help you."

"Sorry, but I can't make explanations. I must see him, at once."

"And General Services is sorry. Mr. Clare is a very busy man; it is impossible to see him without appointment and without explanation."

"Are you recording?"

"Certainly."

"Then please cease doing so."

Above the console, in sight of the client, she switched off the recorder. Underneath the desk she switched it back on again. General Services was sometimes asked to perform illegal acts; its confidential employees took no chances. He fished something out from the folds of his chemise and held it out to her. The stereo effect made it appear as if he were reaching right out through the screen.

Trained features masked her surprise—it was the sigil of a planetary official, and the color of the badge was green.

"I will arrange it," she said.

"Very good. Can you meet me and conduct me in from the waiting room? In ten minutes?"

"I will be there, Mister . . . Mister—" But he had cut off. Grace Cormet switched to the switchboard chief and called for relief. Then, with her board cut out of service, she removed the spool bearing the clandestine record of the interview, stared at it as if undecided, and after a moment, dipped it into an opening in the top of the desk where a strong magnetic field wiped the unfixed patterns from the soft metal.

A girl entered the booth from the rear. She was blonde, decorative, and looked slow and a little dull. She was neither. "Okay, Grace," she said. "Anything to turn over?"

"No. Clear board."

"'S matter? Sick?"

"No." With no further explanation Grace left the booth, went on out past the other booths housing operators who handled unlisted services and into the large hall where the hundreds of catalogue operators worked. These had no such complex equipment as the booth which Grace had quitted. One enormous volume, a copy of the current price list of all of General Services' regular price-marked functions, and an ordinary look-and-listen enabled a catalogue operator to provide for the public almost anything the ordinary customer could wish for. If a call was beyond the scope of the catalogue it was transferred to the aristocrats of resourcefulness, such as Grace.

She took a short cut through the master files room, walked down an alleyway between dozens of chattering punched-card machines, and entered the foyer of that level. A pneumatic lift bounced her up to the level of the President's office. The President's receptionist did not stop her, nor, apparently, announce her. But Grace noted that the girl's hands were busy at the keys of her voder.

Switchboard operators do not walk into the office of the president of a billion-credit corporation. But General Services was not organized like any other business on the planet. It was a *sui generis* business in which special training was a commodity to be listed, bought, and sold, but general resourcefulness and a ready wit were all important. In its hierarchy Jay Clare, the president, came first, his handyman, Saunders Francis, stood second, and the couple of dozen operators, of which Grace was one, who took calls on the unlimited switchboard came immediately after. They, and the field operators who handled the most difficult unclassified commissions—; one group in fact, for the unlimited switchboard operators and the unlimited field operators swapped places indiscriminately.

After them came the tens of thousands of other employees spread over the planet, from the chief accountant, the head of the legal department, the chief clerk of the master files on down through the local managers, the catalogue operators to the last classified part time employee—stenographers prepared to take dictation when and where ordered, gigolos ready to fill an empty place at a dinner, the man who rented both armadillos and trained fleas.

Grace Cormet walked into Mr. Clare's office. It was the only room in the building not cluttered up with electro-mechanical recording and communicating equipment. It contained nothing but his desk (bare), a couple of chairs, and a stereo screen, which, when not in use, seemed to be Krantz' famous painting "The Weeping Buddha." The original was in fact in the sub-basement, a thousand feet below.

"Hello, Grace," he greeted her, and shoved a piece of paper at her. "Tell me what you think of that. Sance says it's lousy." Saunders Francis turned his mild pop eyes from his chief to Grace Cormet, but neither confirmed nor denied the statement.

Miss Cormet read:

CAN YOU AFFORD IT?
Can You Afford GENERAL SERVICES?
Can You Afford NOT to have General Services? ? ? ? ?
*In this jet-speed age can you afford
to go on wasting time doing your own shopping,
paying bills yourself, taking care
of your living compartment?*
We'll spank the baby and feed the cat.
We'll rent you a house and buy your shoes.
We'll write to your mother-in-law
and add up your check stubs.
No job too large; No job too small—
and all amazingly Cheap!
GENERAL SERVICES
Dial H-U-R-R-Y—U-P
P.S. *WE ALSO WALK DOGS*

"Well?" said Clare.
"Sance is right. It smells."

"Why?"

"Too logical. Too verbose. No drive."

"What's your idea of an ad to catch the marginal market?"

She thought a moment, then borrowed his stylus and wrote:

DO YOU WANT SOMEBODY MURDERED?
(Then *don't* call GENERAL SERVICES)
But for *any* other job dial *HURRY-UP—It pays!*
P.S. We also walk dogs.

"Mmmm . . . well, maybe," Mr. Clare said cautiously. "We'll try it. Sance, give this a type B coverage, two weeks, North America, and let me know how it takes." Francis put it away in his kit, still with no change in his mild expression. "Now as I was saying—"

"Chief," broke in Grace Cormet. "I made an appointment for you in—" She glanced at her watchfinger. "—exactly two minutes and forty seconds. Government man."

"Make him happy and send him away. I'm busy."

"Green Badge."

He looked up sharply. Even Francis looked interested. "So?" Clare remarked. "Got the interview transcript with you?"

"I wiped it."

"You did? Well, perhaps you know best. I like your hunches. Bring him in."

She nodded thoughtfully and left.

She found her man just entering the public reception room and escorted him past half a dozen gates whose guardians would otherwise have demanded his identity and the nature of his business. When he was seated in Clare's office, he looked around. "May I speak with you in private, Mr. Clare?"

"Mr. Francis is my right leg. You've already spoken to Miss Cormet."

"Very well." He produced the green sigil again and held it out. "No names are necessary just yet. I am sure of your discretion."

The President of General Services sat up impatiently. "Let's get down to business. You are Pierre Beaumont, Chief of Protocol. Does the administration want a job done?"

Beaumont was unperturbed by the change in pace. "You know me. Very well. We'll get down to business. The government may want a job done. In any case our discussion must not be permitted to leak out—"

"All of General Services relations are confidential."

"This is not confidential; this is secret." He paused.

"I understand you," agreed Clare. "Go on."

"You have an interesting organization here, Mr. Clare. I believe it is your boast that you will undertake any commission whatsoever—for a price."

"If it is legal."

"Ah, yes, of course. But legal is a word capable of interpretation. I admired the way your company handled the outfitting of the Second Plutonian Expedition. Some of your methods were, ah, ingenious."

"If you have any criticism of our actions in that case they are best made to our legal department through the usual channels."

Beaumont pushed a palm in his direction. "Oh, no,

Mr. Clare—please! You misunderstand me. I was not criticising; I was admiring. Such resource! What a diplomat you would have made!"

"Let's quit fencing. What do you want?"

Mr. Beaumont pursed his lips. "Let us suppose that you had to entertain a dozen representatives of each intelligent race in this planetary system and you wanted to make each one of them completely comfortable and happy. Could you do it?"

Clare thought aloud. "Air pressure, humidity, radiation densities, atmosphere, chemistry, temperatures, cultural conditions—those things are all simple. But how about acceleration? We could use a centrifuge for the Jovians, but Martians and Titans—that's another matter. There is no way to reduce earth-normal gravity. No, you would have to entertain them out in space, or on Luna. That makes it not our pigeon; we never give service beyond the stratosphere."

Beaumont shook his head. "It won't be beyond the stratosphere. You may take it as an absolute condition that you are to accomplish your results on the surface of the Earth."

"Why?"

"Is it the custom of General Services to inquire why a client wants a particular type of service?"

"No. Sorry."

"Quite all right. But you do need more information in order to understand what must be accomplished and why it must be secret. There will be a conference, held on this planet, in the near future—ninety days at the outside. Until the conference is called no suspicion that it is to be held must be allowed to leak out. If the plans for it were to be anticipated in certain quarters, it would be useless to hold the conference at all. I suggest that you think of this conference as a round-table of leading, ah, scientists of the system, about of the same size and makeup as the session of the Academy held on Mars last spring. You are to make all preparations for the entertainments of the delegates, but you are to conceal these preparations in the ramifications of your organization until needed. As for the details—"

But Clare interrupted him. "You appear to have assumed that we will take on this commission. As you have explained it, it would involve us in a ridiculous failure. General Services does not like failures. You know and I know that low-gravity people cannot spend more than a few hours in high gravity without seriously endangering their health. Interplanetary get-togethers are always held on a low-gravity planet and always will be."

"Yes," answered Beaumont patiently, "they always have been. Do you realize the tremendous diplomatic handicap which Earth and Venus labor under in consequence?"

"I don't get it."

"It isn't necessary that you should. Political psychology is not your concern. Take it for granted that it does and that the Administration is determined that *this* conference shall take place on Earth."

"Why not Luna?"

Beaumont shook his head. "Not the same thing at all. Even though we administer it, Luna City is a treaty port. Not the same thing, psychologically."

Clare shook his head. "Mr. Beaumont, I don't believe

that you understand the nature of General Services, even as I fail to appreciate the subtle requirements of diplomacy. We don't work miracles and we don't promise to. We are just the handyman of the last century, gone speed-lined and corporate. We are the latter day equivalent of the old servant class, but we are not Aladdin's genie. We don't even maintain research laboratories in the scientific sense. We simply make the best possible use of modern advances in communication and organization to do what already *can* be done." He waved a hand at the far wall, on which there was cut in intaglio the time-honored trademark of the business—a Scottie dog, pulling against a leash and sniffing at a post. "*There* is the spirit of the sort of work we do. We walk dogs for people who are too busy to walk 'em themselves. My grandfather worked his way through college walking dogs. I'm still walking them. I don't promise miracles, nor monkey with politics."

Beaumont fitted his fingertips carefully together. "You walk dogs for a fee. But of course you do—you walk my pair. Five minim-credits seems rather cheap."

"It is. But a hundred thousand dogs, twice a day, soon runs up the gross take."

"The 'take' for walking this 'dog' would be considerable."

"How much?" asked Francis. It was his first sign of interest.

Beaumont turned his eyes on him. "My dear sir, the outcome of this, ah, roundtable should make a difference of literally hundreds of billions of credits to this planet. We will not bind the mouth of the kine that tread the corn, if you pardon the figure of speech."

"How much?"

"Would thirty percent over cost be reasonable?"

Francis shook his head. "Might not come to much."

"Well, I certainly won't haggle. Suppose we leave it up to you gentlemen—your pardon, Miss Cormet!—to decide what the service is worth. I think I can rely on your planetary and racial patriotism to make it reasonable and proper."

Francis sat back, said nothing, but looked pleased.

"Wait a minute," protested Clare. "We haven't taken this job."

"We have discussed the fee," observed Beaumont.

Clare looked from Francis to Grace Cormet, then examined his fingernails. "Give me twenty-four hours to find out whether or not it is possible," he said finally, "and I'll tell you whether or not we will walk your dog."

"I feel sure," answered Beaumont, "that you will." He gathered his cape about him.

"Okay, masterminds," said Clare bitterly, "you've bought it."

"I've been wanting to get back to field work," said Grace.

"Put a crew on everything but the gravity problem," suggested Francis. "It's the only catch. The rest is routine."

"Certainly," agreed Clare, "but you had better deliver on that. If you can't, we are out some mighty expensive preparations that we will never be paid for. Who do you want? Grace?"

"I suppose so," answered Francis. "She can count up to ten."

Grace Cormet looked at him coldly. "There are times, Sance Francis, when I regret having married you."

"Keep your domestic affairs out of the office," warned Clare. "Where do you start?"

"Let's find out who knows most about gravitation," decided Francis. "Grace, better get Doctor Krathwohl on the screen."

"Right," she acknowledged, as she stepped to the stereo controls. "That's the beauty about this business. You don't have to know anything; you just have to know where to find out."

Dr. Krathwohl was a part of the permanent staff of General Services. He had no assigned duties. The company found it worthwhile to support him in comfort while providing him with an unlimited drawing account for scientific journals and for attendance at the meetings which the learned hold from time to time. Dr. Krathwohl lacked the single-minded drive of the research scientist; he was a dilettante by nature.

Occasionally they asked him a question. It paid.

"Oh, hello, my dear!" Doctor Krathwohl's gentle face smiled out at her from the screen. "Look—I've just come across the most amusing fact in the latest issue of *Nature*. It throws a most interesting sidelight on Brownlee's theory of—"

"Just a second, Doc," she interrupted. "I'm kinda in a hurry."

"Yes, my dear?"

"Who knows the most about gravitation?"

"In what way do you mean that? Do you want an astrophysicist, or do you want to deal with the subject from a standpoint of theoretical mechanics? Farquarson would be the man in the first instance, I suppose."

"I want to know what makes it tick."

"Field theory, eh? In that case you don't want Farquarson. He is a descriptive ballistician, primarily. Dr. Julian's work in that subject is authoritative, possibly definitive."

"Where can we get hold of him?"

"Oh, but you can't. He died last year, poor fellow. A great loss."

Grace refrained from telling him how great a loss and asked, "Who stepped into his shoes?"

"Who what? Oh, you were jesting! I see. You want the name of the present top man in field theory. I would say O'Neil."

"Where is he?"

"I'll have to find out. I know him slightly—a difficult man."

"Do, please. In the meantime who could coach us a bit on what it's all about?"

"Why don't you try young Carson, in our engineering department? He was interested in such things before he took a job with us. Intelligent chap—I've had many an interesting talk with him."

"I'll do that. Thanks, Doc. Call the Chief's office as soon as you have located O'Neil. Speed." She cut off.

Carson agreed with Krathwohl's opinion, but looked dubious. "O'Neil is arrogant and non-cooperative. I've worked under him. But he undoubtedly knows more about field theory and space structure than any other living man."

Carson had been taken into the inner circle, the problem explained to him. He had admitted that he saw no solution. "Maybe we are making something hard out of this," Clare suggested. "I've got some ideas. Check me if I'm wrong, Carson."

"Go ahead, Chief."

"Well, the acceleration of gravity is produced by the proximity of a mass—right? Earth-normal gravity being produced by the proximity of the Earth. Well, what would be the effect of placing a large mass just over a particular point on the earth's surface. Would not that serve to counteract the pull of the Earth?"

"Theoretically, yes. But it would have to be a damn big mass."

"No matter."

"You don't understand, Chief. To offset fully the pull of the Earth at a given point would require another planet the size of the Earth in contact with the Earth at that point. Of course since you don't want to cancel the pull completely, but simply to reduce it, you gain a certain advantage through using a smaller mass which would have its center of gravity closer to the point in question than would be the center of gravity of the Earth. Not enough, though. While the attraction builds up inversely as the square of the distance—in this case the half-diameter— the mass and the consequent attraction drops off directly as the *cube* of the diameter."

"What does that give us?"

Carson produced a sliderule and figured for a few

moments. He looked up. "I'm almost afraid to answer. You would need a good-sized asteroid, of lead, to get anywhere at all."

"Asteroids have been moved before this."

"Yes, but what is to *hold it up*? No, Chief, there is no conceivable source of power, or means of applying it, that would enable you to hang a big planetoid over a particular spot on the Earth's surface and keep it there."

"Well, it was a good idea while it lasted," Clare said pensively.

Grace's smooth brow had been wrinkled as she followed the discussion. Now she put in, "I gathered that you could use an extremely heavy small mass more effectively. I seem to have read somewhere about some stuff that weighs *tons* per cubic inch."

"The core of dwarf stars," agreed Carson. "All we would need for that would be a ship capable of going light-years in a few days, some way to mine the interior of a star, and a new space-time theory."

"Oh, well, skip it."

"Wait a minute," Francis observed. "Magnetism is a lot like gravity, isn't it?"

"Well—yes."

"Could there be some way to *magnetize* these gazebos from the little planets? Maybe something odd about their body chemistry?"

"Nice idea," agreed Carson, "but while their internal economy is odd, it's not that odd. They are still organic."

"I suppose not. If pigs had wings they'd be pigeons."

The stereo annunciator blinked. Doctor Krathwohl announced that O'Neil could be found at his summer home in Portage, Wisconsin. He had not screened him and would prefer not to do so, unless the Chief insisted.

Clare thanked him and turned back to the others. "We are wasting time," he announced. "After years in this business we should know better than to try to decide technical questions. I'm not a physicist and I don't give a damn how gravitation works. That's O'Neil's business. And Carson's. Carson, shoot up to Wisconsin and get O'Neil on the job."

"Me?"

"You. You're an operator for this job—with pay to match. Bounce over to the port—there will be a rocket and a credit facsimile waiting for you. You ought to be able to raise ground in seven or eight minutes."

Carson blinked. "How about my job here?"

"The engineering department will be told, likewise the accounting. Get going."

Without replying Carson headed for the door. By the time he reached it he was hurrying.

Carson's departure left them with nothing to do until he reported back—nothing to do, that is, but to start action on the manifold details of reproducing the physical and cultural details of three other planets and four major satellites, exclusive of their characteristic surface-normal gravitational accelerations. The assignment, although new, presented no real difficulties—to General Services. Somewhere there were persons who knew all the answers to these matters. The vast loose organization called General Services was geared to find them, hire them, put them to work. Any of the unlimited operators and a considerable percent of the catalogue operators could take such an assignment and handle it without excitement or hurry.

Francis called in one unlimited operator. He did not even bother to select him, but took the first available on the ready panel—they were all "Can do!" people. He explained in detail the assignment, then promptly forgot about it. It would be done, and on time. The punched-card machines would chatter a bit louder, stereo screens would flash, and bright young people in all parts of the Earth would drop what they were doing and dig out the specialists who would do the actual work.

He turned back to Clare, who said, "I wish I knew what Beaumont is up to. Conference of scientists—phooey!"

"I thought you weren't interested in politics, Jay."

"I'm not. I don't give a hoot in hell about politics, interplanetary or otherwise, except as it affects this business. But if I knew what was being planned, we might be able to squeeze a bigger cut out of it."

"Well," put in Grace, "I think you can take it for granted that the real heavyweights from all the planets are about to meet and divide Gaul into three parts."

"Yes, but who gets cut out?"

"Mars, I suppose."

"Seems likely. With a bone tossed to the Venerians. In that case we might speculate a little in Pan-Jovian Trading Corp."

"Easy, son, easy," Francis warned. "Do that, and you might get people interested. This is a hush-hush job."

"I guess you're right. Still, keep your eyes open. There

ought to be some way to cut a slice of pie before this is over."

Grace Cormet's telephone buzzed. She took it out of her pocket and said, "Yes?"

"A Mrs. Hogbein Johnson wants to speak to you."

"You handle her. I'm off the board."

"She won't talk to anyone but you."

"All right. Put her on the Chief's stereo, but stay in parallel yourself. You'll handle it after I've talked to her."

The screen came to life, showing Mrs. Johnson's fleshy face alone, framed in the middle of the screen in flat picture. "Oh, Miss Cormet," she moaned, "some dreadful mistake has been made. There is no stereo on this ship."

"It will be installed in Cincinnati. That will be in about twenty minutes."

"You are *sure?*"

"Quite sure."

"Oh, thank you! It's such a relief to talk with you. Do you know, I'm *thinking* of making you my social secretary."

"Thank you," Grace replied evenly, "but I am under contract."

"But how stupidly tiresome! You can break it."

"No, I'm sorry Mrs. Johnson. Good-by." She switched off the screen and spoke again into her telephone. "Tell Accounting to double her fee. And I *won't* speak with her again." She cut off and shoved the little instrument savagely back into her pocket. "Social secretary!"

It was after dinner and Clare had retired to his living apartment before Carson called back. Francis took the call in his own office.

"Any luck?" he asked, when Carson's image had built up.

"Quite a bit. I've seen O'Neil."

"Well? Will he do it?"

"You mean can he do it, don't you?"

"Well—can he?"

"Now that is a funny thing—I didn't think it was theoretically possible. But after talking with him, I'm convinced that it is. O'Neil has a new outlook on field theory—stuff he's never published. The man is a genius."

"I don't care," said Francis, "whether he's a genius or a Mongolian idiot—can he build some sort of a gravity thinnerouter?"

"I believe he can. I really do believe he can."

"Fine. You hired him?"

"No. That's the hitch. That's why I called back. It's like this: I happened to catch him in a mellow mood, and because we had worked together once before and because I had not aroused his ire quite as frequently as his other assistants he invited me to stay for dinner. We talked about a lot of things (you can't hurry him) and I broached the proposition. It interested him mildly—the idea, I mean; not the proposition and he discussed the theory with me, or, rather, at me. But he won't work on it."

"Why not? You didn't offer him enough money. I guess I'd better tackle him."

"No, Mr. Francis, no. You don't understand. He's not interested in money. He's independently wealthy and has more than he needs for his research, or anything else he wants. But just at present he is busy on wave mechanics theory and he just won't be bothered with anything else."

"Did you make him realize it was important?"

"Yes and no. Mostly no. I tried to, but there isn't anything important to him but what *he* wants. It's a sort of intellectual snobbishness. Other people simply don't count."

"All right," said Francis. "You've done well so far. Here's what you do: After I switch off, you call EXECUTIVE and make a transcript of everything you can remember of what he said about gravitational theory. We'll hire the next best men, feed it to them, and see if it gives them any ideas to work on. In the meantime I'll put a crew to work on the details of Dr. O'Neil's background. He'll have a weak point somewhere; it's just a matter of finding it. Maybe he's keeping a woman somewhere—"

"He's long past that."

"—or maybe he has a by-blow stashed away somewhere. We'll see, I want you to stay there in Portage. Since you can't hire him, maybe you can persuade him to hire you. You're our pipeline, I want it kept open. We've got to find something he wants, or something he is afraid of."

"He's not afraid of *anything*. I'm positive of that."

"Then he wants something. If it's not money, or women, it's something else. It's a law of nature."

"I doubt it," Carson replied slowly. "Say! Did I tell you about his hobby?"

"No. What is it?"

"It's china. In particular, Ming china. He has the best collection in the world, I'd guess. But I know what he wants!"

"Well, spill it, man, spill it. Don't be dramatic."

"It's a little china dish, or bowl, about four inches

across and two inches high. It's got a Chinese name that means 'Flower of Forgetfulness.'"

"Hmmm—doesn't seem significant. You think he wants it pretty bad?"

"*I know* he does. He has a solid colorgraph of it in his study, where he can look at it. But it hurts him to talk about it."

"Find out who owns it and where it is."

"I know. British Museum. That's why he can't buy it."

"So?" mused Francis. "Well, you can forget it. Carry on."

Clare came down to Francis' office and the three talked it over. "I guess we'll need Beaumont on this," was his comment when he had heard the report. "It will take the Government to get anything loose from the British Museum." Francis looked morose. "Well—what's eating you? What's wrong with that?"

"I know," offered Grace. "You remember the treaty under which Great Britain entered the planetary confederation?"

"I was never much good at history."

"It comes to this: I doubt if the planetary government can touch anything that belongs to the Museum without asking the British Parliament."

"Why not? Treaty or no treaty, the planetary government is sovereign. That was established in the Brazilian Incident."

"Yeah, sure. But it could cause questions to be asked in the House of Commons and that would lead to the one thing Beaumont wants to avoid at all costs—publicity."

"Okay. What do you propose?"

"I'd say that Sance and I had better slide over to England and find out just how tight they have the 'Flower of Forgetfulness' nailed down—and who does the nailing and what his weaknesses are."

Clare's eyes travelled past her to Francis, who was looking blank in the fashion that indicated assent to his intimates. "Okay," agreed Clare, "it's your baby. Taking a special?"

"No, we've got time to get the midnight out of New York. By-by."

"By. Call me tomorrow."

When Grace screened the Chief the next day he took one look at her and exclaimed, "Good Grief, kid! What have you done to your hair?"

"We located the guy," she explained succinctly. "His weakness is blondes."

"You've had your skin bleached, too."

"Of course. How do you like it?"

"It's stupendous—though I preferred you the way you were. But what does Sance think of it?"

"He doesn't mind—it's business. But to get down to cases, Chief, there isn't much to report. This will have to be a left-handed job. In the ordinary way, it would take an earthquake to get anything out of that tomb."

"Don't do anything that can't be fixed!"

"You know me, Chief. I won't get you in trouble. But it will be expensive."

"Of course."

"That's all for now. I'll screen tomorrow."

☆ ☆ ☆

She was a brunette again the next day. "What is this?" asked Clare. "A masquerade?"

"I wasn't the blonde he was weak for," she explained, "but I found the one he was interested in."

"Did it work out?"

"I think it will. Sance is having a facsimile integrated now. With luck, we'll see you tomorrow."

They showed up the next day, apparently empty handed, "Well?" said Clare, "well?"

"Seal the place up, Jay," suggested Francis. "Then we'll talk."

Clare flipped a switch controlling an interference shield which rendered his office somewhat more private than a coffin. "How about it?" he demanded. "Did you get it?"

"Show it to him, Grace."

Grace turned her back, fumbled at her clothing for a moment, then turned around and placed it gently on the Chief's desk.

It was not that it was beautiful—it *was* beauty. Its subtle simple curve had no ornamentation, decoration would have sullied it. One spoke softly in its presence, for fear a sudden noise would shatter it.

Clare reached out to touch, then thought better of it and drew his hand back. But he bent his head over it and stared down into it. It was strangely hard to focus—to allocate—the bottom of the bowl. It seemed as if his sight sank deeper and ever deeper into it, as if he were drowning in a pool of light.

He jerked up his head and blinked. "God," he whispered, "God—I didn't know such things existed."

He looked at Grace and looked away to Francis. Francis had tears in his eyes, or perhaps his own were blurred.

"Look, Chief," said Francis. "Look—couldn't we just keep it and call the whole thing off?"

"There's no use talking about it any longer," said Francis wearily. "We can't keep it, Chief. I shouldn't have suggested it and you shouldn't have listened to me. Let's screen O'Neil."

"We might just wait another day before we do anything about it," Clare ventured. His eyes returned yet again to the "Flower of Forgetfulness."

Grace shook her head. "No good. It will just be harder tomorrow. I *know*." She walked decisively over to the stereo and manipulated the controls.

O'Neil was annoyed at being disturbed and twice annoyed that they had used the emergency signal to call him to his disconnected screen.

"What is this?" he demanded. "What do you mean by disturbing a private citizen when he has disconnected? Speak up—and it had better be good, or, so help me, I'll sue you!"

"We want you to do a little job of work for us, Doctor," Clare began evenly.

"What!" O'Neil seemed almost too surprised to be angry. "Do you mean to stand there, sir, and tell me that you have invaded the privacy of my home to ask *me* to work for *you*?"

"The pay will be satisfactory to you."

O'Neil seemed to be counting up to ten before

answering. "Sir," he said carefully, "there are men in the world who seem to think they can buy anything, or anybody. I grant you that they have much to go on in that belief. But I am not for sale. Since you seem to be one of those persons, I will do my best to make this interview expensive for you. You will hear from my attorneys. Good night!"

"Wait a moment," Clare said urgently. "I believe that you are interested in china—"

"What if I am?"

"Show it to him, Grace." Grace brought the "Flower of Forgetfulness" up near the screen, handling it carefully, reverently.

O'Neil said nothing. He leaned forward and stared. He seemed to be about to climb through the screen. "Where did you get it?" he said at last.

"That doesn't matter."

"I'll buy it from you—at your own price."

"It's not for sale. But you may have it—if we can reach an agreement."

O'Neil eyed him. "It's stolen property."

"You're mistaken. Nor will you find anyone to take an interest in such a charge. Now about this job—"

O'Neil pulled his eyes away from the bowl. "What is it you wish me to do?"

Clare explained the problem to him. When he had concluded O'Neil shook his head. "That's ridiculous," he said.

"We have reason to feel that it is theoretically possible."

"Oh, certainly! It's theoretically possible to live forever, too. But no one has ever managed it."

"We think you can do it."

"Thank you for nothing. Say!" O'Neil stabbed a finger at him out of the screen. "You set that young pup Carson on me!"

"He was acting under my orders."

"Then, sir, I do not like your manners."

"How about the job? And this?" Clare indicated the bowl. O'Neil gazed at it and chewed his whiskers. "Suppose," he said, at last, "I make an honest attempt, to the full extent of my ability, to supply what you want—and I fail."

Clare shook his head. "We pay only for results. Oh, your salary, of course, but not *this*. This is a bonus in addition to your salary, *if* you are successful."

O'Neil seemed about to agree, then said suddenly, "You may be fooling me with a colorgraph. I can't tell through this damned screen."

Clare shrugged. "Come see for yourself."

"I shall. I will. Stay where you are. Where are you? Damn it, sir, what's your *name*?"

He came storming in two hours later. "You've tricked me! The 'Flower' is still in England. I've investigated. I'll . . . I'll *punish* you, sir, with my own two hands."

"See for yourself," answered Clare. He stepped aside, so that his body no longer obscured O'Neil's view of Clare's desk top.

They let him look. They respected his need for quiet and let him look. After a long time he turned to them, but did not speak.

"Well?" asked Clare.

"I'll build your damned gadget," he said huskily. "I figured out an approach on the way here."

✲ ✲ ✲

Beaumont came in person to call the day before the first session of the conference. "Just a social call, Mr. Clare," he stated. "I simply wanted to express to you my personal appreciation for the work you have done. And to deliver this." "This" turned out to be a draft on the Bank Central for the agreed fee. Clare accepted it, glanced at it, nodded, and placed it on his desk.

"I take it, then," he remarked, "that the Government is satisfied with the service rendered."

"That is putting it conservatively," Beaumont assured him. "To be perfectly truthful, I did not think you could do so much. You seem to have thought of everything. The Callistan delegation is out now, riding around and seeing the sights in one of the little tanks you had prepared. They are delighted. Confidentially, I think we can depend on their vote in the coming sessions."

"Gravity shields working all right, eh?"

"Perfectly. I stepped into their sightseeing tank before we turned it over to them. I was as light as the proverbial feather. Too light—I was very nearly spacesick." He smiled in wry amusement. "I entered the Jovian apartments, too. That was quite another matter."

"Yes, it would be," Clare agreed. "Two and a half times normal weight is oppressive to say the least."

"It's a happy ending to a difficult task. I must be going. Oh, yes, one other little matter—I've discussed with Doctor O'Neil the possibility that the Administration may be interested in other uses for his new development. In order to simplify the matter it seems desirable that you provide me with a quitclaim to the O'Neil effect from General Services."

Clare gazed thoughtfully at the "Weeping Buddha" and chewed his thumb. "No," he said slowly, "no. I'm afraid that would be difficult."

"Why not?" asked Beaumont. "It avoids the necessity of adjudication and attendant waste of time. We are prepared to recognize your service and recompense you."

"Hmmm. I don't believe you fully understand the situation, Mr. Beaumont. There is a certain amount of open territory between our contract with Doctor O'Neil and your contract with us. You asked of us certain services and certain chattels with which to achieve that service. We provided them—for a fee. All done. But our contract with Doctor O'Neil made him a full-time employee for the period of his employment. His research results and the patents embodying them are the property of General Services."

"Really?" said Beaumont. "Doctor O'Neil has a different impression."

"Doctor O'Neil is mistaken. Seriously, Mr. Beaumont— you asked us to develop a siege gun, figuratively speaking, to shoot a gnat. Did you expect us, as businessmen, to throw away the siege gun after one shot?"

"No, I suppose not. What do you propose to do?"

"We expect to exploit the gravity modulator commercially. I fancy we could get quite a good price for certain adaptations of it on Mars."

"Yes. Yes, I suppose you could. But to be brutally frank, Mr. Clare, I am afraid that is impossible. It is a matter of imperative public policy that this development be limited to terrestrials. In fact, the administration would find it necessary to intervene and make it government monopoly."

"Have you considered how to keep O'Neil quiet?"

"In view of the change in circumstances, no. What is your thought?"

"A corporation, in which he would hold a block of stock and be president. One of our bright young men would be chairman of the board." Clare thought of Carson. "There would be stock enough to go around," he added, and watched Beaumont's face.

Beaumont ignored the bait. "I suppose that this corporation would be under contract to the Government—its sole customer?"

"That is the idea."

"Mmmm . . . yes, it seems feasible. Perhaps I had better speak with Doctor O'Neil."

"Help yourself."

Beaumont got O'Neil on the screen and talked with him in low tones. Or, more properly, Beaumont's tones were low. O'Neil displayed a tendency to blast the microphone. Clare sent for Francis and Grace and explained to them what had taken place.

Beaumont turned away from the screen. "The Doctor wishes to speak with you, Mr. Clare."

O'Neil looked at him frigidly. "What is this claptrap I've had to listen to, sir? What's this about the O'Neil effect being your property?"

"It was in your contract, Doctor. Don't you recall?"

"Contract! I never read the damned thing. But I can tell you this: I'll take you to court. I'll tie you in knots before I'll let you make a fool of me that way."

"Just a moment, Doctor, please!" Clare soothed. "We have no desire to take advantage of a mere legal technicality, and no one disputes your interest. Let me outline what I had in mind—" He ran rapidly over the plan. O'Neil listened, but his expression was still unmollified at the conclusion.

"I'm not interested," he said gruffly. "So far as I am concerned the Government can have the whole thing. And I'll see to it."

"I had not mentioned one other condition," added Clare.

"Don't bother."

"I must. This will be just a matter of agreement between gentlemen, but it is essential. You have custody of the 'Flower of Forgetfulness.'"

O'Neil was at once on guard. "What do you mean, 'custody.' I own it. Understand me—*own* it."

"'Own it,'" repeated Clare. "Nevertheless, in return for the concessions we are making you with respect to your contract, we want something in return."

"What?" asked O'Neil. The mention of the bowl had upset his confidence.

"You own it and you retain possession of it. But I want your word that I, or Mr. Francis, or Miss Cormet, may come look at it from time to time—frequently."

O'Neil looked unbelieving. "You mean that you simply want to come to *look* at it?"

"That's all."

"Simply to *enjoy* it?"

"That's right."

O'Neil looked at him with new respect. "I did not

understand you before, Mr. Clare. I apologize. As for the corporation nonsense—do as you like. I don't care. You and Mr. Francis and Miss Cormet may come to see the 'Flower' whenever you like. You have my word."

"Thank you, Doctor O'Neil—for all of us." He switched off as quickly as could be managed gracefully.

Beaumont was looking at Clare with added respect, too. "I think," he said, "that the next time I shall not interfere with your handling of the details. I'll take my leave. Adieu, gentlemen—and Miss Cormet."

When the door had rolled down behind him Grace remarked, "That seems to polish it off."

"Yes," said Clare. "We've 'walked his dog' for him; O'Neil has what he wants; Beaumont got what he wanted, and more besides."

"Just what is he after?"

"I don't know, but I suspect that he would like to be first president of the Solar System Federation, if and when there is such a thing. With the aces we have dumped in his lap, he might make it. Do you realize the potentialities of the O'Neil effect?"

"Vaguely," said Francis.

"Have you thought about what it will do to space navigation? Or the possibilities it adds in the way of colonization? Or its recreational uses? There's a fortune in that alone."

"What do we get out of it?"

"What do we get out of it? Money, old son. Gobs and gobs of money. There's always money in giving people what they want." He glanced up at the Scottie dog trademark.

"Money," repeated Francis. "Yeah, I suppose so."

"Anyhow," added Grace, "we can always go look at the 'Flower.'"

Ordeal in Space

MAYBE we should never have ventured out into space. Our race has but two basic, innate fears; noise and the fear of falling. Those terrible heights—Why should any man in his right mind let himself be placed where he could fall . . . and fall . . . and fall—But all spacemen are crazy. Everybody knows that.

The medicos had been very kind, he supposed. "You're lucky. You want to remember that, old fellow. You're still young and your retired pay relieves you of all worry about your future. You've got both arms and legs and are in fine shape."

"Fine shape!" His voice was unintentionally contemptuous. "No, I mean it," the chief psychiatrist had persisted gently. "The little quirk you have does you no harm at all—except that you can't go out into space again. I can't honestly call acrophobia a neurosis; fear of falling is normal and sane. You've just got it a little more strongly than most—but that is not abnormal, in view of what you have been through."

The reminder set him to shaking again. He closed his eyes and saw the stars wheeling below him again. He was falling . . . falling endlessly. The psychiatrist's voice came through to him and pulled him back. "Steady, old man! Look around you."

"Sorry."

"Not at all. Now tell me, what do you plan to do?"

"I don't know. Get a job, I suppose."

"The Company will give you a job, you know."

He shook his head. "I don't want to hang around a spaceport." Wear a little button in his shirt to show that he was once a man, be addressed by a courtesy title of captain, claim the privileges of the pilots' lounge on the basis of what he used to be, hear the shop talk die down whenever he approached a group, wonder what they were saying behind his back—no, thank you!

"I think you're wise. Best to make a clean break, for a while at least, until you are feeling better."

"You think I'll get over it?"

The psychiatrist pursed his lips. "Possible. It's functional, you know. No trauma."

"But you don't think so?"

"I didn't say that. I honestly don't know. We still know very little about what makes a man tick."

"I see. Well, I might as well be leaving."

The psychiatrist stood up and shoved out his hand. "Holler if you want anything. And come back to see us in any case."

"Thanks."

"You're going to be all right. I know it."

But the psychiatrist shook his head as his patient

walked out. The man did not walk like a spaceman; the easy, animal self-confidence was gone.

Only a small part of Great New York was roofed over in those days; he stayed underground until he was in that section, then sought out a passageway lined with bachelor rooms. He stuck a coin in the slot of the first one which displayed a lighted "vacant" sign, chucked his jump bag inside, and left. The monitor at the intersection gave him the address of the nearest placement office. He went there, seated himself at an interview desk, stamped in his finger prints, and started filling out forms. It gave him a curious back-to-the-beginning feeling; he had not looked for a job since pre-cadet days.

He left filling in his name to the last and hesitated even then. He had had more than his bellyful of publicity; he did not want to be recognized; he certainly did not want to be throbbed over—and most of all he did not want anyone telling him he was a hero. Presently he printed in the name "William Saunders" and dropped the forms in the slot.

He was well into his third cigarette and getting ready to strike another when the screen in front of him at last lighted up. He found himself staring at a nice-looking brunette. "Mr. Saunders," the image said, "will you come inside, please? Door seventeen."

The brunette in person was there to offer him a seat and a cigarette. "Make yourself comfortable, Mr. Saunders. I'm Miss Joyce. I'd like to talk with you about your application."

He settled himself and waited, without speaking.

When she saw that he did not intend to speak, she added, "Now take this name 'William Saunders' which you have given us—we know who you are, of course, from your prints."

"I suppose so."

"Of course I know what everybody knows about you, but your action in calling yourself 'William Saunders,' Mr.—"

"Saunders."

"—Mr. Saunders, caused me to query the files." She held up a microfilm spool, turned so that he might read his own name on it. "I know quite a lot about you now— more than the public knows and more than you saw fit to put into your application. It's a good record, Mr. Saunders."

"Thank you."

"But I can't use it in placing you in a job. I can't even refer to it if you insist on designating yourself as 'Saunders.'"

"The name is Saunders." His voice was flat, rather than emphatic.

"Don't be hasty, Mr. Saunders. There are many positions in which the factor of prestige can be used quite legitimately to obtain for a client a much higher beginning rate of pay than—"

"I'm not interested."

She looked at him and decided not to insist. "As you wish. If you will go to reception room B, you can start your classification and skill tests."

"Thank you."

"*If* you should change your mind later, Mr. Saunders,

we will be glad to reopen the case. Through that door, please."

Three days later found him at work for a small firm specializing in custom-built communication systems. His job was calibrating electronic equipment. It was soothing work, demanding enough to occupy his mind, yet easy for a man of his training and experience. At the end of his three months probation he was promoted out of the helper category.

He was building himself a well-insulated rut, working, sleeping, eating, spending an occasional evening at the public library or working out at the YMCA—and never, under any circumstances, going out under the open sky nor up to any height, not even a theater balcony.

He tried to keep his past life shut out of his mind, but his memory of it was still fresh; he would find himself day-dreaming—the star-sharp, frozen sky of Mars, or the roaring night life of Venusburg. He would see again the swollen, ruddy bulk of Jupiter hanging over the port on Ganymede, its oblate bloated shape impossibly huge and crowding the sky.

Or he might, for a time, feel again the sweet quiet of the long watches on the lonely reaches between the planets. But such reveries were dangerous; they cut close to the edge of his new peace of mind. It was easy to slide over and find himself clinging for life to his last handhold on the steel sides of the *Valkyrie*, fingers numb and failing, and nothing below him but the bottomless well of space.

Then he would come back to Earth, shaking uncontrollably and gripping his chair or the workbench.

The first time it had happened at work he had found one of his benchmates, Joe Tully, staring at him curiously. "What's the trouble, Bill?" he had asked. "Hangover?"

"Nothing," he had managed to say. "Just a chill."

"You better take a pill. Come on—let's go to lunch."

Tully led the way to the elevator; they crowded in. Most of the employees—even the women—preferred to go down via the drop chute, but Tully always used the elevator. "Saunders," of course, never used the drop chute; this had eased them into the habit of lunching together. He knew that the chute was safe, that, even if the power should fail, safety nets would snap across at each floor level—but he could not force himself to step off the edge.

Tully said publicly that a drop-chute landing hurt his arches, but he confided privately to Saunders that he did not trust automatic machinery. Saunders nodded understandingly but said nothing. It warmed him toward Tully. He began feeling friendly and not on the defensive with another human being for the first time since the start of his new life. He began to want to tell Tully the truth about himself. If he could be sure that Joe would not insist on treating him as a hero—not that he really objected to the role of hero. As a kid, hanging around spaceports, trying to wangle chances to go inside the ships, cutting classes to watch take-offs, he had dreamed of being a "hero" someday, a hero of the spaceways, returning in triumph from some incredible and dangerous piece of exploration. But he was troubled by the fact that he still had the same picture of what a hero should look like and how he should behave; it did not include shying away from open windows, being fearful of walking across an open square, and growing too upset to speak at the mere thought of boundless depths of space.

Tully invited him home for dinner. He wanted to go, but fended off the invitation while he inquired where Tully lived. The Shelton Homes, Tully told him, naming one of those great, boxlike warrens that used to disfigure the Jersey flats. "It's a long way to come back," Saunders said doubtfully, while turning over in his mind ways to get there without exposing himself to the things he feared.

"You won't have to come back," Tully assured him. "We've got a spare room. Come on. My old lady does her own cooking—that's why I keep her."

"Well, all right," he conceded. "Thanks, Joe." The La Guardia Tube would take him within a quarter of a mile; if he could not find a covered way he would take a ground cab and close the shades.

Tully met him in the hall and apologized in a whisper.

"Meant to have a young lady for you, Bill. Instead we've got my brother-in-law. He's a louse. Sorry."

"Forget it, Joe. I'm glad to be here." He was indeed. The discovery that Bill's flat was on the thirty-fifth floor had dismayed him at first, but he was delighted to find that he had no feeling of height. The lights were on, the windows occulted, the floor under him was rock solid; he felt warm and safe. Mrs. Tully turned out in fact to be a good cook, to his surprise—he had the bachelor's usual distrust of amateur cooking. He let himself go to the pleasure of feeling at home and safe and wanted; he managed not even to hear most of the aggressive and opinionated remarks of Joe's in-law.

After dinner he relaxed in an easy chair, glass of beer in hand, and watched the video screen. It was a musical comedy; he laughed more heartily than he had in months. Presently the comedy gave way to a religious program, the National Cathedral Choir; he let it be, listening with one ear and giving some attention to the conversation with the other.

The choir was more than half way through *Prayer for Travelers* before he became fully aware of what they were singing:

> "—*hear us when we pray to Thee*
> *For those in peril on the sea.*
>
> "*Almighty Ruler of the all*
> *Whose power extends to great and small,*
> *Who guides the stars with steadfast law,*
> *Whose least creation fills with awe;*
> *Oh, grant Thy mercy and Thy grace*
> *To those who venture into space.*"

He wanted to switch it off, but he had to hear it out, he could not stop listening to it, though it hurt him in his heart with the unbearable homesickness of the hopelessly exiled. Even as a cadet this one hymn could fill his eyes with tears; now he kept his face turned away from the others to try to hide from them the drops wetting his cheeks.

When the choir's "amen" let him do so he switched quickly to some other—any other—program and remained bent over the instrument, pretending to fiddle with it, while he composed his features. Then he turned back to the company, outwardly serene, though it seemed to him that anyone could see the hard, aching knot in his middle.

The brother-in-law was still sounding off.

"We ought to annex 'em," he was saying. "That's what we ought to do. Three-Planets Treaty—what a lot of ruddy rot! What right have they got to tell us what we can and can't do on Mars?"

"Well, Ed," Tully said mildly, "it's their planet, isn't it? They were there first."

Ed brushed it aside. "Did we ask the Indians whether or not they wanted us in North America? Nobody has any right to hang on to something he doesn't know how to use. With proper exploitation—"

"You been speculating, Ed?"

"Huh? It wouldn't be speculation if the government wasn't made up of a bunch of weak-spined old women. 'Rights of Natives,' indeed. What rights do a bunch of degenerates have?"

Saunders found himself contrasting Ed Schultz with Knath Sooth, the only Martian he himself had ever known well. Gentle Knath, who had been old before Ed was born, and yet was rated as young among his own kind. Knath . . . why, Knath could sit for hours with a friend or trusted acquaintance, saying nothing, needing to say nothing. "Growing together" they called it—his entire race had so grown together that they had needed no government, until the Earthman came.

Saunders had once asked his friend why he exerted himself so little, was satisfied with so little. More than an hour passed and Saunders was beginning to regret his inquisitiveness when Knath replied, "My fathers have labored and I am weary."

Saunders sat up and faced the brother-in-law. "They are not degenerate."

"Huh? I suppose *you* are an expert!"

"The Martians aren't degenerate, they're just tired," Saunders persisted.

Tully grinned. His brother-in-law saw it and became surly. "What gives you the right to an opinion? Have you ever been to Mars?"

Saunders realized suddenly that he had let his censors down. "Have you?" he answered cautiously.

"That's beside the point. The best minds all agree—" Bill let him go on and did not contradict him again. It was a relief when Tully suggested that, since they all had to be up early, maybe it was about time to think about beginning to get ready to go to bed.

He said goodnight to Mrs. Tully and thanked her for a wonderful dinner, then followed Tully into the guest room. "Only way to get rid of that family curse we're saddled with, Bill," he apologized. "Stay up as long as you like." Tully stepped to the window and opened it. "You'll sleep well here. We're up high enough to get honest-to-goodness fresh air." He stuck his head out and took a couple of big breaths. "Nothing like the real article," he continued as he withdrew from the window. "I'm a country boy at heart. What's the matter, Bill?"

"Nothing. Nothing at all."

"I thought you looked a little pale. Well, sleep tight. I've already set your bed for seven; that'll give us plenty of time."

"Thanks, Joe. Goodnight." As soon as Tully was out of the room he braced himself, then went over and closed the window. Sweating, he turned away and switched the ventilation back on. That done, he sank down on the edge of the bed.

He sat there for a long time, striking one cigarette after another. He knew too well that the peace of mind he thought he had regained was unreal. There was nothing left to him but shame and a long, long hurt. To have reached the point where he had to knuckle under to a tenth-rate knothead like Ed Schultz—it would have been better if he had never come out of the *Valkyrie* business.

Presently he took five grains of "Fly-Rite" from his pouch, swallowed it, and went to bed. He got up almost at once, forced himself to open the window a trifle, then compromised by changing the setting of the bed so that it would not turn out the lights after he got to sleep.

He had been asleep and dreaming for an indefinitely long time. He was back in space again—indeed, he had never been away from it. He was happy, with the full happiness of a man who has awakened to find it was only a bad dream.

The crying disturbed his serenity. At first it made him only vaguely uneasy, then he began to feel in some way responsible—he must do something about it. The transition to falling had only dream logic behind it, but it was real to him. He was grasping, his hands were slipping, had slipped—and there was nothing under him but the black emptiness of space—

He was awake and gasping, on Joe Tully's guest-room bed; the lights burned bright around him.

But the crying persisted.

He shook his head, then listened. It was real all right. Now he had it identified—a cat, a kitten by the sound of it.

He sat up. Even if he had not had the spaceman's traditional fondness for cats, he would have investigated. However, he liked cats for themselves, quite aside from their neat shipboard habits, their ready adaptability to changing accelerations, and their usefulness in keeping the ship free of those other creatures that go wherever man goes. So he got up at once and looked for this one.

A quick look around showed him that the kitten was not in the room, and his ear led him to the correct spot; the sound came in through the slightly opened window. He shied off, stopped, and tried to collect his thoughts.

He told himself that it was unnecessary to do anything more; if the sound came in through his window, then it must be because it came out of some nearby window. But he knew that he was lying to himself; the sound was close by. In some impossible way the cat was just outside his window, thirty-five stories above the street.

He sat down and tried to strike a cigarette, but the tube broke in his fingers. He let the fragments fall to the floor, got up and took six nervous steps toward the window, as if he were being jerked along. He sank down to his knees, grasped the window and threw it wide open, then clung to the windowsill, his eyes tight shut.

After a time the sill seemed to steady a bit. He opened his eyes, gasped, and shut them again. Finally he opened them again, being very careful not to look out at the stars, not to look down at the street. He had half expected to find the cat on a balcony outside his room—it seemed the only reasonable explanation. But there was no balcony, no place at all where a cat could reasonably be.

However, the mewing was louder than ever. It seemed to come from directly under him. Slowly he forced his head out, still clinging to the sill, and made himself look down. Under him, about four feet lower than the edge of the window, a narrow ledge ran around the side of the building. Seated on it was a woebegone ratty-looking kitten. It stared up at him and meowed again.

It was barely possible that, by clinging to the sill with one hand and making a long arm with the other, he could reach it without actually going out the window, he thought—if he could bring himself to do it. He considered calling Tully, then thought better of it. Tully was shorter than he was, had less reach. And the kitten had to be rescued now, before the fluff-brained idiot jumped or fell.

He tried for it. He shoved his shoulders out, clung with his left arm and reached down with his right. Then he opened his eyes and saw that he was a foot or ten inches away from the kitten still. It sniffed curiously in the direction of his hand.

He stretched till his bones cracked. The kitten promptly skittered away from his clutching fingers, stopping a good six feet down the ledge. There it settled down and commenced washing its face.

He inched back inside and collapsed, sobbing, on the floor underneath the window. "I can't do it," he whispered. "I can't do it. Not again—"

The Rocket Ship *Valkyrie* was two hundred and

forty-nine days out from Earth-Luna Space Terminal and approaching Mars Terminal on Deimos, outer Martian satellite. William Cole, Chief Communications Officer and relief pilot, was sleeping sweetly when his assistant shook him. "Hey! Bill! Wake up—we're in a jam."

"Huh? Wazzat?" But he was already reaching for his socks. "What's the trouble, Tom?"

Fifteen minutes later he knew that his junior officer had not exaggerated; he was reporting the facts to the Old Man—the primary piloting radar was out of whack. Tom Sandburg had discovered it during a routine check, made as soon as Mars was inside the maximum range of the radar pilot. The captain had shrugged. "Fix it, Mister—and be quick about it. We need it."

Bill Cole shook his head. "There's nothing wrong with it, Captain—inside. She acts as if the antenna were gone completely."

"That's impossible. We haven't even had a meteor alarm."

"Might be anything, Captain. Might be metal fatigue and it just fell off. But we've got to replace that antenna. Stop the spin on the ship and I'll go out and fix it. I can jury-rig a replacement while she loses her spin."

The *Valkyrie* was a luxury ship, of her day. She was assembled long before anyone had any idea of how to produce an artificial gravity field. Nevertheless she had pseudogravity for the comfort of her passengers. She spun endlessly around her main axis, like a shell from a rifled gun; the resulting angular acceleration—miscalled "centrifugal force"—kept her passengers firm in their beds, or steady on their feet. The spin was started as soon as her rockets stopped blasting at the beginning of a trip and was stopped only when it was necessary to maneuver into a landing. It was accomplished, not by magic, but by reaction against the contrary spin of a flywheel located on her centerline.

The captain looked annoyed. "I've started to take the spin off, but I can't wait that long. Jury-rig the astrogational radar for piloting."

Cole started to explain why the astrogational radar could not be adapted to short-range work, then decided not to try. "It can't be done, sir. It's a technical impossibility."

"When I was your age I could jury-rig anything! Well, find me an answer, Mister. I can't take this ship down blind. Not even for the Harriman Medal."

Bill Cole hesitated for a moment before replying, "I'll have to go out while she's still got spin on her, Captain, and make the replacement. There isn't any other way to do it."

The captain looked away from him, his jaw muscles flexed. "Get the replacement ready. Hurry up about it."

Cole found the captain already at the airlock when he arrived with the gear he needed for the repair. To his surprise the Old Man was suited up. "Explain to me what I'm to do," he ordered Bill.

"You're not going out, sir?" The captain simply nodded.

Bill took a look at his captain's waist line, or where his waist line used to be. Why, the Old Man must be thirty-five if he were a day! "I'm afraid I can't explain too clearly. I had expected to make the repair myself."

"I've never asked a man to do a job I wouldn't do myself. Explain it to me."

"Excuse me, sir—but can you chin yourself with one hand?"

"What's that got to do with it?"

"Well, we've got forty-eight passengers, sir, and—"

"Shut up!"

Sandburg and he, both in space suits, helped the Old Man down the hole after the inner door of the lock was closed and the air exhausted. The space beyond the lock was a vast, starflecked emptiness. With spin still on the ship, every direction outward was "down," down for millions of uncounted miles. They put a safety line on him, of course—nevertheless it gave him a sinking feeling to see the captain's head disappear in the bottomless, black hole.

The line paid out steadily for several feet, then stopped. When it had been stopped for several minutes, Bill leaned over and touched his helmet against Sandburg's. "Hang on to my feet. I'm going to take a look."

He hung head down out the lock and looked around. The captain was stopped, hanging by both hands, nowhere near the antenna fixture. He scrambled back up and reversed himself. "I'm going out."

It was no great trick, he found, to hang by his hands and swing himself along to where the captain was stalled. The *Valkyrie* was a space-to-space ship, not like the sleek-sided jobs we see around earthports; she was covered with handholds for the convenience of repairmen at the terminals. Once he reached him, it was possible, by grasping the same steel rung that the captain clung to, to aid him in swinging back to the last one he had quitted. Five minutes later Sandburg was pulling the Old Man up through the hole and Bill was scrambling after him.

He began at once to unbuckle the repair gear from the captain's suit and transfer it to his own. He lowered himself back down the hole and was on his way before the older man had recovered enough to object, if he still intended to.

Swinging out to where the antenna must be replaced was not too hard, though he had all eternity under his toes. The suit impeded him a little—the gloves were clumsy—but he was used to spacesuits. He was a little winded from helping the captain, but he could not stop to think about that. The increased spin bothered him somewhat; the airlock was nearer the axis of spin than was the antenna—he felt heavier as he moved out.

Getting the replacement antenna shipped was another matter. It was neither large nor heavy, but he found it impossible to fasten it into place. He needed one hand to cling by, one to hold the antenna, and one to handle the wrench. That left him shy one hand, no matter how he tried it.

Finally he jerked his safety line to signal Sandburg for more slack. Then he unshackled it from his waist, working with one hand, passed the end twice through a handhold and knotted it; he left about six feet of it hanging free. The shackle on the free end he fastened to another handhold. The result was a loop, a bight, an improvised bosun's chair, which would support his weight while he man-handled the antenna into place. The job went fairly quickly then.

He was almost through. There remained one bolt to fasten on the far side, away from where he swung. The antenna was already secured at two points and its circuit connection made. He decided he could manage it with one hand. He left his perch and swung over, monkey fashion.

The wrench slipped as he finished tightening the bolt; it slipped from his grasp, fell free. He watched it go, out and out and out, down and down and down, until it was so small he could no longer see it. It made him dizzy to watch it, bright in the sunlight against the deep black of space. He had been too busy to look down, up to now.

He shivered. "Good thing I was through with it," he said. "It would be a long walk to fetch it." He started to make his way back.

He found that he could not.

He had swung past the antenna to reach his present position, using a grip on his safety-line swing to give him a few inches more reach. Now the loop of line hung quietly, just out of reach. There was no way to reverse the process.

He hung by both hands and told himself not to get panicky—he must think his way out. Around the other side? No, the steel skin of the *Valkyrie* was smooth there—no handhold for more than six feet. Even if he were not tired—and he had to admit that he was, tired and getting a little cold—even if he were fresh, it was an impossible swing for anyone not a chimpanzee.

He looked down—and regretted it.

There was nothing below him but stars, down and down, endlessly. Stars, swinging past as the ship spun with him, emptiness of all time and blackness and cold.

He found himself trying to hoist himself bodily onto the single narrow rung he clung to, trying to reach it with his toes. It was a futile, strength-wasting excess. He quieted his panic sufficiently to stop it, then hung limp.

It was easier if he kept his eyes closed. But after a while he always had to open them and look. The Big

Dipper would swing past and then, presently, Orion. He tried to compute the passing minutes in terms of the number of rotations the ship made, but his mind would not work clearly, and, after a while, he would have to shut his eyes.

His hands were becoming stiff—and cold. He tried to rest them by hanging by one hand at a time. He let go with his left hand, felt pins-and-needles course through it, and beat it against his side. Presently it seemed time to spell his right hand.

He could no longer reach up to the rung with his left hand. He did not have the power left in him to make the extra pull; he was fully extended and could not shorten himself enough to get his left hand up.

He could no longer feel his right hand at all.

He could see it slip. It was slipping—

The sudden release in tension let him know that he was falling . . . falling. The ship dropped away from him.

He came to with the captain bending over him. "Just keep quiet, Bill."

"Where—"

"Take it easy. The patrol from Deimos was already close by when you let go. They tracked you on the 'scope, matched orbits with you, and picked you up. First time in history, I guess. Now keep quiet. You're a sick man—you hung there more than two hours, Bill."

The meowing started up again, louder than ever. He got up on his knees and looked out over the windowsill. The kitten was still away to the left on the ledge. He thrust his head cautiously out a little further, remembering not to look at anything but the kitten and the ledge. "Here, kitty!" he called. "Here, kit-kit-kitty! Here, kitty, come kitty!"

The kitten stopped washing and managed to look puzzled.

"Come, kitty," he repeated softly. He let go of the windowsill with his right hand and gestured toward it invitingly. The kitten approached about three inches, then sat down. "Here, kitty," he pleaded and stretched his arm as far as possible.

The fluff ball promptly backed away again.

He withdrew his arm and thought about it. This was getting nowhere, he decided. If he were to slide over the edge and stand on the ledge, he could hang on with one arm and be perfectly safe. He knew that, he knew it would be safe—he needn't look down!

He drew himself back inside, reversed himself, and, with great caution, gripping the sill with both arms, let his legs slide down the face of the building. He focused his eyes carefully on the corner of the bed.

The ledge seemed to have been moved. He could not find it, and was beginning to be sure that he had reached past it, when he touched it with one toe—then he had both feet firmly planted on it. It seemed about six inches wide. He took a deep breath.

Letting go with his right arm, he turned and faced the kitten. It seemed interested in the procedure but not disposed to investigate more closely. If he were to creep along the ledge, holding on with his left hand, he could just about reach it from the corner of the window—

He moved his feet one at a time, baby fashion, rather

than pass one past the other. By bending his knees a trifle, and leaning, he could just manage to reach it. The kitten sniffed his groping fingers, then leaped backward. One tiny paw missed the edge; it scrambled and regained its footing. "You little idiot!" he said indignantly, "do you want to bash your brains out?"

"If any," he added. The situation looked hopeless now; the baby cat was too far away to be reached from his anchorage at the window, no matter how he stretched. He called "Kitty, kitty" rather hopelessly, then stopped to consider the matter.

He could give it up.

He could prepare himself to wait all night in the hope that the kitten would decide to come closer. Or he could go get it.

The ledge was wide enough to take his weight. If he made himself small, flat to the wall, no weight rested on his left arm. He moved slowly forward, retaining the grip on the window as long as possible, inching so gradually that he hardly seemed to move. When the window frame was finally out of reach, when his left hand was flat to smooth wall, he made the mistake of looking down, down, past the sheer wall at the glowing pavement far below.

He pulled his eyes back and fastened them on a spot on the wall, level with his eyes and only a few feet away. He was still there!

And so was the kitten. Slowly he separated his feet, moving his right foot forward, and bent his knees. He stretched his right hand along the wall, until it was over and a little beyond the kitten.

He brought it down in a sudden swipe, as if to swat a

fly. He found himself with a handful of scratching, biting fur.

He held perfectly still then, and made no attempt to check the minor outrages the kitten was giving him. Arms still outstretched, body flat to the wall, he started his return. He could not see where he was going and could not turn his head without losing some little of his margin of balance. It seemed a long way back, longer than he had come, when at last the fingertips of his left hand slipped into the window opening.

He backed up the rest of the way in a matter of seconds, slid both arms over the sill, then got his right knee over. He rested himself on the sill and took a deep breath. "Man!" he said aloud. "That was a tight squeeze. You're a menace to traffic, little cat."

He glanced down at the pavement. It was certainly a long way down—looked hard, too.

He looked up at the stars. Mighty nice they looked and mighty bright. He braced himself in the window frame, back against one side, foot pushed against the other, and looked at them. The kitten settled down in the cradle of his stomach and began to buzz. He stroked it absent-mindedly and reached for a cigarette. He would go out to the port and take his physical and his psycho tomorrow, he decided. He scratched the kitten's ears. "Little fluffhead," he said, "how would you like to take a long, long ride with me?"

The Green Hills of Earth

THIS is the story of Rhysling, the Blind Singer of the Spaceways—but not the official version. You sang his words in school:

> *"I pray for one last landing*
> *On the globe that gave me birth;*
> *Let me rest my eyes on the fleecy skies*
> *And the cool, green hills of Earth."*

Or perhaps you sang in French, or German. Or it might have been Esperanto, while Terra's rainbow banner rippled over your head.

The language does not matter—it was certainly an *Earth* tongue. No one has ever translated *"Green Hills"* into the lisping Venerian speech; no Martian ever croaked and whispered it in the dry corridors. This is ours. We of Earth have exported everything from Hollywood crawlies to synthetic radioactives, but this belongs solely to Terra, and to her sons and daughters wherever they may be.

We have all heard many stories of Rhysling. You may even be one of the many who have sought degrees, or acclaim, by scholarly evaluations of his published works— *Songs of the Spaceways, The Grand Canal, and other Poems, High and Far,* and *"UP SHIP!"*

Nevertheless, although you have sung his songs and read his verses, in school and out your whole life, it is at least an even money bet—unless you are a spaceman yourself—that you have never even heard of most of Rhysling's unpublished songs, such items as *Since the Pusher Met My Cousin, That Red-Headed Venusburg Gal, Keep Your Pants On, Skipper,* or *A Space Suit Built for Two.*

Nor can we quote them in a family magazine.

Rhysling's reputation was protected by a careful literary executor and by the happy chance that he was never interviewed. *Songs of the Spaceways* appeared the week he died; when it became a best seller, the publicity stories about him were pieced together from what people remembered about him plus the highly colored handouts from his publishers.

The resulting traditional picture of Rhysling is about as authentic as George Washington's hatchet or King Alfred's cakes.

In truth you would not have wanted him in your parlor; he was not socially acceptable. He had a permanent case of sun itch, which he scratched continually, adding nothing to his negligible beauty.

Van der Voort's portrait of him for the Harriman Centennial edition of his works shows a figure of high tragedy, a solemn mouth, sightless eyes concealed by black silk bandage. He was never solemn! His mouth was always open, singing, grinning, drinking, or eating. The bandage was any rag, usually dirty. After he lost his sight he became less and less neat about his person.

"Noisy" Rhysling was a jetman, second class, with eyes as good as yours, when he signed on for a loop trip to the Jovian asteroids in the RS *Goshawk*. The crew signed releases for everything in those days; a Lloyd's associate would have laughed in your face at the notion of insuring a spaceman. The Space Precautionary Act had never been heard of, and the Company was responsible only for wages, if and when. Half the ships that went further than Luna City never came back. Spacemen did not care; by preference they signed for shares, and any one of them would have bet you that he could jump from the 200th floor of Harriman Tower and ground safely, if you offered him three to two and allowed him rubber heels for the landing.

Jetmen were the most carefree of the lot and the meanest. Compared with them the masters, the radarmen, and the astrogators (there were no supers or stewards in those days) were gentle vegetarians. Jetmen knew too much. The others trusted the skill of the captain to get them down safely; jetmen knew that skill was useless against the blind and fitful devils chained inside their rocket motors.

The *Goshawk* was the first of Harriman's ships to be converted from chemical fuel to atomic power-piles—or rather the first that did not blow up. Rhysling knew her well; she was an old tub that had plied the Luna City run, Supra-New York space station to Leyport and back, before she was converted for deep space. He had worked the Luna run in her and had been along on the first deep space trip, Drywater on Mars—and back, to everyone's surprise.

He should have made chief engineer by the time he signed for the Jovian loop trip, but, after the Drywater pioneer trip, he had been fired, blacklisted, and grounded at Luna City for having spent his time writing a chorus and several verses at a time when he should have been watching his gauges. The song was the infamous *The Skipper is à Father to his Crew*, with the uproariously unprintable final couplet.

The blacklist did not bother him. He won an accordion from a Chinese barkeep in Luna City by cheating at one-thumb and thereafter kept going by singing to the miners for drinks and tips until the rapid attrition in spacemen caused the Company agent there to give him another chance. He kept his nose clean on the Luna run for a year or two, got back into deep space, helped give Venusburg its original ripe reputation, strolled the banks of the Grand Canal when a second colony was established at the ancient Martian capital, and froze his toes and ears on the second trip to Titan.

Things moved fast in those days. Once the power-pile drive was accepted the number of ships that put out from the Luna-Terra system was limited only by the availability of crews. Jetmen were scarce; the shielding was cut to a minimum to save weight and few married men cared to risk possible exposure to radioactivity. Rhysling did not want to be a father, so jobs were always open to him during the golden days of the claiming boom. He crossed and recrossed the system, singing the doggerel that boiled up in his head and chording it out on his accordion.

The master of the *Goshawk* knew him; Captain Hicks had been astrogator on Rhysling's first trip in her. "Welcome home, Noisy," Hicks had greeted him. "Are you sober, or shall I sign the book for you?"

"You can't get drunk on the bug juice they sell here, Skipper." He signed and went below, lugging his accordion.

Ten minutes later he was back. "Captain," he stated darkly, "that number two jet ain't fit. The cadmium dampers are warped."

"Why tell me? Tell the Chief."

"I did, but he says they will do. He's wrong."

The captain gestured at the book. "Scratch out your name and scram. We raise ship in thirty minutes."

Rhysling looked at him, shrugged, and went below again.

It is a long climb to the Jovian planetoids; a Hawk-class clunker had to blast for three watches before going into free flight. Rhysling had the second watch. Damping was done by hand then, with a multiplying vernier and a danger gauge. When the gauge showed red, he tried to correct it—no luck.

Jetmen don't wait; that's why they are jetmen. He slapped the emergency discover and fished at the hot stuff with the tongs. The lights went out, he went right ahead. A jetman has to know his power room the way your tongue knows the inside of your mouth.

He sneaked a quick look over the top of the lead baffle when the lights went out. The blue radioactive glow did not help him any; he jerked his head back and went on fishing by touch.

When he was done he called over the tube, "Number two jet out. And for crissake get me some light down here!"

There was light—the emergency circuit—but not for him. The blue radioactive glow was the last thing his optic nerve ever responded to.

II

"As Time and Space come bending back to shape
    this starspecked scene,
The tranquil tears of tragic joy still spread their
    silver sheen;
Along the Grand Canal still soar the fragile
    Towers of Truth;
Their fairy grace defends this place of Beauty,
    calm and couth.

"Bone-tired the race that raised the Towers, forgotten
    are their lores;
Long gone the gods who shed the tears that lap
    these crystal shores.
Slow beats the time-worn heart of Mars beneath
    this icy sky;
The thin air whispers voicelessly that all who live
    must die—

"Yet still the lacy Spires of Truth sing Beauty's
    madrigal
And she herself will ever dwell along the Grand
    Canal!"

✾ ✾ ✾

—from *The Grand Canal*, by permission of Lux Transcriptions, Ltd., London and Luna City

On the swing back they set Rhysling down on Mars at Drywater; the boys passed the hat and the skipper kicked in a half month's pay. That was all—*finish*—just another space bum who had not had the good fortune to finish it off when his luck ran out. He holed up with the prospectors and archeologists at How-Far? for a month or so, and could probably have stayed forever in exchange for his songs and his accordion playing. But spacemen die if they stay in one place; he hooked a crawler over to Drywater again and thence to Marsopolis.

The capital was well into its boom; the processing plants lined the Grand Canal on both sides and roiled the ancient waters with the filth of the run-off. This was before the Tri-Planet Treaty forbade disturbing cultural relics for commerce; half the slender, fairylike towers had been torn down, and others were disfigured to adapt them as pressurized buildings for Earthmen.

Now Rhysling had never seen any of these changes and no one described them to him; when he "saw" Marsopolis again, he visualized it as it had been, before it was rationalized for trade. His memory was good. He stood on the riparian esplanade where the ancient great of Mars had taken their ease and saw its beauty spreading out before his blinded eyes—ice blue plain of water unmoved by tide, untouched by breeze, and reflecting serenely the sharp, bright stars of the Martian sky, and beyond the water the lacy buttresses and flying towers of an architecture too delicate for our rumbling, heavy planet.

The result was *Grand Canal*.

The subtle change in his orientation which enabled him to see beauty at Marsopolis where beauty was not now began to affect his whole life. All women became beautiful to him. He knew them by their voices and fitted their appearances to the sounds. It is a mean spirit indeed who will speak to a blind man other than in gentle friendliness; scolds who had given their husbands no peace sweetened their voices to Rhysling.

It populated his world with beautiful women and gracious men. *Dark Star Passing, Berenice's Hair, Death Song of a Wood's Colt,* and his other love songs of the wanderers, the womenless men of space, were the direct result of the fact that his conceptions were unsullied by tawdry truths. It mellowed his approach, changed his doggerel to verse, and sometimes even to poetry.

He had plenty of time to think now, time to get all the lovely words just so, and to worry a verse until it sang true in his head. The monotonous beat of *Jet Song*—

When the field is clear, the reports all seen,
When the lock sighs shut, when the lights wink green,
When the check-off's done, when it's time to pray,
When the Captain nods, when she blasts away—

> *Hear the jets!*
> *Hear them snarl at your back*
> *When you're stretched on the rack;*
> *Feel your ribs clamp your chest,*
> *Feel your neck grind its rest.*
> *Feel the pain in your ship,*

> *Feel her strain in their grip.*
> *Feel her rise! Feel her drive!*
> *Straining steel, come alive,*
> *On her jets!*

—came to him not while he himself was a jetman but later while he was hitchhiking from Mars to Venus and sitting out a watch with an old shipmate.

At Venusburg he sang his new songs and some of the old, in the bars. Someone would start a hat around for him; it would come back with a minstrel's usual take doubled or tripled in recognition of the gallant spirit behind the bandaged eyes.

It was an easy life. Any space port was his home and any ship his private carriage. No skipper cared to refuse to lift the extra mass of blind Rhysling and his squeeze box; he shuttled from Venusburg to Leyport to Drywater to New Shanghai, or back again, as the whim took him.

He never went closer to Earth than Supra-New York Space Station. Even when signing the contract for *Songs of the Spaceways* he made his mark in a cabin-class liner somewhere between Luna City and Ganymede. Horowitz, the original publisher, was aboard for a second honeymoon and heard Rhysling sing at a ship's party. Horowitz knew a good thing for the publishing trade when he heard it; the entire contents of *Songs* were sung directly into the tape in the communications room of the ship before he let Rhysling out of his sight. The next three volumes were squeezed out of Rhysling at Venusburg, where Horowitz had sent an agent to keep him liquored up until he had sung all he could remember.

UP SHIP! is not certainly authentic Rhysling throughout. Much of it is Rhysling's, no doubt, and *Jet Song* is unquestionably his, but most of the verses were collected after his death from people who had known him during his wanderings.

The Green Hills of Earth grew through twenty years. The earliest form we know about was composed before Rhysling was blinded, during a drinking bout with some of the indentured men on Venus. The verses were concerned mostly with the things the labor clients intended to do back on Earth if and when they ever managed to pay their bounties and thereby be allowed to go home. Some of the stanzas were vulgar, some were not, but the chorus was recognizably that of *Green Hills*.

We know exactly where the final form of *Green Hills* came from, and when.

There was a ship in at Venus Ellis Isle which was scheduled for the direct jump from there to Great Lakes, Illinois. She was the old *Falcon,* youngest of the Hawk class and the first ship to apply the Harriman Trust's new policy of extra-fare express service between Earth cities and any colony with scheduled stops.

Rhysling decided to ride her back to Earth. Perhaps his own song had gotten under his skin—or perhaps he just hankered to see his native Ozarks one more time.

The Company no longer permitted deadheads; Rhysling knew this but it never occurred to him that the ruling might apply to him. He was getting old, for a spaceman, and just a little matter of fact about his privileges. Not senile—he simply knew that he was one of the landmarks in space, along with Halley's Comet, the

Rings, and Brewster's Ridge. He walked in the crew's port, went below, and made himself at home in the first empty acceleration couch.

The Captain found him there while making a last minute tour of his ship. "What are you doing here?" he demanded.

"Dragging it back to Earth, Captain." Rhysling needed no eyes to see a skipper's four stripes.

"You can't drag in this ship; you know the rules. Shake a leg and get out of here. We raise ship at once." The Captain was young; he had come up after Rhysling's active time, but Rhysling knew the type—five years at Harriman Hall with only cadet practice trips instead of solid, deep space experience. The two men did not touch in background nor spirit; space was changing.

"Now, Captain, you wouldn't begrudge an old man a trip home."

The officer hesitated—several of the crew had stopped to listen. "I can't do it. 'Space Precautionary Act, Clause Six: No one shall enter space save as a licensed member of a crew of a chartered vessel, or as a paying passenger of such a vessel under such regulations as may be issued pursuant to this act.' Up you get and out you go."

Rhysling lolled back, his hands under his head. "If I've got to go, I'm damned if I'll walk. Carry me."

The Captain bit his lip and said, "Master-at-Arms! Have this man removed."

The ship's policeman fixed his eyes on the overhead struts.

"Can't rightly do it, Captain. I've sprained my shoulder."

The other crew members, present a moment before, had faded into the bulkhead paint.

"Well, get a working party!"

"Aye, aye, sir." He, too, went away.

Rhysling spoke again. "Now look, Skipper—let's not have any hard feelings about this. You've got an out to carry me if you want to—the 'Distressed Spaceman' clause."

"'Distressed Spaceman,' my eye! You're no distressed spaceman; you're a space-lawyer. I know who you are; you've been bumming around the system for years. Well, you won't do it in my ship. That clause was intended to succor men who had missed their ships, not to let a man drag free all over space."

"Well, now, Captain, can you properly say I haven't missed my ship? I've never been back home since my last trip as a signed-on crew member. The law says I can have a trip back."

"But that was years ago. You've used up your chance."

"Have I now? The clause doesn't say a word about how soon a man has to take his trip back; it just says he's got it coming to him. Go look it up, Skipper. If I'm wrong, I'll not only walk out on my two legs, I'll beg your humble pardon in front of your crew. Go on—look it up. Be a sport."

Rhysling could feel the man's glare, but he turned and stomped out of the compartment. Rhysling knew that he had used his blindness to place the Captain in an impossible position, but this did not embarrass Rhysling—he rather enjoyed it.

Ten minutes later the siren sounded, he heard the

orders on the bull horn for Up-Stations. When the soft sighing of the locks and the slight pressure change in his ears let him know that take-off was imminent he got up and shuffled down to the power room, as he wanted to be near the jets when they blasted off. He needed no one to guide him in any ship of the Hawk class.

Trouble started during the first watch. Rhysling had been lounging in the inspector's chair, fiddling with the keys of his accordion and trying out a new version of *Green Hills*.

> *"Let me breathe unrationed air again*
> *Where there's no lack nor dearth*

And something, something, something 'Earth'"—it would not come out right. He tried again.

> *"Let the sweet fresh breezes heal me*
> *As they rove around the girth*
> *Of our lovely mother planet,*
> *Of the cool green hills of Earth."*

That was better, he thought. "How do you like that, Archie?" he asked over the muted roar.

"Pretty good. Give out with the whole thing." Archie Macdougal, Chief Jetman, was an old friend, both spaceside and in bars; he had been an apprentice under Rhysling many years and millions of miles back.

Rhysling obliged, then said, "You youngsters have got it soft. Everything automatic. When I was twisting her tail you had to stay awake."

"You still have to stay awake." They fell to talking shop and Macdougal showed him the direct response damping rig which had replaced the manual vernier control which Rhysling had used. Rhysling felt out the controls and asked questions until he was familiar with the new installation. It was his conceit that he was still a jetman and that his present occupation as a troubadour was simply an expedient during one of the fusses with the company that any man could get into.

"I see you still have the old hand damping plates installed," he remarked, his agile fingers flitting over the equipment.

"All except the links. I unshipped them because they obscure the dials."

"You ought to have them shipped. You might need them."

"Oh, I don't know. I think—" Rhysling never did find out what Macdougal thought for it was at that moment the trouble tore loose. Macdougal caught it square, a blast of radioactivity that burned him down where he stood.

Rhysling sensed what had happened. Automatic reflexes of old habit came out. He slapped the discover and rang the alarm to the control room simultaneously. Then he remembered the unshipped links. He had to grope until he found them, while trying to keep as low as he could to get maximum benefit from the baffles. Nothing but the links bothered him as to location. The place was as light to him as any place could be; he knew every spot, every control, the way he knew the keys of his accordion.

"Power room! Power room! What's the alarm?"

"Stay out!" Rhysling shouted. "The place is 'hot.'" He could feel it on his face and in his bones, like desert sunshine.

The links he got into place, after cursing someone, anyone, for having failed to rack the wrench he needed. Then he commenced trying to reduce the trouble by hand. It was a long job and ticklish. Presently he decided that the jet would have to be spilled, pile and all.

First he reported. "Control!"

"Control aye aye!"

"Spilling jet three—emergency."

"Is this Macdougal?"

"Macdougal is dead. This is Rhysling, on watch. Stand by to record."

There was no answer; dumbfounded the Skipper may have been, but he could not interfere in a power room emergency. He had the ship to consider, and the passengers and crew. The doors had to stay closed.

The Captain must have been still more surprised at what Rhysling sent for record. It was:

> "We rot in the molds of Venus,
> We retch at her tainted breath.
> Foul are her flooded jungles,
> Crawling with unclean death."

Rhysling went on cataloguing the Solar System as he worked, "—harsh bright soil of Luna—," "—Saturn's rainbow rings—," "—the frozen night of Titan—," all the while opening and spilling the jet and fishing it clean. He finished with an alternate chorus—

> "We've tried each spinning space mote
> And reckoned its true worth:
> Take us back again to the homes of men
> On the cool, green hills of Earth."

—then, almost absentmindedly remembered to tack on his revised first verse:

> "The arching sky is calling
> Spacemen back to their trade.
> All hands! Stand by! Free falling!
> And the lights below us fade.
> Out ride the sons of Terra,
> Far drives the thundering jet,
> Up leaps the race of Earthmen,
> Out, far, and onward yet—"

The ship was safe now and ready to limp home shy one jet. As for himself, Rhysling was not so sure. That "sunburn" seemed sharp, he thought. He was unable to see the bright, rosy fog in which he worked but he knew it was there. He went on with the business of flushing the air out through the outer valve, repeating it several times to permit the level of radiation to drop to something a man might stand under suitable armor. While he did this he sent one more chorus, the last bit of authentic Rhysling that ever could be:

> "We pray for one last landing
> On the globe that gave us birth;

Let us rest our eyes on fleecy skies
And the cool, green hills of Earth."

Logic of Empire

"DON'T be a sentimental fool, Sam!"

"Sentimental, or not," Jones persisted, "I know human slavery when I see it. That's what you've got on Venus."

Humphrey Wingate snorted. "That's utterly ridiculous. The company's labor clients are employees, working under legal contracts, freely entered into."

Jones' eyebrows raised slightly. "So? What kind of a contract is it that throws a man into jail if he quits his job?"

"That's not the case. Any client can quit his job on the usual two weeks notice—I ought to know; I—"

"Yes, I know," agreed Jones in a tired voice. "You're a lawyer. You know all about contracts. But the trouble with you, you dunderheaded fool, is that all you understand is legal phrases. Free contract—nuts! What I'm talking about is *facts*, not legalisms. I don't care what the contract says—those people are slaves!"

Wingate emptied his glass and set it down. "So I'm a dunderheaded fool, am I? Well, I'll tell you what you are, Sam Houston Jones—you are a half-baked parlor pink.

You've never had to work for a living in your life and you think it's just too dreadful that anyone else should have to. No, wait a minute," he continued, as Jones opened his mouth, "listen to me. The company's clients on Venus are a damn sight better off than most people of their own class here on Earth. They are certain of a job, of food, and a place to sleep. If they get sick, they're certain of medical attention. The trouble with people of that class is that they don't want to work—"

"Who does?"

"Don't be funny. The trouble is, if they weren't under a fairly tight contract, they'd throw up a good job the minute they got bored with it and expect the company to give 'em a free ride back to Earth. Now it may not have occurred to your fine, free charitable mind, but the company has obligations to its stockholders—you, for instance—and it can't afford to run an interplanetary ferry for the benefit of a class of people that feel that the world owes them a living."

"You got me that time, pal," Jones acknowledged with a wry face, "—that crack about me being a stockholder. I'm ashamed of it."

"Then why don't you sell?"

Jones looked disgusted. "What kind of a solution is that? Do you think I can avoid the responsibility of *knowing* about it just unloading my stock?"

"Oh, the devil with it," said Wingate. "Drink up."

"Righto," agreed Jones. It was his first night aground after a practice cruise as a reserve officer; he needed to catch up on his drinking. Too bad, thought Wingate, that the cruise should have touched at Venus—

✿ ✿ ✿

"All out! All out! Up *aaaall* you idlers! Show a leg there! Show a leg and grab a sock!" The raucous voice sawed its way through Wingate's aching head. He opened his eyes, was blinded by raw white light, and shut them hastily. But the voice would not let him alone. "Ten minutes till breakfast," it rasped. "Come and get it, or we'll throw it out!"

He opened his eyes again, and with trembling willpower forced them to track. Legs moved past his eyes, denim clad legs mostly, though some were bare—repulsive hairy nakedness. A confusion of male voices, from which he could catch words but not sentences, was accompanied by an obligato of metallic sounds, muffled but pervasive— shrrg, shrrg, thump! Shrrg, shrrg, thump! The thump with which the cycle was completed hurt his aching head but was not as nerve stretching as another noise, a toneless whirring sibilance which he could neither locate nor escape.

The air was full of the odor of human beings, too many of them in too small a space. There was nothing so distinct as to be fairly termed a stench, nor was the supply of oxygen inadequate. But the room was filled with the warm, slightly musky smell of bodies still heated by bedclothes, bodies not dirty but not freshly washed. It was oppressive and unappetizing—in his present state almost nauseating.

He began to have some appreciation of the nature of his surroundings; he was in a bunkroom of some sort. It was crowded with men, men getting up, shuffling about, pulling on clothes. He lay on the bottom-most of a tier of four narrow bunks. Through the interstices between the legs which crowded around him and moved past his face he could see other such tiers around the walls and away from the walls, stacked floor to ceiling and supported by stanchions.

Someone sat down on the foot of Wingate's bunk, crowding his broad fundament against Wingate's ankles while he drew on his socks. Wingate squirmed his feet away from the intrusion. The stranger turned his face toward him. "Did I crowd 'ja, bud? Sorry." Then he added, not unkindly, "Better rustle out of there. The Master-at-Arms'll be riding you to get them bunks up." He yawned hugely, and started to get up, quite evidently having dismissed Wingate and Wingate's affairs from his mind.

"Wait a minute!" Wingate demanded hastily.

"Huh?"

"Where am I? In jail?"

The stranger studied Wingate's bloodshot eyes and puffy, unwashed face with detached but unmalicious interest. "Boy, oh boy, you must 'a' done a good job of drinking up your bounty money."

"Bounty money? What the hell are you talking about?"

"Honest to God, don't you know where you are?"

"No."

"Well . . ." The other seemed reluctant to proclaim a truth made silly by its self-evidence until Wingate's expression convinced him that he really wanted to know. "Well, you're in the *Evening Star*, headed for Venus."

☼ ☼ ☼

A couple of minutes later the stranger touched him on the arm. "Don't take it so hard, bud. There's nothing to get excited about."

Wingate took his hands from his face and pressed them against his temples. "It's not real," he said, speaking more to himself than to the other. "It can't be real—"

"Stow it. Come and get your breakfast."

"I couldn't eat anything."

"Nuts. Know how you feel . . . felt that way sometimes myself. Food is just the ticket." The Master-at-Arms settled the issue by coming up and prodding Wingate in the ribs with his truncheon.

"What d'yuh think this is—sickbay, or first class? Get those bunks hooked up."

"Easy, mate, easy," Wingate's new acquaintance conciliated, "our pal's not himself this morning." As he spoke he dragged Wingate to his feet with one massive hand, then with the other shoved the tier of bunks up and against the wall. Hooks clicked into their sockets, and the tier stayed up, flat to the wall.

"He'll be a damn sight less himself if he interferes with my routine," the petty officer predicted. But he moved on. Wingate stood barefooted on the floorplates, immobile and overcome by a feeling of helpless indecision which was reinforced by the fact that he was dressed only in his underwear. His champion studied him.

"You forgot your pillow. Here—" He reached down into the pocket formed by the lowest bunk and the wall and hauled out a flat package covered with transparent plastic. He broke the seal and shook out the contents, a single coverall garment of heavy denim. Wingate put it on gratefully. "You can get the squeezer to issue you a pair of slippers after breakfast," his friend added. "Right now we gotta eat."

The last of the queue had left the galley window by the time they reached it and the window was closed. Wingate's companion pounded on it. "Open up in there!"

It slammed open. "No seconds," a face announced.

The stranger prevented the descent of the window with his hand. "We don't want seconds, shipmate, we want firsts."

"Why the devil can't you show up on time?" the galley functionary groused. But he slapped two ration cartons down on the broad sill of the issuing window. The big fellow handed one to Wingate, and sat down on the floor-plates, his back supported by the galley bulkhead.

"What's your name, bud?" he enquired, as he skinned the cover off his ration. "Mine's Hartley—'Satchel' Hartley."

"Mine is Humphrey Wingate."

"Okay, Hump. Pleased to meet 'cha. Now what's all this song and dance you been giving me?" He spooned up an impossible bite of baked eggs and sucked coffee from the end of his carton.

"Well," said Wingate, his face twisted with worry, "I guess I've been shanghaied." He tried to emulate Hartley's method of drinking, and got the brown liquid over his face.

"Here—that's no way to do," Hartley said hastily. "Put the nipple in your mouth, then don't squeeze any harder than you suck. Like this." He illustrated. "Your theory don't seem very sound to me. The company don't need crimps when there's plenty of guys standing in line for a chance to sign up. What happened? Can't you remember?"

Wingate tried. "The last thing I recall," he said, "is arguing with a gyro driver over his fare."

Hartley nodded. "They'll gyp you every time. D'you think he put the slug on you?"

"Well . . . no, I guess not. I seem to be all right, except for the damndest hangover you can imagine."

"You'll feel better. You ought to be glad the *Evening Star* is a high-gravity ship instead of a trajectory job. Then you'd really be sick, and no foolin'."

"How's that?"

"I mean that she accelerates or decelerates her whole run. Has to because she carries cabin passengers. If we had been sent by a freighter, it'd be a different story. They gun 'em into the right trajectory, then go weightless for the rest of the trip. Man, how the new chums do suffer!" He chuckled.

Wingate was in no condition to dwell on the hardships of space sickness. "What I can't figure out," he said, "is how I landed here. Do you suppose they could have brought me aboard by mistake, thinking I was somebody else?"

"Can't say. Say, aren't you going to finish your breakfast?"

"I've had all I want." Hartley took his statement as an invitation and quickly finished off Wingate's ration. Then he stood up, crumpled the two cartons into a ball, stuffed them down a disposal chute, and said,

"What are you going to do about it?"

"What am I going to do about it?" A look of decision

came over Wingate's face. "I'm going to march right straight up to the Captain and demand an explanation, that's what I'm going to do!"

"I'd take that by easy stages, Hump," Hartley commented doubtfully.

"Easy stages, hell!" He stood up quickly. "Ow! My head!"

The Master-at-Arms referred them to the Chief Master-at-Arms in order to get rid of them. Hartley waited with Wingate outside the stateroom of the Chief Master-at-Arms to keep him company. "Better sell 'em your bill of goods pretty pronto," he advised.

"Why?"

"We'll ground on the Moon in a few hours. The stop to refuel at Luna City for deep space will be your last chance to get out, unless you want to walk back."

"I hadn't thought of that," Wingate agreed delightedly. "I thought I'd have to make the round trip in any case."

"Shouldn't be surprised but what you could pick up the *Morning Star* in a week or two. If it's their mistake, they'll have to return you."

"I can beat that," said Wingate eagerly. "I'll go right straight to the bank at Luna City, have them arrange a letter of credit with my bank, and buy a ticket on the Earth-Moon shuttle."

Hartley's manner underwent a subtle change. He had never in his life "arranged a letter of credit." Perhaps such a man *could* walk up to the Captain and lay down the law.

The Chief Master-at-Arms listened to Wingate's story with obvious impatience, and interrupted him in the middle of it to consult his roster of emigrants. He thumbed through it to the Ws, and pointed to a line. Wingate read it with a sinking feeling. There was his own name, correctly spelled. "Now get out," ordered the official, "and quit wasting my time."

But Wingate stood up to him. "You have no authority in this matter—none whatsoever. I insist that you take me to the Captain."

"Why, you—" Wingate thought momentarily that the man was going to strike him. He interrupted.

"Be careful what you do. You are apparently the victim of an honest mistake—but your legal position will be very shaky indeed, if you disregard the requirements of space-wise law under which this vessel is licensed. I don't think your Captain would be pleased to have to explain such actions on your part in federal court."

That he had gotten the man angry was evident. But a man does not get to be chief police officer of a major transport by jeopardizing his superior officers. His jaw muscles twitched but he pressed a button, saying nothing. A junior master-at-arms appeared. "Take this man to the Purser." He turned his back in dismissal and dialed a number on the ship's intercommunication system.

Wingate was let in to see the Purser, ex-officio company business agent, after only a short wait. "What's this all about?" that officer demanded. "If you have a complaint, why can't you present it at the morning hearings in the regular order?"

Wingate explained his predicament as clearly, convincingly, and persuasively as he knew how. "And so you see," he concluded, "I want to be put aground at

Luna City. I've no desire to cause the company any embarrassment over what was undoubtedly an unintentional mishap—particularly as I am forced to admit that I had been celebrating rather freely and, perhaps, in some manner, contributed to the mistake."

The Purser, who had listened noncommittally to his recital, made no answer. He shuffled through a high stack of file folders which rested on one corner of his desk, selected one, and opened it. It contained a sheaf of legal-size papers clipped together at the top. These he studied leisurely for several minutes, while Wingate stood waiting.

The Purser breathed with an asthmatic noisiness while he read, and, from time to time, drummed on his bared teeth with his fingernails. Wingate had about decided, in his none too steady nervous condition, that if the man approached his hand to his mouth just once more that he, Wingate, would scream and start throwing things. At this point the Purser chucked the dossier across the desk toward Wingate. "Better have a look at these," he said.

Wingate did so. The main exhibit he found to be a contract, duly entered into, between Humphrey Wingate and the Venus Development Company for six years of indentured labor on the planet Venus.

"That your signature?" asked the Purser.

Wingate's professional caution stood him in good stead. He studied the signature closely in order to gain time while he tried to collect his wits. "Well," he said at last, "I will stipulate that it looks very much like my signature, but I will not concede that it is my signature—I'm not a handwriting expert."

The Purser brushed aside the objection with an air of

annoyance. "I haven't time to quibble with you. Let's check the thumbprint. Here." He shoved an impression pad across his desk. For a moment Wingate considered standing on his legal rights by refusing, but no, that would prejudice his case. He had nothing to lose; it *couldn't* be his thumbprint on the contract. Unless—

But it was. Even his untrained eye could see that the two prints matched. He fought back a surge of panic. This was probably a nightmare, inspired by his argument last night with Jones. Or, if by some wild chance it were real, it was a frameup in which he must find the flaw. Men of his sort were not framed; the whole thing was ridiculous. He marshalled his words carefully.

"I won't dispute your position, my dear sir. In some fashion both you and I have been made the victims of a rather sorry joke. It seems hardly necessary to point out that a man who is unconscious, as I must have been last night, may have his thumbprint taken without his knowledge. Superficially this contract is valid and I assume naturally your good faith in the matter. But, in fact, the instrument lacks one necessary element of a contract."

"Which is?"

"The intention on the part of both parties to enter into a contractual relationship. Notwithstanding signature and thumbprint I had no intention of contracting which can easily be shown by other factors. I am a successful lawyer with a good practice, as my tax returns will show. It is not reasonable to believe—and no court *will* believe—that I voluntarily gave up my accustomed life for six years of indenture at a much lower income."

"So you're a lawyer, eh? Perhaps there has been

chicanery—on your part. How does it happen that you represent yourself here as a radio technician?"

Wingate again had to steady himself at this unexpected flank attack. He was in truth a radio expert—it was his cherished hobby—but how had they known? Shut up, he told himself. Don't admit anything. "The whole thing is ridiculous," he protested. "I insist that I be taken to see the Captain—I can break that contract in ten minutes time."

The Purser waited before replying. "Are you through speaking your piece?"

"Yes."

"Very well. You've had your say, now I'll have mine. You listen to me, Mister Spacelawyer. That contract was drawn up by some of the shrewdest legal minds in two planets. They had specifically in mind that worthless bums would sign it, drink up their bounty money, and then decide that they didn't want to go to work after all. That contract has been subjected to every sort of attack possible and revised so that it can't be broken by the devil himself.

"You're not peddling your curbstone law to another stumble-bum in this case; you are talking to a man who knows just where he stands, legally. As for seeing the Captain—if you think the commanding officer of a major vessel has nothing more to do than listen to the *rhira*-dreams of a self-appointed word artist, you've got another think coming! Return to your quarters!"

Wingate started to speak, thought better of it, and turned to go. This would require some thought. The Purser stopped him. "Wait. Here's your copy of the contract." He chucked it, the flimsy white sheets riffled to the deck. Wingate picked them up and left silently.

✿ ✿ ✿

Hartley was waiting for him in the passageway. "How d'ja make out, Hump?"

"Not so well. No, I don't want to talk about it. I've got to think." They walked silently back the way they had come toward the ladder which gave access to the lower decks. A figure ascended from the ladder and came toward them. Wingate noted it without interest.

He looked again. Suddenly the whole preposterous chain of events fell into place; he shouted in relief. "Sam!" he called out. "Sam—you cockeyed old so-and-so. I should have spotted your handiwork." It was all clear now; Sam had framed him with a phony shanghai. Probably the skipper was a pal of Sam's—a reserve officer, maybe—and they had cooked it up between them. It was a rough sort of a joke, but he was too relieved to be angry. Just the same he would make Jones pay for his fun, somehow, on the jump back from Luna City.

It was then that he noticed that Jones was not laughing. Furthermore he was dressed—most unreasonably—in the same blue denim that the contract laborers were. "Hump," he was saying, "are you still drunk?"

"Me? No. What's the i—"

"Don't you realize we're in a jam?"

"Oh hell, Sam, a joke's a joke, but don't keep it up any longer. I've caught on, I tell you. I don't mind—it was a good gag."

"Gag, eh?" said Jones bitterly. "I suppose it was just a gag when you talked me into signing up."

"*I* persuaded *you* to sign up?"

"You certainly did. You were so damn sure you knew

what you were talking about. You claimed that we could sign up, spend a month or so on Venus, and come home. You wanted to bet on it. So we went around to the docks and signed up. It seemed like a good idea then—the only way to settle the argument."

Wingate whistled softly. "Well, I'll be—Sam, I haven't the slightest recollection of it. I must have drawn a blank before I passed out."

"Yeah, I guess so. Too bad you didn't pass out sooner. Not that I'm blaming you; you didn't drag me. Anyhow, I'm on my way up to try to straighten it out."

"Better wait a minute till you hear what happened to me. Oh yes—Sam, this is, uh, Satchel Hartley. Good sort." Hartley had been waiting uncertainly near them; he stepped forward and shook hands.

Wingate brought Jones up to date, and added, "So you see your reception isn't likely to be too friendly. I guess I muffed it. But we are sure to break the contract as soon as we can get a hearing on time alone."

"How do you mean?"

"We were signed up less than twelve hours before ship lifting. That's contrary to the Space Precautionary Act."

"Yes—yes, I see what you mean. The Moon's in her last quarter; they would lift ship some time after midnight to take advantage of favorable earthswing. I wonder what time it was when we signed on?"

Wingate took out his contract copy. The notary's stamp showed a time of eleven thirty-two. "Great Day!" he shouted. "I knew there would be a flaw in it somewhere. This contract is invalid on its face. The ship's log will prove it."

Jones studied it. "Look again," he said. Wingate did so. The stamp showed eleven thirty-two, but A.M., not P.M.

"But that's impossible," he protested.

"Of course it is. But it's official. I think we will find that the story is that we were signed on in the morning, paid our bounty money, and had one last glorious luau before we were carried aboard. I seem to recollect some trouble in getting the recruiter to sign us up. Maybe we convinced him by kicking in our bounty money."

"But we *didn't* sign up in the morning. It's not true and I can prove it."

"Sure you can prove it—*but how can you prove it without going back to Earth first!*"

"So you see it's this way," Jones decided after some minutes of somewhat fruitless discussion, "there is no sense in trying to break our contracts here and now; they'll laugh at us. The thing to do is to make money talk, and talk loud. The only way I can see to get us off at Luna City is to post non-performance bonds with the company bank there—cash, and damn big ones, too."

"How big?"

"Twenty thousand credits, at least, I should guess."

"But that's not equitable—it's all out of proportion."

"Quit worrying about equity, will you? Can't you realize that they've got us where the hair is short? This won't be a bond set by a court ruling; it's got to be big enough to make a minor company official take a chance on doing something that's not in the book."

"I can't raise such a bond."

"Don't worry about that. I'll take care of it."

Wingate wanted to argue the point, but did not. There are times when it is very convenient to have a wealthy friend.

"I've got to get a radiogram off to my sister," Jones went on, "to get this done—"

"Why your sister? Why not your family firm?"

"Because we need fast action, that's why. The lawyers that handle our family finances would fiddle and fume around trying to confirm the message. They'd send a message back to the Captain, asking if Sam Houston Jones were really aboard, and he would answer 'No,' as I'm signed up as Sam Jones. I had some silly idea of staying out of the news broadcasts, on account of the family."

"You can't blame them," protested Wingate, feeling an obscure clannish loyalty to his colleagues in law, "they're handling other peoples' money."

"I'm not blaming them. But I've got to have fast action and Sis'll do what I ask her. I'll phrase the message so she'll know it's me. The only hurdle now is to persuade the Purser to let me send a message on tick."

He was gone for a long time on this mission. Hartley waited with Wingate, both to keep him company and because of a strong human interest in unusual events. When Jones finally appeared he wore a look of tight-lipped annoyance. Wingate, seeing the expression, felt a sudden, chilling apprehension. "Couldn't you send it? Wouldn't he let you?"

"Oh, he let me—finally," Jones admitted, "but that Purser—man, is he tight!"

Even without the alarm gongs Wingate would have

been acutely aware of the grounding at Luna City. The sudden change from the high gravity deceleration of their approach to the weak surface gravity—one-sixth earth normal—of the Moon took immediate toll on his abused stomach. It was well that he had not eaten much. Both Hartley and Jones were deepspace men and regarded enough acceleration to permit normal swallowing as adequate for any purpose. There is a curious lack of sympathy between those who are subject to spacesickness and those who are immune to it. Why the spectacle of a man regurgitating, choked, eyes streaming with tears, stomach knotted with pain, should seem funny is difficult to see, but there it is. It divides the human race into two distinct and antipathetic groups—amused contempt on one side, helpless murderous hatred on the other.

Neither Hartley nor Jones had the inherent sadism which is too frequently evident on such occasions—for example the great wit who suggests salt pork as a remedy—but, feeling no discomfort themselves, they were simply unable to comprehend (having forgotten the soul-twisting intensity of their own experience as new chums) that Wingate was literally suffering "a fate worse than death"—much worse, for it was stretched into a sensible eternity by a distortion of the time sense known only to sufferers from spacesicknesses, seasicknesses, and (we are told) smokers of hashish.

As a matter of fact, the stop on the Moon was less than four hours long. Toward the end of the wait Wingate had quieted down sufficiently again to take an interest in the expected reply to Jones' message, particularly after Jones had assured him that he would be able to spend the expected lay-over under bond at Luna City in a hotel equipped with a centrifuge.

But the answer was delayed. Jones had expected to hear from his sister within an hour, perhaps before the *Evening Star* grounded at the Luna City docks. As the hours stretched out he managed to make himself very unpopular at the radio room by his repeated inquiries. An over-worked clerk had sent him brusquely about his business for the seventeenth time when he heard the alarm sound preparatory to raising ship; he went back and admitted to Wingate that his scheme had apparently failed.

"Of course, we've got ten minutes yet," he finished unhopefully, "if the message should arrive before they raise ship, the Captain could still put us aground at the last minute. We'll go back and haunt 'em some more right up to the last. But it looks like a thin chance."

"Ten minutes—" said Wingate, "couldn't we manage somehow to slip outside and run for it?"

Jones looked exasperated. "Have you ever tried running in a total vacuum?"

Wingate had very little time in which to fret on the passage from Luna City to Venus. He learned a great deal about the care and cleaning of washrooms, and spent ten hours a day perfecting his new skill. Masters-at-Arms have long memories.

The *Evening Star* passed beyond the limits of ship-to-Terra radio communication shortly after leaving Luna City; there was nothing to do but wait until arrival at Adonis, port of the north polar colony. The company radio there was strong enough to remain in communication at all times except for the sixty days bracketing superior conjunction and a shorter period of solar interference at inferior conjunction. "They will probably be waiting for us with a release order when we ground," Jones assured Wingate, "and we'll go back on the return trip of the *Evening Star*—first class, this time. Or, at the very worst, we'll have to wait over for the *Morning Star.* That wouldn't be so bad, once I get some credit transferred; we could spend it at Venusburg,"

"I suppose you went there on your cruise," Wingate said, curiosity showing in his voice. He was no Sybarite, but the lurid reputation of the most infamous, or famous—depending on one's evaluations—pleasure city of three planets was enough to stir the imagination of the least hedonistic.

"No—worse luck!" Jones denied. "I was on a hull inspection board the whole time. Some of my messmates went, though . . . boy!" He whistled softly and shook his head.

But there was no one awaiting their arrival, nor was there any message. Again they stood around the communication office until told sharply and officially to get on back to their quarters and stand by to disembark, "—and be quick about it!"

"I'll see you in the receiving barracks, Hump," were Jones' last words before he hurried off to his own compartment.

The Master-at-Arms responsible for the compartment in which Hartley and Wingate were billeted lined his charges up in a rough column of two's and, when ordered to do so by the metallic bray of the ship's loudspeaker, conducted them through the central passageway and down four decks to the lower passenger port. It stood open; they shuffled through the lock and out of the ship—not into the free air of Venus, but into a sheetmetal tunnel which joined it, after some fifty yards, to a building.

The air within the tunnel was still acrid from the atomized antiseptic with which it had been flushed out, but to Wingate it was nevertheless fresh and stimulating after the stale flatness of the repeatedly reconditioned air of the transport. That, plus the surface gravity of Venus, five-sixths of earth-normal, strong enough to prevent nausea yet low enough to produce a feeling of lightness and strength—these things combined to give him an irrational optimism, an up-and-at-'em frame of mind.

The exit from the tunnel gave into a moderately large room, windowless but brilliantly and glarelessly lighted from concealed sources. It contained no furniture.

"Squaaad—HALT!" called out the Master-at-Arms, and handed papers to a slight, clerkish-appearing man who stood near an inner doorway. The man glanced at the papers, counted the detachment, then signed one sheet, which he handed back to the ship's petty officer who accepted it and returned through the tunnel.

The clerkish man turned to the immigrants. He was dressed, Wingate noted, in nothing but the briefest of shorts, hardly more than a strap, and his entire body, even his feet, was a smooth mellow tan. "Now men," he said in a mild voice, "strip off your clothes and put them in the hopper." He indicated a fixture set in one wall.

"Why?" asked Wingate. His manner was uncontentious but he made no move to comply.

"Come now," he was answered, still mildly but with a note of annoyance, "don't argue. It's for your own protection. We can't afford to import disease."

Wingate checked a reply and unzipped his coverall. Several who had paused to hear the outcome followed his example. Suits, shoes, underclothing, socks, they all went into the hopper. "Follow me," said their guide.

In the next room the naked herd were confronted by four "barbers" armed with electric clippers and rubber gloves who proceeded to clip them smooth. Again Wingate felt disposed to argue, but decided the issue was not worth it. But he wondered if the female labor clients were required to submit to such drastic quarantine precautions. It would be a shame, it seemed to him, to sacrifice a beautiful head of hair that had been twenty years in growing.

The succeeding room was a shower room. A curtain of warm spray completely blocked passage through the room. Wingate entered it unreluctantly, even eagerly, and fairly wallowed in the first decent bath he had been able to take since leaving Earth. They were plentifully supplied with liquid green soap, strong and smelly, but which lathered freely. Half a dozen attendants, dressed as skimpily as their guide, stood on the far side of the wall of water and saw to it that the squad remained under the shower a fixed time and scrubbed. In some cases they made highly personal suggestions to insure thoroughness. Each of them wore a red cross on a white field affixed to his belt which lent justification to their officiousness.

Blasts of warm air in the exit passageway dried them quickly and completely.

"Hold still." Wingate complied, the bored hospital orderly who had spoken dabbed at Wingate's upper arm with a swab which felt cold to touch, then scratched the spot. "That's all, move on." Wingate added himself to the queue at the next table. The experience was repeated on the other arm. By the time he had worked down to the far end of the room the outer sides of each arm were covered with little red scratches, more than twenty of them.

"What's this all about?" he asked the hospital clerk at the end of the line, who had counted his scratches and checked his name off a list.

"Skin tests . . . to check your resistances and immunities."

"Resistance to what?"

"Anything. Both terrestrial and Venerian diseases. Fungoids, the Venus ones are, mostly. Move on, you're holding up the line." He heard more about it later. It took from two to three weeks to recondition the ordinary terrestrial to Venus conditions. Until that reconditioning was complete and immunity was established to the new hazards of another planet it was literally death to an Earth man to expose his skin and particularly his mucous membranes to the ravenous invisible parasites of the surface of Venus.

The ceaseless fight of life against life which is the dominant characteristic of life anywhere proceeds with especial intensity, under conditions of high metabolism, in the steamy jungles of Venus. The general bacteriophage which has so nearly eliminated disease caused by pathogenic microorganisms on Earth was found capable of a subtle modification which made it potent against the analogous but different diseases of Venus. The hungry fungi were another matter.

Imagine the worst of the fungoid-type skin diseases you have ever encountered—ringworm, dhobie itch, athlete's foot, Chinese rot, saltwater itch, seven year itch. Add to that your conception of mold, of damp rot, of scale, of toadstools feeding on decay. Then conceive them speeded up in their processes, visibly crawling as you watch—picture them attacking your eyeballs, your armpits, the soft wet tissues inside your mouth, working down into your lungs.

The first Venus expedition was lost entirely. The second had a surgeon with sufficient imagination to provide what seemed a liberal supply of salicylic acid and mercury salicylate as well as a small ultraviolet radiator. Three of them returned.

But permanent colonization depends on adaptation to environment, not insulating against it. Luna City might be cited as a case which denies this proposition but it is only superficially so. While it is true that the "lunatics" are absolutely dependent on their citywide hermetically-sealed air bubble, Luna City is not a self-sustaining colony; it is an outpost, useful as a mining station, as an observatory, as a refueling stop beyond the densest portion of Terra's gravitational field.

Venus is a colony. The colonists breathe the air of Venus, eat its food, and expose their skins to its climate and natural hazards. Only the cold polar regions—approximately equivalent in weather conditions to an Amazonian jungle on a hot day in the rainy season—are tenable by terrestrials, but here they slop barefooted on the marshy soil in a true ecological balance.

✿ ✿ ✿

Wingate ate the meal that was offered him—satisfactory but roughly served and dull, except for Venus sweet-sour melon, the portion of which he ate would have fetched a price in a Chicago gourmets' restaurant equivalent to the food budget for a week of a middle-class family—and located his assigned sleeping billet. Thereafter he attempted to locate Sam Houston Jones. He could find no sign of him among the other labor clients, nor anyone who remembered having seen him. He was advised by one of the permanent staff of the conditioning station to enquire of the factor's clerk. This he did, in the ingratiating manner he had learned it was wise to use in dealing with minor functionaries.

"Come back in the morning. The lists will be posted."

"Thank you, sir. Sorry to have bothered you, but I can't find him and I was afraid he might have taken sick or something. Could you tell me if he is on the sick list?"

"Oh, well—Wait a minute." The clerk thumbed through his records. "Hmmm . . . you say he was in the *Evening Star*?"

"Yes, sir."

"Well, he's not...Mmmm, no—Oh, yes, here he is. He didn't disembark here."

"What did you say?"

"He went on with the *Evening Star* to New Auckland, South Pole. He's stamped in as a machinist's helper. If you had told me that, I'd 'a' known. All the metal workers in this consignment were sent to work on the new South Power Station."

After a moment Wingate pulled himself together enough to murmur, "Thanks for your trouble."

"'S all right. Don't mention it." The clerk turned away. South Pole Colony! He muttered it to himself. South Pole Colony, his only friend twelve thousand miles away. At last Wingate felt alone, alone and trapped, abandoned. During the short interval between waking up aboard the transport and finding Jones also aboard he had not had time fully to appreciate his predicament, nor had he, then, lost his upper class arrogance, the innate conviction that it could not be serious—such things just don't happen to people, not to people one *knows!*

But in the meantime he had suffered such assaults to his human dignity (the Chief Master-at-Arms had seen to some of it) that he was no longer certain of his essential inviolability from unjust or arbitrary treatment. But now, shaved and bathed without his consent, stripped of his clothing and attired in a harnesslike breechclout, transported millions of miles from his social matrix, subject to the orders of persons indifferent to his feelings and who claimed legal control over his person and actions, and now, most bitterly, cut off from the one human contact which had given him support and courage and hope, he realized at last with chilling thoroughness that anything could happen to him, to *him*, Humphrey Belmont Wingate, successful attorney-at-law and member of all the right clubs.

"Wingate!"

"That's you, Jack. Go on in, don't keep them waiting." Wingate pushed through the doorway and found himself in a fairly crowded room. Thirty-odd men were seated around the sides of the room. Near the door a clerk sat at a desk, busy with papers. One brisk-mannered individual stood in the cleared space between the chairs near a low platform on which all the illumination of the room was concentrated. The clerk at the door looked up to say, "Step up where they can see you." He pointed a stylus at the platform.

Wingate moved forward and did as he was bade, blinking at the brilliant light. "Contract number 482-23-06," read the clerk, "client Humphrey Wingate, six years, radio technician non-certified, pay grade six-D, contract now available for assignment." Three weeks it had taken them to condition him, three weeks with no word from Jones. He had passed his exposure test without infection; he was about to enter the active period of his indenture. The brisk man spoke up close on the last words of the clerk:

"Nowhere, patrons, if you please—we have an exceptionally promising man. I hardly dare tell you the ratings he received on his intelligence, adaptability, and general information tests. In fact I won't, except to tell you that Administration has put in a protective offer of a thousand credits. But it would be a shame to use any such client for the routine work of administration when we need good men so badly to wrest wealth from the wilderness. I venture to predict that the lucky bidder who obtains the services of this client will be using him as a foreman within a month. But look him over for yourselves, talk to him, and see for yourselves."

The clerk whispered something to the speaker. He nodded and added, "I am required to notify you,

gentlemen and patrons, that this client has given the usual
legal notice of two weeks, subject of course to liens of
record." He laughed jovially, and cocked one eyebrow as
if there were some huge joke behind his remarks. No one
paid attention to the announcement; to a limited extent
Wingate appreciated wryly the nature of the jest. He had
given notice the day after he found out that Jones had
been sent to South Pole Colony, and had discovered that
while he was free theoretically to quit, it was freedom to
starve on Venus, unless he first worked out his bounty, and
his passage both ways.

Several of the patrons gathered around the platform
and looked him over, discussing him as they did so. "Not
too well muscled." "I'm not overeager to bid on these
smart boys; they're trouble-makers." "No, but a stupid
client isn't worth his keep." "What can he *do*? I'm going to
have a look at his record." They drifted over to the clerk's
desk and scrutinized the results of the many tests and
examinations that Wingate had undergone during his
period of quarantine. All but one beady-eyed individual
who sidled up closer to Wingate, and, resting one foot on
the platform so that he could bring his face nearer, spoke
in confidential tones.

"I'm not interested in those phony puff-sheets, bub.
Tell me about yourself."

"There's not much to tell."

"Loosen up. You'll like my place. Just like a home—
I run a free crock to Venusburg for my boys. Had any
experience handling niggers?"

"No."

"Well, the natives ain't niggers anyhow, except in a

manner of speaking. You look like you could boss a gang. Had any experience?"

"Not much."

"Well . . . maybe you're modest. I like a man who keeps his mouth shut. And my boys like me. I never let my pusher take kickbacks."

"No," put in another patron who had returned to the side of the platform, "you save that for yourself, Rigsbee."

"You stay out o' this, Van Huysen!"

The newcomer, a heavy-set, middle-aged man, ignored the other and addressed Wingate himself. "You have given notice. Why?"

"The whole thing was a mistake. I was drunk."

"Will you do honest work in the meantime?"

Wingate considered this. "Yes," he said finally. The heavyset man nodded and walked heavily back to his chair, settling his broad girth with care and giving his harness a hitch.

When the others were seated the spokesman announced cheerfully, "Now, gentlemen, if you are quite through—Let's hear an opening offer for this contract. I wish I could afford to bid him in as my assistant, by George, I do! Now . . . do I hear an offer?"

"Six hundred."

"Please, patrons! Did you not hear me mention a protection of one thousand?"

"I don't think you mean it. He's a sleeper."

The company agent raised his eyebrows. "I'm sorry. I'll have to ask the client to step down from the platform."

But before Wingate could do so another voice said, "One thousand."

"Now that's better!" exclaimed the agent. "I should have known that you gentlemen wouldn't let a real opportunity escape you. But a ship can't fly on one jet. Do I hear eleven hundred? Come, patrons, you can't make your fortunes without clients. Do I hear—"

"Eleven hundred."

"Eleven hundred from Patron Rigsbee! And a bargain it would be at that price. But I doubt if you will get it. Do I hear twelve?"

The heavy-set man flicked a thumb upward. "Twelve hundred from Patron van Huysen. I see I've made a mistake and am wasting your time; the intervals should be not less than two hundred. Do I hear fourteen? Do I hear fourteen? Going once for twelve . . . going twi—"

"Fourteen," Rigsbee said sullenly.

"Seventeen," Van Huysen added at once.

"Eighteen," snapped Rigsbee.

"Nooo," said the agent, "no interval of less than two, please."

"All right, dammit, nineteen!"

"Nineteen I hear. It's a hard number to write; who'll make it twenty-one?" Van Huysen's thumb flicked again. "Twenty-one it is. It takes money to make money. What do I hear? What do I hear?" He paused. "Going once for twenty-one . . . going twice for twenty-one. Are you giving up so easily, Patron Rigsbee?"

"Van Huysen is a—" The rest was muttered too indistinctly to hear.

"One more chance, gentlemen. Going, going, . . . GONE!—" He smacked his palms sharply together. "—and sold to Patron van Huysen for twenty-one hundred credits. My congratulations, sir, on a shrewd deal."

Wingate followed his new master out the far door. They were stopped in the passageway by Rigsbee. "All right, Van, you've had your fun. I'll cut your losses for two thousand."

"Out of my way."

"Don't be a fool. He's no bargain. You don't know how to sweat a man—I do." Van Huysen ignored him, pushing on past. Wingate followed him out into warm winter drizzle to the parking lot where steel crocodiles were drawn up in parallel rows. Van Huysen paused beside a thirty-foot Remington. "Get in."

The long boxlike body of the crock was stowed to its load line with supplies Van Huysen had purchased at the base. Sprawled on the tarpaulin which covered the cargo were half a dozen men. One of them stirred as Wingate climbed over the side. "Hump! Oh, Hump!"

It was Hartley. Wingate was surprised at his own surge of emotion. He gripped Hartley's hand and exchanged friendly insults. "Chums," said Hartley, "meet Hump Wingate. He's a right guy. Hump, meet the gang. That's Jimmie right behind you. He rassles this velocipede."

The man designated gave Wingate a bright nod and moved forward into the operator's seat. At a wave from Van Huysen, who had seated his bulk in the little sheltered cabin aft, he pulled back on both control levers and the crocodile crawled away, its caterpillar treads clanking and chunking through the mud.

Three of the six were old-timers, including Jimmie, the driver. They had come along to handle cargo, the ranch products which the patron had brought in to market and the supplies he had purchased to take back. Van Huysen had bought the contracts of two others clients in addition to Wingate and Satchel Hartley. Wingate recognized them as men he had known casually in the *Evening Star* and at the assignment and conditioning station. They looked a little woebegone, which Wingate could thoroughly understand, but the men from the ranch seemed to be enjoying themselves. They appeared to regard the opportunity to ride a load to and from town as an outing. They sprawled on the tarpaulin and passed the time gossiping and getting acquainted with the new chums.

But they asked no personal questions. No labor client on Venus ever asked anything about what he had been before he shipped with the company unless he first volunteered information. It "wasn't done."

Shortly after leaving the outskirts of Adonis the car slithered down a sloping piece of ground, teetered over a low bank, and splashed logily into water. Van Huysen threw up a window in the bulkhead which separated the cabin from the hold and shouted, "Dumkopf! How many times do I tell you to take those launchings slowly?"

"Sorry, Boss," Jimmie answered. "I missed it."

"You keep your eyes peeled, or I get me a new crocker!" He slammed the port. Jimmie glanced around and gave the other clients a sly wink. He had his hands full; the marsh they were traversing looked like solid ground, so heavily was it overgrown with rank vegetation. The crocodile now functioned as a boat, the broad flanges of the treads acting as paddle wheels. The wedge-shaped prow pushed shrubs and marsh grass aside, or struck and ground down small trees. Occasionally the lugs would bite into the mud of a shoal bottom, and, crawling over a bar, return temporarily to the status of a land vehicle. Jimmie's slender, nervous hands moved constantly over the controls, avoiding large trees and continually seeking the easiest, most nearly direct route, while he split his attention between the terrain and the craft's compass.

Presently the conversation lagged and one of the ranch hands started to sing. He had a passable tenor voice and was soon joined by others. Wingate found himself singing the choruses as fast as he learned them. They sang *Pay Book* and *Since the Pusher Met My Cousin* and a mournful thing called *They Found Him in the Bush.* But this was followed by a light number, *The Night the Rain Stopped,* which seemed to have an endless string of verses recounting various unlikely happenings which occurred on that occasion. ("The Squeezer bought a round-a-drinks—")

Jimmie drew applause and enthusiastic support in the choruses with a ditty entitled *That Redheaded Venusburg Gal,* but Wingate considered it inexcusably vulgar. He did not have time to dwell on the matter; it was followed by a song which drove it out of his mind.

The tenor started it, slowly and softly. The others sang the refrains while he rested—all but Wingate; he was silent and thoughtful throughout. In the triplet of the second verse the tenor dropped out and the others sang in his place.

"Oh, you stamp your paper and you sign your name,
     ("Come away! Come away!)
"They pay your bounty and you drown your shame.
     ("Rue the day! Rue the day!)
"They land you down at Ellis Isle and put you in a pen;
"There you see what happens to the Six-Year men—
"They haven't paid their bounty and they sign 'em up again!
     ("Here to stay! Here to stay!)
"But me I'll save my bounty and a ticket on the ship,
     ("So you say! So you say!)
"And then you'll see me leavin' on the very next trip.
     ("Come the day! Come the day!)
"Oh, we've heard that kinda story just a thousand times
     and one.
"Now we wouldn't say you're lyin' but we'd like to see it done.
"We'll see you next at Venusburg apayin' for your fun!
[Spoken slowly] "And you'll never meet your bounty
     on this hitch!
     ("Come away!")

It left Wingate with a feeling of depression not entirely accounted for by the tepid drizzle, the unappetizing landscape, nor by the blanket of pale mist which is the invariable Venetian substitute for the open sky. He withdrew to one corner of the hold and kept to himself, until, much later, Jimmie shouted, "Lights ahead!"

Wingate leaned out and peered eagerly toward his new home.

Four weeks and no word from Sam Houston Jones.

Venus had turned once on its axis, the fortnight long Venetian "winter" had given way to an equally short "summer"—indistinguishable from "winter" except that the rain was a trifle heavier and a little hotter—and now it was "winter" again. Van Huysens' ranch, being near the pole, was, like most of the tenable area of Venus, never in darkness. The miles-thick, everpresent layer of clouds tempered the light of the low-hanging sun during the long day, and, equally, held the heat and diffused the light from a sun just below the horizon to produce a continuing twilight during the two-week periods which were officially "night," or "winter."

Four weeks and no word. Four weeks and no sun, no moon, no stars, no dawn. No clean crisp breath of morning air, no life-quickening beat of noonday sun, no welcome evening shadows, nothing, nothing at all to distinguish one sultry, sticky hour from the next but the treadmill routine of sleep and work and food and sleep again—nothing but the gathering ache in his heart for the cool blue skies of Terra.

He had acceded to the invariable custom that new men should provide a celebration for the other clients and had signed the Squeezer's chits to obtain happywater—*rhira*—for the purpose—to discover, when first he signed the pay book, that his gesture of fellowship had cost him another four months of delay before he could legally quit his "job." Thereupon he had resolved never again to sign a chit, had foresworn the prospect of brief holidays at Venusburg, had promised himself to save every possible credit against his bounty and transportation liens.

Whereupon he discovered that the mild alcoholoid

drink was neither a vice nor a luxury, but a necessity, as necessary to human life on Venus as the ultraviolet factor present in all colonial illuminating systems. It produces, not drunkenness, but lightness of heart, freedom from worry, and without it he could not *get to sleep*. Three nights of self-recrimination and fretting, three days of fatigue-drugged uselessness under the unfriendly eye of the Pusher, and he had signed for his bottle with the rest, even though dully aware that the price of the bottle had washed out more than half of the day's microscopic progress toward freedom.

Nor had he been assigned to radio operation. Van Huysen had an operator. Wingate, although listed on the books as standby operator, went to the swamps with the rest. He discovered on rereading his contract a clause which permitted his patron to do this, and he admitted with half his mind—the detached judicial and legalistic half—that the clause was reasonable and proper, not inequitable.

He went to the swamps. He learned to wheedle and bully the little, mild amphibian people into harvesting the bulbous underwater growth of *Hyacinthus veneris johnsoni*—Venus swamproot—and to bribe the co-operation of their matriarchs with promises of bonuses in the form of "thigarek", a term which meant not only cigarette, but tobacco in any form, the staple medium in trade when dealing with the natives.

He took his turn in the chopping sheds and learned, clumsily and slowly, to cut and strip the spongy outer husk from the pea-sized kernel which alone had commercial value and which must be removed intact, without scratch

or bruise. The juice from the pods made his hands raw
and the odor made him cough and stung his eyes, but he
enjoyed it more than the work in the marshes, for it threw
him into the company of the female labor clients. Women
were quicker at the work than men and their smaller
fingers more dextrous in removing the valuable, easily
damaged capsule. Men were used for such work only
when accumulated crops required extra help.

.   He learned his new trade from a motherly old person
whom the other women addressed as Hazel. She talked as
she worked, her gnarled old hands moving steadily and
without apparent direction or skill. He could close his
eyes and imagine that he was back on earth and a boy
again, hanging around his grandmother's kitchen while
she shelled peas and rambled on. "Don't you fret yourself,
boy," Hazel told him. "Do your work and shame the devil.
There's a great day coming."

"What kind of a great day, Hazel?"

"The day when the Angels of the Lord will rise up and
smite the powers of evil. The day when the Prince of
Darkness will be cast down into the pit and the Prophet
shall reign over the children of Heaven. So don't you
worry; it doesn't matter whether you are here or back
home when the great day comes; the only thing that
matters is your state of grace."

"Are you sure we will live long enough to see the
day?"

She glanced around, then leaned over confidentially.
"The day is almost upon us. Even now the Prophet moves
up and down the land gathering his forces. Out of the
clean farm country of the Mississippi Valley there comes

the Man, known in this world"—she lowered her voice still more—"as *Nehemiah Scudder!*"

Wingate hoped that his start of surprise and amusement did not show externally. He recalled the name. It was that of a pipsqueak, backwoods evangelist, an unimportant nuisance back on Earth, the butt of an occasional guying news story, but a man of no possible consequence.

The chopping shed Pusher moved up to their bench. "Keep your eyes on your work, you! You're way behind now." Wingate hastened to comply, but Hazel came to his aid.

"You leave him be, Joe Tompson. It takes time to learn chopping."

"Okay, Mon," answered the Pusher with a grin, "but keep him pluggin'. See?"

"I will. You worry about the rest of the shed. This bench'll have its quota." Wingate had been docked two days running for spoilage. Hazel was lending him poundage now and the Pusher knew it, but everybody liked her, even pushers, who are reputed to like no one, not even themselves.

Wingate stood just outside the gate of the bachelors' compound. There was yet fifteen minutes before lock-up roll call; he had walked out in a subconscious attempt to rid himself of the pervading feeling of claustrophobia which he had had throughout his stay. The attempt was futile; there was no "outdoorness" about the outdoors on Venus, the bush crowded the clearing in on itself, the leaden misty sky pressed down on his head, and the steamy heat sat on his bare chest. Still, it was better than the bunkroom in spite of the dehydrators.

He had not yet obtained his evening ration of *rhira* and felt, consequently, nervous and despondent, yet residual self-respect caused him to cherish a few minutes' clear thinking before he gave in to the cheerful soporific. It's getting me, he thought, in a few more months I'll be taking every chance to get to Venusburg, or, worse yet, signing a chit for married quarters and condemning myself and my kids to a life-sentence. When he first arrived the women clients, with their uniformly dull minds and usually commonplace faces, had seemed entirely unattractive. Now, he realized with dismay, he was no longer so fussy. Why, he was even beginning to lisp, as the other clients did, in unconscious imitation of the amphibians.

Early, he had observed that the clients could be divided roughly into two categories, the child of nature and the broken men. The first were those of little imagination and simple standards. In all probability they had known nothing better back on earth; they saw in the colonial culture, not slavery, but freedom from responsibility, security, and an occasional spree. The others were the broken men, the outcasts, they who had once been somebody, but, through some defect of character, or some accident, had lost their places in society. Perhaps the judge had said, "Sentence suspended if you ship for the colonies."

He realized with sudden panic that his own status was crystallizing; he was becoming one of the broken men. His background on Earth was becoming dim in his mind; he had put off for the last three days the labor of writing another letter to Jones; he had spent all the last shift rationalizing the necessity for taking a couple of days holiday at Venusburg. Face it, son, face it, he told himself.

You're slipping, you're letting your mind relax into slave psychology. You've unloaded the problem of getting out of this mess onto Jones—how do you know he *can* help you? For all you know he may be dead. Out of the dimness of his memory he recaptured a phrase which he had read somewhere, some philosopher of history: "No slave is ever freed, *save he free himself.*"

All right, all right—pull up your socks, old son. Take a brace. No more *rhira*—no, that wasn't practical; a man had to have sleep. Very well, then, no *rhira* until lights-out, keep your mind clear in the evenings and *plan.* Keep your eyes open, find out all you can, cultivate friendships, and watch for a chance.

Through the gloom he saw a human figure approaching the gate of the compound. As it approached he saw that it was a woman and supposed it to be one of the female clients. She came closer, he saw that he was mistaken. It was Annek van Huysen, daughter of the patron.

She was a husky, overgrown blonde girl with unhappy eyes. He had seen her many times, watching the clients as they returned from their labor, or wandering alone around the ranch clearing. She was neither unsightly, nor in any-wise attractive; her heavy adolescent figure needed more to flatter it than the harness which all colonists wore as the maximum tolerable garment.

She stopped before him, and, unzipping the pouch at her waist which served in lieu of pockets, took out a package of cigarettes. "I found this back there. Did you lose it?"

He knew that she lied; she had picked up nothing since she had come into sight. And the brand was one smoked on Earth and by patrons; no client could afford such. What was she up to?

He noted the eagerness in her face and the rapidity of her breathing, and realized, with confusion, that this girl was trying indirectly to make him a present. Why?

Wingate was not particularly conceited about his own physical beauty, or charm, nor had he any reason to be. But what he had not realized was that among the common run of the clients he stood out like a cock pheasant in a barnyard. But that Annek found him pleasing he was forced to admit; there could be no other explanation for her trumped-up story and her pathetic little present.

His first impulse was to snub her. He wanted nothing of her and resented the invasion of his privacy, and he was vaguely aware that the situation could be awkward, even dangerous to him, involving, as it did, violations of custom which jeopardized the whole social and economic structure. From the viewpoint of the patrons, labor clients were almost as much beyond the pale as the amphibians. A liaison between a labor client and one of the womenfolk of the patrons could easily wake up old Judge Lynch.

But he had not the heart to be brusque with her. He could see the dumb adoration in her eyes; it would have required cold heartlessness to have repulsed her. Besides, there was nothing coy or provocative in her attitude; her manner was naive, almost childlike in its unsophistication. He recalled his determination to make friends; here was friendship offered, a dangerous friendship, but one which might prove useful in winning free.

He felt a momentary wave of shame that he should be weighing the potential usefulness of this defenseless child, but he suppressed it by affirming to himself that he would do her no harm, and, anyhow, there was the old saw about the vindictiveness of a woman scorned.

"Why, perhaps I did lose it," he evaded, then added, "It's my favorite brand."

"Is it?" she said happily. "Then do take it, in any case."

"Thank you. Will you smoke one with me? No, I guess that wouldn't do; your father would not want you to stay here that long."

"Oh, he's busy with his accounts. I saw that before I came out," she answered, and seemed unaware that she had given away her pitiful little deception. "But go ahead, I—I hardly ever smoke."

"Perhaps you prefer a meerschaum pipe, like your father."

She laughed more than the poor witticism deserved. After that they talked aimlessly, both agreeing that the crop was coming in nicely, that the weather seemed a little cooler than last week, and that there was nothing like a little fresh air after supper.

"Do you ever walk for exercise after supper?" she asked. He did not say that a long day in the swamps offered more than enough exercise, but agreed that he did.

"So do I," she blurted out. "Lots of times up near the water tower."

He looked at her. "Is that so? I'll remember that." The signal for roll call gave him a welcome excuse to get away; three more minutes, he thought, and I would have had to make a date with her.

Wingate found himself called for swamp work the

next day, the rush in the chopping sheds having abated.
The crock lumbered and splashed its way around the long,
meandering circuit, leaving one or more Earthmen at
each supervision station. The car was down to four
occupants, Wingate, Satchel, the Pusher, and Jimmie the
Crocker, when the Pusher signalled for another stop. The
flat, bright-eyed heads of amphibian natives broke water
on three sides as soon as they were halted. "All right,
Satchel," ordered the Pusher, "this is your billet. Over the
side."

Satchel looked around. "Where's my skiff?" The
ranchers used small flat-bottomed duralumin skiffs in
which to collect their day's harvest. There was not one left
in the crock.

"You won't need one. You goin' to clean this field for
planting."

"That's okay. Still—I don't see nobody around, and
I don't see no solid ground." The skiffs had a double
purpose; if a man were working out of contact with other
Earthmen and at some distance from safe dry ground, the
skiff became his life boat. If the crocodile which was
supposed to collect him broke down, or if for any other
reason he had need to sit down or lie down while on
station, the skiff gave him a place to do so. The older
clients told grim stories of men who had stood in eighteen
inches of water for twenty-four, forty-eight, seventy-two
hours, and then drowned horribly, out of their heads from
sheer fatigue.

"There's dry ground right over there." The Pusher
waved his hand in the general direction of a clump of trees
which lay perhaps a quarter of a mile away.

"Maybe so," answered Satchel equably. "Let's go see." He glanced at Jimmie, who turned to the Pusher for instructions.

"Damnation! Don't argue with me! Get over the side!"

"Not," said Satchel, "until I've seen something better than two feet of slime to squat on in a pinch."

The little water people had been following the argument with acute interest. They clucked and lisped in their own language; those who knew some pidgin English appeared to be giving newsy and undoubtedly distorted explanations of the events to their less sophisticated brethren. Fuming as he was, this seemed to add to the Pusher's anger.

"For the last time—get out there!"

"Well," said Satchel, settling his gross frame more comfortably on the floorplates, "I'm glad we've finished with that subject."

Wingate was behind the Pusher. This circumstance probably saved Satchel Hartley at least a scalp wound, for he caught the arm of the Pusher as he struck. Hartley closed in at once; the three wrestled for a few seconds on the bottom of the craft.

Hartley sat on the Pusher's chest while Wingate pried a blackjack away from the clenched fingers of the Pusher's right fist. "Glad you saw him reach for that, Hump," Satchel acknowledged, "or I'd be needin' an aspirin about now."

"Yeah, I guess so," Wingate answered, and threw the weapon as far as he could out into the marshy waste. Several of the amphibians streaked after it and dived. "I guess you can let him up now."

The Pusher said nothing to them as he brushed himself off, but he turned to the Crocker who had remained quietly in his saddle at the controls the whole time. "Why the hell didn't you help me?"

"I supposed you could take care of yourself, Boss," Jimmie answered noncommittally.

Wingate and Hartley finished that work period as helpers to labor clients already stationed. The Pusher had completely ignored them except for curt orders necessary to station them. But while they were washing up for supper back at the compound they received word to report to the Big House.

When they were ushered into the Patron's office they found the Pusher already there with his employer and wearing a self-satisfied smirk while Van Huysen's expression was black indeed.

"What's this I hear about you two?" he burst out. "Refusing work. Jumping my foreman. By Joe, I show you a thing or two!"

"Just a moment, Patron van Huysen," began Wingate quietly, suddenly at home in the atmosphere of a trial court, "no one refused duty. Hartley simply protested doing dangerous work without reasonable safeguards. As for the fracas, your foreman attacked us; we acted simply in self-defense, and desisted as soon as we had disarmed him."

The Pusher leaned over Van Huysen and whispered in his ear. The Patron looked more angry than before. "You did this with natives watching. Natives! You know colonial law? I could send you to the mines for this."

"No," Wingate denied, "your foreman did it in the

presence of natives. Our role was passive and defensive throughout—"

"You call jumping my foreman peaceful? Now you listen to me—Your job here is to work. My foreman's job is to tell you where and how to work. He's not such a dummy as to lose me my investment in a man. He judges what work is dangerous, not you." The Pusher whispered again to his chief. Van Huysen shook his head. The other persisted, but the Patron cut him off with a gesture, and turned back to the two labor clients.

"See here—I give every dog one bite, but not two. For you, no supper tonight and no *rhira*. Tomorrow we see how you behave."

"But Patron van Huys—"

"That's all. Get to your quarters."

At lights out Wingate found, on crawling into his bunk, that someone had hidden therein a foodbar. He munched it gratefully in the dark and wondered who his friend could be. The food stayed the complaints of his stomach but was not sufficient, in the absence of *rhira,* to permit him to go to sleep. He lay there, staring into the oppressive blackness of the bunkroom and listening to the assorted irritating noises that men can make while sleeping, and considered his position. It had been bad enough but barely tolerable before; now, he was logically certain, it would be as near hell as a vindictive overseer could make it. He was prepared to believe, from what he had seen and the tales he had heard, that it would be very near indeed!

He had been nursing his troubles for perhaps an hour when he felt a hand touch his side. "Hump! Hump!" came a whisper, "come outside. Something's up." It was Jimmie.

He felt his way cautiously through the stacks of bunks and slipped out the door after Jimmie. Satchel was already outside and with him a fourth figure.

It was Annek van Huysen. He wondered how she had been able to get into the locked compound. Her eyes were puffy, as if she had been crying.

Jimmie started to speak at once, in cautious, low tones. "The kid tells us that I am scheduled to haul you two lugs back into Adonis tomorrow."

"What for?"

"She doesn't know. But she's afraid it's to sell you South. That doesn't seem likely. The Old Man has never sold anyone South—but then nobody ever jumped his pusher before. I don't know."

They wasted some minutes in fruitless discussion, then, after a bemused silence, Wingate asked Jimmie, "Do you know where they keep the keys to the crock?"

"No. Why do y—"

"I could get them for you," offered Annek eagerly.

"You can't drive a crock."

"I've watched you for some weeks."

"Well, suppose you can," Jimmie continued to protest, "suppose you run for it in the crock. You'd be lost in ten miles. If you weren't caught, you'd starve."

Wingate shrugged. "I'm not going to be sold South."

"Nor am I," Hartley added.

"Wait a minute."

"Well, I don't see any bet—"

"Wait a minute," Jimmie reiterated snappishly. "Can't you see I'm trying to think?"

The other three kept silent for several long moments.

At last Jimmie said, "Okay. Kid, you'd better run along and let us talk. The less you know about this the better for you." Annek looked hurt, but complied docilely to the extent of withdrawing out of earshot. The three men conferred for some minutes. At last Wingate motioned for her to rejoin them.

"That's all, Annek," he told her. "Thanks a lot for everything you've done. We've figured a way out." He stopped, and then said awkwardly, "Well, good night."

She looked up at him.

Wingate wondered what to do or say next. Finally he led her around the corner of the barracks and bade her good night again. He returned very quickly, looking shame-faced. They re-entered the barracks.

Patron van Huysen also was having trouble getting to sleep. He hated having to discipline his people. By damn, why couldn't they all be good boys and leave him in peace? Not but what there was precious little peace for a rancher these days. It cost more to make a crop than the crop fetched in Adonis—at least it did after the interest was paid.

He had turned his attention to his accounts after dinner that night to try to get the unpleasantness out of his mind, but he found it hard to concentrate on his figures. That man Wingate, now . . . he had bought him as much to keep him away from that slavedriver Rigsbee as to get another hand. He had too much money invested in hands as it was in spite of his foreman always complaining about being short of labor. He would either have to sell some, or ask the bank to refinance the mortgage again.

Hands weren't worth their keep any more. You didn't get the kind of men on Venus that used to come when he was a boy. He bent over his books again. If the market went up even a little, the bank should be willing to discount his paper for a little more than last season. Maybe that would do it.

He had been interrupted by a visit from his daughter. Annek he was always glad to see, but this time what she had to say, what she finally blurted out, had only served to make him angry. She, preoccupied with her own thoughts, could not know that she hurt her father's heart, with a pain that was actually physical.

But that had settled the matter insofar as Wingate was concerned. He would get rid of the trouble-maker. Van Huysen ordered his daughter to bed with a roughness he had never before used on her.

Of course it was all his own fault, he told himself after he had gone to bed. A ranch on Venus was no place to raise a motherless girl. His Annekchen was almost a grown woman now; how was she to find a husband here in these outlands? What would she do if he should die? She did not know it, but there would be nothing left, nothing, not even a ticket to Terra. No, she would not become a labor client's vrouw; no, not while there was a breath left in his old tired body.

Well, Wingate would have to go, and the one they called Satchel, too. But he would not sell them South. No, he had never done that to one of his people. He thought with distaste of the great, factorylike plantations a few hundred miles further from the pole, where the temperature was always twenty to thirty degrees higher than it was in his marshes and mortality among labor clients was a standard item in cost accounting. No, he would take them in and trade them at the assignment station; what happened to them at auction there would be none of his business. But he would not sell them directly South.

That gave him an idea; he did a little computing in his head and estimated that he might be able to get enough credit on the two unexpired labor contracts to buy Annek a ticket to Earth. He was quite sure that his sister would take her in, reasonably sure anyway, even though she had quarreled with him over marrying Annek's mother. He could send her a little money from time to time. And perhaps she could learn to be a secretary, or one of those other fine jobs a girl could get on Earth.

But what would the ranch be like without Annekchen? He was so immersed in his own troubles that he did not hear his daughter slip out of her room and go outside.

Wingate and Hartley tried to appear surprised when they were left behind at muster for work. Jimmie was told to report to the Big House; they saw him a few minutes later, backing the big Remington out of its shed. He picked them up, then trundled back to the Big House and waited for the Patron to appear. Van Huysen came out shortly and climbed into his cabin with neither word nor look for anyone.

The crocodile started toward Adonis, lumbering a steady ten miles an hour. Wingate and Satchel conversed in subdued voices, waited, and wondered. After an interminable time the crock stopped. The cabin window flew open. "What's the matter?" Van Huysen demanded. "Your engine acting up?"

Jimmie grinned at him. "No, I stopped it."

"For what?"

"Better come up here and find out."

"By damn, I do!" The window slammed; presently Van Huysen reappeared, warping his ponderous bulk around the side of the little cabin. "Now what this monkeyshines?"

"Better get out and walk, Patron. This is the end of the line." Van Huysen seemed to have no remark suitable in answer, but his expression spoke for him.

"No, I mean it," Jimmie went on. "This is the end of the line for you. I've stuck to solid ground the whole way, so you could walk back. You'll be able to follow the trail I broke; you ought to be able to make it in three or four hours, fat as you are."

The Patron looked from Jimmie to the others. Wingate and Satchel closed in slightly, eyes unfriendly. "Better get goin', Fatty," Satchel said softly, "before you get chucked out headfirst."

Van Huysen pressed back against the rail of the crock, his hands gripping it. "I won't get out of my own crock," he said tightly.

Satchel spat in the palm of one hand, then rubbed the two together. "Okay, Hump. He asked for it—"

"Just a second." Wingate addressed Van Huysen, "See here, Patron van Huysen—we don't want to rough you up unless we have to. But there are three of us and we are determined. Better climb out quietly."

The older man's face was dripping with sweat which was not entirely due to the muggy heat. His chest heaved, he seemed about to defy them. Then something went out inside him. His figure sagged, the defiant lines in his face gave way to a whipped expression which was not good to see.

A moment later he climbed quietly, listlessly, over the side into the ankle-deep mud and stood there, stooped, his legs slightly bent at the knees.

When they were out of sight of the place where they had dropped their patron Jimmie turned the crock off in a new direction. "Do you suppose he'll make it?" asked Wingate.

"Who?" asked Jimmie. "Van Huysen? Oh, sure, he'll make it—probably." He was very busy now with his driving; the crock crawled down a slope and lunged into navigable water. In a few minutes the marsh grass gave way to open water. Wingate saw that they were in a broad lake whose further shores were lost in the mist. Jimmie set a compass course.

The far shore was no more than a strand; it concealed an overgrown bayou. Jimmie followed it a short distance, stopped the crock, and said, "This must be just about the place," in an uncertain voice. He dug under the tarpaulin folded up in one corner of the empty hold and drew out a broad flat paddle. He took this to the rail, and, leaning out, he smacked the water loudly with the blade: Slap! . . . slap, slap. . . . Slap!

He waited.

The flat head of an amphibian broke water near the side; it studied Jimmie with bright, merry eyes. "Hello," said Jimmie.

It answered in its own language. Jimmie replied in the

same tongue, stretching his mouth to reproduce the uncouth clucking syllables. The native listened, then slid underwater again.

He—or, more probably, she—was back in a few minutes, another with her. "Thigarek?" the newcomer said hopefully.

"Thigarek when we get there, old girl," Jimmie temporized. "Here . . . climb aboard." He held out a hand, which the native accepted and wriggled gracefully inboard. It perched its unhuman, yet oddly pleasing little figure on the rail near the driver's seat. Jimmie got the car underway.

How long they were guided by their little pilot Wingate did not know, as the timepiece on the control panel was out of order, but his stomach informed him that it was too long. He rummaged through the cabin and dug out an iron ration which he shared with Satchel and Jimmie. He offered some to the native, but she smelled at it and drew her head away.

Shortly after that there was a sharp hissing noise and a column of steam rose up ten yards ahead of them. Jimmie halted the crock at once. "Cease firing!" he called out. "It's just us chickens."

"Who are you?" came a disembodied voice.

"Fellow travelers."

"Climb out where we can see you."

The native poked Jimmie in the ribs. "Thigarek," she stated positively.

"Huh? Oh, sure." He parceled out trade tobacco until she acknowledged the total, then added one more package for good will. She withdrew a piece of string from her left cheek pouch, tied up her pay, and slid over the side. They saw her swimming away, her prize carried high out of the water.

"Hurry up and show yourself!"

"Coming!" They climbed out into waist-deep water and advanced holding their hands overhead. A squad of four broke cover and looked them over, their weapons lowered but ready. The leader searched their harness pouches and sent one of his men on to look over the crocodile.

"You keep a close watch," remarked Wingate.

The leader glanced at him. "Yes," he said, "and no. The little people told us you were coming. They're worth all the watch dogs that were ever littered."

They got underway again with one of the scouting party driving. Their captors were not unfriendly but not disposed to talk. "Wait till you see the Governor," they said.

Their destination turned out to be a wide stretch of moderately high ground. Wingate was amazed at the number of buildings and the numerous population. "How in the world can they keep a place like this a secret?" he asked Jimmie.

"If the state of Texas were covered with fog and had only the population of Waukegan, Illinois, you could hide quite a lot of things."

"But wouldn't it show on a map?"

"How well mapped do you think Venus is? Don't be a dope."

On the basis of the few words he had had with Jimmie beforehand Wingate had expected no more than a camp where fugitive clients lurked in the bush while squeezing a precarious living from the country. What he found was a culture and a government. True, it was a rough frontier culture and a simple government with few laws and an unwritten constitution, but a framework of customs was in actual operation and its gross offenders were punished—with no higher degree of injustice than one finds anywhere.

It surprised Humphrey Wingate that fugitive slaves, the scum of Earth, were able to develop an integrated society. It had surprised his ancestors that the transported criminals of Botany Bay should develop a high civilization in Australia. Not that Wingate found the phenomenon of Botany Bay surprising—that was history, and history is never surprising—after it happens.

The success of the colony was more credible to Wingate when he came to know more of the character of the Governor, who was also generalissimo, and administrator of the low and middle justice. (High justice was voted on by the whole community, a procedure that Wingate considered outrageously sloppy, but which seemed to satisfy the community.) As magistrate the Governor handed out decisions with a casual contempt for rules of evidence and legal theory that reminded Wingate of stories he had heard of the apocryphal Old Judge Bean, "The Law West of Pecos," but again the people seemed to like it.

The great shortage of women in the community (men outnumbered them three to one) caused incidents which more than anything else required the decisions of the Governor. Here, Wingate was forced to admit, was a situation in which traditional custom would have been nothing but a source of trouble; he admired the shrewd common sense and understanding of human nature with which the Governor sorted out conflicting strong human passions and suggested *modus operandi* for getting along together. A man who could maintain a working degree of peace in such matters did not need a legal education.

The Governor held office by election and was advised by an elected council. It was Wingate's private opinion that the Governor would have risen to the top in any society. The man had boundless energy, great gusto for living, a ready thunderous laugh—and the courage and capacity for making decisions. He was a "natural."

The three runaways were given a couple of weeks in which to get their bearings and find some job in which they could make themselves useful and self-supporting. Jimmie stayed with his crock, now confiscated for the community, but which still required a driver. There were other crockers available who probably would have liked the job, but there was tacit consent that the man who brought it in should drive it, if he wished. Satchel found a billet in the fields, doing much the same work he had done for Van Huysen. He told Wingate that he was actually having to work harder; nevertheless he liked it better because the conditions were, as he put it, "looser."

Wingate detested the idea of going back to agricultural work. He had no rational excuse, it was simply that he hated it. His radio experience at last stood him in good stead. The community had a jury-rigged, low-power radio on which a constant listening watch was kept, but which was rarely used for transmission, because of the danger of detection. Earlier runaway slave camps had been wiped out by the company police through careless use of radio.

Nowadays they hardly dared use it, except in extreme emergency.

But they needed radio. The grapevine telegraph maintained through the somewhat slap-happy help of the little people enabled them to keep some contact with the other fugitive communities with which they were loosely confederated, but it was not really fast, and any but the simplest of messages were distorted out of recognition.

Wingate was assigned to the community radio when it was discovered that he had appropriate technical knowledge. The previous operator had been lost in the bush. His opposite number was a pleasant old codger, known as Doc, who could listen for signals but who knew nothing of upkeep and repair.

Wingate threw himself into the job of overhauling the antiquated installation. The problems presented by lack of equipment, the necessity for "making do," gave him a degree of happiness he had not known since he was a boy, but he was not aware of it.

He was intrigued by the problem of safety in radio communication. An idea, derived from some account of the pioneer days in radio, gave him a lead. His installation, like all others, communicated by frequency modulation. Somewhere he had seen a diagram for a totally obsolete type of transmitter, an amplitude modulator. He did not have much to go on, but he worked out a circuit which he believed would oscillate in that fashion and which could be hooked up from the gear at hand.

He asked the Governor for permission to attempt to build it. "Why not? Why not?" the Governor roared at him. "I haven't the slightest idea what you are talking

about, son, but if you think you can build a radio that the
company can't detect, go right ahead. You don't have to
ask me; it's your pigeon."

"I'll have to put the station out of commission for
sending."

"Why not?"

The problem had more knots in it than he had
thought. But he labored at it with the clumsy but willing
assistance of Doc. His first hookup failed; his forty-third
attempt five weeks later worked. Doc, stationed some
miles out in the bush, reported himself able to hear the
broadcast via a small receiver constructed for the purpose,
whereas Wingate picked up nothing whatsoever on the
conventional receiver located in the same room with the
experimental transmitter.

In the meantime he worked on his book.

Why he was writing a book he could not have told
you. Back on earth it could have been termed a political
pamphlet against the colonial system. Here there was no
one to convince of his thesis, nor had he any expectation
of ever being able to present it to a reading public. Venus
was his home. He knew that there was no chance for him
ever to return; the only way lay through Adonis, and there,
waiting for him, were warrants for half the crimes in the
calendar, contract-jumping, theft, kidnapping, criminal
abandonment, conspiracy, subverting government. If the
company police ever laid hands on him, they would jail
him and lose the key.

No, the book arose, not from any expectation of
publication, but from a half-subconscious need to arrange
his thoughts. He had suffered a complete upsetting of all

the evaluations by which he had lived; for his mental health it was necessary that he formulate new ones. It was natural to his orderly, if somewhat unimaginative, mind that he set his reasons and conclusions forth in writing.

Somewhat diffidently he offered the manuscript to Doc. He had learned that the nickname title had derived from the man's former occupation on Earth; he had been a professor of economics and philosophy in one of the smaller universities. Doc had even offered a partial explanation of his presence on Venus. "A little matter involving one of my women students," he confided. "My wife took an unsympathetic view of the matter and so did the board of regents. The board had long considered my opinions a little too radical."

"Were they?"

"Heavens, no! I was a rockbound conservative. But I had an unfortunate tendency to express conservative principles in realistic rather than allegorical language."

"I suppose you're a radical now."

Doc's eyebrows lifted slightly. "Not at all. Radical and conservative are terms for emotional attitudes, not sociological opinions."

Doc accepted the manuscript, read it through, and returned it without comment. But Wingate pressed him for an opinion. "Well, my boy, if you insist—"

"I do."

"—I would say that you have fallen into the commonest fallacy of all in dealing with social and economic subjects— the 'devil theory.'"

"Huh?"

"You have attributed conditions to villainy that simply

result from stupidity. Colonial slavery is nothing new; it is the inevitable result of imperial expansion, the automatic result of an antiquated financial structure—"

"I pointed out the part the banks played in my book."

"No, no, no! You think bankers are scoundrels. They are not. Nor are company officials, nor patrons, nor the governing classes back on earth. Men are constrained by necessity and build up rationalizations to account for their acts. It is not even cupidity. Slavery is economically unsound, non-productive, but men drift into it whenever the circumstances compel it. A different financial system— But that's another story."

"I still think it's rooted in human cussedness," Wingate said stubbornly.

"Not cussedness—simple stupidity. I can't prove it to you, but you will learn."

The success of the "silent radio" caused the Governor to send Wingate on a long swing around the other camps of the free federation to help them rig new equipment and to teach them how to use it. He spent four hard-working and soul-satisfying weeks, and finished with the warm knowledge that he had done more to consolidate the position of the free men against their enemies than could be done by winning a pitched battle.

When he returned to his home community, he found Sam Houston Jones waiting there.

Wingate broke into a run. "Sam!" he shouted, "Sam! Sam!" He grabbed his hand, pounded him on the back, and yelled at him the affectionate insults that sentimental men use in attempting to cover up their weakness. "Sam, you old scoundrel! When did you get here? How did you escape? And how the devil did you manage to come all the way from South Pole? Were you transferred before you escaped?"

"Howdy, Hump," said Sam. "Now one at a time, and not so fast."

But Wingate bubbled on. "My, but it's good to see your ugly face, fellow. And am I glad you came here—this is a great place. We've got the most up-and-coming little state in the whole federation. You'll like it. They're a great bunch—"

"What are you?" Jones asked, eyeing him. "President of the local chamber of commerce?"

Wingate looked at him, and then laughed. "I get it. But seriously, you will like it. Of course, it's a lot different from what you were used to back on Earth—but that's all past and done with. No use crying over spilt milk, eh?"

"Wait a minute. You are under a misapprehension, Hump. Listen. I'm not an escaped slave. *I'm here to take you back.*"

Wingate opened his mouth, closed it, then opened it again.

"But Sam," he said, "that's impossible. You don't know?"

"I think I do."

"But you don't. There's no going back for me. If I did, I'd have to face trial, and they've got me dead to rights. Even if I threw myself on the mercy of the court and managed to get off with a light sentence, it would be twenty years before I'd be a free man. No, Sam, it's impossible. You don't know the things I'm charged with."

"I don't, eh? It's cost me a nice piece of change to clear them up."

"Huh?"

"I know how you escaped. I know you stole a crock and kidnapped your patron and got two other clients to run with you. It took my best blarney and plenty of folding money to fix it. So help me, Hump—why didn't you pull something mild, like murder, or rape, or robbing a post office?"

"Well, now, Sam—I didn't do any of those things to cause you trouble. I had counted you out of my calculations. I was on my own. I'm sorry about the money."

"Forget it. Money isn't an item with me. I'm filthy with the stuff. You know that. It comes from exercising care in the choice of parents. I was just pulling your leg and it came off in my hand."

"Okay. Sorry." Wingate's grin was a little forced. Nobody likes charity. "But tell me what happened. I'm still in the dark."

"Right." Jones had been as much surprised and distressed at being separated from Wingate on grounding as Wingate had been. But there had been nothing for him to do about it until he received assistance from Earth. He had spent long weeks as a metal worker at South Pole, waiting and wondering why his sister did not answer his call for help. He had written letters to her to supplement his first radiogram, that being the only type of communication he could afford, but the days crept past with no answer.

When a message did arrive from her the mystery was cleared up. She had not received his radio to Earth promptly, because she too, was aboard the *Evening Star*—in the first class cabin, traveling, as was her custom, in a stateroom listed under her maid's name. "It was the family habit of avoiding publicity that stymied us," Jones explained. "If I hadn't sent the radio to her rather than to the family lawyers, or if she had been known by name to the purser, we would have gotten together the first day."

The message had not been relayed to her on Venus because the bright planet had by that time crawled to superior opposition on the far side of the sun from the Earth. For a matter of sixty earth days there was no communication, Earth to Venus. The message had rested, recorded but still scrambled, in the hands of the family firm, until she could be reached.

When she received it, she started a small tornado. Jones had been released, the liens against his contract paid, and ample credit posted to his name on Venus, in less than twenty-four hours. "So that was that," concluded Jones, "except that I've got to explain to big sister when I get home just how I got into this mess. She'll burn my ears."

Jones had chartered a rocket for North Pole and had gotten on Wingate's trail at once. "If you had held on one more day, I would have picked you up. We retrieved your ex-patron about a mile from his gates."

"So the old villain made it. I'm glad of that."

"And a good job, too. If he hadn't I might never have been able to square you. He was pretty well done in, and his heart was kicking up plenty. Do you know that abandonment is a capital offense on this planet—with a mandatory death sentence if the victim dies?"

Wingate nodded. "Yeah, I know. Not that I ever heard of a patron being gassed for it, if the corpse was a client. But that's beside the point. Go ahead."

"Well, he was plenty sore. I don't blame him, though I don't blame you, either. Nobody wants to be sold South, and I gather that was what you expected. Well, I paid him for his crock, and I paid him for your contract—take a look at me, I'm your new owner!—and I paid for the contracts of your two friends as well. Still he wasn't satisfied. I finally had to throw in a first-class passage for his daughter back to Earth, and promise to find her a job. She's a big dumb ox, but I guess the family can stand another retainer. Anyhow, old son, you're a free man. The only remaining question is whether or not the Governor will let us leave here. It seems it's not done."

"No, that's a point. Which reminds me—how did you locate the place?"

"A spot of detective work too long to go into now. That's what took me so long. Slaves don't like to talk. Anyhow, we've a date to talk to the Governor tomorrow."

Wingate took a long time to get to sleep. After his first burst of jubilation he began to wonder. Did he want to go back? To return to the law, to citing technicalities in the interest of whichever side employed him, to meaningless social engagements, to the empty, sterile, bunkum-fed life of the fat and prosperous class he had moved among and served—did he want that, he, who had fought and worked with *men*? It seemed to him that his anachronistic little "invention" in radio had been of more worth than all he had ever done on Earth.

Then he recalled his book.

Perhaps he could get it published. Perhaps he could expose this disgraceful, inhuman system which sold men into legal slavery. He was really wide awake now. *There* was a thing to do! That was his job—to go back to Earth and plead the cause of the colonists. Maybe there was destiny that shapes men's lives after all. He was just the man to do it, the right social background, the proper training. *He* could make himself heard.

He fell asleep, and dreamt of cool, dry breezes, of clear blue sky. Of moonlight.

Satchel and Jimmie decided to stay, even though Jones had been able to fix it up with the Governor. "It's like this," said Satchel. "There's nothing for us back on Earth, or we wouldn't have shipped in the first place. And you can't undertake to support a couple of deadheads. And this isn't such a bad place. It's going to be something someday. We'll stay and grow up with it."

They handled the crock which carried Jones and Wingate to Adonis. There was no hazard in it, as Jones was now officially their patron. What the authorities did not know they could not act on. The crock returned to the refugee community loaded with a cargo which Jones insisted on calling their ransom. As a matter of fact, the opportunity to send an agent to obtain badly needed supplies—one who could do so safely and without arousing the suspicions of the company authorities—had been the determining factor in the Governor's unprecedented decision to risk compromising the secrets of his constituency. He had been frankly not interested in Wingate's plans to agitate for the abolishment of the slave trade.

Saying goodbye to Satchel and Jimmie was something Wingate found embarrassing and unexpectedly depressing.

For the first two weeks after grounding on Earth both Wingate and Jones were too busy to see much of each other. Wingate had gotten his manuscript in shape on the return trip and had spent the time getting acquainted with the waiting rooms of publishers. Only one had shown any interest beyond a form letter of rejection.

"I'm sorry, old man," that one had told him. "I'd like to publish your book, in spite of its controversial nature, if it stood any chance at all of success. But it doesn't. Frankly, it has no literary merit whatsoever. I would as soon read a brief."

"I think I understand," Wingate answered sullenly. "A big publishing house can't afford to print anything which might offend the powers-that-be."

The publisher took his cigar from his mouth and looked at the younger man before replying. "I suppose I should resent that," he said quietly, "but I won't. That's a popular misconception. The powers-that-be, as you call them, do not resort to suppression in this country. We publish what the public will buy. We're in business for that purpose.

"I was about to suggest, if you will listen, a means of making your book salable. You need a collaborator, somebody that knows the writing game and can put some guts in it."

Jones called the day that Wingate got his revised manuscript back from his ghost writer. "Listen to this, Sam," he pleaded. "Look what the dirty so-and-so has done to my book. Look. '—I heard again the crack of the overseer's whip. The frail body of my mate shook under the lash. He gave one cough and slid slowly under the waist-deep water, dragged down by his chains.' Honest, Sam, did you ever see such drivel? And look at the new title: *'I Was a Slave on Venus.'* It sounds like a confession magazine."

Jones nodded without replying. "And listen to this," Wingate went on, "'—crowded like cattle in the enclosure, their naked bodies gleaming with sweat, the women slaves shrank from the—' Oh, hell, I can't go on!"

"Well, they did wear nothing but harnesses."

"Yes, yes—but that has nothing to do with the case. Venus costume is a necessary concomitant of the weather. There's no excuse to leer about it. He's turned my book into a damned sex show. And he had the nerve to defend his actions. He claimed that social pamphleteering is dependent on extravagant language."

"Well, maybe he's got something. *Gulliver's Travels* certainly has some racy passages, and the whipping scenes in *Uncle Tom's Cabin* aren't anything to hand a kid to read. Not to mention *Grapes of Wrath.*"

"Well, I'm damned if I'll resort to that kind of cheap sensationalism. I've got a perfectly straightforward case that anyone can understand."

"Have you now?" Jones took his pipe out of his mouth. "I've been wondering how long it would take you to get your eyes opened. What is your case? It's nothing new; it happened in the Old South, it happened again in California, in Mexico, in Australia, in South Africa. Why? Because in any expanding free-enterprise economy which does not have a money system designed to fit its requirements, the use of mother-country capital to develop the colony inevitably results in subsistence-level wages at home and slave labor in the colonies. The rich get richer and the poor get poorer, and all the good will in the world on the part of the so-called ruling classes won't change it, because the basic problem is one requiring scientific analysis and a mathematical mind. Do you think you can explain those issues to the general public?"

"I can try."

"How far did I get when I tried to explain them to you before you had seen the results? And you are a smart hombre. No, Hump, these things are too difficult to explain to people and too abstract to interest them. You spoke before a women's club the other day, didn't you?"

"Yes."

"How did you make out?"

"Well . . . the chairwoman called me up beforehand and asked me to hold my talk down to ten minutes, as their national president was to be there and they would be crowded for time."

"Hmm . . . you see where your great social message rates in competition. But never mind. Ten minutes is long enough to explain the issue to a person if they have the capacity to understand it. Did you sell anybody?"

"Well . . . I'm not sure."

"You're darn tootin' you're not sure. Maybe they clapped for you but how many of them came up afterwards and wanted to sign checks? No, Hump, sweet reasonableness won't get you anywhere in this racket. To make yourself heard you have to be a demagogue, or a rabble-rousing political preacher like this fellow Nehemiah Scudder. We're going merrily to hell and it won't stop until it winds up in a crash."

"But— Oh, the devil! What can we *do* about it?"

"Nothing. Things are bound to get a whole lot worse before they can get any better. Let's have a drink."

The
Menace From
Earth

To Hermann B. Deutsch

The Year of the Jackpot

I

At first Potiphar Breen did not notice the girl who was undressing.

She was standing at a bus stop only ten feet away. He was indoors but that would not have kept him from noticing; he was seated in a drugstore booth adjacent to the bus stop; there was nothing between Potiphar and the young lady but plate glass and an occasional pedestrian.

Nevertheless he did not look up when she began to peel. Propped up in front of him was a Los Angeles *Times*; beside it, still unopened, were the *Herald-Express* and the *Daily News*. He was scanning the newspaper carefully but the headline stories got only a passing glance. He noted the maximum and minimum temperatures in Brownsville, Texas and entered them in a neat black notebook; he did the same with the closing prices of three blue chips and two dogs on the New York Exchange, as well as the total number of shares. He then began a rapid sifting of minor news stories, from time to time entering briefs of them in his little book; the items he recorded seemed randomly unrelated—among them a publicity release in which Miss National Cottage Cheese Week announced that she intended to marry and have twelve children by a man who could prove that he had been a life-long vegetarian, a circumstantial but wildly unlikely flying saucer report, and a call for prayers for rain throughout Southern California.

Potiphar had just written down the names and addresses of three residents of Watts, California who had been miraculously healed at a tent meeting of the God-is-All First Truth Brethren by the Reverend Dickie Bottomley, the eight-year-old evangelist, and was preparing to tackle the *Herald-Express*, when he glanced over his reading glasses and saw the amateur ecdysiast on the street corner outside. He stood up, placed his glasses in their case, folded the newspapers and put them carefully in his right coat pocket, counted out the exact amount of his check and added twenty-five cents. He then took his raincoat from a hook, placed it over his arm, and went outside.

By now the girl was practically down to the buff. It seemed to Potiphar Breen that she had quite a lot of buff. Nevertheless she had not pulled much of a house. The corner newsboy had stopped hawking his disasters and was grinning at her, and a mixed pair of transvestites who were apparently waiting for the bus had their eyes on her. None of the passers-by stopped. They glanced at her, then with the self-conscious indifference to the unusual of the true Southern Californian, they went on their various ways. The transvestites were frankly staring. The male member of the team wore a frilly feminine blouse but his skirt was a conservative Scottish kilt—his female companion wore a business suit and Homburg hat; she stared with lively interest.

As Breen approached the girl hung a scrap of nylon on the bus stop bench, then reached for her shoes. A police officer, looking hot and unhappy, crossed with the lights and came up to them. "Okay," he said in a tired voice, "that'll be all, lady. Get them duds back on and clear out of here."

The female transvestite took a cigar out of her mouth. "Just," she said, "what business is it of yours, officer?"

The cop turned to her. "Keep out of this!" He ran his eyes over her get up, that of her companion. "I ought to run both of you in, too."

The transvestite raised her eyebrows. "Arrest us for being clothed, arrest her for not being. I think I'm going to like this." She turned to the girl, who was standing still and saying nothing, as if she were puzzled by what was going on. "I'm a lawyer, dear." She pulled a card from her vest pocket. "If this uniformed Neanderthal persists in annoying you, I'll be delighted to handle him."

The man in the kilt said, "Grace! Please!"

She shook him off. "Quiet, Norman—this *is* our business." She went on to the policeman, "Well? Call the wagon. In the meantime my client will answer no questions."

The officer looked unhappy enough to cry and his face was getting dangerously red. Breen quietly stepped forward and slipped his raincoat around the shoulders of the girl. She looked startled and spoke for the first time. "Uh—thanks." She pulled the coat about her, cape fashion.

The female attorney glanced at Breen then back to the cop. "Well, officer? Ready to arrest us?"

He shoved his face close to hers. "I ain't going to give you the satisfaction!" He sighed and added, "Thanks, Mr. Breen—you know this lady?"

"I'll take care of her. You can forget it, Kawonski."

"I sure hope so. If she's with you, I'll do just that. But get her out of here, Mr. Breen—please!"

The lawyer interrupted. "Just a moment—you're interfering with my client."

Kawonski said, "Shut up, you! You heard Mr. Breen— she's with him. Right, Mr. Breen?"

"Well—yes. I'm a friend. I'll take care of her."

The transvestite said suspiciously, "I didn't hear *her* say that."

Her companion said, "Grace—please! There's our bus."

"And I didn't hear her say she was your client," the cop retorted. "You look like a—" His words were drowned out by the bus's brakes, "—and besides that, if you don't climb on that bus and get off my territory, I'll . . . I'll . . . "

"You'll what?"

"Grace! We'll miss our bus."

"Just a moment, Norman. Dear, is this man really a friend of yours? Are you with him?"

The girl looked uncertainly at Breen, then said in a low voice, "Uh, yes. That's right."

"Well . . . " The lawyer's companion pulled at her arm. She shoved her card into Breen's hand and got on the bus; it pulled away.

Breen pocketed the card. Kawonski wiped his forehead. "Why did you do it, lady?" he said peevishly.

The girl looked puzzled. "I . . . I don't know."

"You hear that, Mr. Breen? That's what they all say. And if you pull 'em in, there's six more the next day. The Chief said—" He sighed. "The Chief said—well, if I had arrested her like that female shyster wanted me to, I'd be out at a hundred and ninety-sixth and Ploughed Ground tomorrow morning, thinking about retirement. So get her out of here, will you?"

The girl said, "But—"

"No 'buts,' lady. Just be glad a real gentleman like Mr. Breen is willing to help you." He gathered up her clothes, handed them to her. When she reached for them she again exposed an uncustomary amount of skin; Kawonski hastily gave them to Breen instead, who crowded them into his coat pockets.

She let Breen lead her to where his car was parked, got in and tucked the raincoat around her so that she was rather more dressed than a girl usually is. She looked at him.

She saw a medium-sized and undistinguished man who was slipping down the wrong side of thirty-five and looked older. His eyes had that mild and slightly naked look of the habitual spectacles wearer who is not at the moment with glasses; his hair was gray at the temples and thin on top. His herringbone suit, black shoes, white shirt, and neat tie smacked more of the East than of California.

He saw a face which he classified as "pretty" and "wholesome" rather than "beautiful" and "glamorous." It was topped by a healthy mop of light brown hair. He set her age at twenty-five, give or take eighteen months. He smiled gently, climbed in without speaking and started his car.

He turned up Doheny Drive and east on Sunset. Near La Cienega he slowed down. "Feeling better?"

"Uh, I guess so. Mr.—'Breen'?"

"Call me Potiphar. What's your name? Don't tell me if you don't want to."

"Me? I'm . . . I'm Meade Barstow."

"Thank you, Meade. Where do you want to go? Home?"

"I suppose so. I—Oh my, no! I can't go home like *this*." She clutched the coat tightly to her.

"Parents?"

"No. My landlady. She'd be shocked to death."

"Where, then?"

She thought. "Maybe we could stop at a filling station and I could sneak into the ladies' room."

"Mmm . . . maybe. See here, Meade—my house is six blocks from here and has a garage entrance. You could get inside without being seen." He looked at her.

She stared back. "Potiphar—you don't *look* like a wolf?"

"Oh, but I am! The worst sort." He whistled and gnashed his teeth. "See? But Wednesday is my day off from it." She looked at him and dimpled. "Oh, well! I'd rather wrestle with you than with Mrs. Megeath. Let's go."

He turned up into the hills. His bachelor diggings were one of the many little frame houses clinging like fungus to the brown slopes of the Santa Monica Mountains. The garage was notched into this hill; the house sat on it. He drove in, cut the ignition, and led her up a teetery inside stairway into the living room. "In there," he said, pointing. "Help yourself." He pulled her clothes out of his coat pockets and handed them to her.

She blushed and took them, disappeared into his bedroom. He heard her turn the key in the lock. He settled down in his easy chair, took out his notebook, and opened the *Herald-Express.*

He was finishing the *Daily News* and had added several notes to his collection when she came out. Her hair was neatly rolled; her face was restored; she had brushed most of the wrinkles out of her skirt. Her sweater was neither too tight nor deep cut, but it was pleasantly filled. She reminded him of well water and farm breakfasts.

He took his raincoat from her, hung it up, and said, "Sit down, Meade."

She said uncertainly, "I had better go."

"Go if you must—but I had hoped to talk with you."

"Well—" She sat down on the edge of his couch and looked around. The room was small but as neat as his necktie, clean as his collar. The fireplace was swept; the floor was bare and polished. Books crowded bookshelves in every possible space. One corner was filled by an elderly flat-top desk; the papers on it were neatly in order. Near it, on its own stand, was a small electric calculator. To her right, French windows gave out on a tiny porch over the garage. Beyond it she could see the sprawling city; a few neon signs were already blinking.

She sat back a little. "This is a nice room—Potiphar. It looks like you."

"I take that as a compliment. Thank you." She did not answer; he went on, "Would you like a drink?"

"Oh, would I!" She shivered. "I guess I've got the jitters."

He got up. "Not surprising. What'll it be?"

She took Scotch and water, no ice; he was a Bourbon-and-ginger-ale man. She had soaked up half her highball in silence, then put it down, squared her shoulders and said, "Potiphar?"

"Yes, Meade?"

"Look—if you brought me here to make a pass, I wish you'd go ahead and make it. It won't do you a bit of good, but it makes me nervous to wait for it."

He said nothing and did not change his expression. She went on uneasily, "Not that I'd blame you for trying—under the circumstances. And I *am* grateful. But—well—it's just that I don't—"

He came over and took both her hands. "My dear, I haven't the slightest thought of making a pass at you. Nor need you feel grateful. I butted in because I was interested in your case."

"My case? Are you a doctor? A psychiatrist?"

He shook his head. "I'm a mathematician. A statistician, to be precise."

"Huh? I don't get it."

"Don't worry about it. But I would like to ask some questions. May I?"

"Uh, sure, sure! I owe you that much—and then some."

"You owe me nothing. Want your drink sweetened?"

She gulped it and handed him her glass, then followed him out into the kitchen. He did an exact job of measuring and gave it back. "Now tell me why you took your clothes off?"

She frowned. "I don't know. I *don't* know. I don't *know*. I guess I just went crazy." She added round-eyed,

"But I don't feel crazy. Could I go off my rocker and not know it?"

"You're not crazy . . . not more so than the rest of us," he amended. "Tell me, where did you see someone else do this?"

"Huh? But I never have."

"Where did you read about it?"

"But I haven't. Wait a minute—those people up in Canada. Dooka-somethings."

"Doukhobors. That's all? No bareskin swimming parties? No strip poker?"

She shook her head. "No. You may not believe it but I was the kind of a little girl who undressed under her nightie." She colored and added, "I still do—unless I remember to tell myself it's silly."

"I believe it. No news stories?"

"No. Yes, there was too! About two weeks ago, I think it was. Some girl in a theater, in the audience, I mean. But I thought it was just publicity. You know the stunts they pull here."

He shook his head. "It wasn't. February 3rd, the Grand Theater, Mrs. Alvin Copley. Charges dismissed."

"Huh? How did *you* know?"

"Excuse me." He went to his desk, dialed the City News Bureau. "Alf? This is Pot Breen. They still sitting on that story? . . . yes, yes, the Gypsy Rose file. Any new ones today?" He waited; Meade thought that she could make out swearing. "Take it easy, Alf—this hot weather can't last forever. Nine, eh? Well, add another—Santa Monica Boulevard, late this afternoon. No arrest." He added, "Nope, nobody got her name—a middle-aged woman with a cast in one eye. I happened to see it . . . who, me? Why would I want to get mixed up? But it's rounding up into a very, very interesting picture." He put the phone down.

Meade said, "Cast in one eye, indeed!"

"Shall I call him back and give him your name?"

"Oh, no!"

"Very well. Now, Meade, we seemed to have located the point of contagion in your case—Mrs. Copley. What I'd like to know next is how you felt, what you were thinking about, when you did it?"

She was frowning intently. "Wait a minute, Potiphar— do I understand that *nine other* girls have pulled the stunt I pulled?"

"Oh, no—nine others *today*. You are—" He paused briefly. "—the three hundred and nineteenth case in Los Angeles county since the first of the year. I don't have figures on the rest of the country, but the suggestion to clamp down on the stories came from the eastern news services when the papers here put our first cases on the wire. That proves that it's a problem elsewhere, too."

"You mean that women all over the country are peeling off their clothes in public? Why, how shocking!"

He said nothing. She blushed again and insisted, "Well, it is shocking, even if it was me, this time."

"No, Meade. One case is shocking; over three hundred makes it scientifically interesting. That's why I want to know how it felt. Tell me about it."

"But—All right, I'll try. I told you I don't know why I did it; I still don't. I—"

"You remember it?"

"Oh, yes! I remember getting up off the bench and pulling up my sweater. I remember unzipping my skirt. I remember thinking I would have to hurry as I could see my bus stopped two blocks down the street. I remember how *good* it felt when I finally, uh—" She paused and looked puzzled. "But I still don't know why."

"What were you thinking about just before you stood up?"

"I don't remember."

"Visualize the street. What was passing by? Where were your hands? Were your legs crossed or uncrossed? Was there anybody near you? What were you thinking about?"

"Uh . . . nobody was on the bench with me. I had my hands in my lap. Those characters in the mixed-up clothes were standing near by, but I wasn't paying attention. I wasn't thinking much except that my feet hurt and I wanted to get home—and how unbearably hot and sultry it was. Then—" Her eyes became distant, "—suddenly I knew what I had to do and it was very urgent that I do it. So I stood up and I . . . and I—" Her voice became shrill.

"Take it easy!" he said. "Don't do it again."

"Huh? Why, Mr. Breen! I wouldn't do anything like that."

"Of course not. Then what?"

"Why, you put your raincoat around me and you know the rest." She faced him. "Say, Potiphar, what were you doing with a raincoat? It hasn't rained in weeks—this is the driest, hottest rainy season in years."

"In sixty-eight years, to be exact."

"Huh?"

"I carry a raincoat anyhow. Uh, just a notion of mine, but I feel that when it does rain, it's going to rain awfully hard." He added, "Forty days and forty nights, maybe."

She decided that he was being humorous and laughed. He went on, "Can you remember how you got the idea?"

She swirled her glass and thought. "I simply don't know."

He nodded. "That's what I expected."

"I don't understand you—unless you think I'm crazy. Do you?"

"No. I think you had to do it and could not help it and don't know why and can't know why."

"But *you* know." She said it accusingly.

"Maybe. At least I have some figures. Ever take any interest in statistics, Meade?"

She shook her head. "Figures confuse me. Never mind statistics—*I want to know why I did what I did!*"

He looked at her very soberly. "I think we're lemmings, Meade."

She looked puzzled, then horrified. "You mean those little furry mouselike creatures? The ones that—"

"Yes. The ones that periodically make a death migration, until millions, hundreds of millions of them drown themselves in the sea. Ask a lemming why he does it. If you could get him to slow up his rush toward death, even money says he would rationalize his answer as well as any college graduate. But he does it because he has to—and so do we."

"That's a horrid idea, Potiphar."

"Maybe. Come here, Meade. I'll show you figures that

confuse me, too." He went to his desk and opened a drawer, took out a packet of cards. "Here's one. Two weeks ago—a man sues an entire state legislature for alienation of his wife's affection—and the judge lets the suit be tried. Or this one—a patent application for a device to lay the globe over on its side and warm up the arctic regions. Patent denied, but the inventor took in over three hundred thousand dollars in down payments on South Pole real estate before the postal authorities stepped in. Now he's fighting the case and it looks as if he might win. And here—prominent bishop proposes applied courses in the so-called facts of life in high schools." He put the card away hastily. "Here's a dilly: a bill introduced in the Alabama lower house to repeal the laws of atomic energy—not the present statutes, but the natural laws concerning nuclear physics; the wording makes that plain." He shrugged. "How silly can you get?"

"They're crazy."

"No, Meade. One such is crazy; a lot of them is a lemming death march. No, don't object—I've plotted them on a curve. The last time we had anything like this was the so-called Era of Wonderful Nonsense. But this one is much worse." He delved into a lower drawer, hauled out a graph. "The amplitude is more than twice as great and we haven't reached peak. What the peak will be I don't dare guess—three separate rhythms, reinforcing."

She peered at the curves. "You mean that the laddy with the arctic real estate deal is somewhere on this line?"

"He adds to it. And back here on the last crest are the flagpole sitters and the goldfish swallowers and the Ponzi hoax and the marathon dancers and the man who pushed a peanut up Pikes Peak with his nose. You're on the new crest—or you will be when I add you in."

She made a face. "I don't like it."

"Neither do I. But it's as clear as a bank statement. This year the human race is letting down its hair, flipping its lip with a finger, and saying, '*Wubba, wubba, wubba.*'"

She shivered. "Do you suppose I could have another drink? Then I'll go."

"I have a better idea. I owe you a dinner for answering questions. Pick a place and we'll have a cocktail before."

She chewed her lip. "You don't owe me anything. And I don't feel up to facing a restaurant crowd. I might . . . I might—"

"No, you wouldn't," he said sharply. "It doesn't hit twice."

"You're sure? Anyhow, I don't want to face a crowd." She glanced at his kitchen door. "Have you anything to eat in there? I can cook."

"Um, breakfast things. And there's a pound of ground round in the freezer compartment and some rolls. I sometimes make hamburgers when I don't want to go out."

She headed for the kitchen. "Drunk or sober, fully dressed or—or naked, I can cook. You'll see."

He did see. Open-faced sandwiches with the meat married to toasted buns and the flavor garnished rather than suppressed by scraped Bermuda onion and thin-sliced dill, a salad made from things she had scrounged out of his refrigerator, potatoes crisp but not vulcanized. They ate it on the tiny balcony, sopping it down with cold beer.

He sighed and wiped his mouth. "Yes, Meade, you can cook."

"Some day I'll arrive with proper materials and pay you back. Then I'll prove it."

"You've already proved it. Nevertheless I accept. But I tell you three times, you owe me nothing."

"No? If you hadn't been a Boy Scout, I'd be in jail."

Breen shook his head. "The police have orders to keep it quiet at all costs—to keep it from growing. You saw that. And, my dear, you weren't a person to me at the time. I didn't even see your face; I—"

"You saw plenty else!"

"Truthfully, I didn't look. You were just a—a statistic."

She toyed with her knife and said slowly, "I'm not sure, but I think I've just been insulted. In all the twenty-five years that I've fought men off, more or less successfully, I've been called a lot of names—but a 'statistic'—why, I ought to take your slide rule and beat you to death with it."

"My dear young lady—"

"I'm not a lady, that's for sure. But I'm *not* a statistic."

"My dear Meade, then. I wanted to tell you, before you did anything hasty, that in college I wrestled varsity middle-weight."

She grinned and dimpled. "That's more the talk a girl likes to hear. I was beginning to be afraid you had been assembled in an adding machine factory. Potty, you're rather a dear."

"If that is a diminutive of my given name, I like it. But if it refers to my waist line, I resent it."

She reached across and patted his stomach. "I like your waist line; lean and hungry men are difficult. If I were cooking for you regularly, I'd really pad it."

"Is that a proposal?"

"Let it lie, let it lie—Potty, do you really think the whole country is losing its buttons?"

He sobered at once. "It's worse than that."

"Huh?"

"Come inside. I'll show you." They gathered up dishes and dumped them in the sink, Breen talking all the while. "As a kid I was fascinated by numbers. Numbers are pretty things and they combine in such interesting configurations. I took my degree in math, of course, and got a job as a junior actuary with Midwestern Mutual—the insurance outfit. That was fun—no way on Earth to tell when a particular man is going to die, but an absolute certainty that so many men of a certain age group would die before a certain date. The curves were so lovely—and they always worked out. Always. You didn't have to know *why;* you could predict with dead certainty and never know why. The equations worked; the curves were right.

"I was interested in astronomy too; it was the one science where individual figures worked out neatly, completely, and accurately, down to the last decimal point the instruments were good for. Compared with astronomy the other sciences were mere carpentry and kitchen chemistry.

"I found there were nooks and crannies in astronomy where individual numbers won't do, where you have to go over to statistics, and I became even more interested. I joined the Variable Star Association and I might have gone into astronomy professionally, instead of what I'm in now—business consultation—if I hadn't gotten interested in something else."

"'Business consultation'?" repeated Meade. "Income tax work?"

"Oh, no—that's too elementary. I'm the numbers boy for a firm of industrial engineers. I can tell a rancher exactly how many of his Hereford bull calves will be sterile. Or I tell a motion picture producer how much rain insurance to carry on location. Or maybe how big a company in a particular line must be to carry its own risk in industrial accidents. And I'm right. I'm always right."

"Wait a minute. Seems to me a big company would *have* to have insurance."

"Contrariwise. A really big corporation begins to resemble a statistical universe."

"Huh?"

"Never mind. I got interested in something else— cycles. Cycles are everything, Meade. And everywhere. The tides. The seasons. Wars. Love. Everybody knows that in the spring the young man's fancy lightly turns to what the girls never stopped thinking about, but did you know that it runs in an eighteen-year-plus cycle as well? And that a girl born at the wrong swing of the curve doesn't stand nearly as good a chance as her older or younger sister?"

"What? Is *that* why I'm a doddering old maid?"

"You're twenty-five?" He pondered. "Maybe—but your chances are picking up again; the curve is swinging up. Anyhow, remember you are just one statistic; the curve applies to the group. Some girls get married every year anyhow."

"Don't call me a statistic."

"Sorry. And marriages match up with acreage planted

to wheat, with wheat cresting ahead. You could almost say that planting wheat makes people get married."

"Sounds silly."

"It *is* silly. The whole notion of cause-and-effect is probably superstition. But the same cycle shows a peak in house building right after a peak in marriages, every time."

"Now that makes sense."

"Does it? How many newlyweds do you know who can afford to build a house? You might as well blame it on wheat acreage. We don't know *why;* it just *is.*"

"Sunspots, maybe?"

"You can correlate sunspots with stock prices, or Columbia River salmon, or women's skirts. And you are just as much justified in blaming short skirts for sunspots as you are in blaming sunspots for salmon. We don't know. But the curves go on just the same."

"But there has to be some *reason* behind it."

"Does there? That's mere assumption. A fact has no 'why.' There it stands, self demonstrating. Why did you take your clothes off today?"

She frowned. "That's not fair."

"Maybe not. But I want to show you why I'm worried." He went into the bedroom, came out with a large roll of tracing paper. "We'll spread it on the floor. Here they are, all of them. The 54-year cycle—see the Civil War there? See how it matches in? The 18 & 1/3 year cycle, the 9-plus cycle, the 41-month shorty, the three rhythms of sunspots—everything, all combined in one grand chart. Mississippi River floods, fur catches in Canada, stock market prices, marriages, epidemics, freight-car loadings, bank clearings, locust plagues, divorces, tree growth, wars, rainfall, Earth magnetism, building construction, patents applied for, murders—you name it; I've got it there."

She stared at the bewildering array of wavy lines. "But, Potty, what does it mean?"

"It means that these things all happen, in regular rhythm, whether we like it or not. It means that when skirts are due to go up, all the stylists in Paris can't make 'em go down. It means that when prices are going down, all the controls and supports and government planning can't make 'em go up." He pointed to a curve. "Take a look at the grocery ads. Then turn to the financial page and read how the Big Brains try to double-talk their way out of it. It means that when an epidemic is due, it happens, despite all the public health efforts. It means we're lemmings."

She pulled her lip. "I don't like it. 'I am the master of my fate,' and so forth. I've got free will, Potty. I know I have—I can feel it."

"I imagine every little neutron in an atom bomb feels the same way. He can go *spung!* or he can sit still, just as he pleases. But statistical mechanics work out anyhow. And the bomb goes off—which is what I'm leading up to. See anything odd there, Meade?"

She studied the chart, trying not to let the curving lines confuse her. "They sort of bunch up over at the right end."

"You're dern tootin' they do! See that dotted vertical line? That's right now—and things are bad enough. But take a look at that solid vertical; that's about six months from now and that's when we get it. Look at the cycles—the long ones, the short ones, all of them. Every single last one of them reaches either a trough or a crest exactly on—or almost on—that line."

"That's bad?"

"What do you think? Three of the big ones troughed in 1929 and the depression almost ruined us . . . even with the big 54-year cycle supporting things. Now we've got the big one troughing—and the few crests are not things that help. I mean to say, tent caterpillars and influenza don't do us any good. Meade, if statistics mean anything, this tired old planet hasn't seen a jackpot like this since Eve went into the apple business. I'm scared."

She searched his face. "Potty—you're not simply having fun with me? You know I can't check up on you."

"I wish to heaven I were. No, Meade, I can't fool about numbers; I wouldn't know how. This is it. The Year of the Jackpot."

She was very silent as he drove her home. As they approached West Los Angeles, she said, "Potty?"

"Yes, Meade?"

"What do we *do* about it?"

"What do you do about a hurricane? You pull in your ears. What can you do about an atom bomb? You try to out-guess it, not be there when it goes off. What else can you do?"

"Oh." She was silent for a few moments, then added, "Potty? Will you tell me which way to jump?"

"Huh? Oh, sure! If I can figure it out."

He took her to her door, turned to go. She said, "Potty!"

He faced her. "Yes, Meade?"

She grabbed his head, shook it—then kissed him fiercely on the mouth. "There—is that just a statistic?"

"Uh, no."

"It had better not be," she said dangerously. "Potty, I think I'm going to have to change your curve."

"RUSSIANS REJECT UN NOTE"
"MISSOURI FLOOD DAMAGE EXCEEDS 1951 RECORD"
"MISSISSIPPI MESSIAH DEFIES COURT"
"NUDIST CONVENTION STORMS BAILEY'S BEACH"
"BRITISH-IRAN TALKS STILL DEAD-LOCKED"
"FASTER-THAN-LIGHT WEAPON PROMISED"
"TYPHOON DOUBLING BACK ON MANILA"

"MARRIAGE SOLEMNIZED ON FLOOR OF HUDSON—New York, 13 July, *In a specially-constructed diving suit built for two, Merydith Smithe, café society headline girl, and Prince Augie Schleswieg of New York and the Riviera were united today by Bishop Dalton in a service televised with the aid of the Navy's ultra-new—*"

As the Year of the Jackpot progressed Breen took melancholy pleasure in adding to the data which proved that the curve was sagging as predicted. The undeclared World War continued its bloody, blundering way at half a dozen spots around a tortured globe. Breen did not chart it; the headlines were there for anyone to read. He concentrated on the odd facts in the other pages of the papers, facts which, taken singly, meant nothing, but taken together showed a disastrous trend.

He listed stock market prices, rainfall, wheat futures, but it was the "silly season" items which fascinated him. To be sure, some humans were always doing silly things— but at what point had prime damfoolishness become commonplace? When, for example, had the zombie-like professional models become accepted ideals of American womanhood? What were the gradations between National Cancer Week and National Athlete's Foot Week? On what day had the American people finally taken leave of horse sense?

Take transvestism—male-and-female dress customs were arbitrary, but they had seemed to be deeply rooted in the culture. When did the breakdown start? With Marlene Dietrich's tailored suits? By the late forties there was no "male" article of clothing that a woman could not wear in public—but when had men started to slip over the line? Should he count the psychological cripples who had made the word "drag" a byword in Greenwich Village and Hollywood long before this outbreak? Or were they "wild shots" not belonging on the curve? Did it start with some unknown normal man attending a masquerade and there discovering that skirts actually were more comfortable and practical than trousers? Or had it started with the resurgence of Scottish nationalism reflected in the wearing of kilts by many Scottish-Americans?

Ask a lemming to state his motives! The outcome was in

front of him, a news story. Transvestism by draft-dodgers had at last resulted in a mass arrest in Chicago which was to have ended in a giant joint trial—only to have the deputy prosecutor show up in a pinafore and defy the judge to submit to an examination to determine the judge's true sex. The judge suffered a stroke and died and the trial was postponed—postponed forever in Breen's opinion; he doubted that this particular blue law would ever again be enforced.

Or the laws about indecent exposure, for that matter. The attempt to limit the Gypsy-Rose syndrome by ignoring it had taken the starch out of enforcement; now here was a report about the All Souls Community Church of Springfield: the pastor had reinstituted ceremonial nudity. Probably the first time this thousand years, Breen thought, aside from some screwball cults in Los Angeles. The reverend gentleman claimed that the ceremony was identical with the "dance of the high priestess" in the ancient temple of Karnak.

Could be—but Breen had private information that the "priestess" had been working the burlesque & nightclub circuit before her present engagement. In any case the holy leader was packing them in and had not been arrested.

Two weeks later a hundred and nine churches in thirty-three states offered equivalent attractions. Breen entered them on his curves.

This queasy oddity seemed to him to have no relation to the startling rise in the dissident evangelical cults throughout the country. These churches were sincere, earnest and poor—but growing, ever since the War. Now they were multiplying like yeast. It seemed a statistical cinch that the United States was about to become god-struck again. He correlated it with Transcendentalism and the trek of the Latter Day Saints—hmm . . . yes, it fitted. And the curve was pushing toward a crest.

Billions in war bonds were now falling due; wartime marriages were reflected in the swollen peak of the Los Angeles school population. The Colorado River was at a record low and the towers in Lake Mead stood high out of the water. But the Angelenos committed slow suicide by watering lawns as usual. The Metropolitan Water District commissioners tried to stop it—it fell between the stools of the police powers of fifty "sovereign" cities. The taps remained open, trickling away the life blood of the desert paradise.

The four regular party conventions—Dixiecrats, Regular Republicans, the other Regular Republicans, and the Democrats—attracted scant attention, as the Know-Nothings had not yet met. The fact that the "American Rally," as the Know-Nothings preferred to be called, claimed not to be a party but an educational society did not detract from their strength. But what was their strength? Their beginnings had been so obscure that Breen had had to go back and dig into the December 1951 files—but he had been approached twice this very week to join them, right inside his own office—once by his boss, once by the janitor.

He hadn't been able to chart the Know-Nothings. They gave him chills in his spine. He kept column-inches on them, found that their publicity was shrinking while their numbers were obviously zooming.

Krakatau blew up on July 8th. It provided the first

important transPacific TV-cast; its effect on sunsets, on solar constant, on mean temperature, and on rainfall would not be felt until later in the year. The San Andreas fault, its stresses unrelieved since the Long Beach disaster of 1933 continued to build up imbalance—an unhealed wound running the full length of the West Coast. Pelée and Etna erupted; Mauna Loa was still quiet.

Flying saucers seemed to be landing daily in every state. No one had exhibited one on the ground—or had the Department of Defense sat on them? Breen was unsatisfied with the off-the-record reports he had been able to get; the alcoholic content of some of them had been high. But the sea serpent on Ventura Beach was real; he had seen it. The troglodyte in Tennessee he was not in a position to verify.

Thirty-one domestic air crashes the last week in July . . . was it sabotage? Or was it a sagging curve on a chart? And that neo-polio epidemic that skipped from Seattle to New York? Time for a big epidemic? Breen's chart said it was. But how about B.W.? Could a chart *know* that a Slav biochemist would perfect an efficient virus-and-vector at the right time? Nonsense!

But the curves, if they meant anything at all, included "free will;" they averaged in all the individual "wills" of a statistical universe—and came out as a smooth function. Every morning three million "free wills" flowed toward the center of the New York megapolis; every evening they flowed out again—all by "free will," and on a smooth and predictable curve.

Ask a lemming! Ask *all* the lemmings, dead and alive—let them take a vote on it! Breen tossed his notebook aside and called Meade. "Is this my favorite statistic?"

"Potty! I was thinking about you."

"Naturally. This is your night off."

"Yes, but another reason, too. Potiphar, have you ever taken a look at the Great Pyramid?"

"I haven't even been to Niagara Falls. I'm looking for a rich woman, so I can travel."

"Yes, yes, I'll let you know when I get my first million, but—"

"That's the first time you've proposed to me this week."

"Shut up. Have you ever looked into the prophecies they found inside the pyramid?"

"Huh? Look, Meade, that's in the same class with astrology—strictly for squirrels. Grow up."

"Yes, of course. But Potty, I thought you were interested in anything odd. This is odd."

"Oh. Sorry. If it's 'silly season' stuff, let's see it."

"All right. Am I cooking for you tonight?"

"It's Wednesday, isn't it?"

"How soon?"

He glanced at his watch. "Pick you up in eleven minutes." He felt his whiskers. "No, twelve and a half."

"I'll be ready. Mrs. Megeath says that these regular dates mean that you are going to marry me."

"Pay no attention to her. She's just a statistic. And I'm a wild datum."

"Oh, well, I've got two hundred and forty-seven dollars toward that million. 'Bye!"

Meade's prize was the usual Rosicrucian come-on,

elaborately printed, and including a photograph (retouched, he was sure) of the much disputed line on the corridor wall which was alleged to prophesy, by its various discontinuities, the entire future. This one had an unusual time scale but the major events were all marked on it— the fall of Rome, the Norman Invasion, the Discovery of America, Napoleon, the World Wars.

What made it interesting was that it suddenly stopped—now.

"What about it, Potty?"

"I guess the stonecutter got tired. Or got fired. Or they got a new head priest with new ideas." He tucked it into his desk. "Thanks. I'll think about how to list it." But he got it out again, applied dividers and a magnifying glass. "It says here," he announced, "that the end comes late in August—unless that's a fly speck."

"Morning or afternoon? I have to know how to dress."

"Shoes will be worn. All God's chilluns got shoes." He put it away.

She was quiet for a moment, then said, "Potty, isn't it about time to jump?"

"Huh? Girl, don't let *that* thing affect you! That's 'silly season' stuff."

"Yes. But take a look at *your* chart."

Nevertheless he took the next afternoon off, spent it in the reference room of the main library, confirmed his opinion of soothsayers. Nostradamus was pretentiously silly, Mother Shippey was worse. In any of them you could find what you looked for.

He did find one item in Nostradamus that he liked: "The Oriental shall come forth from his seat . . . he shall pass through the sky, through the waters and the snow, and he shall strike each one with his weapon."

That sounded like what the Department of Defense expected the commies to try to do to the Western Allies.

But it was also a description of every invasion that had come out of the "heartland" in the memory of mankind. Nuts!

When he got home he found himself taking down his father's Bible and turning to Revelations. He could not find anything that he could understand but he got fascinated by the recurring use of precise numbers. Presently he thumbed through the Book at random; his eye lit on: "Boast not thyself of tomorrow; for thou knowest not what a day may bring forth." He put the Book away, feeling humbled but not cheered.

The rains started the next morning. The Master Plumbers elected Miss Star Morning "Miss Sanitary Engineering" on the same day that the morticians designated her as "The Body I would Like Best to Prepare," and her option was dropped by Fragrant Features. Congress voted $1.37 to compensate Thomas Jefferson Meeks for losses incurred while an emergency postman for the Christmas rush of 1936, approved the appointment of five lieutenant generals and one ambassador and adjourned in eight minutes. The fire extinguishers in a midwest orphanage turned out to be filled with air. The chancellor of the leading football institution sponsored a fund to send peace messages and vitamins to the Politburo. The stock market slumped nineteen points and the tickers ran two hours late. Wichita, Kansas, remained flooded while Phoenix, Arizona, cut off drinking water to areas outside city limits. And Potiphar Breen found that he had left his raincoat at Meade Barstow's rooming house.

He phoned her landlady, but Mrs. Megeath turned him over to Meade. "What are you doing home on a Friday?" he demanded.

"The theater manager laid me off. Now you'll have to marry me."

"You can't afford me. Meade—seriously, baby, what happened?"

"I was ready to leave the dump anyway. For the last six weeks the popcorn machine has been carrying the place. Today I sat through *I Was A Teen-Age Beatnik* twice. Nothing to do."

"I'll be along."

"Eleven minutes?"

"It's raining. Twenty—with luck."

It was more nearly sixty. Santa Monica Boulevard was a navigable stream; Sunset Boulevard was a subway jam. When he tried to ford the streams leading to Mrs. Megeath's house, he found that changing tires with the wheel wedged against a storm drain presented problems.

"Potty! You look like a drowned rat."

"I'll live." But presently he found himself wrapped in a blanket robe belonging to the late Mr. Megeath and sipping hot cocoa while Mrs. Megeath dried his clothing in the kitchen.

"Meade . . . . I'm 'at liberty,' too."

"Huh? You quit your job?"

"Not exactly. Old Man Wiley and I have been having differences of opinion about my answers for months—too much 'Jackpot factor' in the figures I give him to turn over to clients. Not that I call it that, but he has felt that I was unduly pessimistic."

"But you were right!"

"Since when has being right endeared a man to his boss? But that wasn't why he fired me; that was just the excuse. He wants a man willing to back up the Know-Nothing program with scientific double-talk. And I wouldn't join." He went to the window. "It's raining harder."

"But they haven't got any program."

"I know that."

"Potty, you should have joined. It doesn't mean anything—I joined three months ago."

"The hell you did!"

She shrugged. "You pay your dollar and you turn up for two meetings and they leave you alone. It kept my job for another three months. What of it?"

"Uh, well—I'm sorry you did it; that's all. Forget it. Meade, the water is over the curbs out there."

"You had better stay here overnight."

"Mmm . . . I don't like to leave 'Entropy' parked out in this stuff all night. Meade?"

"Yes, Potty?"

"We're both out of jobs. How would you like to duck north into the Mojave and find a dry spot?"

"I'd love it. But look, Potty—is this a proposal, or just a proposition?"

"Don't pull that 'either-or' stuff on me. It's just a suggestion for a vacation. Do you want to take a chaperone?"

"No."

"Then pack a bag."

"Right away. But look, Potiphar—pack a bag *how?* Are you trying to tell me it's *time to jump?*"

He faced her, then looked back at the window. "I don't know," he said slowly, "but this rain might go on quite a while. Don't take anything you don't have to have—but don't leave anything behind you can't get along without."

He repossessed his clothing from Mrs. Megeath while Meade was upstairs. She came down dressed in slacks and carrying two large bags; under one arm was a battered and rakish Teddy bear. "This is Winnie."

"Winnie the Pooh?"

"No, Winnie Churchill. When I feel bad he promises me 'blood, toil, tears, and sweat;' then I feel better. You said to bring anything I couldn't do without?" She looked at him anxiously.

"Right." He took the bags. Mrs. Megeath had seemed satisfied with his explanation that they were going to visit his (mythical) aunt in Bakersfield before looking for jobs; nevertheless she embarrassed him by kissing him good-by and telling him to "take care of my little girl."

Santa Monica Boulevard was blocked off from use. While stalled in traffic in Beverly Hills he fiddled with the car radio, getting squawks and crackling noises, then finally one station nearby: "—in effect," a harsh, high, staccato voice was saying, "the Kremlin has given us till sundown to get out of town. This is your New York Reporter, who thinks that in days like these every American must personally keep his powder dry. And now for a word from—" Breen switched it off and glanced at her face. "Don't worry," he said. "They've been talking that way for years."

"You think they are bluffing?"

"I didn't say that. I said, 'don't worry.'"

But his own packing, with her help, was clearly on a "Survival Kit" basis—canned goods, all his warm clothing, a sporting rifle he had not fired in over two years, a first-aid kit and the contents of his medicine chest. He dumped the stuff from his desk into a carton, shoved it into the back seat along with cans and books and coats and covered the plunder with all the blankets in the house. They went back up the rickety stairs for a last check.

"Potty—where's your chart?"

"Rolled up on the back seat shelf. I guess that's all— hey, wait a minute!" He went to a shelf over his desk and began taking down small, sober-looking magazines. "I dern near left behind my file of *The Western Astronomer* and of the *Proceedings of the Variable Star Association*."

"Why take them?"

"Huh? I must be nearly a year behind on both of them. Now maybe I'll have time to read."

"Hmm . . . Potty, watching you read professional journals is not my notion of a vacation."

"Quiet, woman! You took Winnie; I take these."

She shut up and helped him. He cast a longing eye at his electric calculator but decided it was too much like the White Knight's mouse trap. He could get by with his slide rule.

As the car splashed out into the street she said, "Potty, how are you fixed for cash?"

"Huh? Okay, I guess."

"I mean, leaving while the banks are closed and everything." She held up her purse. "Here's my bank. It isn't much, but we can use it."

He smiled and patted her knee. "Stout fellow! I'm sitting on my bank; I started turning everything to cash about the first of the year."

"Oh. I closed out my bank account right after we met."

"You did? You must have taken my maunderings seriously."

"I always take you seriously."

Mint Canyon was a five-mile-an-hour nightmare, with visibility limited to the tail lights of the truck ahead. When they stopped for coffee at Halfway, they confirmed what seemed evident: Cajon Pass was closed and long-haul traffic for Route 66 was being detoured through the secondary pass. At long, long last they reached the Victorville cut-off and lost some of the traffic—a good thing, as the windshield wiper on his side had quit working and they were driving by the committee system. Just short of Lancaster she said suddenly, "Potty, is this buggy equipped with a snorkel?"

"Nope."

"Then we had better stop. But I see a light off the road."

The light was an auto court. Meade settled the matter of economy versus convention by signing the book herself; they were placed in one cabin. He saw that it had twin beds and let the matter ride. Meade went to bed with her teddy bear without even asking to be kissed goodnight. It was already gray, wet dawn.

They got up in the late afternoon and decided to stay over one more night, then push north toward Bakersfield. A high pressure area was alleged to be moving south, crowding the warm, wet mass that smothered Southern California. They wanted to get into it. Breen had the wiper repaired and bought two new tires to replace his ruined spare, added some camping items to his cargo, and bought for Meade a .32 automatic, a lady's social-purposes gun; he gave it to her somewhat sheepishly.

"What's this for?"

"Well, you're carrying quite a bit of cash."

"Oh. I thought maybe I was to use it to fight you off."

"Now, Meade—"

"Never mind. Thanks, Potty."

They had finished supper and were packing the car with their afternoon's purchases when the quake struck. Five inches of rain in twenty-four hours, more than three billion tons of mass suddenly loaded on a fault already overstrained, all cut loose in one subsonic, stomach-twisting rumble.

Meade sat down on the wet ground very suddenly; Breen stayed upright by dancing like a logroller. When the ground quieted down somewhat, thirty seconds later, he helped her up. "You all right?"

"My slacks are soaked." She added pettishly, "But, Potty, it never quakes in wet weather. *Never*."

"It did this time."

"But—"

"Keep quiet, can't you?" He opened the car door and switched on the radio, waited impatiently for it to warm up. Shortly he was searching the entire dial. "Not a confounded Los Angeles station on the air!"

"Maybe the shock busted one of your tubes?"

"Pipe down." He passed a squeal and dialed back to it: "—your Sunshine Station in Riverside, California. Keep tuned to this station for the latest developments. It is as of now impossible to tell the size of the disaster. The Colorado River aqueduct is broken; nothing is known of the extent of the damage nor how long it will take to repair it. So far as we know the Owens River Valley aqueduct may be intact, but all persons in the Los Angeles area are advised to conserve water. My personal advice is to stick your washtubs out into this rain; it can't last forever. If we had time, we'd play *Cool Water*, just to give you the idea. I now read from the standard disaster instructions, quote: 'Boil all water. Remain quietly in your homes and do not panic. Stay off the highways. Cooperate with the police and render—' Joe! Joe! Catch that phone! '—render aid where necessary. Do not use the telephone except for—' Flash! an unconfirmed report from Long Beach states that the Wilmington and San Pedro waterfront is under five feet of water. I repeat, this is unconfirmed. Here's a message from the commanding general, March Field: 'official, all military personnel will report—'"

Breen switched it off. "Get in the car."

"Where are we going?"

"North."

"We've paid for the cabin. Should we—"

"Get in!"

He stopped in the town, managed to buy six five-gallon tins and a jeep tank. He filled them with gasoline and packed them with blankets in the back seat, topping off the mess with a dozen cans of oil. Then they were rolling.

"What are we doing, Potiphar?"

"I want to get west on the valley highway."

"Any particular place west?"

"I think so. We'll see. You work the radio, but keep

an eye on the road, too. That gas back there makes me nervous."

Through the town of Mojave and northwest on 466 into the Tehachapi Mountains—Reception was poor in the pass but what Meade could pick up confirmed the first impression—worse than the quake of '06, worse than San Francisco, Managua, and Long Beach taken together.

When they got down out of the mountains it was clearing locally; a few stars appeared. Breen swung left off the highway and ducked south of Bakersfield by the county road, reached the Route 99 superhighway just south of Greenfield. It was, as he had feared, already jammed with refugees; he was forced to go along with the flow for a couple of miles before he could cut west at Greenfield toward Taft. They stopped on the western outskirts of the town and ate at an all-night truckers' joint.

They were about to climb back into the car when there was suddenly "sunrise" due south. The rosy light swelled almost instantaneously, filled the sky, and died; where it had been a red-and-purple pillar of cloud was mounting, mounting—spreading to a mushroom top.

Breen stared at it, glanced at his watch, then said harshly, "Get in the car."

"Potty—that was . . . that was—"

"That was—that used to be—Los Angeles. Get in the car!"

He simply drove for several minutes. Meade seemed to be in a state of shock, unable to speak. When the sound reached them he again glanced at his watch. "Six minutes and nineteen seconds. That's about right."

"Potty—*we should have brought Mrs. Megeath.*"

"How was I to know?" he said angrily. "Anyhow, you can't transplant an old tree. If she got it, she never knew it."

"Oh, I hope so!"

"Forget it; straighten out and fly right. We're going to have all we can do to take care of ourselves. Take the flashlight and check the map. I want to turn north at Taft and over toward the coast."

"Yes, Potiphar."

"And try the radio."

She quieted down and did as she was told. The radio gave nothing, not even the Riverside station; the whole broadcast range was covered by a curious static, like rain on a window. He slowed down as they approached Taft, let her spot the turn north onto the state road, and turned into it. Almost at once a figure jumped out into the road in front of them, waved his arms violently. Breen tromped on the brake.

The man came up on the left side of the car, rapped on the window; Breen ran the glass down. Then he stared stupidly at the gun in the man's left hand. "Out of the car," the stranger said sharply. "I've got to have it." He reached inside with his right hand, groped for the door lever.

Meade reached across Breen, stuck her little lady's gun in the man's face, pulled the trigger. Breen could feel the flash on his own face, never noticed the report. The man looked puzzled, with a neat, not-yet-bloody hole in his upper lip—then slowly sagged away from the car.

"Drive on!" Meade said in a high voice.

Breen caught his breath. "Good girl—"

"Drive on! *Get rolling*!"

They followed the state road through Los Padres

National Forest, stopping once to fill the tank from their cans. They turned off onto a dirt road. Meade kept trying the radio, got San Francisco once but it was too jammed with static to read. Then she got Salt Lake City, faint but clear: "—since there are no reports of anything passing our radar screen the Kansas City bomb must be assumed to have been planted rather than delivered. This is a tentative theory but—" They passed into a deep cut and lost the rest.

When the squawk box again came to life it was a new voice: "Conelrad," said a crisp voice, "coming to you over the combined networks. The rumor that Los Angeles has been hit by an atom bomb is totally unfounded. It is true that the western metropolis has suffered a severe earthquake shock but that is all. Government officials and the Red Cross are on the spot to care for the victims, but—and I repeat—there has *been no atomic bombing*. So relax and stay in your homes. Such wild rumors can damage the United States quite as much as enemy's bombs. Stay off the highways and listen for—" Breen snapped it off.

"Somebody," he said bitterly, "has again decided that 'Mama knows best.' They won't tell us any bad news."

"Potiphar," Meade said sharply, "that *was* an atom bomb . . . wasn't it?"

"It was. And now we don't know whether it was just Los Angeles—and Kansas City—or all the big cities in the country. All we know is that they are lying to us."

"Maybe I can get another station?"

"The hell with it." He concentrated on driving. The road was very bad.

As it began to get light she said, "Potty—do you know where we're going? Are we just keeping out of cities?"

"I think I do. If I'm not lost." He stared around them. "Nope, it's all right. See that hill up forward with the triple gendarmes on its profile?"

"Gendarmes?"

"Big rock pillars. That's a sure landmark. I'm looking for a private road now. It leads to a hunting lodge belonging to two of my friends—an old ranch house actually, but as a ranch it didn't pay."

"Oh. They won't mind us using it?"

He shrugged. "If they show up, we'll ask them. If they show up. They lived in Los Angeles, Meade."

"Oh. Yes, I guess so."

The private road had once been a poor grade of wagon trail; now it was almost impassable. But they finally topped a hogback from which they could see almost to the Pacific, then dropped down into a sheltered bowl where the cabin was. "All out, girl. End of the line."

Meade sighed. "It looks heavenly."

"Think you can rustle breakfast while I unload? There's probably wood in the shed. Or can you manage a wood range?"

"Just try me."

Two hours later Breen was standing on the hogback, smoking a cigarette, and staring off down to the west. He wondered if that was a mushroom cloud up San Francisco way? Probably his imagination, he decided, in view of the distance. Certainly there was nothing to be seen to the south.

Meade came out of the cabin. "Potty!"

"Up here."

She joined him, took his hand, and smiled, then

snitched his cigarette and took a deep drag. She expelled it and said, "I know it's sinful of me, but I feel more peaceful than I have in months and months."

"I know."

"Did you see the canned goods in that pantry? We could pull through a hard winter here."

"We might have to."

"I suppose. I wish we had a cow."

"What would you do with a cow?"

"I used to milk four cows before I caught the school bus, every morning. I can butcher a hog, too."

"I'll try to find one."

"You do and I'll manage to smoke it." She yawned. "I'm suddenly terribly sleepy."

"So am I. And small wonder."

"Let's go to bed."

"Uh, yes. Meade?"

"Yes, Potty?"

"We may be here quite a while. You know that, don't you?"

"Yes, Potty."

"In fact it might be smart to stay put until those curves all start turning up again. They will, you know."

"Yes. I had figured that out."

He hesitated, then went on, "Meade . . . will you marry me?"

"Yes." She moved up to him.

After a time he pushed her gently away and said, "My dear, my very dear, uh—we could drive down and find a minister in some little town?"

She looked at him steadily. "That wouldn't be very

bright, would it? I mean, nobody knows we're here and that's the way we want it. And besides, your car might not make it back up that road."

"No, it wouldn't be very bright. But I want to do the right thing."

"It's all right, Potty. It's *all right.*"

"Well, then . . . kneel down here with me. We'll say them together."

"Yes, Potiphar." She knelt and he took her hand. He closed his eyes and prayed wordlessly.

When he opened them he said, "What's the matter?"

"Uh, the gravel hurts my knees."

"We'll stand up, then."

"No. Look, Potty, why don't we just go in the house and say them there?"

"Huh? Hell's bells, woman, we might forget to say them entirely. Now repeat after me: I, Potiphar, take thee, Meade—"

"Yes, Potiphar. I, Meade, take thee, Potiphar—"

"OFFICIAL: STATIONS WITHIN RANGE RELAY TWICE. EXECUTIVE BULLETIN NUMBER NINE— ROAD LAWS PREVIOUSLY PUBLISHED HAVE BEEN IGNORED IN MANY INSTANCES. PATROLS ARE ORDERED TO SHOOT WITHOUT WARNING AND PROVOST MARSHALS ABE DIRECTED TO USE DEATH PENALTY FOR UNAUTHORIZED POS-SESSION OF GASOLINE. B.W. AND RADIATION

QUARANTINE REGULATIONS PREVIOUSLY ISSUED WILL BE RIGIDLY ENFORCED. LONG LIVE THE UNITED STATES! HARLEY J. NEAL, LIEUTENANT GENERAL, ACTING CHIEF OF GOVERNMENT. ALL STATIONS RELAY TWICE."

"THIS IS THE FREE RADIO AMERICA RELAY NETWORK. PASS THIS ALONG, BOYS! GOVERNOR BRANDLEY WAS SWORN IN TODAY AS PRESIDENT BY ACTING CHIEF JUSTICE ROBERTS UNDER THE RULE-OF-SUCCESSION. THE PRESIDENT NAMED THOMAS DEWEY AS SECRETARY OF STATE AND PAUL DOUGLAS AS SECRETARY OF DEFENSE. HIS SECOND OFFICIAL ACT WAS TO STRIP THE RENEGADE NEAL OF RANK AND TO DIRECT HIS ARREST BY ANY CITIZEN OR OFFICIAL. MORE LATER. PASS THE WORD ALONG.

"HELLO, CQ, CQ, CQ. THIS IS W5KMR, FREEPORT, QRR, QRR! ANYBODY READ ME? ANYBODY? WE'RE DYING LIKE FLIES DOWN HERE. WHAT'S HAPPENED? STARTS WITH FEVER AND A BURNING THIRST BUT YOU CAN'T SWALLOW. WE NEED HELP. ANYBODY READ ME? HELLO, CQ 75, CQ 75 THIS IS W5 KILO METRO ROMEO CALLING QRR AND CQ 75. BY FOR SOMEBODY . . . . ANYBODY!!!"

"THIS IS THE LORD'S TIME, SPONSORED BY SWAN'S ELIXIR, THE TONIC THAT MAKES

WAITING FOR THE KINGDOM OF GOD WORTH-
WHILE. YOU ARE ABOUT TO HEAR A MESSAGE
OF CHEER FROM JUDGE BROOMFIELD,
ANOINTED VICAR OF THE KINGDOM ON
EARTH. BUT FIRST A BULLETIN: SEND YOUR
CONTRIBUTIONS TO 'MESSIAH,' CLINT, TEXAS.
DON'T TRY TO MAIL THEM: SEND THEM BY A
KINGDOM MESSENGER OR BY SOME PILGRIM
JOURNEYING THIS WAY. AND NOW THE TABER-
NACLE CHOIR FOLLOWED BY THE VOICE OF
THE VICAR ON EARTH—"

"—THE FIRST SYMPTOM IS LITTLE RED SPOTS
IN THE ARMPITS. THEY ITCH. PUT 'EM TO BED
AT ONCE AND KEEP 'EM COVERED UP WARM.
THEN GO SCRUB YOURSELF AND WEAR A MASK:
WE DON'T KNOW YET HOW YOU CATCH IT. PASS
IT ALONG, ED."

"—NO NEW LANDINGS REPORTED ANYWHERE
ON THIS CONTINENT. THE PARATROOPERS WHO
ESCAPED THE ORIGINAL SLAUGHTER ARE
THOUGHT TO BE HIDING OUT IN THE
POCONOS. SHOOT—BUT BE CAREFUL; IT MIGHT
BE AUNT TESSIE. OFF AND CLEAR, UNTIL NOON
TOMORROW—"

The curves were turning up again. There was no
longer doubt in Breen's mind about that. It might not
even be necessary to stay up here in the Sierra Madres
through the winter—though he rather thought they

would. He had picked their spot to keep them west of the fallout; it would be silly to be mowed down by the tail of a dying epidemic, or be shot by a nervous vigilante, when a few months' wait would take care of everything.

Besides, he had chopped all that firewood. He looked at his calloused hands—he had done all that work and, by George, he was going to enjoy the benefits!

He was headed out to the hogback to wait for sunset and do an hour's reading; he glanced at his car as he passed it, thinking that he would like to try the radio. He suppressed the yen; two thirds of his reserve gasoline was gone already just from keeping the battery charged for the radio—and here it was only December. He really ought to cut it down to twice a week. But it meant a lot to catch the noon bulletin of Free America and then twiddle the dial a few minutes to see what else he could pick up.

But for the past three days Free America had not been on the air—solar static maybe, or perhaps just a power failure. But that rumor that President Brandley had been assassinated—while it hadn't come from the Free radio . . . and it hadn't been denied by them, either, which was a good sign. Still, it worried him.

And that other story that lost Atlantis had pushed up during the quake period and that the Azores were now a little continent—almost certainly a hang-over of the "silly season"—but it would be nice to hear a follow-up.

Rather sheepishly he let his feet carry him to the car. It wasn't fair to listen when Meade wasn't around. He warmed it up, slowly spun the dial, once around and back. Not a peep at full gain, nothing but a terrible amount of static. Served him right.

He climbed the hogback, sat down on the bench he had dragged up there—their "memorial bench," sacred to the memory of the time Meade had hurt her knees on the gravel—sat down and sighed. His lean belly was stuffed with venison and corn fritters; he lacked only tobacco to make him completely happy. The evening cloud colors were spectacularly beautiful and the weather was extremely balmy for December; both, he thought, caused by volcanic dust, with perhaps an assist from atom bombs.

Surprising how fast things went to pieces when they started to skid! And surprising how quickly they were going back together, judging by the signs. A curve reaches trough and then starts right back up. World War III was the shortest big war on record—forty cities gone, counting Moscow and the other slave cities as well as the American ones—and then *whoosh!* neither side fit to fight. Of course, the fact that both sides had thrown their ICBMs over the pole through the most freakish arctic weather since Peary invented the place had a lot to do with it, he supposed. It was amazing that any of the Russian paratroop transports had gotten through at all.

He sighed and pulled the November 1951 copy of the *Western Astronomer* out of his pocket. Where was he? Oh, yes, *Some Notes on the Stability of G-Type Stars with Especial Reference to Sol* , by A. G. M. Dynkowski, Lenin Institute, translated by Heinrich Ley, F. R. A. S. Good boy, Ski—sound mathematician. Very clever application of harmonic series and tightly reasoned. He started to thumb for his place when he noticed a footnote that he had missed. Dynkowski's own name carried down to it: "This monograph was denounced by *Pravda* as romantic reactionariism shortly after it was published. Professor Dynkowski has been unreported since and must be presumed to be liquidated."

The poor geek! Well, he probably would have been atomized by now anyway, along with the goons who did him in. He wondered if they really had gotten all the Russki paratroopers? Well, he had killed his quota; if he hadn't gotten that doe within a quarter mile of the cabin and headed right back, Meade would have had a bad time. He had shot them in the back, the swine! and buried them beyond the woodpile—and then it had seemed a shame to skin and eat an innocent deer while those lice got decent burial.

Aside from mathematics, just two things worth doing—kill a man and love a woman. He had done both; he was rich.

He settled down to some solid pleasure. Dynkowski was a treat. Of course, it was old stuff that a G-type star, such as the Sun, was potentially unstable; a G-O star could explode, slide right off the Russell diagram, and end up as a white dwarf. But no one before Dynkowski had defined the exact conditions for such a catastrophe, nor had anyone else devised mathematical means of diagnosing the instability and describing its progress.

He looked up to rest his eyes from the fine print and saw that the Sun was obscured by a thin low cloud—one of those unusual conditions where the filtering effect is just right to permit a man to view the Sun clearly with the naked eye. Probably volcanic dust in the air, he decided, acting almost like smoked glass.

He looked again. Either he had spots before his eyes

or that was one fancy big sunspot. He had heard of being able to see them with the naked eye, but it had never happened to him. He longed for a telescope.

He blinked. Yep, it was still there, upper right. A *big* spot—no wonder the car radio sounded like a Hitler speech.

He turned back and continued on to the end of the article, being anxious to finish before the light failed. At first his mood was sheerest intellectual pleasure at the man's tight mathematical reasoning. A 3% imbalance in the solar constant—yes, that was standard stuff; the sun would *nova* with that much change. But Dynkowski went further; by means of a novel mathematical operator which he had dubbed "yokes" he bracketed the period in a star's history when this could happen and tied it down further with secondary, tertiary, and quaternary yokes, showing exactly the time of highest probability. Beautiful! Dynkowski even assigned dates to the extreme limit of his primary yoke, as a good statistician should.

But, as he went back and reviewed the equations, his mood changed from intellectual to personal. Dynkowski was not talking about just any G-O star; in the latter part he meant old Sol himself, Breen's personal sun, the big boy out there with the oversized freckle on his face.

That was one hell of a big freckle! It was a hole you could chuck Jupiter into and not make a splash. He could see it very clearly now.

Everybody talks about "when the stars grow old and the Sun grows cold"—but it's an impersonal concept, like one's own death. Breen started thinking about it very personally. How long would it take, from the instant the imbalance was triggered until the expanding wave front engulfed Earth? The mechanics couldn't be solved without a calculator even though they were implicit in the equations in front of him. Half an hour, for a horseback guess, from incitement until the Earth went *phutt!*

It hit him with gentle melancholy. No more? Never again? Colorado on a cool morning . . . the Boston Post road with autumn wood smoke tanging the air . . . Bucks county bursting in the spring. The wet smells of the Fulton Fish Market—no, that was gone already. Coffee at the *Morning Call.* No more wild strawberries on a hillside in Jersey, hot and sweet as lips. Dawn in the South Pacific with the light airs cool velvet under your shirt and never a sound but the chuckling of the water against the sides of the old rust bucket—what was her name? That was a long time ago—the *S. S. Mary Brewster.*

No more Moon if the Earth was gone. Stars—but no one to look at them.

He looked back at the dates bracketing Dynkowski's probability yoke. "Thine Alabaster Cities gleam, undimmed by—"

He suddenly felt the need for Meade and stood up.

She was coming out to meet him. "Hello, Potty! Safe to come in now—I've finished the dishes."

"I should help."

"You do the man's work; I'll do the woman's work. That's fair." She shaded her eyes. "What a sunset! We ought to have volcanoes blowing their tops every year."

"Sit down and we'll watch it."

She sat beside him and he took her hand. "Notice the sunspot? You can see it with your naked eye."

She stared. "Is that a sunspot? It looks as if somebody had taken a bite out of it."

He squinted his eyes at it again. Damned if it didn't look bigger!

Meade shivered. "I'm chilly. Put your arm around me."

He did so with his free arm, continuing to hold hands with the other. It *was* bigger—the thing was growing.

What good is the race of man? Monkeys, he thought, monkeys with a spot of poetry in them, cluttering and wasting a second-string planet near a third-string star. But sometimes they finish in style.

She snuggled to him. "Keep me warm."

"It will be warmer soon. I mean . . . I'll keep you warm."

"Dear Potty."

She looked up. "Potty—something funny is happening to the sunset."

"No, darling—to the Sun."

"I'm frightened."

"I'm here, dear."

He glanced down at the journal, still open beside him. He did not need to add up the two figures and divide by two to reach the answer. Instead he clutched fiercely at her hand, knowing with an unexpected and overpowering burst of sorrow that this was

The End

By His Bootstraps

Bob Wilson did not see the circle grow.

Nor, for that matter, did he see the stranger who stepped out of the circle and stood staring at the back of Wilson's neck—stared, and breathed heavily, as if laboring under strong and unusual emotion.

Wilson had no reason to suspect that anyone else was in his room; he had every reason to expect the contrary. He had locked himself in his room for the purpose of completing his thesis in one sustained drive. He *had* to—tomorrow was the last day for submission, yesterday the thesis had been no more than a title: "An Investigation Into Certain Mathematical Aspects of a Rigor of Metaphysics."

Fifty-two cigarettes, four pots of coffee, and thirteen hours of continuous work had added seven thousand words to the title. As to the validity of his thesis he was far too groggy to give a damn. Get it done, was his only thought, get it done, turn it in, take three stiff drinks and sleep for a week.

He glanced up and let his eyes rest on his wardrobe door, behind which he had cached a gin bottle, nearly full. No, he admonished himself, one more drink and you'll never finish it, Bob, old son.

The stranger behind him said nothing.

Wilson resumed typing. "—nor is it valid to assume that a conceivable proposition is necessarily a possible proposition, even when it is possible to formulate mathematics which describes the proposition with exactness. A case in point is the concept 'Time Travel.' Time travel may be imagined and its necessities may be formulated under any and all theories of time, formulae which resolve the paradoxes of each theory. Nevertheless, we know certain things about the empirical nature of time which preclude the possibility of the conceivable proposition. Duration is an attribute of consciousness and not of the plenum. It has no *Ding an Sich.* Therefore—"

A key of the typewriter stuck, three more jammed up on top of it. Wilson swore dully and reached forward to straighten out the cantankerous machinery. "Don't bother with it," he heard a voice say. "It's a lot of utter hogwash anyhow."

Wilson sat up with a jerk, then turned his head slowly around. He fervently hoped that there was someone behind him. Otherwise—

He perceived the stranger with relief. "Thank God," he said to himself. "For a moment I thought I had come unstuck." His relief turned to extreme annoyance. "What the devil are you doing in my room?" he demanded. He shoved back his chair, got up and strode over to the one door. It was still locked, and bolted on the inside.

The windows were no help; they were adjacent to his desk and three stories above a busy street. "How *did* you get in?" he added.

"Through that," answered the stranger, hooking a thumb toward the circle. Wilson noticed it for the first time, blinked his eyes and looked again. There it hung between them and the wall, a great disk of nothing, of the color one sees when the eyes are shut tight.

Wilson shook his head vigorously. The circle remained. "Gosh," he thought, "I was right the first time. I wonder when I slipped my trolley?" He advanced toward the disk, put out a hand to touch it.

"Don't!" snapped the stranger.

"Why not?" said Wilson edgily. Nevertheless he paused.

"I'll explain. But let's have a drink first." He walked directly to the wardrobe, opened it, reached in and took out the bottle of gin without looking.

"Hey!" yelled Wilson. "What are you doing there? That's *my* liquor."

"*Your* liquor—" The stranger paused for a moment. "Sorry. You don't mind if I have a drink, do you?"

"I suppose not," Bob Wilson conceded in a surly tone. "Pour me one while you're about it."

"Okay," agreed the stranger, "then I'll explain."

"It had better be good," Wilson said ominously. Nevertheless he drank his drink and looked the stranger over.

He saw a chap about the same size as himself and much the same age—perhaps a little older, though a three-day growth of beard may have accounted for that impression. The stranger had a black eye and a freshly cut and badly swollen upper lip. Wilson decided he did not like the chap's face. Still, there was something familiar about the face; he felt that he should have recognized it, that he had seen it many times before under different circumstances.

"Who are you?" he asked suddenly.

"Me?" said his guest. "Don't you recognize me?"

"I'm not sure," admitted Wilson. "Have I ever seen you before?"

"Well—not exactly," the other temporized. "Skip it—you wouldn't know about it."

"What's your name?"

"My name? Uh . . . just call me Joe."

Wilson set down his glass. "Okay, Joe Whatever-your-name-is, trot out that explanation and make it snappy."

"I'll do that," agreed Joe. "That dingus I came through"—he pointed to the circle—"that's a Time Gate."

"A what?"

"A Time Gate. Time flows along side by side on each side of the Gate, but some thousands of years apart—just how many thousands I don't know. But for the next couple of hours that Gate is open. You can walk into the future just by stepping through that circle." The stranger paused.

Bob drummed on the desk. "Go ahead. I'm listening. It's a nice story."

"You don't believe me, do you? I'll show you." Joe got up, went again to the wardrobe and obtained Bob's hat, his prized and only hat, which he had mistreated into its present battered grandeur through six years of undergraduate and graduate life. Joe chucked it toward the impalpable disk.

It struck the surface, went on through with no apparent resistance, disappeared from sight.

Wilson got up, walked carefully around the circle and examined the bare floor. "A neat trick," he conceded. "Now I'll thank you to return to me my hat."

The stranger shook his head. "You can get it for yourself when you pass through."

"Huh?"

"That's right. Listen—" Briefly the stranger repeated his explanation about the Time Gate. Wilson, he insisted, had an opportunity that comes once in a millennium— if he would only hurry up and climb through that circle. Furthermore, though Joe could not explain in detail at the moment, it was very important that Wilson go through.

Bob Wilson helped himself to a second drink, and then a third. He was beginning to feel both good and argumentative. "Why?" he said flatly.

Joe looked exasperated. "Dammit, if you'd just step through once, explanations wouldn't be necessary. However—" According to Joe, there was an old guy on the other side who needed Wilson's help. With Wilson's help the three of them would run the country. The exact nature of the help Joe could not or would not specify. Instead he bore down on the unique possibilities for high adventure. "You don't want to slave your life away teaching numskulls in some freshwater college," he insisted. "This is your chance. Grab it!"

Bob Wilson admitted to himself that a Ph.D. and an appointment as an instructor was not his idea of existence. Still, it beat working for a living. His eye fell on the gin bottle, its level now deplorably lowered. That explained it. He got up unsteadily.

"No, my dear fellow," he stated, "I'm not going to climb on your merry-go-round. You know why?"

"Why?"

"Because I'm drunk, that's why. You're not there at all. *That* ain't there." He gestured widely at the circle. "There ain't anybody here but me, and I'm drunk. Been working too hard," he added apologetically. "I'm goin' to bed."

"You're not drunk."

"I *am* drunk. Peter Piper pepped a pick of pippered peckles." He moved toward his bed.

Joe grabbed his arm. "You can't do that," he said.

"Let him alone!"

They both swung around. Facing them, standing directly in front of the circle was a third man. Bob looked at the newcomer, looked back at Joe, blinked his eyes and tried to focus them. The two looked a good bit alike, he thought, enough alike to be brothers. Or maybe he was seeing double. Bad stuff, gin. Should 'ave switched to rum a long time ago. Good stuff, rum. You could drink it, or take a bath in it. No, that was gin—he meant Joe.

How silly! Joe was the one with the black eye. He wondered why he had ever been confused.

Then who was this other lug? Couldn't a couple of friends have a quiet drink together without people butting in?

"Who are you?" he said with quiet dignity.

The newcomer turned his head, then looked at Joe. "*He* knows me," he said meaningly.

Joe looked him over slowly. "Yes," he said, "yes, I suppose I do. But what the deuce are you here for? And why are you trying to bust up the plan?"

"No time for long-winded explanations. I know more about it than you do—you'll concede that—and my judgment is bound to be better than yours. He doesn't go through the Gate."

"I don't concede anything of the sort—"

The telephone rang.

"Answer it!" snapped the newcomer.

Bob was about to protest the peremptory tone, but decided he wouldn't. He lacked the phlegmatic temperament necessary to ignore a ringing telephone. "Hello?"

"Hello," he was answered. "Is that Bob Wilson?"

"Yes. Who is this?"

"Never mind. I just wanted to be sure you were there. I *thought* you would be. You're right in the groove, kid, right in the groove."

Wilson heard a chuckle, then the click of the disconnection. "Hello," he said. "Hello!" He jiggled the bar a couple of times, then hung up.

"What was it?" asked Joe.

"Nothing. Some nut with a misplaced sense of humor." The telephone bell rang again. Wilson added, "There he is again," and picked up the receiver. "Listen, you butterfly-brained ape! I'm a busy man, and this is *not* a public telephone."

"Why, Bob!" came a hurt feminine voice.

"Huh? Oh, it's you, Genevieve. Look—I'm sorry. I apologize—"

"Well, I should think you would!"

"You don't understand, honey. A guy has been pestering me over the phone and I thought it was him. You know I wouldn't talk that way to you, Babe."

"Well, I should think not. Particularly after all you said to me this afternoon, and all we *meant* to each other."

"Huh? This afternoon? Did you say *this* afternoon?"

"Of course. But what I called up about was this: you left your hat in my apartment. I noticed it a few minutes after you had gone and just thought I'd call and tell you where it is. Anyhow," she added coyly, "it gave me an excuse to hear your voice again."

"Sure. Fine," he said mechanically. "Look, Babe, I'm a little mixed up about this. Trouble I've had all day long, and more trouble now. I'll look you up tonight and straighten it out. But I *know* I didn't leave your hat in my apartment—"

"*Your* hat, silly!"

"Huh? Oh, sure! Anyhow, I'll see you tonight. 'Bye." He rang off hurriedly. Gosh, he thought, that woman is getting to be a problem. Hallucinations. He turned to his two companions.

"Very well, Joe. I'm ready to go if you are." He was not sure just when or why he had decided to go through the time gadget, but he had. Who did this other mug think he was, anyhow, trying to interfere with a man's freedom of choice?

"Fine!" said Joe, in a relieved voice. "Just step through. That's all there is to it."

"No, you don't!" It was the ubiquitous stranger. He stepped between Wilson and the Gate.

Bob Wilson faced him. "Listen, you! You come butting in here like you think I was a bum. If you don't like it, go jump in the lake—and I'm just the kind of guy who can do it! You and who else?"

The stranger reached out and tried to collar him. Wilson let go a swing, but not a good one. It went by nothing faster than parcel post. The stranger walked under it and let him have a mouthful of knuckles—large, hard ones. Joe closed in rapidly, coming to Bob's aid. They traded punches in a free-for-all, with Bob joining in enthusiastically but inefficiently. The only punch he landed was on Joe, theoretically his ally. However, he had intended it for the third man.

It was this *faux pas* which gave the stranger an opportunity to land a clean left jab on Wilson's face. It was inches higher than the button, but in Bob's bemused condition it was sufficient to cause him to cease taking part in the activities.

Bob Wilson came slowly to awareness of his surroundings. He was seated on a floor which seemed a little unsteady. Someone was bending over him. "Are you all right?" the figure inquired.

"I guess so," he answered thickly. His mouth pained him; he put his hand to it, got it sticky with blood. "My head hurts."

"I should think it would. You came through head over heels. I think you hit your head when you landed."

Wilson's thoughts were coming back into confused focus. Came through? He looked more closely at his succorer. He saw a middle-aged man with gray-shot bushy hair and a short, neatly trimmed beard. He was dressed in what Wilson took to be purple lounging pajamas.

But the room in which he found himself bothered him even more. It was circular and the ceiling was arched so subtly that it was difficult to say how high it was. A steady glareless light filled the room from no apparent source. There was no furniture save for a high dais or pulpit-shaped object near the wall facing him. "Came through? Came through what?"

"The Gate, of course." There was something odd about the man's accent. Wilson could not place it, save for a feeling that English was not a tongue he was accustomed to speaking.

Wilson looked over his shoulder in the direction of the other's gaze, and saw the circle.

That made his head ache even more. "Oh, Lord," he thought, "now I really am nuts. Why don't I wake up?" He shook his head to clear it.

That was a mistake. The top of his head did not quite come off—not quite. And the circle stayed where it was, a simple locus hanging in the air, its flat depth filled with the amorphous colors and shapes of no-vision. "Did I come through that?"

"Yes."

"Where am I?"

"In the Hall of the Gate in the High Palace of Norkaal. But what is more important is *when* you are. You have gone forward a little more than thirty thousand years."

"Now I know I'm crazy," thought Wilson. He got up unsteadily and moved toward the Gate.

The older man put a hand on his shoulder. "Where are you going?"

"Back!"

"Not so fast. You will go back all right—I give you my word on that. But let me dress your wounds first. And you should rest. I have some explanations to make to you, and there is an errand you can do for me when you get back—to our mutual advantage. There is a great future in store for you and me, my boy—a great future!"

Wilson paused uncertainly. The elder man's insistence was vaguely disquieting. "I don't like this."

The other eyed him narrowly. "Wouldn't you like a drink before you go?"

Wilson most assuredly would. Right at the moment a stiff drink seemed the most desirable thing on Earth—or in time. "Okay."

"Come with me." The older man led him back of the structure near the wall and through a door which led into a passageway. He walked briskly; Wilson hurried to keep up.

"By the way," he asked, as they continued down the long passage, "what is your name?"

"My name? You may call me Diktor—everyone else does."

"Okay, Diktor. Do you want my name?"

"Your name?" Diktor chuckled. "I know your name. It's Bob Wilson."

"Huh? Oh—I suppose Joe told you."

"Joe? I know no one by that name."

"You don't? He seemed to know you. Say—maybe you aren't that guy I was supposed to see."

"But I am. I have been expecting you—in a way. Joe . . . Joe—Oh!" Diktor chuckled. "It had slipped my mind for a moment. He told you to call him Joe, didn't he?"

"Isn't it his name?"

"It's as good a name as any other. Here we are." He ushered Wilson into a small, but cheerful room. It contained no furniture of any sort, but the floor was soft and warm as live flesh. "Sit down. I'll be back in a moment."

Bob looked around for something to sit on, then turned to ask Diktor for a chair. But Diktor was gone, furthermore the door through which they had entered was gone. Bob sat down on the comfortable floor and tried not to worry.

Diktor returned promptly. Wilson saw the door dilate to let him in, but did not catch on to how it was done. Diktor was carrying a carafe, which gurgled pleasantly, and a cup. "Mud in your eye," he said heartily and poured a good four fingers. "Drink up."

Bob accepted the cup. "Aren't you drinking?"

"Presently. I want to attend to your wounds first."

"Okay." Wilson tossed off the first drink in almost indecent haste—it was good stuff, a little like Scotch, he decided, but smoother and not as dry—while Diktor worked deftly with salves that smarted at first, then soothed. "Mind if I have another?"

"Help yourself."

Bob drank more slowly the second cup. He did not finish it; it slipped from relaxed fingers, spilling a ruddy, brown stain across the floor. He snored.

Bob Wilson woke up feeling fine and completely rested. He was cheerful without knowing why. He lay relaxed, eyes still closed, for a few moments and let his soul snuggle back into his body. This was going to be a good day, he felt. Oh, yes—he had finished that double-damned thesis. No, he hadn't either! He sat up with a start.

The sight of the strange walls around him brought him back into continuity. But before he had time to worry—at once, in fact—the door relaxed and Diktor stepped in. "Feeling better?"

"Why, yes, I do. Say, what is this?"

"We'll get to that. How about some breakfast?"

In Wilson's scale of evaluations breakfast rated just after life itself and ahead of the chance of immortality. Diktor conducted him to another room—the first that he had seen possessing windows. As a matter of fact half the room was open, a balcony hanging high over a green countryside. A soft, warm, summer breeze wafted through the place. They broke their fast in luxury, Roman style, while Diktor explained.

Bob Wilson did not follow the explanations as closely as he might have done, because his attention was diverted by the maidservants who served the meal. The first came in bearing a great tray of fruit on her head. The fruit was gorgeous. So was the girl. Search as he would he could discern no fault in her.

Her costume lent itself to the search.

She came first to Diktor, and with a single, graceful movement dropped to one knee, removed the tray from her head, and offered it to him. He helped himself to a small, red fruit and waved her away. She then offered it to Bob in the same delightful manner.

"As I was saying," continued Diktor, "it is not certain

where the High Ones came from or where they went when they left Earth. I am inclined to think they went away into Time. In any case they ruled more than twenty thousand years and completely obliterated human culture as you knew it. What is more important to you and to me is the effect they had on the human psyche. One twentieth-century style go-getter can accomplish just about anything he wants to accomplish around here—Aren't you listening?"

"Huh? Oh, yes, sure. Say, that's one mighty pretty girl." His eyes still rested on the exit through which she had disappeared.

"Who? Oh, yes, I suppose so. She's not exceptionally beautiful as women go around here."

"That's hard to believe. I could learn to get along with a girl like that."

"You like her? Very well, she is yours."

"Huh?"

"She's a slave. Don't get indignant. They are slaves by nature. If you like her, I'll make you a present of her. It will make her happy." The girl had just returned. Diktor called to her in a language strange to Bob. "Her name is Arma," he said in an aside, then spoke to her briefly.

Arma giggled. She composed her face quickly, and, moving over to where Wilson reclined, dropped on both knees to the floor and lowered her head, with both hands cupped before her. "Touch her forehead," Diktor instructed.

Bob did so. The girl arose and stood waiting placidly by his side. Diktor spoke to her. She looked puzzled, but moved out of the room. "I told her that, notwithstanding her new status, you wished her to continue serving breakfast."

✧ ✧ ✧

Diktor resumed his explanations while the service of the meal continued. The next course was brought in by Arma and another girl. When Bob saw the second girl he let out a low whistle. He realized he had been a little hasty in letting Diktor give him Arma. Either the standard of pulchritude had gone up incredibly, he decided, or Diktor went to a lot of trouble in selecting his servants.

"—for that reason," Diktor was saying, "it is necessary that you go back through the Time Gate at once. Your first job is to bring this other chap back. Then there is one other task for you to do, and we'll be sitting pretty. After that it is share and share alike for you and me. And there is plenty to share, I—You aren't listening!"

"Sure I was, chief. I heard every word you said." He fingered his chin. "Say, have you got a razor I could borrow? I'd like to shave."

Diktor swore softly in two languages. "Keep your eyes off those wenches and listen to me! There's work to be done."

"Sure, sure. I understand that—and I'm your man. When do we start?" Wilson had made up his mind some time ago—just shortly after Arma had entered with the tray of fruit, in fact. He felt as if he had walked into some extremely pleasant dream. If cooperation with Diktor would cause that dream to continue, so be it. To hell with an academic career!

Anyhow, all Diktor wanted was for him to go back where he started and persuade another guy to go through the Gate. The worst that could happen was for him to find himself back in the twentieth century. What could he lose?

Diktor stood up. "Let's get on with it," he said shortly, "before you get your attention diverted again. Follow me." He set off at a brisk pace with Wilson behind him.

Diktor took him to the Hall of the Gate and stopped. "All you have to do," he said, "is to step through the Gate. You will find yourself back in your own room, in your own time. Persuade the man you find there to go through the Gate. We have need of him. Then come back yourself."

Bob held up a hand and pinched thumb and forefinger together. "It's in the bag, boss. Consider it done." He started to step through the Gate.

"Wait!" commanded Diktor. "You are not used to time travel. I warn you that you are going to get one hell of a shock when you step through. This other chap—you'll recognize him."

"Who is he?"

"I won't tell you because you wouldn't understand. But you will when you see him. Just remember this— There are some very strange paradoxes connected with time travel. Don't let anything you see throw you. You do what I tell you to and you'll be all right."

"Paradoxes don't worry me," Bob said confidently. "Is that all? I'm ready."

"One minute." Diktor stepped behind the raised dais. His head appeared above the side a moment later. "I've set the controls. O.K. Go!"

Bob Wilson stepped through the locus known as the Time Gate.

There was no particular sensation connected with the transition. It was like stepping through a curtained door-way into a darker room. He paused for a moment on the other side and let his eyes adjust to the dimmer light. He was, he saw, indeed in his own room.

There was a man in it, seated at his own desk. Diktor had been right about that. This, then, was the chap he was to send back through the Gate. Diktor had said he would recognize him. Well, let's see who it is.

He felt a passing resentment at finding someone at *his* desk in *his* room, then thought better of it. After all, it was just a rented room; when he disappeared, no doubt it had been rented again. He had no way of telling how long he had been gone—shucks, it might be the middle of next week!

The chap did look vaguely familiar, although all he could see was his back. Who was it? Should he speak to him, cause him to turn around? He felt vaguely reluctant to do so until he knew who it was. He rationalized the feeling by telling himself that it was desirable to know with whom he was dealing before he attempted anything as outlandish as persuading this man to go through the Gate.

The man at the desk continued typing, paused to snuff out a cigarette by laying it in an ash tray, then stamping it with a paper weight.

Bob Wilson knew that gesture.

Chills trickled down his back. "If he lights his next one," he whispered to himself, "the way I think he is going to—"

The man at the desk took out another cigarette, tamped it on one end, turned it and tamped the other, straightened and crimped the paper on one end carefully against his left thumbnail and placed that end in his mouth.

Wilson felt the blood beating in his neck. *Sitting there with his back to him was himself, Bob Wilson!*

He felt that he was going to faint. He closed his eyes and steadied himself on a chair back. "I knew it," he thought, "the whole thing is absurd. I'm crazy. I know I'm crazy. Some sort of split personality. I shouldn't have worked so hard."

The sound of typing continued.

He pulled himself together, and reconsidered the matter.

Diktor had warned him that he was due for a shock, a shock that could not be explained ahead of time, because it could not be believed. "All right—suppose I'm not crazy. If time travel can happen at all, there is no reason why I can't come back and see myself doing something I did in the past. If I'm sane, that is what I'm doing.

"And if I am crazy, it doesn't make a damn bit of difference what I do!

"And furthermore," he added to himself, "if I'm crazy, maybe I can stay crazy and go back through the Gate! No, that does not make sense. Neither does anything else— the hell with it!"

He crept forward softly and peered over the shoulder of his double. "Duration is an attribute of the consciousness," he read, "and not of the plenum."

"That tears it," he thought, "right back where I started, and watching myself write my thesis."

The typing continued. "It has no *Ding an Sich*. Therefore—" A key stuck, and others piled up on top of it. His double at the desk swore and reached out a hand to straighten the keys.

"Don't bother with it," Wilson said on sudden impulse. "It's a lot of utter hogwash anyhow."

The other Bob Wilson sat up with a jerk, then looked slowly around. An expression of surprise gave way to annoyance. "What the devil are you doing in my room?" he demanded. Without waiting for an answer he got up, went quickly to the door and examined the lock. "How did you get in?"

"This," thought Wilson, "is going to be difficult."

"Through that," Wilson answered, pointing to the Time Gate. His double looked where he had pointed, did a double take, then advanced cautiously and started to touch it.

"Don't!" yelled Wilson.

The other checked himself. "Why not?" he demanded.

Just why he must not permit his other self to touch the Gate was not clear to Wilson, but he had had an unmistakable feeling of impending disaster when he saw it about to happen. He temporized by saying, "I'll explain. But let's have a drink." A drink was a good idea in any case. There had never been a time when he needed one more than he did right now. Quite automatically he went to his usual cache of liquor in the wardrobe and took out the bottle he expected to find there.

"Hey!" protested the other. "What are you doing there? That's *my* liquor."

"Your liquor—" Hell's bells! It was *his* liquor. No, it wasn't; it was—*their* liquor. Oh, the devil! It was much too mixed up to try to explain. "Sorry. You don't mind if I have a drink, do you?"

"I suppose not," his double said grudgingly. "Pour me one while you're about it."

"O.K.," Wilson assented, "then I'll explain." It was going to be much, much too difficult to explain until he had had a drink, he felt. As it was, he couldn't explain it fully to himself.

"It had better be good," the other warned him, and looked Wilson over carefully while he drank his drink.

Wilson watched his younger self scrutinizing him with confused and almost insupportable emotions. Couldn't the stupid fool recognize his own face when he saw it in front of him? If he could not *see* what the situation was, how in the world was he ever going to make it clear to him?

It had slipped his mind that his face was barely recognizable in any case, being decidedly battered and unshaven. Even more important, he failed to take into account the fact that a person does not look at his own face, even in mirrors, in the same frame of mind with which he regards another's face. No sane person ever expects to see his own face hanging on another.

Wilson could see that his companion was puzzled by his appearance, but it was equally clear that no recognition took place. "Who are you?" the other man asked suddenly.

"Me?" replied Wilson. "Don't you recognize me?"

"I'm not sure. Have I ever seen you before?"

"Well—not exactly," Wilson stalled. How did you go about telling another guy that the two of you were a trifle closer than twins? "Skip it—you wouldn't know about it."

"What's your name?"

"My name? Uh—" Oh, oh! This was going to be sticky! The whole situation was utterly ridiculous. He opened his mouth, tried to form the words "Bob Wilson," then gave up with a feeling of utter futility. Like many a man before him, he found himself forced into a lie because the truth simply would not be believed. "Just call me Joe," he finished lamely.

He felt suddenly startled at his own words. It was at this point that he realized that he was, *in fact*, "Joe," the Joe whom he had encountered once before. That he had landed back in his own room at the very time at which he had ceased working on his thesis he already realized, but he had not had time to think the matter through. Hearing himself refer to himself as Joe slapped him in the face with the realization that this was not simply a similar scene, but the *same* scene he had lived through once before—save that he was living through it from a different viewpoint.

At least he thought it was the same scene. Did it differ in any respect? He could not be sure as he could not recall, word for word, what the conversation had been.

For a complete transcript of the scene that lay dormant in his memory he felt willing to pay twenty-five dollars cash, plus sales tax.

Wait a minute now—he was under no compulsion. He was sure of that. Everything he did and said was the result of his own free will. Even if he couldn't remember the script, there were some things he *knew* "Joe" hadn't said. "Mary had a little lamb," for example. He would recite a nursery rhyme and get off this damned repetitious treadmill. He opened his mouth—

"Okay, Joe Whatever-your-name-is," his alter ego remarked, setting down a glass which had contained, until recently, a quarter pint of gin, "trot out that explanation and make it snappy."

He opened his mouth again to answer the question, then closed it. "Steady, son, steady," he told himself. "You're a free agent. You want to recite a nursery rhyme—go ahead and do it. Don't answer him; go ahead and recite it—and break this vicious circle."

But under the unfriendly, suspicious eye of the man opposite him he found himself totally unable to recall any nursery rhyme. His mental processes stuck on dead center.

He capitulated. "I'll do that. That dingus I came through—that's a Time Gate."

"A what?"

"A Time Gate. Time flows along side by side on each side—" As he talked he felt sweat breaking out on him; he felt reasonably sure that he was explaining in exactly the same words in which explanation had first been offered to *him*. "—into the future just by stepping through that circle." He stopped and wiped his forehead.

"Go ahead," said the other implacably. "I'm listening. It's a nice story."

Bob suddenly wondered if the other man *could* be himself. The stupid arrogant dogmatism of the man's manner infuriated him. All right, all right! He'd show him. He strode suddenly over to the wardrobe, took out his hat and threw it through the Gate.

His opposite number watched the hat snuff out of existence with expressionless eyes, then stood up and went around in back of the Gate, walking with the careful steps of a man who is a little bit drunk, but determined not to show it. "A neat trick," he applauded, after satisfying himself that the hat was gone, "now I'll thank you to return to me my hat."

Wilson shook his head. "You can get it for yourself when you pass through," he answered absentmindedly. He was pondering the problem of how many hats there were on the other side of the Gate.

"Huh?"

"That's right. Listen—" Wilson did his best to explain persuasively what it was he wanted his earlier *persona* to do. Or rather to cajole. Explanations were out of the question, in any honest sense of the word. He would have preferred attempting to explain tensor calculus to an Australian aborigine, even though he did not understand that esoteric mathematics himself.

The other man was not helpful. He seemed more interested in nursing the gin than he did in following Wilson's implausible protestations.

"Why?" he interrupted pugnaciously.

"Dammit," Wilson answered, "if you'd just step through once, explanations wouldn't be necessary. However—" He continued with a synopsis of Diktor's proposition. He realized with irritation that Diktor had been exceedingly sketchy with *his* explanations. He was forced to hit only the high spots in the logical parts of his argument, and bear down on the emotional appeal. He was on safe ground there—no one knew better than he did himself how fed up the earlier Bob Wilson had been with the petty drudgery and stuffy atmosphere of an academic career. "You don't want to slave your life away teaching numskulls in some freshwater college," he concluded. "This is your chance. Grab it!"

Wilson watched his companion narrowly and thought he detected a favorable response. He definitely seemed interested. But the other set his glass down carefully, stared at the gin bottle and at last replied:

"My dear fellow, I am not going to climb on your merry-go-round. You know why?"

"Why?"

"Because I'm drunk, that's why. You're not there at all. *That* ain't there." He gestured widely at the Gate, nearly fell, and recovered himself with effort. "There ain't anybody here but me, and I'm drunk. Been working too hard," he mumbled, "'m goin' to bed."

"You're not drunk," Wilson protested unhopefully. "Damnation," he thought, "a man who can't hold his liquor shouldn't drink."

"I *am* drunk. Peter Piper pepped a pick of pippered peckles." He lumbered over toward the bed.

Wilson grabbed his arm. "You can't do that."

"Let him alone!"

Wilson swung around, saw a third man standing in front of the Gate—recognized him with a sudden shock. His own recollection of the sequence of events was none too clear in his memory, since he had been somewhat intoxicated—damned near boiled, he admitted—the first time he had experienced this particular busy afternoon. He realized that he should have anticipated the arrival of a third party. But his memory had not prepared him for who the third party would turn out to be.

He recognized himself—another carbon copy.

He stood silent for a minute, trying to assimilate this new fact and force it into some reasonable integration. He closed his eyes helplessly. This was just a little too much. He felt that he wanted to have a few plain words with Diktor.

"Who the hell are you?" He opened his eyes to find that his other self, the drunk one, was addressing the latest edition. The newcomer turned away from his interrogator and looked sharply at Wilson.

"*He* knows me."

Wilson took his time about replying. This thing was getting out of hand. "Yes," he admitted, "yes, I suppose I do. But what the deuce are you here for? And why are you trying to bust up the plan?"

His facsimile cut him short. "No time for long-winded explanations. I know more about it than you do—you'll concede that—and my judgment is bound to be better than yours. He doesn't go through the Gate."

The offhand arrogance of the other antagonized Wilson. "I don't concede anything of the sort—" he began.

He was interrupted by the telephone bell. "Answer it!" snapped Number Three.

The tipsy Number One looked belligerent but picked up the handset. "Hello . . . .Yes. Who is this? . . . Hello . . . Hello!" He tapped the bar of the instrument, then slammed the receiver back into its cradle.

"Who was that?" Wilson asked, somewhat annoyed that he had not had a chance to answer it himself.

"Nothing. Some nut with a misplaced sense of humor." At that instant the telephone rang again. "There he is again!" Wilson tried to answer it, but his alcoholic counterpart beat him to it, brushed him aside. "Listen, you butterfly-brained ape! I'm a busy man and this is *not* a public telephone . . . Huh? Oh, it's you, Genevieve. Look—I'm sorry. I apologize— . . . You don't understand, honey. A guy has been pestering me over the phone and I thought it was him. You know I wouldn't talk to you that way, Babe . . . Huh? This afternoon? Did you say *this* afternoon? Sure. Fine. Look, Babe, I'm a little mixed up about this. Trouble I've had all day long and more trouble now. I'll look you up tonight and straighten it out. But I *know* I didn't leave your hat in my apartment— . . . Huh? Oh, sure! Anyhow, I'll see you tonight. 'Bye."

It almost nauseated Wilson to hear his earlier self catering to the demands of that clinging female. Why didn't he just hang up on her? The contrast with Arma—there was a dish!—was acute; it made him more determined than ever to go ahead with the plan, despite the warning of the latest arrival.

After hanging up the phone his earlier self faced him, pointedly ignoring the presence of the third copy. "Very well, Joe," he announced. "I'm ready to go if you are."

"Fine!" Wilson agreed with relief. "Just step through. That's all there is to it."

"No, you don't!" Number Three barred the way.

Wilson started to argue, but his erratic comrade was ahead of him. "Listen, you! You come butting in here like you think I was a bum. If you don't like it, go jump in the lake—and I'm just the kind of a guy who can do it! You and who else?"

They started trading punches almost at once. Wilson stepped in warily, looking for an opening that would enable him to put the slug on Number Three with one decisive blow.

He should have watched his drunken ally as well. A wild swing from that quarter glanced off his already damaged features and caused him excruciating pain. His upper lip, cut, puffy and tender from his other encounter, took the blow and became an area of pure agony. He flinched and jumped back.

A sound cut through his fog of pain, a dull *Smack!* He forced his eyes to track and saw the feet of a man disappear through the Gate. Number Three was still standing by the Gate. "Now you've done it!" he said bitterly to Wilson, and nursed the knuckles of his left hand.

The obviously unfair allegation reached Wilson at just the wrong moment. His face still felt like an experiment in sadism. "Me?" he said angrily. "*You* knocked him through. I never laid a finger on him."

"Yes, but it's your fault. If you hadn't interfered, I wouldn't have had to do it."

"*Me* interfere? Why, you bald-faced hypocrite—*you* butted in and tried to queer the pitch. Which reminds me—you owe me some explanations and I damn well mean to have 'em. What's the idea of—"

But his opposite number cut in on him. "Stow it," he said gloomily. "It's too late now. He's gone through."

"Too late for what?" Wilson wanted to know.

"Too late to put a stop to this chain of events."

"Why should we?"

"Because," Number Three said bitterly, "Diktor has played me—I mean has played you . . . us—for a dope, for a couple of dopes. Look, he told you that he was going to

set you up as a big shot over *there*"—he indicated the
Gate—" didn't he?"

"Yes," Wilson admitted.

"Well, that's a lot of malarkey. All he means to do is to
get us so incredibly tangled up in this Time Gate thing
that we'll never get straightened out again."

Wilson felt a sudden doubt nibbling at his mind. It
could be true. Certainly there had not been much sense to
what had happened so far. After all, why should Diktor
want his help, want it bad enough to offer to split with
him, even-steven, what was obviously a cushy spot? "How
do you know?" he demanded.

"Why go into it?" the other answered wearily. "Why
don't you just take my word for it?"

"Why should I?"

His companion turned a look of complete exasperation
on him. "If you can't take my word, whose word can you
take?"

The inescapable logic of the question simply annoyed
Wilson. He resented this interloping duplicate of himself
anyhow; to be asked to follow his lead blindly irked him.
"I'm from Missouri," he said. "I'll see for myself." He
moved toward the Gate.

"Where are you going?"

"Through! I'm going to look up Diktor and have it out
with him."

"Don't!" the other said. "Maybe we can break the chain
even now." Wilson felt and looked stubborn. The other
sighed. "Go ahead," he surrendered. "It's your funeral. I
wash my hands of you."

Wilson paused as he was about to step through the

Gate. "It is, eh? H-m-m-m—how can it be *my* funeral unless it's *your* funeral, too?"

The other man looked blank, then an expression of apprehension raced over his face. That was the last Wilson saw of him as he stepped through.

The Hall of the Gate was empty of other occupants when Bob Wilson came through on the other side. He looked for his hat, but did not find it, then stepped around back of the raised platform, seeking the exit he remembered. He nearly bumped into Diktor.

"Ah, there you are!" the older man greeted him. "Fine! Fine! Now there is just one more little thing to take care of, then we will be all squared away. I must say I am pleased with you, Bob, very pleased indeed."

"Oh, you are, are you?" Bob faced him truculently. "Well, it's too bad I can't say the same about you! I'm not a damn bit pleased. What was the idea of shoving me into that . . . that daisy chain without warning me? What's the meaning of all this nonsense? Why didn't you warn me?"

"Easy, easy," said the older man, "don't get excited. Tell the truth now—if I had told you that you were going back to meet yourself face to face, would you have believed me? Come now, 'fess up."

Wilson admitted that he would not have believed it.

"Well, then," Diktor continued with a shrug, "there was no point in me telling you, was there? If I had told you, you would not have believed me, which is another way of saying that you would have believed false data. Is it not better to be in ignorance than to believe falsely?"

"I suppose so, but—"

"Wait! I did not intentionally deceive you. I did not deceive you at all. But had I told you the full truth, you would have been deceived because you would have rejected the truth. It was better for you to learn the truth with your own eyes. Otherwise—"

"Wait a minute! Wait a minute!" Wilson cut in. "You're getting me all tangled up. I'm willing to let bygones be bygones, if you'll come clean with me. Why did you send me back at all?"

"'Let bygones be bygones,'" Diktor repeated. "Ah, if we only could! But we can't. That's why I sent you back—in order that you might come through the Gate in the first place."

"Huh? Wait a minute—I already *had* come through the Gate."

Diktor shook his head. "Had you, now? Think a moment. When you got back into your own time and your own place you found your earlier self there, didn't you?"

"Mmmm—yes."

"*He*—your earlier self—had not yet been through the Gate, had he?"

"No. I—"

"How could you have *been* through the Gate, unless you persuaded him to *go* through the Gate?"

Bob Wilson's head was beginning to whirl. He was beginning to wonder who did what to whom and who got paid. "But that's impossible! You are telling me that I did something because I was going to do something."

"Well, didn't you? You were there."

"No, I didn't—no . . . well, maybe I did, but it didn't *feel* like it."

"Why should you expect it to? It was something totally new to your experience."

"But . . . but—" Wilson took a deep breath and got control of himself. Then he reached back into his academic philosophical concepts and produced the notion he had been struggling to express. "It denies all reasonable theories of causation. You would have me believe that causation can be completely circular. I went through because I came back from going through to persuade myself to go through. That's silly."

"Well, didn't you?"

Wilson did not have an answer ready for that one. Diktor continued with, "Don't worry about it. The causation you have been accustomed to is valid enough in its own field but is simply a special case under the general case. *Causation in a plenum need not be and is not limited by a man's perception of duration.*"

Wilson thought about that for a moment. It sounded nice, but there was something slippery about it. "Just a second," he said. "How about entropy? You can't get around entropy."

"Oh, for heaven's sake," protested Diktor, "shut up, will you? You remind me of the mathematician who proved that airplanes couldn't fly." He turned and started out the door. "Come on. There's work to be done."

Wilson hurried after him. "Dammit, you can't do this to me. What happened to the other two?"

"The other two what?"

"The other two of me? Where are they? How am I ever going to get unsnarled?"

"You aren't snarled up. You don't feel like more than one person, do you?"

"No, but—"

'Then don't worry about it."

"But I've got to worry about it. What happened to the guy that came through just ahead of me?"

"You remember, don't you? However—" Diktor hurried on ahead, led him down a passageway, and dilated a door. "Take a look inside," he directed.

Wilson did so. He found himself looking into a small windowless unfurnished room, a room that he recognized. Sprawled on the floor, snoring steadily, was another edition of himself.

"When you first came through the Gate," explained Diktor at his elbow, "I brought you in here, attended to your hurts, and gave you a drink. The drink contained a soporific which will cause you to sleep about thirty-six hours, sleep that you badly needed. When you wake up, I will give you breakfast and explain to you what needs to be done."

Wilson's head started to ache again. "Don't do that," he pleaded. "Don't refer to that guy as if he were me. *This* is *me*, standing here."

"Have it your own way," said Diktor. "That is the man you *were*. You remember the things that are about to happen to him, don't you?"

"Yes, but it makes me dizzy. Close the door, please."

"O.K.," said Diktor, and complied. "We've got to hurry, anyhow. Once a sequence like this is established there is no time to waste. Come on." He led the way back to the Hall of the Gate.

"I want you to return to the twentieth century and obtain certain things for us, things that can't be obtained on this side but which will be very useful to us in, ah, developing—yes, that is the word—developing this country."

"What sort of things?"

"Quite a number of items. I've prepared a list for you—certain reference books, certain items of commerce. Excuse me, please. I must adjust the controls of the Gate." He mounted the raised platform from the rear. Wilson followed him and found that the structure was boxlike, open at the top, and had a raised floor. The Gate could be seen by looking over the high sides.

The controls were unique.

Four colored spheres the size of marbles hung on crystal rods arranged with respect to each other as the four major axes of a tetrahedron. The three spheres which bounded the base of the tetrahedron were red, yellow, and blue; the fourth at the apex was white. "Three spatial controls, one time control," explained Diktor. "It's very simple. Using here-and-now as zero reference, displacing any control away from the center moves the other end of the Gate farther from here-and-now. Forward or back, right or left, up or down, past or future—they are all controlled by moving the proper sphere in or out on its rod."

Wilson studied the system. "Yes," he said, "but how do you tell where the other end of the Gate is? Or when? I don't see any graduations."

"You don't need them. You can see where you are. Look." He touched a point under the control framework on the side toward the Gate. A panel rolled back and

Wilson saw there was a small image of the Gate itself. Diktor made another adjustment and Wilson found that he could see through the image.

He was gazing into his own room, as if through the wrong end of a telescope. He could make out two figures, but the scale was too small for him to see clearly what they were doing, nor could he tell which editions of himself were there present—if they were in truth himself! He found it quite upsetting. "Shut it off," he said.

Diktor did so and said, "I must not forget to give you your list." He fumbled in his sleeve and produced a slip of paper which he handed to Wilson. "Here—take it."

Wilson accepted it mechanically and stuffed it into his pocket. "See here," he began, "everywhere I go I keep running into myself. I don't like it at all. It's disconcerting. I feel like a whole batch of guinea pigs. I don't half-understand what this is all about and now you want to rush me through the Gate again with a bunch of half-baked excuses. Come clean. Tell me what it's all about."

Diktor showed temper in his face for the first time. "You are a stupid and ignorant young fool. I've told you all that you are able to understand. This is a period in history entirely beyond your comprehension. It would take weeks before you would even begin to understand it. I am offering you half a world in return for a few hours' cooperation and you stand there arguing about it. Stow it, I tell you. Now—where shall we set you down?" He reached for the controls.

"Get away from those controls!" Wilson rapped out. He was getting the glimmering of an idea. "Who are you, anyhow?"

"Me? I'm Diktor."

"That's not what I mean and you know it. How did you learn English?"

Diktor did not answer. His face became expressionless.

"Go on," Wilson persisted. "You didn't learn it here; that's a cinch. You're from the twentieth century, *aren't you?*"

Diktor smiled sourly. "I wondered how long it would take you to figure that out."

Wilson nodded. "Maybe I'm not bright, but I'm not as stupid as you think I am. Come on. Give me the rest of the story."

Diktor shook his head. "It's immaterial. Besides, we're wasting time."

Wilson laughed. "You've tried to hurry me with that excuse once too often. How can we waste time when we have *that?*" He pointed to the controls and to the Gate beyond it. "Unless you lied to me, we can use any slice of time we want to, any time. No, I think I know why you tried to rush me. Either you want to get me out of the picture here, or there is something devilishly dangerous about the job you want me to do. And I know how to settle it—you're going with me!"

"You don't know what you're saying," Diktor answered slowly. "That's impossible. I've got to stay here and manage the controls."

"That's just what you aren't going to do. You could send me through and lose me. I prefer to keep you in sight."

"Out of the question," answered Diktor. "You'll have to trust me." He bent over the controls again.

"Get away from there!" shouted Wilson. "Back out of there before I bop you one." Under Wilson's menacing fist Diktor withdrew from the control pulpit entirely. "There. That's better," he added when both of them were once more on the floor of the hall.

The idea which had been forming in his mind took full shape. The controls, he knew, were still set on his room in the boardinghouse where he lived—or had lived—back in the twentieth century. From what he had seen through the speculum of the controls, the time control was set to take him right back to the day in 1952 from which he had started. "Stand there," he commanded Diktor, "I want to see something."

He walked over to the Gate as if to inspect it. Instead of stopping when he reached it, he stepped on through.

He was better prepared for what he found on the other side than he had been on the two earlier occasions of time translation— "earlier" in the sense of sequence in his memory track. Nevertheless it is never too easy on the nerves to catch up with one's self.

For he had done it again. He was back in his own room, but there were two of himself there before him. They were very much preoccupied with each other; he had a few seconds in which to get them straightened out in his mind. One of them had a beautiful black eye and a badly battered mouth. Beside that he was very much in need of a shave. That tagged him. He had been through the Gate at least once. The other, though somewhat in need of shaving himself, showed no marks of a fist fight.

He had them sorted out now, and knew where and *when* he was. It was all still mostly damnably confusing, but after former—no, not *former,* he amended—*other* experiences with time translation he knew better what to expect. He was back at the beginning again; this time he would put a stop to the crazy nonsense once and for all.

The other two were arguing. One of them swayed drunkenly toward the bed. The other grabbed him by the arm. "You can't do that," he said.

"Let him alone!" snapped Wilson.

The other two swung around and looked him over. Wilson watched the more sober of the pair size him up, saw his expression of amazement change to startled recognition. The other, the earliest Wilson, seemed to have trouble in focusing on him at all. "This is going to be a job," thought Wilson. "The man is positively stinking." He wondered why anyone would be foolish enough to drink on an empty stomach. It was not only stupid, it was a waste of good liquor.

He wondered if they had left a drink for him.

"Who are you?" demanded his drunken double.

Wilson turned to "Joe." "He knows me," he said significantly.

"Joe" studied him. "Yes," he conceded, "yes, I suppose I do. But what the deuce are you here for? And why are you trying to bust up the plan?"

Wilson interrupted him. "No time for long-winded explanations. I know more about it than you do—you'll concede that—and my judgment is bound to be better than yours. He doesn't go through the Gate."

"I don't concede anything of the sort—"

The ringing of the telephone checked the argument. Wilson greeted the interruption with relief, for he realized that he had started out on the wrong tack. Was it possible that he was really as dense himself as this lug appeared to be? Did *he* look that way to other people? But the time was too short for self-doubts and soul-searching. "Answer it!" he commanded Bob (Boiled) Wilson.

The drunk looked belligerent, but acceded when he saw that Bob (Joe) Wilson was about to beat him to it. "Hello . . . Yes. Who is this? . . . Hello . . . Hello!"

"Who was that?" asked "Joe."

"Nothing. Some nut with a misplaced sense of humor." The telephone rang again. "There he is again." The drunk grabbed the phone before the others could reach it. "Listen, you butterfly-brained ape! I'm a busy man and this is *not* a public telephone . . . . Huh? Oh, it's you, Genevieve—" Wilson paid little attention to the telephone conversation—he had heard it too many times before, and he had too much on his mind. His earliest *persona* was much too drunk to be reasonable, he realized; he must concentrate on some argument that would appeal to "Joe"— otherwise he was outnumbered. "—Huh? Oh, sure!" the call concluded. "Anyhow, I'll see you tonight. 'Bye."

Now was the time, thought Wilson, before this dumb yap can open his mouth. What would he say? What would sound convincing?

But the boiled edition spoke first. "Very well, Joe," he stated, "I'm ready to go if you are."

"Fine!" said "Joe." "Just step through. That's all there is to it."

This was getting out of hand, not the way he had planned it at all. "No, you don't!" he barked and jumped in front of the Gate. He would have to make them realize, and quickly.

But he got no chance to do so. The drunk cussed him out, then swung on him; his temper snapped. He knew with sudden fierce exultation that he had been wanting to take a punch at someone for some time. Who did they think they were to be taking chances with his future?

The drunk was clumsy; Wilson stepped under his guard and hit him hard in the face. It was a solid enough punch to have convinced a sober man, but his opponent shook his head and came back for more. "Joe" closed in. Wilson decided that he would have to put his original opponent away in a hurry, and give his attention to "Joe,"—by far the more dangerous of the two.

A slight mix-up between the two allies gave him his chance. He stepped back, aimed carefully, and landed a long jab with his left, one of the hardest blows he had ever struck in his life. It lifted his target right off his feet.

As the blow landed, Wilson realized his orientation with respect to the Gate, knew with bitter certainty that he had again played through the scene to its inescapable climax.

He was alone with "Joe;" their companion had disappeared through the Gate.

His first impulse was the illogical but quite human and very common feeling of look-what-you-made-me-do. "Now you've done it!" he said angrily.

"Me?" "Joe" protested. "You knocked him through. I never laid a finger on him."

"Yes," Wilson was forced to admit. "But it's your fault," he added, "if you hadn't interfered, I wouldn't have had to do it."

"*Me* interfere? Why, you bald-faced hypocrite, *you*

butted in and tried to queer the pitch. Which reminds me—you owe me some explanations and I damn well mean to have them. What's the idea of—"

"Stow it," Wilson headed him off. He hated to be wrong and he hated still more to have to admit that he was wrong. It had been hopeless from the start, he now realized. He felt bowed down by the utter futility of it. "It's too late now. He's gone through."

"Too late for what?"

"Too late to put a stop to this chain of events." He was aware now that it always had been too late, regardless of what time it was, what year it was, or how many times he came back and tried to stop it. He *remembered* having gone through the first time, he had *seen* himself asleep on the other side. Events would have to work out their weary way.

"Why should we?"

It was not worthwhile to explain, but he felt the need for self-justification. "Because," he said, "Diktor has played me—I mean has played *you* .,. *us*—for a dope, for a couple of dopes. Look, he told you that he was going to set you up as a big shot over there, didn't he?"

"Yes—"

"Well, that's a lot of malarkey. All he means to do is to get us so incredibly tangled up in this Gate thing that we'll never get straightened out again."

"Joe" looked at him sharply. "How do you know?"

Since it was largely hunch, he felt pressed for a reason-able explanation. "Why go into it?" he evaded. "Why don't you just take my word for it?"

"Why should I?"

"Why should you? Why, you lunk, can't you see? I'm yourself, older and more experienced—you *have* to believe me." Aloud he answered, "If you can't take my word, whose word can you take?"

"Joe" grunted. "I'm from Missouri," he said. "I'll see for myself."

Wilson was suddenly aware that "Joe" was about to step through the Gate. "Where are you going?"

"Through! I'm going to look up Diktor and have it out with him."

"Don't!" Wilson pleaded. "Maybe we can break the chain even now." But the stubborn sulky look on the other's face made him realize how futile it was. He was still enmeshed in inevitability; it *had* to happen. "Go ahead," he shrugged. "It's your funeral. I wash my hands of you."

"Joe" paused at the Gate. "It is, eh? Hm-m-m—how can it be *my* funeral unless it's *your* funeral, too?"

Wilson stared speechlessly while "Joe" stepped through the Gate. Whose funeral? He had not thought of it in quite that way. He felt a sudden impulse to rush through the Gate, catch up with his alter ego, and watch over him. The stupid fool might do anything. Suppose he got himself killed? Where would that leave Bob Wilson? Dead, of course.

Or would it? Could the death of a man thousands of years in the future kill *him* in the year 1952? He saw the absurdity of the situation suddenly, and felt very much relieved. "Joe's" actions could not endanger him; he remembered everything that "Joe" had done—was going to do. "Joe" would get into an argument with Diktor and, in due course of events, would come back through the Time Gate. No, *had* come back through the Time Gate. He was "Joe." It was hard to remember that.

Yes, he was "Joe." As well as the first guy. They would thread their courses, in and out and roundabout and end up here, with *him*. Had to.

Wait a minute—in that case the whole crazy business was straightened out. He had gotten away from Diktor, had all of his various personalities sorted out, and was back where he started from, no worse for the wear except for a crop of whiskers and, possibly, a scar on his lip. Well, he knew when to let well enough alone. Shave, and get back to work, kid.

As he shaved he stared at his face and wondered why he had failed to recognize it the first time. He had to admit that he had never looked at it objectively before. He had always taken it for granted.

He acquired a crick in his neck from trying to look at his own profile through the corner of one eye.

On leaving the bathroom the Gate caught his eye forcibly. For some reason he had assumed that it would be gone. It was not. He inspected it, walked around it, carefully refrained from touching it. Wasn't the damned thing ever going to go away? It had served its purpose; why didn't Diktor shut it off?

He stood in front of it, felt a sudden surge of the compulsion that leads men to jump from high places. What would happen if he went through? What would he find? He thought of Arma. And the other one—what was her name? Perhaps Diktor had not told him. The other maidservant, anyhow, the second one.

But he restrained himself and forced himself to sit back down at the desk. If he was going to stay here—and of course he was, he was resolved on that point—he must finish the thesis. He had to eat; he needed the degree to get a decent job. Now where was he?

Twenty minutes later he had come to the conclusion that the thesis would have to be rewritten from one end to the other. His prime theme, the application of the empirical method to the problems of speculative metaphysics and its expression in rigorous formulae, was still valid, he decided, but he had acquired a mass of new and not yet digested data to incorporate in it. In re-reading his manuscript he was amazed to find how dogmatic he had been. Time after time he had fallen into the Cartesian fallacy, mistaking clear reasoning for correct reasoning.

He tried to brief a new version of the thesis, but discovered that there were two problems he was forced to deal with which were decidedly not clear in his mind: the problem of the ego and the problem of free will. When there had been three of him in the room, which one was the ego—was *himself*? And how was it that he had been unable to change the course of events?

An absurdly obvious answer to the first question occurred to him at once. The ego was himself. Self is self, an unproved and unprovable first statement, directly experienced. What, then, of the other two? Surely they had been equally sure of ego-being—he remembered it. He thought of a way to state it: Ego is the point of consciousness, the latest term in a continuously expanding series along the line of memory duration. That sounded like a general statement, but he was not sure; he would

have to try to formulate it mathematically before he could
trust it. Verbal language had such queer booby traps in it.

The telephone rang.

He answered it absent-mindedly. "Yes?"

"Is that you, Bob?"

"Yes. Who is this?"

"Why, it's Genevieve, of course, darling. What's come
over you today? That's the second time you've failed to
recognize my voice."

Annoyance and frustration rose up in him. Here was
another problem he had failed to settle—well, he'd settle it
now. He ignored her complaint. "Look here, Genevieve, I've
told you not to telephone me while I'm working. Good-bye!"

"Well, of all the—You can't talk that way to me, Bob
Wilson! In the first place, you weren't working today. In
the second place, what makes you think you can use honey
and sweet words on me and two hours later snarl at me?
I'm not any too sure I want to marry you."

"Marry you? What put that silly idea in your head?"

The phone sputtered for several seconds. When it had
abated somewhat he resumed with, "Now just calm down.
This isn't the Gay Nineties, you know. You can't assume
that a fellow who takes you out a few times intends to
marry you."

There was a short silence. "So that's the game, is it?"
came an answer at last in a voice so cold and hard and
completely shrewish that he almost failed to recognize it.
"Well, there's a way to handle men like you. A woman isn't
unprotected in this State!"

"You ought to know," he answered savagely. "You've
hung around the campus enough years."

The receiver clicked in his ear.

He wiped the sweat from his forehead. That dame, he knew, was quite capable of causing him lots of trouble. He had been warned before he ever started running around with her, but he had been so sure of his own ability to take care of himself. He should have known better—but then he had not expected anything quite as raw as this.

He tried to get back to work on his thesis, but found himself unable to concentrate. The deadline of 10 A.M. the next morning seemed to be racing toward him. He looked at his watch. It had stopped. He set it by the desk clock—four fifteen in the afternoon. Even if he sat up all night he could not possibly finish it properly.

Besides there was Genevieve—

The telephone rang again. He let it ring. It continued; he took the receiver off the cradle. He would *not* talk to her again.

He thought of Arma. There was a proper girl with the right attitude. He walked over to the window and stared down into the dusty, noisy street. Half subconsciously he compared it with the green and placid countryside he had seen from the balcony where he and Diktor had breakfasted. This was a crummy world full of crummy people. He wished poignantly that Diktor had been on the up-and-up with him.

An idea broke surface in his brain and plunged around frantically. The Gate was still open. *The Gate was still open!* Why worry about Diktor? He was his own master. Go back and play it out—everything to gain, nothing to lose.

He stepped up to the Gate, then hesitated. Was he

wise to do it? After all, how much did he know about the future?

He heard footsteps climbing the stairs, coming down the hall, no—yes, stopping at his door. He was suddenly convinced that it was Genevieve; that decided him. He stepped through.

The Hall of the Gate was empty on his arrival. He hurried around the control box to the door and was just in time to hear, "Come on. There's work to be done." Two figures were retreating down the corridor. He recognized both of them and stopped suddenly.

That was a near thing, he told himself; I'll just have to wait until they get clear. He looked around for a place to conceal himself, but found nothing but the control box. That was useless; they were coming back. Still—

He entered the control box with a plan vaguely forming in his mind. If he found that he could dope out the controls, the Gate might give him all the advantage he needed. First he needed to turn on the speculum gadget. He felt around where he recalled having seen Diktor reach to turn it on, then reached in his pocket for a match.

Instead he pulled out a piece of paper. It was the list that Diktor had given him, the things he was to obtain in the twentieth century. Up to the present moment there had been too much going on for him to look it over.

His eyebrows crawled up his forehead as he read. It was a funny list, he decided. He had subconsciously expected it to call for technical reference books, samples of modern gadgets, weapons. There was nothing of the sort. Still, there was a sort of mad logic to the assortment.

After all, Diktor knew these people better than he did. It might be just what was needed.

He revised his plans, subject to being able to work the Gate. He decided to make one more trip back and do the shopping Diktor's list called for—but for his own benefit, not Diktor's. He fumbled in the semidarkness of the control booth, seeking the switch or control for the speculum. His hand encountered a soft mass. He grasped it, and pulled it out.

It was his hat.

He placed it on his head, guessing idly that Diktor had stowed it there, and reached again. This time he brought forth a small notebook. It looked like a find—very possibly Diktor's own notes on the operation of the controls. He opened it eagerly.

It was not what he had hoped. But it did contain page after page of handwritten notes. There were three columns to the page; the first was in English, the second in international phonetic symbols, the third in a completely strange sort of writing. It took no brilliance for him to identify it as a vocabulary. He slipped it into a pocket with a broad smile; it might have taken Diktor months or even years to work out the relationship between the two languages; he would be able to ride on Diktor's shoulders in the matter.

The third try located the control and the speculum lighted up. He felt again the curious uneasiness he had felt before, for he was gazing again into his own room and again it was inhabited by two figures. He did not want to break into that scene again, he was sure. Cautiously he touched one of the colored beads.

The scene shifted, panned out through the walls of the boardinghouse and came to rest in the air, three stories above the campus. He was pleased to have gotten the Gate out of the house, but three stories was too much of a jump. He fiddled with the other two colored beads and established that one of them caused the scene in the speculum to move toward him or away from him while the other moved it up or down.

He wanted a reasonably inconspicuous place to locate the Gate, some place where it would not attract the attention of the curious. This bothered him a bit; there was no ideal place, but he compromised on a blind alley, a little court formed by the campus powerhouse and the rear wall of the library. Cautiously and clumsily he maneuvered his flying eye to the neighborhood he wanted and set it down carefully between the two buildings. He then readjusted his position so that he stared right into a blank wall. Good enough!

Leaving the controls as they were, he hurried out of the booth and stepped unceremoniously back into his own period.

He bumped his nose against the brick wall. "I cut that a little too fine," he mused as he slid cautiously out from between the confining limits of the wall and the Gate. The Gate hung in the air, about fifteen inches from the wall and roughly parallel to it. But there was room enough, he decided—no need to go back and readjust the controls. He ducked out of the areaway and cut across the campus toward the Students' Co-op, wasting no time. He entered and went to the cashier's window.

"Hi, Bob."

"H'lo, Soupy. Cash a check for me?"

"How much?"

"Twenty dollars."

"Well—I suppose so. Is it a good check?"

"Not very. It's my own."

"Well, I might invest in it as a curiosity." He counted out a ten, a five, and five ones.

"Do that," advised Wilson. "My autographs are going to be rare collectors' items." He passed over the check, took the money and proceeded to the bookstore in the same building. Most of the books on the list were for sale there. Ten minutes later he had acquired title to:

The Prince, by Niccolo Machiavelli.

Behind the Ballots, by James Farley.

Mein Kampf (unexpurgated), by Adolf Schicklgruber.

How to Make Friends and Influence People, by Dale Carnegie.

The other titles he wanted were not available in the bookstore; he went from there to the university library where he drew out *Real Estate Broker's Manual, History of Musical Instruments,* and a quarto titled *Evolution of Dress Styles.* The latter was a handsome volume with beautiful colored plates and was classified as reference. He had to argue a little to get a twenty-four hour permission for it.

He was fairly well loaded down by then; he left the campus, went to a pawnshop and purchased two used, but sturdy, suitcases into one of which he packed the books. From there he went to the largest music store in the town and spent forty-five minutes in selecting and rejecting phonograph records, with emphasis on swing and torch—highly emotional stuff, all of it. He did not neglect classical and semi-classical, but he applied the same rule to those categories—a piece of music had to be sensuous and compelling, rather than cerebral. In consequence his collection included such strangely assorted items as the "Marseillaise," Ravel's "Bolero," four Cole Porters, and "L'Après-midi d'un Faune."

He insisted on buying the best mechanical reproducer on the market in the face of the clerk's insistence that what he needed was an electrical one. But he finally got his own way, wrote a check for the order, packed it all in his suitcases, and had the clerk get a taxi for him.

He had a bad moment over the check. It was pure rubber, as the one he had cashed at the Students' Co-op had cleaned out his balance. He had urged them to phone the bank, since that was what he wished them not to do. It had worked. He had established, he reflected, the all-time record for kiting checks—thirty thousand years.

When the taxi drew up opposite the court where he had located the Gate, he jumped out and hurried in.

The Gate was gone.

He stood there for several minutes, whistling softly and assessing—unfavorably—his own abilities, mental processes, et cetera. The consequences of writing bad checks no longer seemed quite so hypothetical.

He felt a touch at his sleeve. "See here, Bud, do you want my hack, or don't you? The meter's still clicking."

"Huh? Oh, sure." He followed the driver, climbed back in.

"Where to?"

That was a problem. He glanced at his watch, then realized that the usually reliable instrument had been through a process which rendered its reading irrelevant. "What time is it?"

"Two fifteen." He reset his watch.

Two fifteen. There would be a jamboree going on in his room at that time of a particularly confusing sort. He did not want to go *there*—not yet. Not until his blood brothers got through playing happy fun games with the Gate.

The Gate!

It would be in his room until sometime after four fifteen. If he timed it right—"Drive to the corner of Fourth and McKinley," he directed, naming the intersection closest to his boardinghouse.

He paid off the taxi driver there, and lugged his bags into the filling station at that corner, where he obtained permission from the attendant to leave them and assurance that they would be safe. He had nearly two hours to kill. He was reluctant to go very far from the house for fear some hitch would upset his timing.

It occurred to him that there was one piece of unfinished business in the immediate neighborhood—and time enough to take care of it. He walked briskly to a point two streets away, whistling cheerfully and turned in at an apartment house.

In response to his knock the door of Apartment 211 was opened a crack, then wider. "Bob darling! I thought you were working today."

"Hi, Genevieve. Not at all—I've got time to burn."

She glanced back over her shoulder. "I don't know

whether I should let you come in—I wasn't expecting you. I haven't washed the dishes, or made the bed. I was just putting on my make-up."

"Don't be coy." He pushed the door open wide, and went on in.

When he came out he glanced at his watch. Three thirty—plenty of time. He went down the street wearing the expression of the canary that ate the cat.

He thanked the service station salesman and gave him a quarter for his trouble, which left him with a lone dime. He looked at this coin, grinned to himself and inserted it in the pay phone in the office of the station. He dialed his own number.

"Hello," he heard.

"Hello," he replied. "Is that Bob Wilson?"

"Yes. Who is this?"

"Never mind," he chuckled. "I just wanted to be sure you were there. I *thought* you would be. You're right in the groove, kid, right in the groove." He replaced the receiver with a grin.

At four ten he was too nervous to wait any longer. Struggling under the load of the heavy suitcases he made his way to the boardinghouse. He let himself in and heard a telephone ringing upstairs. He glanced at his watch—four fifteen. He waited in the hall for three interminable minutes, then labored up the stairs and down the upper hallway to his own door. He unlocked the door and let himself in.

The room was empty, the Gate still there.

Without stopping for anything, filled with apprehension lest the Gate should flicker and disappear while he crossed the floor, he hurried to it, took a firm grip on his bags, and strode through it.

The Hall of the Gate was empty, to his great relief. What a break, he told himself thankfully. Just five minutes, that's all I ask. Five uninterrupted minutes. He set the suitcases down near the Gate to be ready for a quick departure. As he did so he noticed that a large chunk was missing from a corner of one case. Half a book showed through the opening, sheared as neatly as with a printer's trimmer. He identified it as *Mein Kampf*.

He did not mind the loss of the book but the implications made him slightly sick at his stomach. Suppose he had not described a clear arc when he had first been knocked through the Gate, had hit the edge, half in and half out? Man Sawed in Half—and no illusion!

He wiped his face and went to the control booth. Following Diktor's simple instructions he brought all four spheres together at the center of the tetrahedron. He glanced over the side of the booth and saw that the Gate had disappeared entirely. "Check!" he thought. "Everything on zero—no Gate." He moved the white sphere slightly. The Gate reappeared. Turning on the speculum he was able to see that the miniature scene showed the inside of the Hall of the Gate itself. So far so good—but he would not be able to tell what time the Gate was set for by looking into the hall. He displaced a space control slightly; the scene flickered past the walls of the palace and hung in the open air. Returning the white time control to zero he then displaced it very, very slightly. In the miniature scene the Sun became a streak of brightness across the sky; the days flickered past like light from a low frequency source of illumination. He increased the displacement a little, saw the ground become sere and brown, then snow covered, and finally green again.

Working cautiously, steadying his right hand with his left, he made the seasons march past. He had counted ten winters when he became aware of voices somewhere in the distance. He stopped and listened, then very hastily returned the space controls to zero, leaving the time control as it was—set for ten years in the past—and rushed out of the booth.

He hardly had time to grasp his bags, lift them, and swing them through the Gate, himself with them. This time he was exceedingly careful not to touch the edge of the circle.

He found himself, as he had planned to, still in the Hall of the Gate, but, if he had interpreted the controls correctly, ten years away from the events he had recently participated in. He had intended to give Diktor a wider berth than that, but there had been no time for it. However, he reflected, since Diktor was, by his own statement and the evidence of the little notebook Wilson had lifted from him, a native of the twentieth century, it was quite possible that ten years was enough. Diktor might not be in this era. If he was, there was always the Time Gate for a getaway. But it was reasonable to scout out the situation first before making any more jumps.

It suddenly occurred to him that Diktor might be looking at him through the speculum of the Time Gate. Without stopping to consider that speed was no protection—since the speculum could be used to view *any* time sector—he hurriedly dragged his two suitcases into the cover of the control booth. Once inside the protecting walls of the booth he calmed down a bit. Spying could work both ways. He found the controls set at zero; making use of the same process he had used once before, he ran the scene in the speculum forward through ten years, then cautiously hunted with the space controls on zero. It was a very difficult task; the time scale necessary to hunt through several months in a few minutes caused any figure which might appear in the speculum to flash past at an apparent speed too fast for his eye to follow. Several times he thought he detected flitting shadows which might be human beings but he was never able to find them when he stopped moving the time control.

He wondered in great exasperation why whoever had built the double-damned gadget had failed to provide it with graduations and some sort of delicate control mechanism—a vernier, or the like. It was not until much later that it occurred to him that the creator of the Time Gate might have no need of such gross aids to his senses. He would have given up, was about to give up, when, purely by accident, one more fruitless scanning happened to terminate with a figure in the field.

It was himself, carrying two suitcases. He saw himself walking directly into the field of view, grow large, disappear. He looked over the rail, half expecting to see himself step out of the Gate.

But nothing came out of the Gate. It puzzled him, until he recalled that it was the setting at *that* end, ten years in the future, which controlled the time of egress. But he had what he wanted; he sat back and watched. Almost immediately Diktor and another edition of himself appeared in the scene. He recalled the situation when he saw it portrayed in the speculum. It was Bob Wilson Number Three, about to quarrel with Diktor and make his escape back to the twentieth century.

That was that—Diktor had not seen him, did not know that he had made unauthorized use of the Gate, did not know that he was hiding ten years in the "past," would not look for him there. He returned the controls to zero, and dismissed the matter.

But other matters needed his attention—food, especially. It seemed obvious, in retrospect, that he should have brought along food to last him for a day or two at least. And maybe a .45. He had to admit that he had not been very foresighted. But he easily forgave himself—it was hard to be foresighted when the future kept slipping up behind one. "All right, Bob, old boy," he told himself aloud, "let's see if the natives are friendly—as advertised."

A cautious reconnoiter of the small part of the Palace with which he was acquainted turned up no human beings nor life of any sort, not even insect life. The place was dead, sterile, as static and unlived-in as a window display. He shouted once just to hear a voice. The echoes caused him to shiver; he did not do it again.

The architecture of the place confused him. Not only was it strange to his experience—he had expected that— but the place, with minor exceptions, seemed totally unadapted to the uses of human beings. Great halls large enough to hold ten thousand people at once—had there been floors for them to stand on. For there frequently were no floors in the accepted meaning of a level or reasonably level platform. In following a passageway he came suddenly to one of the great mysterious openings in the structure and almost fell in before he realized that his path had terminated. He crawled gingerly forward and looked over the edge. The mouth of the passage debouched high up on a wall of the place; below him the wall was cut back so that there was not even a vertical surface for the eye to follow. Far below him, the wall curved back and met its mate of the opposite side—not decently, in a horizontal plane, but at an acute angle.

There were other openings scattered around the walls, openings as unserviceable to human beings as the one in which he crouched. "The High Ones," he whispered to himself. All his cockiness was gone out of him. He retraced his steps through the fine dust and reached the almost friendly familiarity of the Hall of the Gate.

On his second try he attempted only those passages and compartments which seemed obviously adapted to men. He had already decided what such parts of the Palace must be—servants' quarters, or, more probably, slaves' quarters. He regained his courage by sticking to such areas. Though deserted completely, by contrast with the rest of the great structure a room or a passage which seemed to have been built for men was friendly and cheerful. The sourceless ever-present illuminations and the unbroken silence still bothered him, but not to the degree to which he had been upset by the gargantuan and mysteriously convoluted chambers of the "High Ones."

He had almost despaired of finding his way out of the palace and was thinking of retracing his steps when the corridor he was following turned and he found himself in bright sunlight.

He was standing at the top of a broad steep ramp which spread fanlike down to the base of the building. Ahead of him and below him, distant at least five hundred yards, the pavement of the ramp met the green of sod and bush and tree. It was the same placid, lush and familiar scene he had looked out over when he breakfasted with Diktor—a few hours ago and ten years in the future.

He stood quietly for a short time, drinking in the sunshine, soaking up the heart-lifting beauty of the warm, spring day. "This is going to be all right," he exulted. "It's a grand place."

He moved slowly down the ramp, his eyes searching for human beings. He was halfway down when he saw a small figure emerge from the trees into a clearing near the foot of the ramp. He called out to it in joyous excitement. The child—it was a child he saw—looked up, stared at him for a moment, then fled back into the shelter of the trees.

"Impetuous, Robert—that's what you are," he chided himself. "Don't scare 'em. Take it easy." But he was not made downhearted by the incident. Where there were children there would be parents, society, opportunities for a bright, young fellow who took a broad view of things. He moved on down at a leisurely pace.

A man showed up at the point where the child had disappeared. Wilson stood still. The man looked him over and advanced hesitantly a step or two. "Come here!" Wilson invited in a friendly voice. "I won't hurt you."

The man could hardly have understood his words, but he advanced slowly. At the edge of the pavement he stopped, eyed it and would not proceed farther.

Something about the behavior pattern clicked in

Wilson's brain, fitted in with what he had seen in the Palace, and with the little that Diktor had told him. "Unless," he told himself, "the time I spent in 'Anthropology I' was totally wasted, this Palace is tabu, the ramp I'm standing on is tabu, and, by contagion, I'm tabu. Play your cards, son, play your cards!"

He advanced to the edge of the pavement, being careful not to step off it. The man dropped to his knees and cupped his hands in front of him, head bowed. Without hesitation Wilson touched him on the forehead. The man got back to his feet, his face radiant.

"This isn't even sporting," Wilson said. "I ought to shoot him on the rise."

His Man Friday cocked his head, looked puzzled and answered in a deep, melodious voice. The words were liquid and strange and sounded like a phrase from a song. "You ought to commercialize that voice," Wilson said admiringly. "Some stars get by on less. However—Get along now, and fetch something to eat. Food." He pointed to his mouth.

The man looked hesitant, spoke again. Bob Wilson reached into his pocket and took out the stolen notebook. He looked up *eat*, then looked up *food*. It was the same word. "Blellan," he said carefully.

"Blellaaaan?"

"Blellaaaaaaaan," agreed Wilson. "You'll have to excuse my accent. Hurry up." He tried to find *hurry* in the vocabulary, but it was not there. Either the language did not contain the idea or Diktor had not thought it worthwhile to record it. But we'll soon fix that, Wilson thought—if there isn't such a word, I'll give 'em one.

The man departed.

Wilson sat himself down Turk-fashion and passed the time by studying the notebook. The speed of his rise in these parts, he decided, was limited only by the time it took him to get into full communication. But he had only time enough to look up a few common substantives when his first acquaintance returned, in company.

The procession was headed by an extremely elderly man, white-haired but beardless. All of the men were beardless. He walked under a canopy carried by four male striplings. Only he of all the crowd wore enough clothes to get by anywhere but on a beach. He was looking uncomfortable in a sort of toga effect which appeared to have started life as a Roman-striped awning. That he was the head man was evident.

Wilson hurriedly looked up the word for "chief."

The word for chief was "Diktor."

It should not have surprised him, but it did. It was, of course, a logical probability that the word "Diktor" was a title rather than a proper name. It simply had not occurred to him.

Diktor—*the* Diktor—had added a note under the word. "One of the few words," Wilson read, "which shows some probability of having been derived from the dead languages. This word, a few dozen others, and the grammatical structure of the language itself, appear to be the only link between the language of the 'Forsaken Ones' and the English language."

The chief stopped in front of Wilson, just short of the pavement.

"O.K., Diktor," Wilson ordered, "kneel down. You're

not exempt." He pointed to the ground. The chief knelt down. Wilson touched his forehead.

The food that had been fetched along was plentiful and very palatable. Wilson ate slowly and with dignity, keeping in mind the importance of face. While he ate he was serenaded by the entire assemblage. The singing was excellent, he was bound to admit. Their ideas of harmony he found a little strange and the performance, as a whole, seemed primitive, but their voices were all clear and mellow and they sang as if they enjoyed it.

The concert gave Wilson an idea. After he had satisfied his hunger he made the chief understand, with the aid of the indispensable little notebook, that he and his flock were to wait where they were. He then returned to the Hall of the Gate and brought back from there the phonograph and a dozen assorted records. He treated them to a recorded concert of "modern" music.

The reaction exceeded his hopes. "Begin the Beguine" caused tears to stream down the face of the old chief. The first movement of Tchaikovsky's "Concerto Number One in B Flat Minor" practically stampeded them. They jerked. They held their heads and moaned. They shouted their applause. Wilson refrained from giving them the second movement, tapered them off instead with the compelling monotony of the "Bolero."

"Diktor," he said—he was not thinking of the old chief—"Diktor, old chum, you certainly had these people doped out when you sent me shopping. By the time you show up—if you ever do—I'll own the place."

Wilson's rise to power was more in the nature of a triumphal progress than a struggle for supremacy; it contained little that was dramatic. Whatever it was that the High Ones had done to the human race it had left them with only physical resemblance and with temperament largely changed. The docile friendly children with whom Wilson dealt had little in common with the brawling, vulgar, lusty, dynamic swarms who had once called themselves the people of the United States.

The relationship was like that of Jersey cattle to longhorns, or cocker spaniels to wolves. The fight was gone out of them. It was not that they lacked intelligence, nor civilized arts; it was the competitive spirit that was gone, the will-to-power.

Wilson had a monopoly on that.

But even he lost interest in playing a game that he always won. Having established himself as boss man by taking up residence in the palace and representing himself as the viceroy of the departed High Ones, he, for a time, busied himself in organizing certain projects intended to bring the culture "up-to-date"—the reinvention of musical instruments, establishment of a systematic system of mail service, redevelopment of the idea of styles in dress and a tabu against wearing the same fashion more than one season. There was cunning in the latter project. He figured that arousing a hearty interest in display in the minds of the womenfolk would force the men to hustle to satisfy their wishes. What the culture lacked was drive—it was slipping downhill. He tried to give them the drive they lacked.

His subjects cooperated with his wishes, but in a bemused fashion, like a dog performing a trick, not because he understands it, but because his master and godhead desires it.

He soon tired of it.

But the mystery of the High Ones, and especially the mystery of their Time Gate, still remained to occupy his mind. His was a mixed nature, half-hustler, half-philosopher. The philosopher had his inning.

It was intellectually necessary to him that he be able to construct in his mind a physio-mathematical model for the phenomena exhibited by the Time Gate. He achieved one, not a good one perhaps, but one which satisfied all of the requirements. Think of a plane surface, a sheet of paper or, better yet, a silk handkerchief—silk, because it has no rigidity, folds easily, while maintaining all of the relative attributes of a two-dimensional continuum on the surface of the silk itself. Let the threads of the woof be the dimension—or direction—of time; let the threads of the warp represent all three of the space dimensions.

An ink spot on the handkerchief becomes the Time Gate. By folding the handkerchief that spot may be superposed on any other spot on the silk. Press the two spots together between thumb and forefinger; the controls are set, the Time Gate is open, a microscopic inhabitant of this piece of silk may crawl from one fold to the other without traversing any other part of the cloth.

The model is imperfect; the picture is static—but a physical picture is necessarily limited by the sensory experience of the person visualizing it.

He could not make up his mind whether or not the concept of folding the four-dimensional continuum—three of space, one of time—back on itself so that the Gate was "open" required the concept of higher dimensions through which to fold it. It seemed so, yet it might simply be an intellectual shortcoming of the human mind. Nothing but empty space was required for the "folding," but "empty space" was itself a term totally lacking in meaning—he was enough of a mathematician to know that.

If higher dimensions were required to "hold" a four-dimensional continuum, then the number of dimensions of space and of time were necessarily infinite; each order requires the next higher order to maintain it.

But "infinite" was another meaningless term. "Open series" was a little better, but not much.

Another consideration forced him to conclude that there was probably at least one more dimension than the four his senses could perceive—the Time Gate itself. He became quite skilled in handling its controls, but he never acquired the foggiest notion of how it worked, or how it had been built. It seemed to him that the creatures who built it must necessarily have been able to stand outside the limits that confined him in order to anchor the Gate to the structure of space time. The concept escaped him.

He suspected that the controls he saw were simply the part that stuck through into the space he knew. The very palace itself might be no more than a three-dimensional section of a more involved structure. Such a condition would help to explain the otherwise inexplicable nature of its architecture.

He became possessed of an overpowering desire to know more about these strange creatures, the "High Ones," who had come and ruled the human race and built this Palace and this Gate, and gone away again—and in whose backwash he had been flung out of his setting some thirty millennia. To the human race they were no more than a sacred myth, a contradictory mass of tradition. No picture of them remained, no trace of their writing, nothing of their works save the High Palace of Norkaal and the Gate. And a sense of irreparable loss in the hearts of the race they had ruled, a loss expressed by their own term for themselves—the Forsaken Ones.

With controls and speculum he hunted back through time, seeking the Builders. It was slow work, as he had found before. A passing shadow, a tedious retracing—and failure.

Once he was sure that he had seen such a shadow in the speculum. He set the controls back far enough to be sure that he had repassed it, armed himself with food and drink and waited.

He waited three weeks.

The shadow might have passed during the hours he was forced to take out for sleep. But he felt sure that he was in the right period; he kept up the vigil.

He saw it.

It was moving toward the Gate.

When he pulled himself together he was halfway down the passageway leading away from the hall. He realized that he had been screaming. He still had an attack of the shakes.

Somewhat later he forced himself to return to the hall, and, with eyes averted, enter the control booth and return the spheres to zero. He backed out hastily and left the hall for his apartment. He did not touch the controls or enter the hall for more than two years.

It had not been fear of physical menace that had

shaken his reason, nor the appearance of the creature—
he could recall nothing of *how* it looked. It had been a
feeling of sadness infinitely compounded which had flooded
through him at the instant, a sense of tragedy, of grief
insupportable and unescapable, of infinite weariness. He
had been flicked with emotions many times too strong for
his spiritual fiber and which he was no more fitted to
experience than an oyster is to play a violin.

He felt that he had learned all about the High Ones a
man could learn and still endure. He was no longer
curious. The shadow of that vicarious emotion ruined his
sleep, brought him sweating out of dreams.

One other problem bothered him—the problem of
himself and his meanders through time. It still worried
him that he had met himself coming back, so to speak, had
talked with himself, fought with himself.

Which one was *himself*?

He was all of them, he knew, for he remembered
being each one. How about the times when there had
been more than one present?

By sheer necessity he was forced to expand the principle
of nonidentity—"Nothing is identical with anything
else, not even with itself"—to include the ego. In a four-
dimensional continuum each event is an absolute individual, it has its space coordinates and its date. The Bob
Wilson he was right now was *not* the Bob Wilson he had
been ten minutes ago. Each was a discrete section of a
four-dimensional process. One resembled the other in
many particulars, as one slice of bread resembles the slice
next to it. But they were *not* the same Bob Wilson—they
differed by a length of time.

When he had doubled back on himself, the difference had become apparent, for the separation was now in space rather than in time, and he happened to be so equipped as to be able to *see* a space length, whereas he could only remember a time difference. Thinking back he could remember a great many different Bob Wilsons, baby, small child, adolescent, young man. They were all different—he knew that. The only thing that bound them together into a feeling of identity was continuity of memory.

And that was the same thing that bound together the three—no, four, Bob Wilsons on a certain crowded afternoon, a memory track that ran through all of them. The only thing about it that remained remarkable was time travel itself.

And a few other little items—the nature of "free will," the problem of entropy, the law of the conservation of energy and mass. The last two, he now realized, needed to be extended or generalized to include the cases in which the Gate, or something like it, permitted a leak of mass, energy, or entropy from one neighborhood in the continuum to another. They were otherwise unchanged and valid. Free will was another matter. It could not be laughed off, because it could be directly experienced—yet his own free will had worked to create the same scene over and over again. Apparently human will must be considered as one of the factors which make up the processes in the continuum—"free" to the ego, mechanistic from the outside.

And yet his last act of evading Diktor had apparently changed the course of events. He was here and running the country, had been for many years, but Diktor had not showed up. Could it be that each act of "true" free will created a new and different future? Many philosophers had thought so.

This future appeared to have no such person as Diktor—*the* Diktor—in it, anywhere or anywhen.

As the end of his first ten years in the future approached, he became more and more nervous, less and less certain of his opinion. Damnation, he thought, if Diktor is going to show up it was high time that he did so. He was anxious to come to grips with him, establish which was to be boss.

He had agents posted throughout the country of the Forsaken Ones with instructions to arrest any man with hair on his face and fetch him forthwith to the Palace. The Hall of the Gate he watched himself.

He tried fishing the future for Diktor, but had no significant luck. He thrice located a shadow and tracked it down; each time it was himself. From tedium and partly from curiosity he attempted to see the other end of the process; he tried to relocate his original home, thirty thousand years in the past.

It was a long chore. The further the time button was displaced from the center, the poorer the control became. It took patient practice to be able to stop the image within a century or so of the period he wanted. It was in the course of this experimentation that he discovered what he had once looked for, a fractional control—a vernier, in effect. It was as simple as the primary control, but twist the bead instead of moving it directly.

He steadied down on the twentieth century, approximated the year by the models of automobiles, types of architecture, and other gross evidence, and stopped in what he believed to be 1952. Careful displacement of the space controls took him to the university town where he had started—after several false tries; the image did not enable him to read road signs.

He located his boardinghouse, brought the Gate into his own room. It was vacant, no furniture in it.

He panned away from the room, and tried again, a year earlier. Success—his own room, his own furniture, but empty. He ran rapidly back, looking for shadows.

There! He checked the swing of the image. There were three figures in the room, the image was too small, the light too poor for him to be sure whether or not one of them was himself. He leaned over and studied the scene.

He heard a dull thump outside the booth. He straightened up and looked over the side. Sprawled on the floor was a limp human figure. Near it lay a crushed and battered hat.

He stood perfectly still for an uncounted time, staring at the two redundant figures, hat and man, while the winds of unreason swept through his mind and shook it. He did not need to examine the unconscious form to identify it. He knew . . . *he knew*—it was his younger self, knocked willy-nilly through the Time Gate.

It was not that fact in itself which shook him. He had not particularly expected it to happen, having come tentatively to the conclusion that he was living in a different, an alternative, future from the one in which he had originally transited the Time Gate. He had been aware that it might happen nevertheless, that it did happen did not surprise him.

When it did happen, *he himself had been the only spectator!*

He was Diktor. He was *the* Diktor. He was *the only* Diktor!

He would never find Diktor, nor have it out with him. He need never fear his coming. There never had been, never would be, any other person called Diktor, because Diktor never had been or ever would be anyone but himself.

In review, it seemed obvious that he must be Diktor; there were so many bits of evidence pointing to it. And yet it had not been obvious. Each point of similarity between himself and *the* Diktor, he recalled, had arisen from rational causes—usually from his desire to ape the gross characteristics of the "other" and thereby consolidate his own position of power and authority before the "other" Diktor showed up. For that reason he had established himself in the very apartments that "Diktor" had used—so that they would be "his" first.

To be sure his people called him Diktor, but he had thought nothing of that—they called anyone who ruled by that title, even the little sub-chieftains who were his local administrators.

He had grown a beard, such as Diktor had worn, partly in imitation of the "other" man's precedent, but more to set him apart from the hairless males of the Forsaken Ones. It gave him prestige, increased his tabu. He fingered his bearded chin. Still, it seemed strange that he had not recalled that his own present appearance checked with the appearance of "Diktor." "Diktor" had been an older man. He himself was only thirty-two, ten here, twenty-two *there*.

Diktor he had judged to be about forty-five. Perhaps

an unprejudiced witness would believe himself to be that age. His hair and beard were shot with gray—had been, ever since the year he had succeeded too well in spying on the High Ones. His face was lined. Uneasy lies the head and so forth. Running a country, even a peaceful Arcadia, will worry a man, keep him awake nights.

Not that he was complaining—it had been a good life, a grand life, and it beat anything the ancient past had to offer.

In any case, he had been looking for a man in his middle forties, whose face he remembered dimly after ten years and whose picture he did not have. It had never occurred to him to connect that blurred face with his present one. Naturally not.

But there were other little things. Arma, for example. He had selected a likely-looking lass some three years back and made her one of his household staff, renaming her Arma in sentimental memory of the girl he had once fancied. It was logically necessary that they were the same girl, not two Armas, but one.

But, as he recalled her, the "first" Arma had been much prettier.

Hm-m-m—it must be his own point of view that had changed. He admitted that he had had much more opportunity to become bored with exquisite female beauty than his young friend over there on the floor. He recalled with a chuckle how he had found it necessary to surround himself with an elaborate system of tabus to keep the nubile daughters of his subjects out of his hair—most of the time. He had caused a particular pool in the river adjacent to the palace to be dedicated to his use in order that he might swim without getting tangled up in mermaids.

The man on the floor groaned, but did not open his eyes.

Wilson, the Diktor, bent over him but made no effort to revive him. That the man was not seriously injured he had reason to be certain. He did not wish him to wake up until he had had time to get his own thoughts entirely in order.

For he had work to do, work which must be done meticulously, without mistake. Everyone, he thought with a wry smile, makes plans to provide for their future.

He was about to provide for his past.

There was the matter of the setting of the Time Gate when he got around to sending his early self back. When he had tuned in on the scene in his room a few minutes ago, he had picked up the action just before his early self had been knocked through. In sending him back he must make a slight readjustment in the time setting to an instant around two o'clock of that particular afternoon. That would be simple enough; he need only search a short sector until he found his early self alone and working at his desk.

But the Time Gate had appeared in that room at a later hour; he had just caused it to do so. He felt confused.

Wait a minute, now—if he changed the setting of the time control, the Gate would appear in his room at the earlier time, remain there and simply blend into its "reappearance" an hour or so later. Yes, that was right. To a person in the room it would simply be as if the Time Gate had been there all along, from about two o'clock.

Which it had been. He would see to that.

Experienced as he was with the phenomena exhibited by the Time Gate, it nevertheless required a strong and subtle intellectual effort to think other than in durational terms, to take an *eternal* viewpoint.

And there was the hat. He picked it up and tried it on. It did not fit very well, no doubt because he was wearing his hair longer now. The hat must be placed where it would be found—Oh, yes, in the control booth. And the notebook, too.

The notebook, the notebook—Mm-m-m—Something funny, there. When the notebook he had stolen had become dog-eared and tattered almost to illegibility some four years back, he had carefully recopied its contents in a new notebook—to refresh his memory of English rather than from any need for it as a guide. The worn-out notebook he had destroyed; it was the new one he intended to obtain, and leave to be found.

In that case, *there never had been two notebooks.* The one he had now would become, after being taken through the Gate to a point ten years in the past, the notebook from which he had copied it. They were simply different segments of the same physical process, manipulated by means of the Gate to run concurrently, side by side, for a certain length of time.

As he had himself—one afternoon.

He wished that he had not thrown away the worn-out notebook. If he had it at hand, he could compare them and convince himself that they were identical save for the wear and tear of increasing entropy.

But when had he learned the language, in order that

he might prepare such a vocabulary? To be sure, when he copied it he then *knew* the language—copying had not actually been necessary.

But he *had* copied it.

The physical process he had all straightened out in his mind, but the intellectual process it represented was completely circular. His older self had taught his younger self a language which the older self knew because the younger self, after being taught, grew up to be the older self and was, therefore, capable of teaching.

But where had it started?

Which comes first, the hen or the egg?

You feed the rats to the cats, skin the cats, and feed the carcasses of the cats to the rats who are in turn fed to the cats. The perpetual motion fur farm.

If God created the world, who created God?

Who wrote the notebook? Who started the chain?

He felt the intellectual desperation of any honest philosopher. He knew that he had about as much chance of understanding such problems as a collie has of understanding how dog food gets into cans. Applied psychology was more his size—which reminded him that there were certain books which his early self would find very useful in learning how to deal with the political affairs of the country he was to run. He made a mental note to make a list.

The man on the floor stirred again, sat up. Wilson knew that the time had come when he must insure his past. He was not worried; he felt the sure confidence of the gambler who is "hot," who *knows* what the next roll of the dice will show.

He bent over his alter ego. "Are you all right?" he asked.

"I guess so," the younger man mumbled. He put his hand to his bloody face. "My head hurts."

"I should think it would," Wilson agreed. "You came through head over heels. I think you hit your head when you landed."

His younger self did not appear fully to comprehend the words at first. He looked around dazedly, as if to get his bearings. Presently he said, "Came through? Came through what?"

"The Gate, of course," Wilson told him. He nodded his head toward the Gate, feeling that the sight of it would orient the still groggy younger Bob.

Young Wilson looked over his shoulder in the direction indicated, sat up with a jerk, shuddered and closed his eyes. He opened them again after what seemed to be a short period of prayer, looked again, and said, "Did I come through that?"

"Yes," Wilson assured him.

"Where am I?"

"In the Hall of the Gate in the High Palace of Norkaal. But what is more important," Wilson added, "is *when* you are. You have gone forward a little more than thirty thousand years."

The knowledge did not seem to reassure him. He got up and stumbled toward the Gate. Wilson put a restraining hand on his shoulder. "Where are you going?"

"Back!"

"Not so fast." He did not dare let him go back yet, not until the Gate had been reset. Besides he was still drunk—his breath was staggering. "You will go back all right—I give you my word on that. But let me dress your wounds first. And you should rest. I have some explanations to make to you, and there is an errand you can do for me when you get back—to our mutual advantage. There is a great future in store for you and me, my boy—a great future!"

A great future!

Columbus Was a Dope

"I do like to wet down a sale," the fat man said happily, raising his voice above the sighing of the air-conditioner. "Drink up, Professor, I'm two ahead of you."

He glanced up from their table as the elevator door opposite them opened. A man stepped out into the cool dark of the bar and stood blinking, as if he had just come from the desert glare outside.

"Hey, Fred—Fred Nolan," the fat man called out. "Come over!" He turned to his guest. "Man I met on the hop from New York. Siddown, Fred. Shake hands with Professor Appleby, Chief Engineer of the Starship *Pegasus*—or will be when she's built. I just sold the Professor an order of bum steel for his crate. Have a drink on it."

"Glad to, Mr. Barnes," Nolan agreed. "I've met Dr. Appleby. On business—Climax Instrument Company."

"Huh?"

"Climax is supplying us with precision equipment," offered Appleby.

Barnes looked surprised, then grinned. "That's one on me. I took Fred for a government man, or one of your scientific johnnies. What'll it be, Fred? Old-fashioned? The same, Professor?"

"Right. But please don't call me 'Professor.' I'm not one and it ages me. I'm still young."

"I'll say you are, uh—Doc, Pete! Two old-fashioneds and another double Manhattan! I guess I expected a comic book scientist, with a long white beard. But now that I've met you, I can't figure out one thing."

"Which is?"

"Well, at your age you bury yourself in this god-forsaken place—"

"We couldn't build the *Pegasus* on Long Island," Appleby pointed out, "and this is the ideal spot for the take-off."

"Yeah, sure, but that's not it. It's—well, mind you, I sell steel. You want special alloys for a starship; I sell it to you. But just the same, now that business is out of the way, why do you want to do it? Why try to go to Proxima Centauri, or any other star?"

Appleby looked amused. "It can't be explained. Why do men try to climb Mount Everest? What took Perry to the North Pole? Why did Columbus get the Queen to hock her jewels? Nobody has ever been to Proxima Centauri—so we're going."

Barnes turned to Nolan. "Do you get it, Fred?"

Nolan shrugged. "I sell precision instruments. Some people raise chrysanthemums; some build starships. I sell instruments."

Barnes' friendly face looked puzzled. "Well—"

The bartender put down their drinks. "Say, Pete, tell me something. Would you go along on the *Pegasus* expedition if you could?"

"Nope."

"Why not?"

"I like it here."

Dr. Appleby nodded. "There's your answer, Barnes, in reverse. Some have the Columbus spirit and some haven't."

"It's all very well to talk about Columbus," Barnes persisted, "but he expected to come back. You guys don't expect to. Sixty years—you told me it would take sixty years. Why, you may not even live to get there."

"No, but our children will. And our grandchildren will come back."

"But—say, you're not *married?*"

"Certainly, I am. Family men only on the expedition. It's a two-to-three generation job. You know that." He hauled out a wallet. "There's Mrs. Appleby with Diane. Diane is three and a half."

"She's a pretty baby," Barnes said soberly and passed it on to Nolan, who smiled at it and handed it back to Appleby. Barnes went on. "What happens to her?"

"She goes with us, naturally. You wouldn't want her put in an orphanage, would you?"

"No, but—" Barnes tossed off the rest of his drink, "I don't get it," he admitted. "Who'll have another drink?"

"Not for me, thanks," Appleby declined, finishing his more slowly and standing up. "I'm due home. Family man, you know." He smiled.

Barnes did not try to stop him. He said goodnight and

watched Appleby leave.

"My round," said Nolan. "The same?"

"Huh? Yeah, sure." Barnes stood up. "Let's get up to the bar, Fred, where we can drink properly. I need about six."

"Okay," Nolan agreed, standing up. "What's the trouble?"

"Trouble? Did you see that picture?"

"Well?"

"Well, how do *you* feel about it? I'm a salesman too, Fred. I sell steel. It don't matter what the customer wants to use it for; I sell it to him. I'd sell a man a rope to hang himself. But I do love kids. I can't stand to think of that cute little kid going along on that—that crazy expedition!"

"Why not? She's better off with her parents. She'll get as used to steel decks as most kids are to sidewalks."

"But look, Fred. You don't have any silly idea they'll make it, do you?"

"They might."

"Well, they won't. They don't stand a chance. I know. I talked it over with our technical staff before I left the home office. Nine chances out of ten they'll burn up on the take-off. That's the best that can happen to them. If they get out of the solar system, which ain't likely, they'll still never make it. They'll never reach the stars."

Pete put another drink down in front of Barnes. He drained it and said:

"Set up another one, Pete. They can't. It's a theoretical impossibility. They'll freeze—or they'll roast—or they'll starve. But they'll never get there."

"Maybe so."

"No maybe about it. They're *crazy*. Hurry up with that drink, Pete. Have one yourself."

"Coming up. Don't mind if I do, thanks." Pete mixed the cocktail, drew a glass of beer, and joined them.

"Pete, here, is a wise man," Barnes said confidentially. "You don't catch him monkeying around with any trips to the stars. Columbus—Pfui! Columbus was a dope. He shoulda stood in bed."

The bartender shook his head. "You got me wrong, Mr. Barnes. If it wasn't for men like Columbus, we wouldn't be here today—now, would we? I'm just not the explorer type. But I'm a believer. I got nothing against the *Pegasus* expedition."

"You don't approve of them taking kids on it, do you?"

"Well, there were kids on the *Mayflower*, so they tell me."

"It's not the same thing." Barnes looked at Nolan, then back to the bartender. "If the Lord had intended us to go to the stars, he would have equipped us with jet propulsion. Fix me another drink, Pete."

"You've had about enough for a while, Mr. Barnes."

The troubled fat man seemed about to argue, thought better of it.

"I'm going up to the Sky Room and find somebody that'll dance with me," he announced. "G'night." He swayed softly toward the elevator.

Nolan watched him leave. "Poor old Barnes." He shrugged. "I guess you and I are hard-hearted, Pete."

"No. I believe in progress, that's all. I remember my old man wanted a law passed about flying machines, keep 'em from breaking their fool necks. Claimed nobody ever

could fly, and the government should put a stop to it. He
was wrong. I'm not the adventurous type myself but I've
seen enough people to know they'll try anything once, and
that's how progress is made."

"You don't look old enough to remember when men
couldn't fly."

"I've been around a long time. Ten years in this one
spot."

"Ten years, eh? Don't you ever get a hankering for a
job that'll let you breathe a little fresh air?"

"Nope. I didn't get any fresh air when I served drinks
on Forty-second Street and I don't miss it now. I like it
here. Always something new going on here, first the atom
laboratories and then the big observatory and now the
Starship. But that's not the real reason. I like it here. It's
my home. Watch this."

He picked up a brandy inhaler, a great fragile crystal
globe, spun it and threw it, straight up, toward the ceiling.
It rose slowly and gracefully, paused for a long reluctant
wait at the top of its rise, then settled slowly, slowly, like a
diver in a slow-motion movie. Pete watched it float past
his nose, then reached out with thumb and forefinger,
nipped it easily by the stem, and returned it to the rack.

"See that," he said. "One-sixth gravity. When I was
tending bar on Earth my bunions gave me the dickens all
the time. Here I weigh only thirty-five pounds. I like it on
the Moon."

The Menace from Earth

My name is Holly Jones and I'm fifteen. I'm very intelligent but it doesn't show, because I look like an underdone angel. Insipid.

I was born right here in Luna City, which seems to surprise Earthside types. Actually, I'm third generation; my grandparents pioneered in Site One, where the Memorial is. I live with my parents in Artemis Apartments, the new co-op in Pressure Five, eight hundred feet down near City Hall. But I'm not there much; I'm too busy.

Mornings I attend Tech High and afternoons I study or go flying with Jeff Hardesty—he's my partner—or whenever a tourist ship is in I guide groundhogs. This day the *Gripsholm* grounded at noon so I went straight from school to American Express.

The first gaggle of tourists was trickling in from Quarantine but I didn't push forward as Mr. Dorcas, the manager, knows I'm the best. Guiding is just temporary (I'm really a spaceship designer), but if you're doing a job you ought to do it well.

Mr. Dorcas spotted me. "Holly! Here, please. Miss Brentwood, Holly Jones will be your guide."

"'Holly,'" she repeated. "What a quaint name. Are you really a guide, dear?"

I'm tolerant of groundhogs—some of my best friends are from Earth. As Daddy says, being born on Luna is luck, not judgment, and most people Earthside are stuck there. After all, Jesus and Gautama Buddha and Dr. Einstein were all groundhogs.

But they can be irritating. If high school kids weren't guides, whom could they hire? "My license says so," I said briskly and looked her over the way she was looking me over.

Her face was sort of familiar and I thought perhaps I had seen her picture in those society things you see in Earthside magazines—one of the rich playgirls we get too many of. She was almost loathsomely lovely . . . nylon skin, soft, wavy, silver blond hair, basic specs about 35-24-34 and enough this and that to make me feel like a matchstick drawing, a low intimate voice and everything necessary to make plainer females think about pacts with the Devil. But I did not feel apprehensive; she was a groundhog and groundhogs don't count.

"All city guides are girls," Mr. Dorcas explained. "Holly is very competent."

"Oh, I'm sure," she answered quickly and went into tourist routine number one: surprise that a guide was needed just to find her hotel, amazement at no taxicabs, same for no porters, and raised eyebrows at the prospect of two girls walking alone through "an underground city."

Mr. Dorcas was patient, ending with: "Miss Brentwood,

Luna City is the only metropolis in the Solar System where a woman is really safe—no dark alleys, no deserted neighborhoods, no criminal element."

I didn't listen; I just held out my tariff card for Mr. Dorcas to stamp and picked up her bags. Guides shouldn't carry bags and most tourists are delighted to experience the fact that their thirty-pound allowance weighs only five pounds. But I wanted to get her moving.

We were in the tunnel outside and me with a foot on the slidebelt when she stopped. "I forgot! I want a city map."

"None available."

"Really?"

"There's only one. That's why you need a guide."

"But why don't they supply them? Or would that throw you guides out of work?"

See? "You think guiding is makework? Miss Brentwood, labor is so scarce they'd hire monkeys if they could."

"Then why not print maps?"

"Because Luna City isn't flat like—" I almost said, "—groundhog cities," but I caught myself.

"—like Earthside cities," I went on. "All you saw from space was the meteor shield. Underneath it spreads out and goes down for miles in a dozen pressure zones."

"Yes, I know, but why not a map for each level?"

Groundhogs always say, "Yes, I know, but—"

"I can show you the one city map. It's a stereo tank twenty feet high and even so all you see clearly are big things like the Hall of the Mountain King and hydroponics farms and the Bats' Cave."

"'The Bats' Cave,'" she repeated. "That's where they fly, isn't it?"

"Yes, that's where we fly."

"Oh, I want to see it!"

"OK. It first . . . or the city map?"

She decided to go to her hotel first. The regular route to the Zurich is to slide up the west through Gray's Tunnel past the Martian Embassy, get off at the Mormon Temple, and take a pressure lock down to Diana Boulevard. But I know all the shortcuts; we got off at Macy-Gimbel Upper to go down their personnel hoist. I thought she would enjoy it.

But when I told her to grab a hand grip as it dropped past her, she peered down the shaft and edged back. "You're joking."

I was about to take her back the regular way when a neighbor of ours came down the hoist. I said, "Hello, Mrs. Greenberg," and she called back, "Hi, Holly. How are your folks?"

Susie Greenberg is more than plump. She was hanging by one hand with young David tucked in her other arm and holding the *Daily Lunatic*, reading as she dropped. Miss Brentwood stared, bit her lip, and said, "How do I do it?"

I said, "Oh, use both hands; I'll take the bags." I tied the handles together with my hanky and went first.

She was shaking when we got to the bottom. "Goodness, Holly, how do you stand it? Don't you get homesick?"

Tourist question number six . . . I said, "I've been to Earth," and let it drop. Two years ago Mother made me visit my aunt in Omaha and I was *miserable*—hot and cold and dirty and beset by creepy-crawlies. I weighed a ton and I ached and my aunt was always chivvying me to go outdoors and exercise when all I wanted was to crawl into a tub and be quietly wretched. And I had hay fever. Probably you've never heard of hay fever—you don't die but you wish you could.

I was supposed to go to a girls' boarding school but I phoned Daddy and told him I was desperate and he let me come home. What groundhogs can't understand is that *they* live in savagery. But groundhogs are groundhogs and loonies are loonies and never the twain shall meet.

Like all the best hotels the Zurich is in Pressure One on the west side so that it can have a view of Earth. I helped Miss Brentwood register with the roboclerk and found her room; it had its own port. She went straight to it, began staring at Earth and going *ooh!* and *ahh!*

I glanced past her and saw that it was a few minutes past thirteen; sunset sliced straight down the tip of India—early enough to snag another client. "Will that be all, Miss Brentwood?"

Instead of answering she said in an awed voice, "Holly, isn't that the most beautiful sight you ever saw?"

"It's nice," I agreed. The view on that side is monotonous except for Earth hanging in the sky—but Earth is what tourists always look at even though they've just left it. Still, Earth is pretty. The changing weather is interesting if you don't have to be in it. Did you ever endure a summer in Omaha?

"It's gorgeous," she whispered.

"Sure," I agreed. "Do you want to go somewhere? Or will you sign my card?"

"What? Excuse me, I was daydreaming. No, not right now—yes, I do! Holly, I want to go out *there!* I must! Is there time? How much longer will it be light?"

"Huh? It's two days to sunset."

She looked startled. "How quaint. Holly, can you get us space suits? I've got to go outside."

I didn't wince—I'm used to tourist talk. I suppose a pressure suit looked like a space suit to them. I simply said, "We girls aren't licensed outside. But I can phone a friend."

Jeff Hardesty is my partner in spaceship designing, so I throw business his way. Jeff is eighteen and already in Goddard Institute, but I'm pushing hard to catch up so that we can set up offices for our firm: "Jones & Hardesty, Spaceship Engineers." I'm very bright in mathematics, which is everything in space engineering, so I'll get my degree pretty fast. Meanwhile we design ships anyhow.

I didn't tell Miss Brentwood this, as tourists think that a girl my age can't possibly be a spaceship designer.

Jeff has arranged his classes to let him guide on Tuesdays and Thursdays; he waits at West City Lock and studies between clients. I reached him on the lockmaster's phone. Jeff grinned and said, "Hi, Scale Model."

"Hi, Penalty Weight. Free to take a client?"

"Well, I was supposed to guide a family party, but they're late."

"Cancel them. Miss Brentwood . . . step into pickup, please. This is Mr. Hardesty."

Jeff's eyes widened and I felt uneasy. But it did not occur to me that Jeff could be attracted by a *groundhog* . . . even though it is conceded that men are robot slaves of their body chemistry in such matters. I knew she was exceptionally decorative, but it was unthinkable that Jeff could be captivated by any groundhog, no matter how well designed. They don't speak our language!

I am not romantic about Jeff; we are simply partners. But anything that affects Jones & Hardesty affects me.

When we joined him at West Lock he almost stepped on his tongue in a disgusting display of adolescent rut. I was ashamed of him and, for the first time, apprehensive. Why are males so childish?

Miss Brentwood didn't seem to mind his behavior. Jeff is a big hulk; suited up for outside he looks like a Frost Giant from *Das Rheingold* ; she smiled up at him and thanked him for changing his schedule. He looked even sillier and told her it was a pleasure.

I keep my pressure suit at West Lock so that when I switch a client to Jeff he can invite me to come along for the walk. This time he hardly spoke to me after that platinum menace was in sight. But I helped her pick out a suit and took her into the dressing room and fitted it. Those rental suits take careful adjusting or they will pinch you in tender places once out in vacuum . . . besides those things about them that one girl ought to explain to another.

When I came out with her, not wearing my own, Jeff didn't even ask why I hadn't suited up—he took her arm and started toward the lock. I had to butt in to get her to sign my tariff card.

The days that followed were the longest of my life. I saw Jeff only once . . . on the slidebelt in Diana Boulevard, going the other way. She was with him.

Though I saw him but once, I knew what was going on.

He was cutting classes and three nights running he took her to the Earthview Room of the Duncan Hines. None of my business!—I hope she had more luck teaching him to dance than I had. Jeff is a free citizen and if he wanted to make an utter fool of himself neglecting school and losing sleep over an upholstered groundhog that was his business.

But he should not have neglected the firm's business!

Jones & Hardesty had a tremendous backlog because we were designing Starship *Prometheus* This project we had been slaving over for a year, flying not more than twice a week in order to devote time to it—and that's a sacrifice.

Of course you can't build a starship today, because of the power plant. But Daddy thinks that there will soon be a technological break-through and mass-conversion power plants will be built—which means starships. Daddy ought to know—he's Luna Chief Engineer for Space Lanes and Fermi Lecturer at Goddard Institute. So Jeff and I are designing a self-supporting interstellar ship on that assumption: quarters, auxiliaries, surgery, labs— everything.

Daddy thinks it's just practice but Mother knows better—Mother is a mathematical chemist for General Synthetics of Luna and is nearly as smart as I am. She realizes that Jones & Hardesty plans to be ready with a finished proposal while other designers are still floundering.

Which was why I was furious with Jeff for wasting time over this creature. We had been working every possible chance. Jeff would show up after dinner, we would finish our homework, then get down to real work, the *Prometheus* . . .

checking each other's computations, fighting bitterly over details, and having a wonderful time. But the very day I introduced him to Ariel Brentwood, he failed to appear. I had finished my lessons and was wondering whether to start or wait for him—we were making a radical change in power plant shielding—when his mother phoned me. "Jeff asked me to call you, dear. He's having dinner with a tourist client and can't come over."

Mrs. Hardesty was watching me so I looked puzzled and said, "Jeff thought I was expecting him? He has his dates mixed." I don't think she believed me; she agreed too quickly.

All that week I was slowly convinced against my will that Jones & Hardesty was being liquidated. Jeff didn't break any more dates—how can you break a date that hasn't been made?—but we always went flying Thursday afternoons unless one of us was guiding. He didn't call. Oh, I know where he was; he took her ice skating in Fingal's Cave.

I stayed home and worked on the *Prometheus*, recalculating masses and moment arms for hydroponics and stores on the basis of the shielding change. But I made mistakes and twice I had to look up logarithms instead of remembering, I was so used to wrangling with Jeff over everything that I just couldn't function.

Presently I looked at the name plate of the sheet I was revising. "Jones & Hardesty" it read, like all the rest. I said to myself, "Holly Jones, quit bluffing; this may be The End. You knew that someday Jeff would fall for somebody."

"Of course . . . but not a *groundhog*."

"But he *did*. What kind of an engineer are you if you

can't face facts? She's beautiful and rich—she'll get her father to give him a job Earthside. You hear me? *Earthside!* So you look for another partner . . . or go into business on your own."

I erased "Jones & Hardesty" and lettered "Jones & Company" and stared at it. Then I started to erase that, too—but it smeared; I had dripped a tear on it. Which was ridiculous!

The following Tuesday both Daddy and Mother were home for lunch which was unusual as Daddy lunches at the spaceport. Now Daddy can't even see you unless you're a spaceship but that day he picked to notice that I had dialed only a salad and hadn't finished it. "That plate is about eight hundred calories short," he said, peering at it. "You can't boost without fuel—aren't you well?"

"Quite well, thank you," I answered with dignity.

"Mmm . . . now that I think back, you've been moping for several days. Maybe you need a checkup." He looked at Mother.

"I do not either need a checkup!" I had *not* been moping—doesn't a woman have a right not to chatter?

But I hate to have doctors poking at me so I added, "It happens I'm eating lightly because I'm going flying this afternoon. But if you insist, I'll order pot roast and potatoes and sleep instead!"

"Easy, punkin'," he answered gently. "I didn't mean to intrude. Get yourself a snack when you're through, and say hello to Jeff for me."

I simply answered, "OK," and asked to be excused; I was humiliated by the assumption that I couldn't fly without Mr. Jefferson Hardesty but did not wish to discuss it.

Daddy called after me, "Don't be late for dinner," and Mother said, "Now, Jacob—" and to me, "Fly until you're tired, dear; you haven't been getting much exercise. I'll leave your dinner in the warmer. Anything you'd like?"

"No, whatever you dial for yourself." I just wasn't interested in food, which isn't like me. As I headed for Bats' Cave I wondered if I had caught something. But my cheeks didn't feel warm and my stomach wasn't upset even if I wasn't hungry.

Then I had a horrible thought. Could it be that I was jealous? *Me?*

It was unthinkable. I am not romantic; I am a career woman. Jeff had been my partner and pal, and under my guidance he could have become a great spaceship designer, but our relationship was straightforward . . . a mutual respect for each other's abilities, with never any of that lovey-dovey stuff. A career woman can't afford such things—why look at all the professional time Mother had lost over having me!

No, I couldn't be jealous; I was simply worried sick because my partner had become involved with a groundhog. Jeff isn't bright about women and, besides, he's never been to Earth and has illusions about it. If she lured him Earthside, Jones & Hardesty was finished.

And somehow, "Jones & Company" wasn't a substitute: the *Prometheus* might never be built.

I was at Bats' Cave when I reached this dismal conclusion. I didn't feel like flying but I went to the locker room and got my wings anyhow.

Most of the stuff written about Bats' Cave gives a wrong impression. It's the air storage tank for the city, just like all the colonies have—the place where the scavenger pumps, deep down, deliver the air until it's needed. We just happen to be lucky enough to have one big enough to fly in. But it never was built, or anything like that; it's just a big volcanic bubble, two miles across, and if it had broken through, way back when, it would have been a crater.

Tourists sometimes pity us loonies because we have no chance to swim. Well, I tried it in Omaha and got water up my nose and scared myself silly. Water is for drinking, not playing in; I'll take flying. I've heard groundhogs say, oh yes, they had "flown" many times. But that's not *flying*. I did what they talk about, between White Sands and Omaha. I felt awful and got sick. Those things aren't safe.

I left my shoes and skirt in the locker room and slipped my tail surfaces on my feet, then zipped into my wings and got someone to tighten the shoulder straps. My wings aren't ready-made condors; they are Storer-Gulls, custom-made for my weight distribution and dimensions. I've cost Daddy a pretty penny in wings, outgrowing them so often, but these latest I bought myself with guide fees.

They're lovely!—titanalloy struts as light and strong as bird bones, tension-compensated wrist-pinion and shoulder joints, natural action in the alula slots, and automatic flap action in stalling. The wing skeleton is dressed in styrene feather-foils with individual quilling of scapulars and primaries. They almost fly themselves.

I folded my wings and went into the lock. While it was cycling I opened my left wing and thumbed the alula control—I had noticed a tendency to sideslip the last time I was airborne. But the alula opened properly and I decided I must have been overcontrolling, easy to do with Storer-Gulls; they're extremely maneuverable. Then the door showed green and I folded the wing and hurried out, while glancing at the barometer. Seventeen pounds— two more than Earth sea-level and nearly twice what we use in the city; even an ostrich could fly in that. I perked up and felt sorry for all groundhogs, tied down by six times proper weight, who never, never, *never* could fly.

Not even I could, on Earth. My wing loading is less than a pound per square foot, as wings and all I weigh less than twenty pounds. Earthside that would be over a hundred pounds and I could flap forever and never get off the ground.

I felt so good that I forgot about Jeff and his weakness. I spread my wings, ran a few steps, warped for lift and grabbed air—lifted my feet and was airborne.

I sculled gently and let myself glide towards the air intake at the middle of the floor—the Baby's Ladder, we call it, because you can ride the updraft clear to the roof, half a mile above, and never move a wing. When I felt it I leaned right, spoiling with right primaries, corrected, and settled in a counterclockwise soaring glide and let it carry me toward the roof.

A couple of hundred feet up, I looked around. The cave was almost empty, not more than two hundred in the air and half that number perched or on the ground—room enough for didoes. So as soon as I was up five hundred feet I leaned out of the updraft and began to beat. Gliding is no effort but flying is as hard work as you care to make it. In gliding I support a mere ten pounds on each arm— shucks, on Earth you work harder than that lying in bed. The lift that keeps you in the air doesn't take any work;

you get it free from the shape of your wings just as long as there is air pouring past them.

Even without an updraft all a level glide takes is gentle sculling with your finger tips to maintain air speed; a feeble old lady could do it. The lift comes from differential air pressures but you don't have to understand it; you just scull a little and the air supports you, as if you were lying in an utterly perfect bed. Sculling keeps you moving forward just like sculling a rowboat . . . or so I'm told; I've never been in a rowboat. I had a chance to in Nebraska but I'm not that foolhardy.

But when you're really flying, you scull with forearms as well as hands and add power with your shoulder muscles. Instead of only the outer quills of your primaries changing pitch (as in gliding), now your primaries and secondaries clear back to the joint warp sharply on each downbeat and recovery; they no longer lift, they force you forward—while your weight is carried by your scapulars, up under your armpits.

So you fly faster, or climb, or both, through controlling the angle of attack with your feet—with the tail surfaces you wear on your feet, I mean.

Oh dear, this sounds complicated and isn't—you just *do* it. You fly exactly as a bird flies. Baby birds can learn it and they aren't very bright. Anyhow, it's easy as breathing after you learn . . . and more fun than you can imagine!

I climbed to the roof with powerful beats, increasing my angle of attack and slotting my alulae for lift without burble—climbing at an angle that would stall most fliers. I'm little but it's all muscle and I've been flying since I was six. Once up there I glided and looked around. Down at the floor near the south wall tourists were trying glide wings—if you call those things "wings." Along the west wall the visitors' gallery was loaded with goggling tourists. I wondered if Jeff and his Circe character were there and decided to go down and find out.

So I went into a steep dive and swooped toward the gallery, leveled off and flew very fast along it. I didn't spot Jeff and his groundhoggess but I wasn't watching where I was going and overtook another flier, almost collided. I glimpsed him just in time to stall and drop under, and fell fifty feet before I got control. Neither of us was in danger as the gallery is two hundred feet up, but I looked silly and it was my own fault; I had violated a safety rule.

There aren't many rules but they are necessary; the first is that orange wings always have the right of way—they're beginners. This flier did not have orange wings but I was overtaking. The flier underneath—or being overtaken—or nearer to wall—or turning counterclockwise, in that order, has the right of way.

I felt foolish and wondered who had seen me, so I went all the way back up, made sure I had clear air, then stooped like a hawk toward the gallery, spilling wings, lifting tail, and letting myself fall like a rock.

I completed my stoop in front of the gallery, lowering and spreading my tail so hard I could feel leg muscles knot and grabbing air with both wings, alulae slotted. I pulled level in an extremely fast glide along the gallery. I could see their eyes pop and thought smugly, "There! That'll show 'em!"

When darn if somebody didn't stoop on me! The blast from a flier braking right over me almost knocked me out of control. I grabbed air and stopped a sideslip, used some shipyard words and looked around to see who had blitzed me. I knew the black-and-gold wing pattern—Mary Muhlenburg, my best girl friend. She swung toward me, pivoting on a wing tip. "Hi, Holly! Scared you, didn't I?"

"You did not! You better be careful; the flightmaster'll ground you for a month."

"Slim chance! He's down for coffee."

I flew away, still annoyed, and started to climb. Mary called after me, but I ignored her, thinking, "Mary, my girl, I'm going to get over you and fly you right out of the air."

That was a foolish thought as Mary flies every day and has shoulders and pectoral muscles like Mrs. Hercules. By the time she caught up with me I had cooled off and we flew side by side, still climbing. "Perch?" she called out.

"Perch," I agreed. Mary has lovely gossip and I could use a breather. We turned toward our usual perch, a ceiling brace for flood lamps—it isn't supposed to be a perch but the flightmaster hardly ever comes up there.

Mary flew in ahead of me, braked and stalled dead to a perfect landing. I skidded a little but Mary stuck out a wing and steadied me. It isn't easy to come into a perch, especially when you have to approach level. Two years ago a boy who had just graduated from orange wings tried it . . . knocked off his left alula and primaries on a strut— went fluttering and spinning down two thousand feet and crashed. He could have saved himself —you can come in safely with a badly damaged wing if you spill air with the other and accept the steeper glide, then stall as you land.

But this poor kid didn't know how; he broke his neck, dead as Icarus. I haven't used that perch since.

We folded our wings and Mary sidled over. "Jeff is looking for you," she said with a sly grin.

My insides jumped but I answered coolly, "So? I didn't know he was here."

"Sure. Down there," she added, pointing with her left wing. "Spot him?"

Jeff wears striped red and silver, but she was pointing at the tourist glide slope, a mile away. "No."

"He's there all right." She looked at me sidewise. "But I wouldn't look him up if I were you."

"Why not? Or for that matter, why should I?" Mary can be exasperating.

"Huh? You always run when he whistles. But he has that Earthside siren in tow again today; you might find it embarrassing."

"Mary, whatever are you talking about?"

"Huh? Don't kid me, Holly Jones; you know what I mean."

"I'm sure I don't," I answered with cold dignity.

"Humph! Then you're the only person in Luna City who doesn't. Everybody knows you're crazy about Jeff; everybody knows she's cut you out . . . and that you are simply simmering with jealousy."

Mary is my dearest friend but someday I'm going to skin her for a rug. "Mary, that's preposterously ridiculous! How can you even think such a thing?"

"Look, darling, you don't have to pretend. I'm for you." She patted my shoulders with her secondaries.

So I pushed her over backwards. She fell a hundred

feet, straightened out, circled and climbed, and came in beside me, still grinning. It gave me time to decide what to say.

"Mary Muhlenburg, in the first place I am not crazy about anyone, least of all Jeff Hardesty. He and I are simply friends. So it's utterly nonsensical to talk about me being 'jealous.' In the second place Miss Brentwood is a lady and doesn't go around 'cutting out' anyone, least of all me. In the third place she is simply a tourist Jeff is guiding—business, nothing more."

"Sure, sure," Mary agreed placidly. "I was wrong. Still—" She shrugged her wings and shut up.

"'Still' what? Mary, don't be mealy-mouthed."

"Mmm . . . I was wondering how you knew I was talking about Ariel Brentwood—since there isn't anything to it."

"Why, you mentioned her name."

"I did not."

I thought frantically. "Uh, maybe not. But it's perfectly simple. Miss Brentwood is a client I turned over to Jeff myself, so I assumed that she must be the tourist you meant."

"So? I don't recall even saying she was a tourist. But since she is just a tourist you two are splitting, why aren't you doing the inside guiding while Jeff sticks to outside work? I thought you guides had an agreement?"

"Huh? If he has been guiding her inside the city, I'm not aware of it—"

"You're the only one who isn't."

"—and I'm not interested; that's up to the grievance committee. But Jeff wouldn't take a fee for inside guiding in any case."

"Oh, sure!—not one he could *bank*. Well, Holly, seeing I was wrong, why don't you give him a hand with her? She wants to learn to glide."

Butting in on that pair was farthest from my mind. "If Mr. Hardesty wants my help, he will ask me. In the meantime I shall mind my own business . . . a practice I recommend to you!"

"Relax, shipmate," she answered, unruffled. "I was doing you a favor."

"Thank you, I don't need one."

"So I'll be on my way—got to practice for the gymkhana." She leaned forward and dropped off. But she didn't practice aerobatics; she dived straight for the tourist slope.

I watched her out of sight, then sneaked my left hand out the hand slit and got at my hanky—awkward when you are wearing wings but the floodlights had made my eyes water. I wiped them and blew my nose and put my hanky away and wiggled my hand back into place, then checked everything, thumbs, toes, and fingers, preparatory to dropping off.

But I didn't. I just sat there, wings drooping, and thought. I had to admit that Mary was partly right; Jeff's head was turned completely . . . over a *groundhog*. So sooner or later he would go Earthside and Jones & Hardesty was finished.

Then I reminded myself that I had been planning to be a spaceship designer like Daddy long before Jeff and I teamed up. I wasn't dependent on anyone; I could stand alone, like Joan of Arc, or Lise Meitner.

I felt better . . . a cold, stern pride, like Lucifer in *Paradise Lost*.

I recognized the red and silver of Jeff's wings while he was far off and I thought about slipping quietly away. But Jeff can overtake me if he tries, so I decided, "Holly, don't be a fool! You've no reason to run . . . just be coolly polite."

He landed by me but didn't sidle up. "Hi, Decimal Point."

"Hi, Zero. Uh, stolen much lately?"

"Just the City Bank but they made me put it back." He frowned and added, "Holly, are you mad at me?"

"Why, Jeff, whatever gave you such a silly notion?"

"Uh . . . something Mary the Mouth said."

"Her? Don't pay any attention to what *she* says. Half of it's always wrong and she doesn't mean the rest."

"Yeah, a short circuit between her ears. Then you aren't mad?"

"Of *course* not. Why should I be?"

"No reason I know of. I haven't been around to work on the ship for a few days . . . but I've been awfully busy."

"Think nothing of it. I've been terribly busy myself."

"Uh, that's fine. Look, Test Sample, do me a favor. Help me out with a friend—a client, that is—well, she's a friend, too. She wants to learn to use glide wings."

I pretended to consider it. "Anyone I know?"

"Oh, yes. Fact is, you introduced us. Ariel Brentwood."

"'Brentwood?' Jeff, there are so many tourists. Let me think. Tall girl? Blonde? Extremely pretty?"

He grinned like a goof and I almost pushed him off. "That's Ariel!"

"I recall her . . . she expected me to carry her bags.

But you don't need help, Jeff. She seemed very clever. Good sense of balance."

"Oh, yes, sure, all of that. Well, the fact is, I want you two to know each other. She's . . . well, she's just wonderful, Holly. A real person all the way through. You'll love her when you know her better. Uh . . . this seemed like a good chance."

I felt dizzy. "Why, that's very thoughtful, Jeff, but I doubt if she wants to know me better. I'm just a servant she hired—you know groundhogs."

"But she's not at all like the ordinary groundhog. And she does want to know you better—she *told* me so!"

After you told her to think so! I muttered. But I had talked myself into a corner. If I had not been hampered by polite upbringing I would have said, "On your way, vacuum skull! I'm not interested in your groundhog girl friends"— but what I did say was, "OK, Jeff," then gathered the fox to my bosom and dropped off into a glide.

So I taught Ariel Brentwood to "fly." Look, those so-called wings they let tourists wear have fifty square feet of lift surface, no controls except warp in the primaries, a built-in dihedral to make them stable as a table, and a few meaningless degrees of hinging to let the wearer think that he is "flying" by waving his arms. The tail is rigid, and canted so that if you stall (almost impossible) you land on your feet. All a tourist does is run a few yards, lift up his feet (he can't avoid it) and slide down a blanket of air. Then he can tell his grandchildren how he flew, really *flew*, "just like a bird."

An ape could learn to "fly" that much.

I put myself to the humiliation of strapping on a set of

the silly things and had Ariel watch while I swung into the
Baby's Ladder and let it carry me up a hundred feet to
show her that you really and truly could "fly" with them.
Then I thankfully got rid of them, strapped her into a larger
set, and put on my beautiful Storer-Gulls. I had chased
Jeff away (two instructors is too many), but when he saw
her wing up, he swooped down and landed by us.

I looked up. "You again."

"Hello, Ariel. Hi, Blip. Say, you've got her shoulder
straps too tight."

"Tut, tut," I said. "One coach at a time, remember? If
you want to help, shuck those gaudy fins and put on some
gliders . . . then I'll use you to show how not to. Otherwise
get above two hundred feet and stay there; we don't need
any dining-lounge pilots."

Jeff pouted like a brat but Ariel backed me up. "Do
what teacher says, Jeff. That's a good boy."

He wouldn't put on gliders but he didn't stay clear,
either. He circled around us, watching, and got bawled
out by the flightmaster for cluttering the tourist area.

I admit Ariel was a good pupil. She didn't even get sore
when I suggested that she was rather mature across the hips
to balance well; she just said that she had noticed that I had
the slimmest behind around there and she envied me. So I
quit trying to get her goat, and found myself almost liking
her as long as I kept my mind firmly on teaching. She tried
hard and learned fast—good reflexes and (despite my dirty
crack) good balance. I remarked on it and she admitted
diffidently that she had had ballet training.

About mid-afternoon she said, "Could I possibly try
real wings?"

"Huh? Gee, Ariel, I don't think so."

"Why not?"

There she had me. She had already done all that could be done with those atrocious gliders. If she was to learn more, she had to have real wings. "Ariel, it's dangerous. It's not what you've been doing, believe me. You might get hurt, even killed."

"Would you be held responsible?"

"No. You signed a release when you came in."

"Then I'd like to try it."

I bit my lip. If she had cracked up without my help, I wouldn't have shed a tear—but to let her do something too dangerous while she was my pupil . . . well, it smacked of David and Uriah. "Ariel, I can't stop you but I should put my wings away and not have anything to do with it."

It was her turn to bite her lip. "If you feel that way, I can't ask you to coach me. But I still want to. Perhaps Jeff will help me."

"He probably will," I blurted out, "if he is as big a fool as I think he is!"

Her company face slipped but she didn't say anything because just then Jeff stalled in beside us. "What's the discussion?"

We both tried to tell him and confused him for he got the idea I had suggested it, and started bawling me out. Was I crazy? Was I trying to get Ariel hurt? Didn't I have any sense?

"*Shut up!*" I yelled, then added quietly but firmly, "Jefferson Hardesty, you wanted me to teach your girl friend, so I agreed. But don't butt in and don't think you can get away with talking to me like that. Now beat it! Take wing. Grab air!"

He swelled up and said slowly, "I absolutely forbid it."

Silence for five long counts. Then Ariel said quietly, "Come, Holly. Let's get me some wings."

"Right, Ariel."

But they don't rent real wings. Fliers have their own; they have to. However, there are second-hand ones for sale because kids outgrow them, or people shift to custom-made ones, or something. I found Mr. Schultz who keeps the key, and said that Ariel was thinking of buying but I wouldn't let her without a tryout. After picking over forty-odd pairs I found a set which Johnny Queveras had outgrown but which I knew were all right. Nevertheless I inspected them carefully. I could hardly reach the finger controls but they fitted Ariel.

While I was helping her into the tail surfaces I said, "Ariel? This is still a bad idea."

"I know. But we can't let men think they own us."

"I suppose not."

"They do own us, of course. But we shouldn't let them know it." She was feeling out the tail controls. "The big toes spread them?"

"Yes. But don't do it. Just keep your feet together and toes pointed. Look, Ariel, you really aren't ready. Today all you will do is glide, just as you've been doing. Promise?"

She looked me in the eye. "I'll do exactly what you say . . . not even take wing unless you OK it."

"OK. Ready?"

"I'm ready."

"All right. Wups! I goofed. They aren't orange."

"Does it matter?"

"It sure does." There followed a weary argument because Mr. Schultz didn't want to spray them orange for a tryout. Ariel settled it by buying them, then we had to wait a bit while the solvent dried.

We went back to the tourist slope and I let her glide, cautioning her to hold both alulae open with her thumbs for more lift at slow speeds, while barely sculling with her fingers. She did fine, and stumbled in landing only once. Jeff stuck around, cutting figure eights above us, but we ignored him. Presently I taught her to turn in a wide, gentle bank—you can turn those awful glider things but it takes skill; they're only meant for straight glide.

Finally I landed by her and said, "Had enough?"

"I'll never have enough! But I'll unwing if you say."

"Tired?"

"No." She glanced over her wing at the Baby's Ladder; a dozen fliers were going up it, wings motionless, soaring lazily. "I wish I could do that just once. It must be heaven."

I chewed it over. "Actually, the higher you are, the safer you are."

"Then why not?"

"Mmm . . . safer *provided* you know what you're doing. Going up that draft is just gliding like you've been doing. You lie still and let it lift you half a mile high. Then you come down the same way, circling the wall in a gentle glide. But you're going to be tempted to do something you don't understand yet—flap your wings, or cut some caper."

She shook her head solemnly. "I won't do anything you haven't taught me."

I was still worried. "Look, it's only half a mile up but you cover five miles getting there and more getting down. Half an hour at least. Will your arms take it?"

"I'm sure they will."

"Well . . . you can start down anytime; you don't have to go all the way. Flex your arms a little now and then, so they won't cramp. Just don't flap your wings."

"I won't."

"O.K." I spread my wings. "Follow me."

I led her into the updraft, leaned gently right, then back left to start the counterclockwise climb, all the while sculling very slowly so that she could keep up. Once we were in the groove I called out, "Steady as you are!" and cut out suddenly, climbed and took station thirty feet over and behind her. "Ariel?"

"Yes, Holly?"

"I'll stay over you. Don't crane your neck; you don't have to watch me, I have to watch you. You're doing fine."

"I feel fine!"

"Wiggle a little. Don't stiffen up. It's a long way to the roof. You can scull harder if you want to."

"Aye aye, Cap'n!"

"Not tired?"

"Heavens, no! Girl, I'm living!" She giggled. "And mama said I'd never be an angel!"

I didn't answer because red-and-silver wings came charging at me, braked suddenly and settled into the circle between me and Ariel. Jeff's face was almost as red as his wings. "What the devil do you think you are doing?"

"Orange wings!" I yelled. "Keep clear!"

"Get down out of here! Both of you!"

"Get out from between me and my pupil. You know the rules."

"Ariel!" Jeff shouted. "Lean out of the circle and glide down. I'll stay with you."

"Jeff Hardesty," I said savagely, "I give you three seconds to get out from between us—then I'm going to report you for violation of Rule One. For the third time—*Orange Wings!*"

Jeff growled something, dipped his right wing and dropped out of formation. The idiot sideslipped within five feet of Ariel's wing tip. I should have reported him for that; all the room you can give a beginner is none too much.

I said, "OK, Ariel?"

"OK, Holly. I'm sorry Jeff is angry."

"He'll get over it. Tell me if you feel tired."

"I'm not. I want to go all the way up. How high are we?"

"Four hundred feet, maybe."

Jeff flew below us a while, then climbed and flew over us . . . probably for the same reason I did: to see better. It suited me to have two of us watching her as long as he didn't interfere; I was beginning to fret that Ariel might not realize that the way down was going to be as long and tiring as the way up. I was hoping she would cry uncle. I knew I could glide until forced down by starvation. But a beginner gets tense.

Jeff stayed generally over us, sweeping back and forth—he's too active to glide very long—while Ariel and I continued to soar, winding slowly up toward the roof. It finally occurred to me when we were about halfway up that I could cry uncle myself; I didn't have to wait for Ariel to weaken. So I called out, "Ariel? Tired now?"

"No."

"Well, I am. Could we go down, please?"

She didn't argue, she just said, "All right. What am I to do?"

"Lean right and get out of the circle." I intended to have her move out five or six hundred feet, get into the return down draft, and circle the cave down instead of up. I glanced up, looking for Jeff. I finally spotted him some distance away and much higher but coming toward us. I called out, "Jeff! See you on the ground." He might not have heard me but he would see if he didn't hear; I glanced back at Ariel.

I couldn't find her.

Then I saw her, a hundred feet below—flailing her wings and falling, out of control.

I didn't know how it happened. Maybe she leaned too far, went into a sideslip and started to struggle. But I didn't try to figure it out; I was simply filled with horror. I seemed to hang there frozen for an hour while I watched her.

But the fact appears to be that I screamed *"Jeff!"* and broke into a stoop.

But I didn't seem to fall, couldn't overtake her. I spilled my wings completely—but couldn't manage to fall; she was as far away as ever.

You do start slowly, of course; our low gravity is the only thing that makes human flying possible. Even a stone falls a scant three feet in the first second. But the first second seemed endless.

Then I knew I was falling. I could feel rushing

air—but I still didn't seem to close on her. Her struggles must have slowed her somewhat, while I was in an intentional stoop, wings spilled and raised over my head, falling as fast as possible. I had a wild notion that if I could pull even with her, I could shout sense into her head, get her to dive, then straighten out in a glide. But I couldn't *reach* her.

This nightmare dragged on for hours.

Actually we didn't have room to fall for more than twenty seconds; that's all it takes to stoop a thousand feet. But twenty seconds can be horribly long . . . long enough to regret every foolish thing I had ever done or said, long enough to say a prayer for us both . . . and to say good-bye to Jeff in my heart. Long enough to see the floor rushing toward us and know that we were both going to crash if I didn't overtake her mighty quick.

I glanced up and Jeff was stooping right over us but a long way up. I looked down at once . . . and I was overtaking her . . . I was passing her—*I was under her!*

Then I was braking with everything I had, almost pulling my wings off. I grabbed air, held it, and started to beat without ever going to level flight. I beat once, twice, three times . . . and hit her from below, jarring us both.

Then the floor hit us.

I felt feeble and dreamily contented. I was on my back in a dim room. I think Mother was with me and I know Daddy was. My nose itched and I tried to scratch it, but my arms wouldn't work. I fell asleep again.

I woke up hungry and wide awake. I was in a hospital bed and my arms still wouldn't work, which wasn't surprising as they were both in casts. A nurse came in with a tray. "Hungry?" she asked.

"Starved," I admitted.

"We'll fix that." She started feeding me like a baby.

I dodged the third spoonful and demanded, "What happened to my arms?"

"Hush," she said and gagged me with a spoon.

But a nice doctor came in later and answered my question. "Nothing much. Three simple fractures. At your age you'll heal in no time. But we like your company so I'm holding you for observation of possible internal injury."

"I'm not hurt inside," I told him. "At least, I don't hurt."

"I told you it was just an excuse."

"Uh, Doctor?"

"Well?"

"Will I be able to fly again?" I waited, scared.

"Certainly. I've seen men hurt worse get up and go three rounds."

"Oh. Well, thanks. Doctor? What happened to the other girl? Is she . . . did she . . . ?"

"Brentwood? She's here."

"She's right here," Ariel agreed from the door. "May I come in?"

My jaw dropped, then I said, "Yeah. Sure. Come in."

The doctor said, "Don't stay long," and left. I said, "Well, sit down."

"Thanks." She hopped instead of walked and I saw that one foot was bandaged. She got on the end of the bed.

"You hurt your foot."

She shrugged. "Nothing. A sprain and a torn ligament. Two cracked ribs. But I would have been dead. You know why I'm not?"

I didn't answer. She touched one of my casts. "That's why. You broke my fall and I landed on top of you. You saved my life and I broke both your arms."

"You don't have to thank me. I would have done it for anybody."

"I believe you and I wasn't thanking you. You can't thank a person for saving your life. I just wanted to make sure you knew that I knew it."

I didn't have an answer so I said, "Where's Jeff? Is he all right?"

"He'll be along soon. Jeff's not hurt . . . though I'm surprised he didn't break both ankles. He stalled in beside us so hard that he should have. But Holly . . . Holly my very dear . . . I slipped in so that you and I could talk about him before he got here."

I changed the subject quickly. Whatever they had given me made me feel dreamy and good, but not beyond being embarrassed. "Ariel, what happened? You were getting along fine—then suddenly you were in trouble."

She looked sheepish. "My own fault. You said we were going down, so I looked down. Really looked, I mean. Before that, all my thoughts had been about climbing to the roof; I hadn't thought about how far down the floor was. Then I looked down . . . and got dizzy and panicky and went all to pieces." She shrugged. "You were right. I wasn't ready."

I thought about it and nodded. "I see. But don't worry—when my arms are well, I'll take you up again."

She touched my foot. "Dear Holly. But I won't be flying again; I'm going back where I belong."

"Earthside?"

"Yes. I'm taking the *Billy Mitchell* on Wednesday."

"Oh. I'm sorry."

She frowned slightly. "Are you? Holly, you don't like me, do you?"

I was startled silly. What can you say? Especially when it's true? "Well," I said slowly, "I don't dislike you. I just don't know you very well."

She nodded. "And I don't know you very well . . . even though I got to know you a lot better in a very few seconds. But Holly . . . listen please and don't get angry. It's about Jeff. He hasn't treated you very well the last few days—while I've been here, I mean. But don't be angry with him. I'm leaving and everything will be the same."

That ripped it open and I couldn't ignore it, because if I did, she would assume all sorts of things that weren't so. So I had to explain . . . about me being a career woman . . . how, if I had seemed upset, it was simply distress at breaking up the firm of Jones & Hardesty before it even finished its first starship . . . how I was *not* in love with Jeff but simply valued him as a friend and associate . . . but if Jones & Hardesty couldn't carry on, then Jones & Company would. "So you see, Ariel, it isn't necessary for you to give up Jeff. If you feel you owe me something, just forget it. It isn't necessary."

She blinked and I saw with amazement that she was holding back tears. "Holly, Holly . . . you don't understand at all."

"I understand all right. I'm not a child."

"No, you're a grown woman . . . but you haven't found it out." She held up a finger. "One—Jeff doesn't love me."

"I don't believe it."

"Two . . . I don't love him."

"I don't believe that, either."

"Three . . . you say you don't love him—but we'll take that up when we come to it. Holly, am I beautiful?"

Changing the subject is a female trait but I'll never learn to do it that fast. "Huh?"

"I said, 'Am I beautiful?'"

"You know darn well you are!"

"Yes. I can sing a bit and dance, but I would get few parts if I were not, because I'm no better than a third-rate actress. So I have to be beautiful. How old am I?"

I managed not to boggle. "Huh? Older than Jeff thinks you are. Twenty-one, at least. Maybe twenty-two."

She sighed. "Holly, I'm old enough to be your mother."

"Huh? I don't believe that, either."

"I'm glad it doesn't show. But that's why, though Jeff is a dear, there never was a chance that I could fall in love with him. But how I feel about him doesn't matter; the important thing is that he loves *you*."

"*What?* That's the silliest thing you've said yet! Oh, he *likes* me—or did. But that's all." I gulped. "And it's all I want. Why, you should hear the way he talks to me."

"I have. But boys that age can't say what they mean; they get embarrassed."

"But—"

"Wait, Holly. I saw something you didn't because you were knocked cold. When you and I bumped, do you know what happened?"

"Uh, no."

"Jeff arrived like an avenging angel, a split second behind us. He was ripping his wings off as he hit, getting his arms free. He didn't even look at me. He just stepped across me and picked you up and cradled you in his arms, all the while bawling his eyes out."

"He *did?*"

"He did."

I mulled it over. Maybe the big lunk did kind of like me, after all.

Ariel went on, "So you see, Holly, even if you don't love him, you must be very gentle with him, because he loves you and you can hurt him terribly."

I tried to think. Romance was still something that a career woman should shun . . . but if Jeff really did feel that way—well . . . would it be compromising my ideals to marry him just to keep him happy? To keep the firm together? Eventually, that is?

But if I did, it wouldn't be Jones & Hardesty; it would be Hardesty & Hardesty.

Ariel was still talking: "—you might even fall in love with him. It does happen, hon, and if it did, you'd be sorry if you had chased him away. Some other girl would grab him; he's awfully nice."

"But . . . " I shut up for I heard Jeff's step—I can always tell it. He stopped in the door and looked at us, frowning.

"Hi, Ariel."

"Hi, Jeff."

"Hi, Fraction." He looked me over. "My, but you're a mess."

"You aren't pretty yourself. I hear you have flat feet."

"Permanently. How do you brush your teeth with those things on your arms?"

"I don't."

Ariel slid off the bed, balanced on one foot. "Must run. See you later, kids."

"So long, Ariel."

"Good-bye, Ariel. Uh . . . thanks."

Jeff closed the door after she hopped away, came to the bed and said gruffly, "Hold still."

Then he put his arms around me and kissed me.

Well, I couldn't stop him, could I? With both arms broken? Besides, it was consonant with the new policy for the firm. I was startled speechless because Jeff never kisses me, except birthday kisses, which don't count. But I tried to kiss back and show that I appreciated it.

I don't know what the stuff was they had been giving me but my ears began to ring and I felt dizzy again.

Then he was leaning over me. "Runt," he said mournfully, "you sure give me a lot of grief."

"You're no bargain yourself, flathead," I answered with dignity.

"I suppose not." He looked me over sadly. "What are you crying for?"

I didn't know that I had been. Then I remembered why. "Oh, Jeff—I busted my pretty wings!"

"We'll get you more. Uh, brace yourself. I'm going to do it again."

"All right." He did.

I suppose Hardesty & Hardesty has more rhythm than Jones & Hardesty.

It really sounds better.

Sky Lift

"All torch pilots! Report to the Commodore!" The call echoed through Earth Satellite Station.

Joe Appleby flipped off the shower to listen. "You don't mean me," he said happily, "I'm on leave—but I'd better shove before you change your mind."

He dressed and hurried along a passageway. He was in the outer ring of the Station; its slow revolution, a giant wheel in the sky, produced gravity-like force against his feet. As he reached his room the loud-speakers repeated, "All torch pilots, report to the Commodore," then added, "Lieutenant Appleby, report to the Commodore." Appleby uttered a rude monosyllable.

The Commodore's office was crowded. All present wore the torch, except a flight surgeon and Commodore Berrio himself, who wore the jets of a rocketship pilot. Berrio glanced up and went on talking: "—the situation. If we are to save Proserpina Station, an emergency run must be made out to Pluto. Any questions?"

No one spoke. Appleby wanted to, but did not wish to

remind Berrio that he had been late. "Very well," Berrio went on. "Gentlemen, it's a job for torch pilots. I must ask for volunteers."

Good! thought Appleby. Let the eager lads volunteer and then adjourn. He decided that he might still catch the next shuttle to Earth. The Commodore continued, "Volunteers please remain. The rest are dismissed."

Excellent, Appleby decided. Don't rush for the door, me lad. Be dignified—sneak out between two taller men.

No one left. Joe Appleby felt swindled but lacked the nerve to start the exodus. The Commodore said soberly, "Thank you, gentlemen. Will you wait in the wardroom, please?" Muttering, Appleby left with the crowd. He wanted to go out to Pluto someday—sure!—but not now, not with Earthside leave papers in his pocket.

He held a torcher's contempt for the vast distance itself. Older pilots thought of interplanetary trips with a rocket man's bias, in terms of years—trips that a torch ship with steady acceleration covered in days. By the orbits that a rocketship must use the round trip to Jupiter takes over five years; Saturn is twice as far, Uranus twice again, Neptune still farther. No rocketship ever attempted Pluto; a round trip would take more than ninety years. But torch ships had won a foothold even there: Proserpina Station— cryology laboratory, cosmic radiation station, parallax observatory, physics laboratory, all in one quintuple dome against the unspeakable cold.

Nearly four billion miles from Proserpina Station Appleby followed a classmate into the wardroom. "Hey, Jerry," he said, "tell me what it is I seem to have volunteered for?"

Jerry Price looked around. "Oh, it's late Joe Appleby. Okay, buy me a drink."

A radiogram had come from Proserpina, Jerry told him, reporting an epidemic: "Larkin's disease." Appleby whistled. Larkin's disease was a mutated virus, possibly of Martian origin; a victim's red-cell count fell rapidly, soon he was dead. The only treatment was massive transfusions while the disease ran its course. "So, m'boy, somebody has to trot out to Pluto with a blood bank."

Appleby frowned. "My pappy warned me. 'Joe,' he said, 'keep your mouth shut and never volunteer.'"

Jerry grinned. "We didn't exactly volunteer."

"How long is the boost? Eighteen days or so? I've got social obligations Earthside."

"Eighteen days at one g—but this will be higher. They are running out of blood donors."

"How high? A g-and-a-half?"

Price shook his head. "I'd guess two gravities."

"Two g's!"

"What's hard about that? Men have lived through a lot more."

"Sure, for a short pull-out—not for days on end. Two g's strains your heart if you stand up."

"Don't moan, they won't pick you—I'm more the hero type. While you're on leave, think of me out in those lonely wastes, a grim-jawed angel of mercy. Buy me another drink."

Appleby decided that Jerry was right; with only two pilots needed he stood a good chance of catching the next Earth shuttle. He got out his little black book and was picking phone numbers when a messenger arrived. "Lieutenant Appleby, sir?" Joe admitted it.

"The-Commodore's-compliments-and-will-you-report-at-once,-sir?"

"On my way." Joe caught Jerry's eye. "Who is what type?"

Jerry said, "Shall I take care of your social obligations?"

"Not likely!"

"I was afraid not. Good luck, boy."

With Commodore Berrio was the flight surgeon and an older lieutenant. Berrio said, "Sit down, Appleby. You know Lieutenant Kleuger? He's your skipper. You will be co-pilot."

"Very good, sir."

"Appleby, Mr. Kleuger is the most experienced torch pilot available. You were picked because medical records show you have exceptional tolerance for acceleration. This is a high-boost trip."

"How high, sir?"

Berrio hesitated. "Three and one-half gravities."

Three and a half *g*'s! That wasn't a boost—that was a pullout. Joe heard the surgeon protest, "I'm sorry, sir, but three gravities is all I can approve."

Berrio frowned. "Legally, it's up to the captain. But three hundred lives depend on it."

Kleuger said, "Doctor, let's see that curve." The surgeon slid a paper across the desk; Kleuger moved it so that Joe could see it. "Here's the scoop, Appleby—"

A curve started high, dropped very slowly, made a sudden "knee" and dropped rapidly. The surgeon put his finger on the "knee." "Here," he said soberly, "is where the donors are suffering from loss of blood as much as the patients. After that it's hopeless, without a new source of blood."

"How did you get this curve?" Joe asked.

"It's the empirical equation of Larkin's disease applied to two hundred eighty-nine people."

Appleby noted vertical lines each marked with an acceleration and a time. Far to the right was one marked: "1 g—18 days." That was the standard trip; it would arrive after the epidemic had burned out. Two gravities cut it to twelve days seventeen hours; even so, half the colony would be dead. Three g's was better but still bad. He could see why the Commodore wanted them to risk three-and-a-half kicks; that line touched the "knee," at nine days fifteen hours. That way they could save almost everybody . . . but, oh, brother!

The time advantage dropped off by inverse squares. Eighteen days required one gravity, so nine days took four, while four-and-a-half days required a fantastic sixteen gravities. But someone had drawn a line at "16 g—4.5 days." "Hey! This plot must be for a robot-torch—that's the ticket! Is there one available?"

Berrio said gently, "Yes. But what are its chances?"

Joe shut up. Even between the inner planets robots often went astray. In four-billion-odd miles the chance that one could hit close enough to be caught by radio control was slim. "We'll try," Berrio promised. "If it succeeds, I'll call you at once." He looked at Kleuger. "Captain, time is short. I must have your decision."

Kleuger turned to the surgeon. "Doctor, why not another half gravity? I recall a report on a chimpanzee who was centrifuged at high g for an amazingly long time."

"A chimpanzee is not a man."

Joe blurted out, "How much did this chimp stand, Surgeon?"

"Three and a quarter gravities for twenty-seven days."

"He *did?* What shape was he in when the test ended?"

"He wasn't," the doctor grunted.

Kleuger looked at the graph, glanced at Joe, then said to the Commodore, "The boost will be at three and one-half gravities, sir."

Berrio merely said, "Very well, sir. Hurry over to sick bay. You haven't much time."

Forty-seven minutes later they were being packed into the scout torchship *Salamander*. She was in orbit close by; Joe, Kleuger, and their handlers came by tube linking the hub of the Station to her airlock. Joe was weak and dopey from a thorough washing-out plus a dozen treatments and injections. A good thing, he thought, that light-off would be automatic.

The ship was built for high boost; controls were over the pilots' tanks, where they could be fingered without lifting a hand. The flight surgeon and an assistant fitted Kleuger into one tank while two medical technicians arranged Joe in his. One of them asked, "Underwear smooth? No wrinkles?"

"I guess."

"I'll check." He did so, then arranged fittings necessary to a man who must remain in one position for days. "The nipple left of your mouth is water; the two on your right are glucose and bouillon."

"No solids?"

The surgeon turned in the air and answered, "You

don't need any, you won't want any, and you mustn't have any. And be careful in swallowing."

"I've boosted before."

"Sure, sure. But be careful."

Each tank was like an oversized bathtub filled with a liquid denser than water. The top was covered by a rubbery sheet, gasketed at the edges; during boost each man would float with the sheet conforming to his body. The *Salamander* being still in free orbit, everything was weightless and the sheet now served to keep the fluid from floating out. The attendants centered Appleby against the sheet and fastened him with sticky tape, then placed his own acceleration collar, tailored to him, behind his head. The surgeon came over and inspected. "You okay?"

"Sure."

"Mind that swallowing." He added, "Okay, Captain. Permission to leave your ship, sir?"

"Certainly. Thank you, Surgeon."

"Good luck." He left with the technicians.

The room had no ports and needed none. The area in front of Joe's face was filled with screens, instruments, radar, and data displays; near his forehead was his eyepiece for the coelostat. A light blinked green as the passenger tube broke its anchors; Kleuger caught Joe's eye in a mirror mounted opposite them. "Report, Mister."

"Minus seven minutes oh four. Tracking. Torch warm and idle. Green for light-off."

"Stand by while I check orientation." Kleuger's eyes disappeared into his coelostat eyepiece. Presently he said, "Check me, Joe."

"Aye aye, sir." Joe twisted a knob and his eyepiece swung down. He found three star images brought together perfectly in the cross hairs. "Couldn't be better, Skipper."

"Ask for clearance."

"*Salamander to Control—clearance requested to Proserpina. Automatic light-off on tape. All green.*"

"*Control to Salamander. You are cleared. Good luck!*"

"Cleared, Skipper. Minus three . . . *Double oh!*" Joe thought morosely that he should be half way to Earth now. Why the hell did the military always get stuck with these succor-&-rescue jobs?

When the counter flashed the last thirty seconds he forgot his foregone leave. The lust to travel possessed him. To go, no matter where, anywhere . . . go! He smiled as the torch lit off.

Then weight hit him.

At three and one-half gravities he weighed six hundred and thirty pounds. It felt as if a load of sand had landed on him, squeezing his chest, making him helpless, forcing his head against his collar. He strove to relax, to let the supporting liquid hold him together. It was all right to tighten up for a pull-out, but for a long boost one must relax. He breathed shallowly and slowly; the air was pure oxygen, little lung action was needed. But he labored just to breathe. He could feel his heart struggling to pump blood grown heavy through squeezed vessels. This is awful, he admitted. I'm not sure I can take it. He had once had four g for nine minutes but he had forgotten how bad it was.

"Joe! *Joe!*"

He opened his eyes and tried to shake his head. "Yes, Skipper." He looked for Kleuger in the mirror; the pilot's face was sagging and drawn, pulled into the mirthless grin of high acceleration.

"Check orientation!"

Joe let his arms float as he worked controls with leaden fingers. "Dead on, Skipper."

"Very well. Call Luna."

Earth Station was blanketed by their torch but the Moon was on their bow. Appleby called Luna tracking center and received their data on the departure plus data relayed from Earth Station. He called figures and times to Kleuger, who fed them into the computer. Joe then found that he had forgotten, while working, his unbearable weight. It felt worse than ever. His neck ached and he suspected that there was a wrinkle under his left calf. He wiggled in the tank to smooth it, but it made it worse. "How's she look, Skipper?"

"Okay. You're relieved, Joe. I'll take first watch."

"Right, Skipper." He tried to rest—as if a man could when buried under sandbags. His bones ached and the wrinkle became a nagging nuisance. The pain in his neck got worse; apparently he had wrenched it at light-off. He turned his head, but there were just two positions—bad and worse. Closing his eyes, he attempted to sleep. Ten minutes later he was wider awake than ever, his mind on three things, the lump in his neck, the irritation under his leg, and the squeezing weight.

Look, bud, he told himself, this is a long boost. Take it easy, or adrenalin exhaustion will get you. As the book says, *"The ideal pilot is relaxed and unworried. Sanguine in temperament, he never borrows trouble.*" Why, you chair-warming so-and-so! Were *you* at three and a half g's when you wrote that twaddle?

Cut it out, boy! He turned his mind to his favorite subject—girls, bless their hearts. Such self-hypnosis he had used to pass many a lonely million miles. Presently he realized wryly that his phantom harem had failed him. He could not conjure them up, so he banished them and spent his time being miserable.

He awoke in a sweat. His last dream had been a nightmare that he was headed out to Pluto at an impossibly high boost.

My God! So he was!

The pressure seemed worse. When he moved his head there was a stabbing pain down his side. He was panting and sweat was pouring off. It ran into his eyes; he tried to wipe them, found that his arm did not respond and that his fingertips were numb. He inched his arm across his body and dabbed at his eyes; it did not help.

He stared at the elapsed time dial of the integrating accelerograph and tried to remember when he was due on watch. It took a while to understand that six and a half hours had passed since light-off. He then realized with a jerk that it was long past time to relieve the watch. Kleuger's face in the mirror was still split in the grin of high g; his eyes were closed. "Skipper!" Joe shouted. Kleuger did not stir. Joe felt for the alarm button, thought better of it. Let the poor goop sleep!

But somebody had to feed the hogs—better get the clouds out of his brain. The accelerometer showed three and a half exactly; the torch dials were all in operating range; the radiometer showed leakage less than ten percent of danger level.

The integrating accelerograph displayed elapsed time, velocity, and distance, in dead-reckoning for empty space. Under these windows were three more which showed the same by the precomputed tape controlling the torch; by comparing, Joe could tell how results matched predictions. The torch had been lit off for less than seven hours, speed was nearly two million miles per hour and they were over six million miles out. A third display corrected these figures for the Sun's field, but Joe ignored this; near Earth's orbit the Sun pulls only one two-thousandth of a gravity—a gnat's whisker, allowed for in precomputation. Joe merely noted that tape and D.R. agreed; he wanted an outside check.

Both Earth and Moon now being blanketed by the same cone of disturbance, he twisted knobs until their radar beacon beamed toward Mars and let it pulse the signal meaning "Where am I?" He did not wait for answer; Mars was eighteen minutes away by radio. He turned instead to the coelostat. The triple image had wandered slightly but the error was too small to correct.

He dictated what he had done into the log, whereupon he felt worse. His ribs hurt, each breath carried the stab of pleurisy. His hands and feet felt "pins-and-needles" from scanty circulation. He wiggled them, which produced crawling sensations and wearied him. So he held still and watched the speed soar. It increased seventy-seven miles per hour every second, more than a quarter million miles per hour every hour. For once he envied rocketship pilots; they took forever to get anywhere but they got there in comfort.

Without the torch, men would never have ventured much past Mars. $E = Mc^2$, mass is energy, and a pound of sand equals fifteen billion horsepower-hours. An atomic rocketship uses but a fraction of one percent of that energy, whereas the new torchers used better than eighty percent. The conversion chamber of a torch was a tiny sun; particles expelled from it approached the speed of light.

Appleby was proud to be a torcher, but not at the moment. The crick had grown into a splitting headache, he wanted to bend his knees and could not, and he was nauseated from the load on his stomach. Kleuger seemed able to sleep through it, damn his eyes! How did they expect a man to *stand* this? Only eight hours and already he felt done in, bushed—how could he last nine days?

Later—time was beginning to be uncertain—some indefinite time later he heard his name called. "Joe! *Joe!*"

Couldn't a man die in peace? His eyes wandered around, found the mirror; he struggled to focus. "Joe! You've got to relieve me—I'm groggy."

"Aye aye, sir."

"Make a check, Joe. I'm too goofed up to do it."

"I already did, sir."

"*Huh?* When?"

Joe's eyes swam around to the elapsed-time dial. He closed one eye to read it. "Uh, about six hours ago."

"What? *What time is it?*"

Joe didn't answer. He wished peevishly that Kleuger would go away. Kleuger added soberly, "I must have blacked out, kid. What's the situation?" Presently he insisted, "Answer me, Mister."

"Huh? Oh, we're all right—down the groove. Skipper, is my left leg twisted? I can't see it."

"Eh? Oh, never mind your leg! What were the figures?"

"What figures?"

"'What figures?' Snap out of it, Mister! You're on duty."

A fine one to talk, Joe thought fretfully. If that's how he's going to act, I'll just close my eyes and ignore him.

Kleuger repeated, "The figures, Mister."

"Huh? Oh, play 'em off the log if you're so damned eager!" He expected a blast at that, but none came. When next he opened his eyes Kleuger's eyes were closed. He couldn't recall whether the Skipper had played his figures back or not—nor whether he had logged them. He decided that it was time for another check but he was dreadfully thirsty; he needed a drink first. He drank carefully but still got a drop down his windpipe. A coughing spasm hurt him all over and left him so weak that he had to rest.

He pulled himself together and scanned the dials. Twelve hours and—No, wait a minute! One *day* and twelve hours—that *couldn't* be right. But their speed was over ten million miles per hour and their distance more than ninety million miles from Earth; they were beyond the orbit of Mars. "Skipper! Hey! Lieutenant Kleuger!"

Kleuger's face was a grinning mask. In dull panic Joe tried to find their situation. The coelostat showed them balanced; either the ship had wobbled back, or Kleuger had corrected it. Or had he himself? He decided to run over the log and see. Fumbling among buttons he found the one to rewind the log.

Since he didn't remember to stop it the wire ran all the

way back to light-off, then played back, zipping through silent stretches and slowing for speech. He listened to his record of the first check, then found that Phobos Station, Mars, had answered with a favorable report—to which a voice added, *"Where's the fire?"*

Yes, Kleuger had corrected balance hours earlier. The wire hurried through a blank spot, slowed again—Kleuger had dictated a letter to someone; it was unfinished and incoherent. Once Kleuger had stopped to shout, *"Joe! Joe!"* and Joe heard himself answer, *"Oh, shut up!"* He had no memory of it.

There was something he should do but he was too tired to think and he hurt all over—except his legs, he couldn't feel them. He shut his eyes and tried not to think. When he opened them the elapsed time was turning three days; he closed them and leaked tears.

A bell rang endlessly; he became aware that it was the general alarm, but he felt no interest other than a need to stop it. It was hard to find the switch, his fingers were numb. But he managed it and was about to rest from the effort, when he heard Kleuger call him. "Joe!"

"Huh?"

"Joe—don't go back to sleep or I'll turn the alarm on again. You hear me?"

"Yeah—" So Kleuger had done that—why, damn him!

"Joe, I've got to talk to you. I can't stand any more."

"'Any more' what?"

"High boost. I can't take any more—it's killing me."

"Oh, rats!" Turn on that loud bell, would he?

"I'm dying, Joe. I can't see—my eyes are shot. Joe, I've got to shut down the boost. I've got to."

"Well, what's stopping you?" Joe answered irritably.

"Don't you see, Joe? You've got to back me up. We tried and we couldn't. We'll both log it. Then it'll be all right."

"Log what?"

"Eh? Dammit, Joe, pay attention. I can't talk much. You've got to say—to say that the strain became unendurable and you advised me to shut down. I'll confirm it and it will be all right." His labored whisper was barely audible.

Joe couldn't figure out what Kleuger meant. He couldn't remember why Kleuger had put them in high boost anyhow. "*Hurry, Joe.*"

There he went, nagging him! Wake him up and then nag him—to hell with him. "Oh, go back to sleep!" He dozed off and was again jerked awake by the alarm. This time he knew where the switch was and flipped it quickly. Kleuger switched it on again, Joe turned it off. Kleuger quit trying and Joe passed out.

He came awake in free fall. He was still realizing the ecstasy of being weightless when he managed to reorient; he was in the *Salamander,* headed for Pluto. Had they reached the end of the run? No, the dial said four days and some hours. Had the tape broken? The autopilot gone haywire? He then recalled the last time he had been awake.

Kleuger had shut off the torch!

The stretched grin was gone from Kleuger's face, the features seemed slack and old. Joe called out, "Captain! Captain Kleuger!" Kleuger's eyes fluttered and lips moved but Joe heard nothing. He slithered out of the tank, moved in front of Kleuger, floated there. "Captain, can you hear me?"

The lips whispered, "I had to, boy. I saved us. Can you get us back, Joe?" His eyes opened but did not track.

"Captain, listen to me. I've got to light off again."

"Huh? No, Joe, no!"

"I've got to."

"*No!* That's an order, Mister."

Appleby stared, then with a judo chop caught the sick man on the jaw. Kleuger's head bobbed loosely. Joe pulled himself between the tanks, located a three-position switch, turned it from "Pilot & Co-Pilot" to "Co-Pilot Only"; Kleuger's controls were now dead. He glanced at Kleuger, saw that his head was not square in his collar, so he taped him properly into place, then got back in his tank. He settled his head and fumbled for the switch that would put the autopilot back on tape. There was some reason why they must finish this run—but for the life of him he could not remember why. He squeezed the switch and weight pinned him down.

He was awakened by a dizzy feeling added to the pressure. It went on for seconds, he retched futilely. When the motion stopped he peered at the dials. The *Salamander* had just completed the somersault from acceleration to deceleration. They had come half way, about eighteen hundred million miles; their speed was over three million miles per hour and beginning to drop. Joe felt that he should report it to the skipper—he had no recollection of any trouble with him. "Skipper! Hey!" Kleuger did not move. Joe called again, then resorted to the alarm.

The clangor woke, not Kleuger, but Joe's memory. He

shut it off, feeling soul sick. Topping his physical misery was shame and loss and panic as he recalled the shabby facts. He felt that he ought to log it but could not decide what to say. Beaten and ever lower in mind he gave up and tried to rest.

He woke later with something gnawing at his mind . . . something he should do for the Captain . . . something about a cargo robot—

That was it! If the robot-torch had reached Pluto, they could quit! Let's see—elapsed-time from light-off was over five days. Yes, if it ever got there, then—

He ran the wire back, listened for a recorded message. It was there: *"EarthStation to Salamander—Extremely sorry to report that robot failed rendezvous. We are depending on you.—Berrio."*

Tears of weakness and disappointment sped down his cheeks, pulled along by three and one-half gravities.

It was on the eighth day that Joe realized that Kleuger was dead. It was not the stench—he was unable to tell that from his own ripe body odors. Nor was it that the Captain had not roused since flip-over; Joe's time sense was so fogged that he did not realize this. But he had dreamt that Kleuger was shouting for him to get up, to stand up— "Hurry up, Joe!" But the weight pressed him down.

So sharp was the dream that Joe tried to answer after he woke up. Then he looked for Kleuger in the mirror. Kleuger's face was much the same, but he knew with sick horror that the captain was dead. Nevertheless he tried to arouse him with the alarm. Presently he gave up; his fingers were purple and he could feel nothing below his waist; he wondered if he were dying and hoped that he was. He slipped into that lethargy which had become his normal state.

He did not become conscious when, after more than nine days, the autopilot quenched the torch. Awareness found him floating in midroom, having somehow squirmed out of his station. He felt deliciously lazy and quite hungry; the latter eventually brought him awake.

His surroundings put past events somewhat into place. He pulled himself to his tank and examined the dials. Good grief!—it had been two hours since the ship had gone into free fall. The plan called for approach to be computed before the tape ran out, corrected on entering free fall, a new tape cut and fed in without delay, then let the autopilot make the approach. He had done nothing and wasted two hours.

He slid between tank and controls, discovering then that his legs were paralyzed. No matter—legs weren't needed in free fall, nor in the tank. His hands did not behave well, but he could use them. He was stunned when he found Kleuger's body, but steadied down and got to work. He had no idea where he was; Pluto might be millions of miles away, or almost in his lap—perhaps they had spotted him and were already sending approach data. He decided to check the wire.

He found their messages at once:

"Proserpina to Salamander—Thank God you are coming. Here are your elements at quench out—": followed by time reference, range-and-bearing figures, and doppler data.

And again: *"Here are later and better figures, Salamander—hurry!"*

And finally, only a few minutes before: *"Salamander, why the delay in light-off? Is your computer broken down? Shall we compute a ballistic for you?"*

The idea that anyone but a torcher could work a torch ballistic did not sink in. He tried to work fast, but his hands bothered him—he punched wrong numbers and had to correct them. It took him a half hour to realize that the trouble was not just his fingers. Ballistics, a subject as easy for him as checkers, was confused in his mind.

He could not work the ballistic.

"Salamander to Proserpina—Request ballistic for approach into parking orbit around Pluto."

The answer came so quickly that he knew that they had not waited for his okay. With ponderous care he cut the tape and fed it into the autopilot. It was then that he noticed the boost . . . four point oh three.

Four gravities for the approach—He had assumed that the approach would be a normal one—and so it might have been if he had not wasted three hours.

But it wasn't fair! It was too much to expect. He cursed childishly as he settled himself, fitted the collar, and squeezed the button that turned control to the autopilot. He had a few minutes of waiting time; he spent it muttering peevishly. They could have figured him a better ballistic— hell, he should have figured it. They were always pushing him around. Good old Joe, anybody's punching bag! That so-and-so Kleuger over there, grinning like a fool and leaving the work for him—if Kleuger hadn't been so confounded eager—

Acceleration hit him and he blacked out.

When the shuttle came up to meet him, they found one man dead, one nearly dead, and the cargo of whole blood.

The supply ship brought pilots for the *Salamander* and fetched Appleby home. He stayed in sick bay until ordered to Luna for treatment; on being detached he reported to Berrio, escorted by the flight surgeon. The Commodore let him know brusquely that he had done a fine job, a damn fine job! The interview ended and the surgeon helped Joe to stand; instead of leaving Joe said, "Uh, Commodore?"

"Yes, son?"

"Uh, there's one thing I don't understand, uh, what I don't understand is, uh, this: why do I have to go, uh, to the geriatrics clinic at Luna City? That's for old people, uh? That's what I've always understood—the way I understand it. Sir?"

The surgeon cut in, "I told you, Joe. They have the very best physiotherapy. We got special permission for you."

Joe looked perplexed. "Is that right, sir? I feel funny, going to an old folks', uh, hospital?"

"That's right, son."

Joe grinned sheepishly. "Okay, sir, uh, if you say so."

They started to leave. "Doctor—stay a moment. Messenger, help Mr. Appleby."

"Joe, can you make it?"

"Uh, sure! My legs are lots better—see?" He went out, leaning on the messenger.

Berrio said, "Doctor, tell me straight: will Joe get well?"

"No, sir."

"Will he get better?"

"Some, perhaps. Lunar gravity makes it easy to get the most out of what a man has left."

"But will his mind clear up?"

The doctor hesitated. "It's this way, sir. Heavy acceleration is a speeded-up aging process. Tissues break down, capillaries rupture, the heart does many times its proper work. And there is hypoxia, from failure to deliver enough oxygen to the brain."

The Commodore struck his desk an angry blow. The surgeon said gently, "Don't take it so hard, sir."

"Damn it, man—think of the way he was. Just a kid, all bounce and vinegar—now look at him! He's an old man—senile."

"Look at it this way," urged the surgeon, "you expended one man, but you saved two hundred and seventy."

"'Expended one man'? If you mean Kleuger, he gets a medal and his wife gets a pension. That's the best any of us can expect. I wasn't thinking of Kleuger."

"Neither was I," answered the surgeon.

Goldfish Bowl

On the horizon lay the immobile cloud which capped the incredible waterspouts known as the Pillars of Hawaii.

Captain Blake lowered his binoculars. "There they stand, gentlemen."

In addition to the naval personnel of the watch, the bridge of the hydrographic survey ship U.S.S. *Mahan* held two civilians; the captain's words were addressed to them. The elder and smaller of the pair peered intently through a spyglass he had borrowed from the quartermaster. "I can't make them out," he complained.

"Here—try my glasses, doctor," Blake suggested, passing over his binoculars. He turned to the officer of the deck and added, "Have the forward range finder manned, if you please, Mr. Mott." Lieutenant Mott caught the eye of the bos'n's mate of the watch, listening from a discreet distance, and jerked a thumb upward. The petty officer stepped to the microphone, piped a shrill stand-by, and the metallic voice of the loud-speaker filled the ship, drowning out the next words of the captain:

"Raaaaange one! Maaaaaaaan and cast loose!"

"I asked," the captain repeated, "if that was any better."

"I think I see them," Jacobson Graves acknowledged. "Two dark vertical stripes, from the cloud to the horizon."

"That's it."

The other civilian, Bill Eisenberg, had taken the telescope when Graves had surrendered it for the binoculars. "I got 'em too," he announced. "There's nothing wrong with this 'scope, Doc. But they don't look as big as I had expected," he admitted.

"They are still beyond the horizon," Blake explained. "You see only the upper segments. But they stand just under eleven thousand feet from water line to cloud—if they are still running true to form."

Graves looked up quickly. "Why the mental reservation? Haven't they been?"

Captain Blake shrugged. "Sure. Right on the nose. But they ought not to be there at all—four months ago they did not exist. How do I know what they will be doing today—or tomorrow?"

Graves nodded. "I see your point—and agree with it. Can we estimate their height from the distance?"

"I'll see." Blake stuck his head into the charthouse. "Any reading, Archie?"

"Just a second, captain." The navigator stuck his face against a voice tube and called out, "Range!"

A muffled voice replied, "Range one—no reading."

"Something greater than twenty miles," Blake told Graves cheerfully. "You'll have to wait, doctor."

Lieutenant Mott directed the quartermaster to make three bells; the captain left the bridge, leaving word that he was to be informed when the ship approached the critical limit of three miles from the Pillars. Somewhat reluctantly, Graves and Eisenberg followed him down; they had barely time enough to dress before dining with the captain.

Captain Blake's manners were old-fashioned; he did not permit the conversation to turn to shop talk until the dinner had reached the coffee and cigars stage. "Well, gentlemen," he began, as he lit up, "just what is it you propose to do?

"Didn't the Navy Department tell you?" Graves asked with a quick look.

"Not much. I have had one letter, directing me to place my ship and command at your disposal for research concerning the Pillars, and a dispatch two days ago telling me to take you aboard this morning. No details."

Graves looked nervously at Eisenberg, then back to the captain. He cleared his throat. "Uh—we propose, captain, to go up the Kanaka column and down the Wahini."

Blake gave him a sharp look, started to speak, reconsidered, and started again. "Doctor—you'll forgive me, I hope; I don't mean to be rude—but that sounds utterly crazy. A fancy way to commit suicide."

"It may be a little dangerous—"

"Hummph!"

"—but we have the means to accomplish it, if, as we believe to be true, the Kanaka column supplies the water which becomes the Wahini column on the return trip." He outlined the method. He and Eisenberg totaled between them nearly twenty-five years of bathysphere experience, eight for Eisenberg, seventeen for himself. They had brought aboard the *Mahan*, at present in an uncouth crate on the fantail, a modified bathysphere. Externally it was a bathysphere with its anchor weights removed; internally it much more nearly resembled some of the complicated barrels in which foolhardy exhibitionists have essayed the spectacular, useless trip over Niagara Falls. It would supply air, stuffy but breathable, for forty-eight hours; it held water and concentrated food for at least that period; there were even rude but adequate sanitary arrangements.

But its principal feature was an anti-shock harness, a glorified corset, a strait jacket, in which a man could hang suspended clear of the walls by means of a network of Gideon cord and steel springs. In it, a man might reasonably hope to survive most violent pummeling. He could perhaps be shot from a cannon, bounced down a hillside, subjected to the sadistic mercy of a baggage smasher, and still survive with bones intact and viscera unruptured.

Blake poked a finger at a line sketch with which Graves had illustrated his description. "You actually intend to try to ascend the Pillars in that?"

Eisenberg replied. "Not him, captain. Me."

Graves reddened. "My damned doctor—"

"*And* your colleagues," Eisenberg added. "It's this way, captain: There's nothing wrong with Doc's nerve, but he has a leaky heart, a pair of submarine ears, and a set of not-so-good arteries. So the Institute has delegated me to kinda watch over him."

"Now look here," Graves protested, "Bill, you're not going to be stuffy about this. I'm an old man; I'll never have another such chance."

"No go," Eisenberg denied. "Captain, I wish to inform you that the Institute vested title of record to that gear we brought aboard in me, just to keep the old war horse from doing anything foolish."

"That's your pidgin," Blake answered testily. "My instructions are to facilitate Dr. Graves' research. Assuming that one or the other of you wish to commit suicide in that steel coffin, how do you propose to enter the Kanaka Pillar?"

"Why, that's your job, captain. You put the sphere into the up column and pick it up again when it comes down the down column."

Blake pursed his lips, then slowly shook his head. "I can't do that."

"Huh? Why not?"

"I will not take my ship closer than three miles to the Pillars. The *Mahan* is a sound ship, but she is not built for speed. She can't make more than twelve knots. Some place inside that circle the surface current which feeds the Kanaka column will exceed twelve knots. I don't care to find out where, by losing my ship.

"There have been an unprecedented number of unreported fishing vessels out of the islands lately. I don't care to have the *Mahan* listed."

"You think they went up the column?"

"I do."

"But, look, captain," suggested Bill Eisenberg, "you wouldn't have to risk the ship. You could launch the sphere from a power boat."

Blake shook his head. "Out of the question," he said grimly. "Even if the ship's boats were built for the job, which they aren't, I will not risk naval personnel. This isn't war."

"I wonder," said Graves softly.

"What's that?"

Eisenberg chuckled. "Doc has a romantic notion that all the odd phenomena turned up in the past few years can be hooked together into one smooth theory with a single, sinister cause—everything from the Pillars to LaGrange's fireballs."

"LaGrange's fireballs? How could there be any connection there? They are simply static electricity, allee samee heat lightning. I know; I've seen 'em."

The scientists were at once attentive, Graves' pique and Eisenberg's amusement alike buried in truth-tropism. "You did? When? Where?"

"Golf course at Hilo. Last March. I was—"

"*That* case! That was one of the disappearance cases!"

"Yes, of course. I'm trying to tell you. I was standing in a sand trap near the thirteenth green, when I happened to look up—" A clear, balmy island day. No clouds, barometer normal, light breeze. Nothing to suggest atmospheric disturbance, no maxima of sunspots, no static on the radio. Without warning a half dozen, or more, giant fireballs— ball "lightning" on a unprecedented scale—floated across the golf course in a sort of skirmish line, a line described by some observers as mathematically even—an assertion denied by others.

A woman player, a tourist from the mainland, screamed and began to run. The flanking ball nearest her left its place in line and danced after her. No one seemed sure that the ball touched her—Blake could not say although he had watched it happen—but when the ball had passed on, there she lay on the grass, dead.

A local medico of somewhat flamboyant reputation insisted that he found evidence in the cadaver of both coagulation and electrolysis, but the jury that sat on the case followed the coroner's advice in calling it heart failure, a verdict heartily approved by the local chamber of commerce and tourist bureau.

The man who disappeared did not try to run; his fate came to meet him. He was a caddy, a Japanese-Portygee-Kanaka mixed breed, with no known relatives, a fact which should have made it easy to leave his name out of the news reports had not a reporter smelled it out. "He was standing on the green, not more than twenty-five yards away from me," Blake recounted, "when the fireballs approached. One passed on each side of me. My skin itched, and my hair stood up. I could smell ozone. I stood still—"

"That saved you," observed Graves.

"Nuts," said Eisenberg. "Standing in the dry sand of the trap was what saved him."

"Bill, you're a fool," Graves said wearily. "These fireball things perform with intelligent awareness."

Blake checked his account. "Why do you assume that, doctor?"

"Never mind, for the moment, please. Go on with your story."

"Hm-m-m. Well, they passed on by me. The caddy fellow was directly in the course of one of them. I don't believe he saw it—back toward it, you see. It reached him, enveloped him, passed on—but the boy was gone."

Graves nodded. "That checks with the accounts I have seen. Odd that I did not recall your name from the reports."

"I stayed in the background," Blake said shortly. "Don't like reporters."

"Hm-m-m. Anything to add to the reports that did come out? Any errors in them?"

"None that I can recall. Did the reports mention the bag of golf clubs he was carrying?"

"I think not."

"They were found on the beach, six miles away."

Eisenberg sat up. "That's news," he said. "Tell me: Was there anything to suggest how far they had fallen? Were they smashed or broken?"

Blake shook his head. "They weren't even scratched, nor was the beach sand disturbed. But they were—ice-cold."

Graves waited for him to go on; when the captain did not do so he inquired, "What do you make of it?"

"Me? I make nothing of it."

"How do you explain it?"

"I don't. Unclassified electrical phenomena. However, if you want a rough guess, I'll give you one. This fireball is a static field of high potential. It englobes the caddy and charges him, whereupon he bounces away like a pith ball—electrocuted, incidentally. When the charge dissipates, he falls into the sea."

"So? There was a case like it in Kansas, rather too far from the sea."

"The body might simply never have been found."

"They never are. But even so—how do you account for the clubs being deposited so gently? And why were they cold?"

"Dammit, man, *I* don't know! I'm no theoretician; I'm a maritime engineer by profession, an empiricist by disposition. Suppose you tell me."

"All right—but bear in mind that my hypothesis is merely tentative, a basis for investigation. I see in these several phenomena, the Pillars, the giant fireballs, a number of other assorted phenomena which should never have happened, but did—including the curious case of a small mountain peak south of Boulder, Colorado, which had its tip leveled off 'spontaneously'—I see in these things evidence of intelligent direction, a single conscious cause." He shrugged. "Call it the 'X' factor. I'm looking for X."

Eisenberg assumed a look of mock sympathy. "Poor old Doc," he sighed. "Sprung a leak at last."

The other two ignored the crack. Blake inquired, "You are primarily an ichthyologist, aren't you?"

"Yes."

"How did you get started along this line?"

"I don't know. Curiosity, I suppose. My boisterous young friend here would tell you that ichthyology is derived from 'icky.'"

Blake turned to Eisenberg. "But aren't *you* an ichthyologist?"

"Hell, no! I'm an oceanographer specializing in ecology."

"He's quibbling," observed Graves. "Tell Captain Blake about Cleo and Pat."

Eisenberg looked embarrassed. "They're damned nice pets," he said defensively.

Blake looked puzzled; Graves explained. "He kids me, but *his* secret shame is a pair of goldfish. Goldfish! You'll find 'em in the washbasin in his stateroom this minute."

"Scientific interest?" Blake inquired with a dead pan.

"Oh, no! He thinks they are devoted to him."

"They're damned nice pets," Eisenberg insisted. "They don't bark, they don't scratch, they don't make messes. And Cleo does so have expression!"

In spite of his initial resistance to their plans Blake cooperated actively in trying to find a dodge whereby the proposed experiment could be performed without endangering naval personnel or material. He liked these two; he understood their curious mixture of selfless recklessness and extreme caution; it matched his own—it was professionalism, as distinguished from economic motivation.

He offered the services of his master diver, an elderly commissioned warrant officer, and his technical crew in checking their gear. "You know," he added, "there is some reason to believe that your bathysphere could make the round trip, aside from the proposition that what goes up must come down. You know of the VJ-14?"

"Was that the naval plane lost in the early investigation?"

"Yes." He buzzed for his orderly. "Have my writer bring up the jacket on the VJ-14," he directed.

Attempts to reconnoiter the strange "permanent" cloud and its incredible waterspouts had been made by air soon after its discovery. Little was learned. A plane would penetrate the cloud. Its ignition would fail; out it would glide, unharmed, whereupon the engines would fire again. Back into the cloud—engine failure. The vertical reach of the cloud was greater than the ceiling of any plane.

"The VJ-14," Blake stated, referring occasionally to the file jacket which had been fetched, "made an air reconnaissance of the Pillars themselves on 12 May, attended by the U.S.S. *Pelican*. Besides the pilot and radioman she carried a cinematographer and a chief aerographer. Mm-m-m—only the last two entries seem to be pertinent: 'Changing course. Will fly between the Pillars—14,' and '0913—Ship does not respond to controls—14.' Telescopic observation from the *Pelican* shows that she made a tight upward spiral around the Kanaka Pillar, about one and a half turns, and was sucked into the column itself. Nothing was seen to fall.

"Incidentally the pilot, Lieutenant—m-m-m-m, yes— Mattson—Lieutenant Mattson was exonerated posthumously by the court of inquiry. Oh, yes, here's the point pertinent to our question: From the log of the *Pelican*: '1709—Picked up wreckage identified as part of VJ-14. See additional sheet for itemized description.' We needn't bother with that. Point is, they picked it up four miles from the base of the Wahini Pillar on the side away from the Kanaka. The inference is obvious and your scheme might work. Not that you'd live through it."

"I'll chance it," Eisenberg stated.

"Mm-m-m—yes. But I was going to suggest we send up a dead load, say a crate of eggs packed into a hogshead." The buzzer from the bridge sounded; Captain Blake raised his voice toward the brass funnel of a voice tube in the overhead. "Yes?"

"Eight o'clock, Captain. Eight o'clock lights and galley fires out; prisoners secured."

"Thank you, sir." Blake stood up. "We can get together on the details in the morning."

A fifty-foot motor launch bobbed listlessly astern the *Mahan*. A nine-inch coir line joined it to its mother ship; bound to it at fathom intervals was a telephone line ending in a pair of headphones worn by a signalman seated in the stern sheets of the launch. A pair of flags and a spyglass lay on the thwart beside him; his blouse had crawled up, exposing part of the lurid cover of a copy of *Dynamic Tales*, smuggled along as a precaution against boredom.

Already in the boat were the coxswain, the engineman, the boat officer, Graves, and Eisenberg. With them, forward in the boat, was a breaker of water rations, two fifty-gallon drums of gasoline—and a hogshead. It contained not only a carefully packed crate of eggs but also a jury-rigged smoke-signal device, armed three ways—delayed action set for eight, nine and ten hours; radio relay triggered from the ship; and simple salt-water penetration to complete an electrical circuit. The torpedo gunner in charge of diving hoped that one of them might work and thereby aid in locating the hogshead. He was busy trying to devise more nearly foolproof gear for the bathysphere.

The boat officer signaled ready to the bridge. A megaphoned bellow responded, "Pay her out handsomely!" The boat drifted slowly away from the ship and directly toward the Kanaka Pillar, three miles away.

The Kanaka Pillar loomed above them, still nearly a

mile away but loweringly impressive nevertheless. The place where it disappeared in cloud seemed almost overhead, falling toward them. Its five-hundred-foot-thick trunk gleamed purplish-black, more like polished steel than water.

"Try your engine again, coxswain."

"Aye, aye, sir!" The engine coughed, took hold; the engineman eased in the clutch, the screw bit in, and the boat surged forward, taking the strain off the towline. "Slack line, sir."

"Stop your engine." The boat officer turned to his passengers. "What's the trouble, Mr. Eisenberg? Cold feet?"

"No, dammit—seasick. I *hate* a small boat."

"Oh, that's too bad. I'll see if we haven't got a pickle in that chow up forward."

"Thanks, but pickles don't help me. Never mind, I can stand it."

The boat officer shrugged, turned and let his eye travel up the dizzy length of the column. He whistled, something which he had done every time he had looked at it. Eisenberg, made nervous by his nausea, was beginning to find it cause for homicide. "*Whew!* You really intend to try to go up that thing, Mr. Eisenberg?"

"I do!"

The boat officer looked startled at the tone, laughed uneasily, and added, "Well, you'll be worse than seasick, if you ask me."

Nobody had. Graves knew his friend's temperament; he made conversation for the next few minutes.

"Try your engine, coxswain." The petty officer acknowledged, and reported back quickly:

"Starter doesn't work, sir."

"Help the engineman get a line on the flywheel. I'll take the tiller."

The two men cranked the engine over easily, but got no answering cough. "Prime it!" Still no results.

The boat officer abandoned the useless tiller and jumped down into the engine space to lend his muscle to heaving on the cranking line. Over his shoulder he ordered the signalman to notify the ship.

"Launch Three, calling bridge. Launch Three, calling bridge. Bridge—reply! Testing—testing." The signalman slipped a phone off one ear. "Phone's dead, sir."

"Get busy with your flags. Tell 'em to haul us in!" The officer wiped sweat from his face and straightened up. He glanced nervously at the current *slap-slapping* against the boat's side.

Graves touched his arm. "How about the barrel?"

"Put it over the side if you like. I'm busy. Can't you raise them, Sears?"

"I'm trying, sir."

"Come on, Bill," Graves said to Eisenberg. The two of them slipped forward in the boat, threading their way past the engine on the side away from the three men sweating over the flywheel. Graves cut the hogshead loose from its lashings, then the two attempted to get a purchase on the awkward, unhandy object. It and its light load weighed less than two hundred pounds, but it was hard to manage, especially on the uncertain footing of heaving floorboards.

They wrestled it outboard somehow, with one smashed finger for Eisenberg, a badly banged shin for Graves. It splashed heavily, drenching them with sticky salt water, and bobbed astern, carried rapidly toward the Kanaka Pillar by the current which fed it.

"Ship answers, sir!"

"Good! Tell them to haul us in—*carefully*." The boat officer jumped out of the engine space and ran forward, where he checked again the secureness with which the towline was fastened.

Graves tapped him on the shoulder. "Can't we stay here until we see the barrel enter the column?"

"No! Right now you had better pray that that line holds, instead of worrying about the barrel—or we go up the column, too. Sears, has the ship acknowledged?"

"Just now, sir."

"Why a coir line, Mr. Parker?" Eisenberg inquired, his nausea forgotten in the excitement. "I'd rather depend on steel, or even good stout Manila."

"Because coir floats, and the others don't," the officer answered snappishly. "Two miles of line would drag us to the bottom. *Sears!* Tell them to ease the strain. We're shipping water."

"Aye, aye, sir!"

The hogshead took less than four minutes to reach the column, enter it, a fact which Graves ascertained by borrowing the signalman's glass to follow it on the last leg of its trip—which action won him a dirty look from the nervous boat officer. Some minutes later, when the boat was about five hundred yards farther from the Pillar than it had been at nearest approach, the telephone came suddenly to life. The starter of the engine was tested immediately; the engine roared into action.

The trip back was made with engine running to take

the strain off the towline—at half speed and with some maneuvering, in order to avoid fouling the screw with the slack bight of the line.

The smoke signal worked—one circuit or another. The plume of smoke was sighted two miles south of the Wahini Pillar, elapsed time from the moment the vessel had entered the Kanaka column just over eight hours.

Bill Eisenberg climbed into the saddle of the exerciser in which he was to receive antibends treatment—thirty minutes of hard work to stir up his circulation while breathing an atmosphere of helium and oxygen, at the end of which time the nitrogen normally dissolved in his blood stream would be largely replaced by helium. The exerciser itself was simply an old bicycle mounted on a stationary platform. Blake looked it over. "You needn't have bothered to bring this," he remarked. "We've a better one aboard. Standard practice for diving operations these days."

"We didn't know that," Graves answered. "Anyhow this one will do. All set, Bill?"

"I guess so." He glanced over his shoulder to where the steel bulk of the bathysphere lay, uncrated, checked and equipped, ready to be swung outboard by the boat crane. "Got the gasket-sealing compound?"

"Sure. The Iron Maiden is all right. The gunner and will seal you in. Here's your mask."

Eisenberg accepted the inhaling mask, started to strap it on, checked himself. Graves noticed the look on his face. "What's the trouble, son?"

"Doc . . . uh—"

"Yes?"

"I say—you'll look out for Cleo and Pat, won't you?"

"Why, sure. But they won't need anything in the length of time you'll be gone."

"Um-m-m, no, I suppose not. But you'll look out for 'em?"

"Sure."

"O.K." Eisenberg slipped the inhaler over his face, waved his hand to the gunner waiting by the gas bottles. The gunner eased open the cut-off valves, the gas lines hissed, and Eisenberg began to pedal like a six-day racer.

With thirty minutes to kill, Blake invited Graves to go forward with him for a smoke and a stroll on the fo'c's'le. They had completed about twenty turns when Blake paused by the wildcat, took his cigar from his mouth and remarked, "Do you know, I believe he has a good chance of completing the trip."

"So? I'm glad to hear that."

"Yes, I do, really. The success of the trial with the dead load convinced me. And whether the smoke gear works or not, if that globe comes back down the Wahini Pillar, *I'll find it.*"

"I know you will. It was a good idea of yours, to paint it yellow."

"Help us to spot it, all right. I don't think he'll learn anything, however. He won't see a thing through those ports but blue water, from the time he enters the column to the time we pick him up."

"Perhaps so."

"What else *could* he see?"

"I don't know. Whatever it is that *made* those Pillars, perhaps."

Blake dumped the ashes from his cigar carefully over the rail before replying. "Doctor, I don't understand you. To my mind, those Pillars are a natural, even though strange, phenomenon."

"And to me it's equally obvious that they are not 'natural.' They exhibit intelligent interference with the ordinary processes of nature as clearly as if they had a sign saying so hung on them."

"I don't see how you can say that. Obviously, they are not man-made."

"No."

"Then who did make them—if they were made?"

"I don't know."

Blake started to speak, shrugged, and held his tongue. They resumed their stroll. Graves turned aside to chuck his cigarette overboard, glancing outboard as he did so.

He stopped, stared, then called out: "Captain Blake!"

"Eh?" The captain turned and looked where Graves pointed. "Great God! Fireballs!"

"That's what I thought."

"They're some distance away," Blake observed, more to himself than to Graves. He turned decisively. "Bridge!" he shouted. "Bridge! Bridge ahoy!"

"Bridge, aye aye!"

"Mr. Weems—pass the word: 'All hands, below decks. Dog down all ports. Close all hatches. And close up the bridge itself! Sound the general alarm."

"Aye aye, sir!"

"Move!" Turning to Graves, he added, "Come inside." Graves followed him; the captain stopped to dog down the door by which they entered himself. Blake pounded up the inner ladders to the bridge, Graves in his train. The ship was filled with the whine of the bos'n pipe, the raucous voice of the loud-speaker, the clomp of hurrying feet, and the monotonous, menacing *cling-cling-cling!* of the general alarm.

The watch on the bridge were still struggling with the last of the heavy glass shutters of the bridge when the captain burst into their midst. "I'll take it, Mr. Weems," he snapped. In one continuous motion he moved from one side of the bridge to the other, letting his eye sweep the port side aft, the fo'c's'le, the starboard side aft, and finally rest on the fireballs—distinctly nearer and heading straight for the ship. He cursed. "Your friend did not get the news," he said to Graves. He grasped the crank which could open or close the after starboard shutter of the bridge.

Graves looked past his shoulder, saw what he meant— the afterdeck was empty, save for one lonely figure pedaling away on the stationary bicycle. The LaGrange fireballs were closing in.

The shutter stuck, jammed tight, would not open. Blake stopped trying, swung quickly to the loud-speaker control panel, and cut in the whole board without bothering to select the proper circuit. "Eisenberg! *Get below!*"

Eisenberg must have heard his name called, for he turned his head and looked over his shoulder—Graves saw distinctly—just as the fireball reached him. It passed on, and the saddle of the exerciser was empty.

The exerciser was undamaged, they found, when they were able to examine it. The rubber hose to the inhaler mask had been cut smoothly. There was no blood, no marks. Bill Eisenberg was simply gone.

"I'm going up."

"You are in no physical shape to do so, doctor."

"You are in no way responsible, Captain Blake."

"I know that. You may go if you like—after we have searched for your friend's body."

"Search be damned! I'm going up to *look* for him."

"Huh? Eh? How's that?"

"If you are right, he's dead, and there is no point in searching for his body. If I'm right, there is just an outside chance of finding him—up there!" He pointed toward the cloud cap of the Pillars.

Blake looked him over slowly, then turned to the master diver. "Mr. Hargreave, find an inhaler mask for Dr. Graves."

They gave him thirty minutes of conditioning against the caisson disease while Blake looked on with expressionless silence. The ship's company, bluejackets and officers alike, stood back and kept quiet; they walked on eggs when the Old Man had that look.

Exercise completed, the diver crew dressed Graves rapidly and strapped him into the bathysphere with dispatch, in order not to expose him too long to the nitrogen in the air. Just before the escape port was dogged down Graves spoke up. "Captain Blake."

"Yes, doctor?"

"Bill's goldfish—will you look out for them?"

"Certainly, doctor."

"Thanks."

"Not at all. Are you ready?"

"Ready."

Blake stepped forward, stuck an arm through the port of the sphere and shook hands with Graves. "Good luck." He withdrew his arm. "Seal it up."

They lowered it over the side; two motor launches nosed it half a mile in the direction of the Kanaka Pillar where the current was strong enough to carry it along. There they left it and bucked the current back to the ship, were hoisted in.

Blake followed it with his glasses from the bridge. It drifted slowly at first, then with increased speed as it approached the base of the column. It whipped into rapid motion the last few hundred yards; Blake saw a flash of yellow just above the water line, then nothing more.

Eight hours—no plume of smoke. Nine hours, ten hours, nothing. After twenty-four hours of steady patrol in the vicinity of the Wahini Pillar, Blake radioed the Bureau.

Four days of vigilance—Blake knew that the bathysphere's passenger must be dead; whether by suffocation, drowning, implosion, or other means was not important. He so reported and received orders to proceed on duty assigned. The ship's company was called to quarters; Captain Blake read the service for the dead aloud in a harsh voice, dropped over the side some rather wilted hibiscus blooms—all that his steward could produce at the time—and went to the bridge to set his course for Pearl Harbor.

On the way to the bridge he stopped for a moment at his cabin and called to his steward: "You'll find some goldfish in the stateroom occupied by Mr. Eisenberg. Find an appropriate container and place them in my cabin."

"Yes, suh, Cap'n."

When Bill Eisenberg came to his senses he was in a Place.

Sorry, but no other description is suitable; it lacked features. Oh, not entirely, of course—it was not dark where he was, nor was it in a state of vacuum, nor was it cold, nor was it too small for comfort. But it did lack features to such a remarkable extent that he had difficulty in estimating the size of the place. Consider—stereo vision, by which we estimate the size of things *directly*, does not work beyond twenty feet or so. At greater distances we depend on previous knowledge of the true size of familiar objects, usually making our estimates subconsciously—a man *so high* is about *that far* away, and vice versa.

But the Place contained no familiar objects. The ceiling was a considerable distance over his head, too far to touch by jumping. The floor curved up to join the ceiling and thus prevented further lateral progress of more than a dozen paces or so. He would become aware of the obstacle by losing his balance. (He had no reference lines by which to judge the vertical; furthermore, his sense of innate balance was affected by the mistreatment his inner ears had undergone through years of diving. It was easier to sit than to walk, nor was there any reason to walk, after the first futile attempt at exploration.)

When he first woke up he stretched and opened his eyes, looked around. The lack of detail confused him.

It was as if he were on the inside of a giant eggshell, illuminated from without by a soft, mellow, slightly amber light. The formless vagueness bothered him; he closed his eyes, shook his head, and opened them again—no better.

He was beginning to remember his last experience before losing consciousness—the fireball swooping down, his frenzied, useless attempt to duck, the "Hold your hats, boys!" thought that flashed through his mind in the long-drawn-out split second before contact. His orderly mind began to look for explanations. Knocked cold, he thought, and my optic nerve paralyzed. Wonder if I'm blind for good.

Anyhow, they ought not to leave him alone like this in his present helpless condition. "Doc!" he shouted. "Doc Graves!"

No answer, no echo—he became aware that there was *no* sound, save for his own voice, none of the random little sounds that fill completely the normal "dead" silence. This place was as silent as the inside of a sack of flour. Were his ears shot, too?

No, he had heard his own voice. At that moment he realized that he was looking at his own hands. Why, there was nothing wrong with his eyes—he could see them plainly!

And the rest of himself, too. He was naked.

It might have been several hours later, it might have been moments, when he reached the conclusion that he was dead. It was the only hypothesis which seemed to cover the facts. A dogmatic agnostic by faith, he had expected no survival after death; he had expected to go out like a light, with a sudden termination of consciousness.

However, he had been subjected to a charge of static electricity more than sufficient to kill a man; when he regained awareness, he found himself without all the usual experience which makes up living. Therefore—he was dead. Q.E.D.

To be sure, he seemed to have a body, but he was acquainted with the subjective-objective paradox. He still had memory, the strongest pattern in one's memory is body awareness. This was not his body, but his detailed sensation memory of it. So he reasoned. Probably, he thought, my dream-body will slough away as my memory of the object-body fades.

There was nothing to do, nothing to experience, nothing to distract his mind. He fell asleep at last, thinking that, if this were death, it was damned dull!

He awoke refreshed, but quite hungry and extremely thirsty. The, matter of dead, or not-dead, no longer concerned him; he was interested in neither theology nor metaphysics. He was hungry.

Furthermore, he experienced on awakening a phenomenon which destroyed most of the basis for his intellectual belief in his own death—it had never reached the stage of emotional conviction. Present there with him in the Place he found material objects other than himself, objects which could be seen and touched.

And eaten.

Which last was not immediately evident, for they did not look like food. There were two sorts. The first was an amorphous lump of nothing in particular, resembling a grayish cheese in appearance, slightly greasy to the touch, and not appetizing. The second sort was a group of objects of uniform and delightful appearance. They were spheres, a couple of dozen; each one seemed to Bill Eisenberg to be a duplicate of a crystal ball he had once purchased— true Brazilian rock crystal the perfect beauty of which he had not been able to resist; he had bought it and smuggled it home to gloat over in private.

The little spheres were like that in appearance. He touched one. It was smooth as crystal and had the same chaste coolness, but it was soft as jelly. It quivered like jelly, causing the lights within it to dance delightfully, before resuming its perfect roundness.

Pleasant as they were, they did not look like food, whereas the cheesy, soapy lump might be. He broke off a small piece, sniffed it, and tasted it tentatively. It was sour, nauseating, unpleasant. He spat it out, made a wry face, and wished heartily that he could brush his teeth. If that was food, he would have to be much hungrier—

He turned his attention back to the delightful little spheres of crystal-like jelly. He balanced them in his palms, savoring their soft, smooth touch. In the heart of each he saw his own reflection, imagined in miniature, made elfin and graceful. He became aware almost for the first time of the serene beauty of the human figure, almost any human figure, when viewed as a composition and not as a mass of colloidal detail.

But thirst became more pressing than narcissist admiration. It occurred to him that the smooth, cool spheres, if held in the mouth, might promote salivation, as pebbles will. He tried it; the sphere he selected struck against his lower teeth as he placed it in his mouth, and his lips and chin were suddenly wet, while drops trickled down his chest. The spheres were water, nothing but water, no cellophane skin, no container of any sort. Water had been delivered to him, neatly packaged, by some esoteric trick of surface tension.

He tried another, handling it more carefully to insure that it was not pricked by his teeth until he had it in his mouth. It worked; his mouth was filled with cool, pure water—too quickly; he choked. But he had caught on to the trick; he drank four of the spheres.

His thirst satisfied, he became interested in the strange trick whereby water became its own container. The spheres were tough; he could not squeeze them into breaking down, nor did smashing them hard against the floor disturb their precarious balance. They bounced like golf balls and came up for more. He managed to pinch the surface of one between thumb and fingernail. It broke down at once, and the water trickled between his fingers—water alone, no skin nor foreign substance. It seemed that a cut alone could disturb the balance of tensions; even wetting had no effect; for he could hold one carefully in his mouth, remove it, and dry it off on his own skin.

He decided that, since his supply was limited, and no more water was in prospect, it would be wise to conserve what he had and experiment no further.

The relief of thirst increased the demands of hunger. He turned his attention again to the other substance and found that he could force himself to chew and swallow. It might not be food, it might even be poison, but it filled his stomach and stayed the pangs. He even felt well fed, once he had cleared out the taste with another sphere of water.

After eating he rearranged his thoughts. He was not dead, or, if he were, the difference between living and being dead was imperceptible, verbal. OK, he was alive. But he was shut up alone. Somebody knew where he was and was aware of him, for he had been supplied with food and drink—mysteriously but cleverly. *Ergo*—he was a prisoner, a word which implies a warden.

Whose prisoner? He had been struck by a LaGrange fireball and had awakened in his cell. It looked, he was forced to admit, as if Doc Graves had been right; the fireballs were intelligently controlled. Furthermore, the person or persons behind them had novel ideas as to how to care for prisoners as well as strange ways of capturing them.

Eisenberg was a brave man, as brave as the ordinary run of the race from which he sprang—a race as foolhardy as Pekingese dogs. He had the high degree of courage so common in the human race, a race capable of conceiving death, yet able to face its probability daily, on the highway, on the obstetrics table, on the battlefield, in the air, in the subway—and to face lightheartedly the certainty of death in the end.

Eisenberg was apprehensive, but not panic-stricken. His situation was decidedly interesting; he was no longer bored. If he were a prisoner, it seemed likely that his captor would come to investigate him presently, perhaps to question him, perhaps to attempt to use him in some fashion. The fact that he had been saved and not killed implied some sort of plans for his future. Very well, he would concentrate on meeting whatever exigency might come with a calm and resourceful mind. In the meantime, there was nothing he could do toward freeing himself; he had satisfied himself of that. This was a prison which would baffle Houdini—smooth continuous walls, no way to get a purchase.

He had thought once that he had a clue to escape; the cells had sanitary arrangements of some sort, for that which his body rejected went elsewhere. But he got no further with that lead; the cage was self-cleaning—and that was that. He could not tell how it was done. It baffled him.

Presently he slept again.

When he awoke, one element only was changed—the food and water had been replenished. The "day" passed without incident, save for his own busy fruitless thoughts.

And the next "day." And the next.

He determined to stay awake long enough to find out how food and water were placed in his cell. He made a colossal effort to do so, using drastic measures to stimulate his body into consciousness. He bit his lips, he bit his tongue. He nipped the lobes of his ears viciously with his nails. He concentrated on difficult mental feats.

Presently he dozed off; when he awoke, the food and water had been replenished.

The waking periods were followed by sleep, renewed hunger and thirst, the satisfying of same, and more sleep. It was after the sixth or seventh sleep that he decided that some sort of a calendar was necessary to his mental health. He had no means of measuring time except by his sleeps; he arbitrarily designated them as days. He had no means of keeping records, save his own body. He made that do. A thumbnail shred, torn off, made a rough tattooing needle. Continued scratching of the same area on his thigh produced a red welt which persisted for a day or two, and could be renewed. Seven welts made a week. The progression of such welts along ten fingers and ten toes gave him the means to measure twenty weeks— which was a much longer period than he anticipated any need to measure.

He had tallied the second set of seven thigh welts on the ring finger of his left hand when the next event occurred to disturb his solitude. When he awoke from the sleep following said tally, he became suddenly and overwhelmingly aware that he was not alone!

There was a human figure sleeping beside him. When he had convinced himself that he was truly wide awake— his dreams were thoroughly populated—he grasped the figure by the shoulder and shook it. "Doc!" he yelled. "Doc! Wake up!"

Graves opened his eyes, focused them, sat up, and put out his hand. "Hi, Bill," he remarked. "I'm damned glad to see you."

"Doc!" He pounded the older man on the back. "Doc! For Criminy sake! You don't know how glad *I* am to see *you.*"

"I can guess."

"Look, Doc—where have you been? How did you get here? Did the fireballs snag you, too?"

"One thing at a time, son. Let's have breakfast." There was a double ration of food and water on the "floor" near them. Graves picked up a sphere, nicked it expertly, and drank it without losing a drop. Eisenberg watched him knowingly.

"You've been here for some time."

"That's right."

"Did the fireballs get you the same time they got me?"

"No." He reached for the food. "I came up the Kanaka Pillar."

"What!"

"That's right. Matter of fact, I was looking for you."

"The hell you say!"

"But I do say. It looks as if my wild hypothesis was right; the Pillars and the fireballs are different manifestations of the same cause—X!"

It seemed almost possible to hear the wheels whir in Eisenberg's head. "But, Doc . . . look here, Doc, that means your whole hypothesis was correct. Somebody *did* the whole thing. Somebody has us locked up here now."

"That's right." He munched slowly. He seemed tired, older and thinner than the way Eisenberg remembered him. "Evidence of intelligent control. Always was. No other explanation."

"But *who?*"

"Ah!"

"Some foreign power? Are we up against something utterly new in the way of an attack?"

"Hummph! Do you think the Russians, for instance, would bother to serve us water like *this?*" He held up one of the dainty little spheres.

"Who, then?"

"I wouldn't know. Call 'em Martians—that's a convenient way to think of them."

"Why Martians?"

"No reason. I said that was a convenient way to think of them."

"Convenient how?"

"Convenient because it keeps you from thinking of them as human beings—which they obviously aren't. Nor animals. Something very intelligent, but not animals, because they are smarter than we are. Martians."

"But . . . but—Wait a minute. Why do you assume that your X people aren't human? Why not humans who have a lot of stuff on the ball that we don't have? New scientific advances?"

"That's a fair question," Graves answered, picking his teeth with a forefinger. "I'll give you a fair answer. Because in the present state of the world we know pretty near where all the best minds are and what they are doing. Advances like these couldn't be hidden and would be a long time in developing. X indicates evidence of a half a dozen different lines of development that are clear beyond our ken and which would require years of work by hundreds of researchers, to say the very least. *Ipso facto*, nonhuman science.

"Of course," he continued, "if you want to postulate a mad scientist and a secret laboratory, I can't argue with you. But I'm not writing Sunday supplements."

Bill Eisenberg kept very quiet for some time, while he considered what Graves said in the light of his own experience. "You're right, Doc," he finally admitted. "Shucks—you're usually right when we have an argument. It has to be Martians. Oh, I don't mean inhabitants of Mars; I mean some form of intelligent life from outside this planet."

"Maybe."

"But you just said so!"

"No, I said it was a convenient way to look at it."

"But it has to be by elimination."

"Elimination is a tricky line of reasoning."

"What else could it be?"

"Mm-m-m. I'm not prepared to say just what I do think—yet. But there are stronger reasons than we have mentioned for concluding that we are up against nonhumans. Psychological reasons."

"What sort?"

"X doesn't treat prisoners in any fashion that arises out of human behavior patterns. Think it over."

They had a lot to talk about; much more than X, even though X was a subject they were bound to return to. Graves gave Bill a simple bald account of how he happened to go up the Pillar—an account which Bill found very moving for what was left out, rather than told. He felt suddenly very humble and unworthy as he looked at his elderly, frail friend. "Doc, you don't look well."

"I'll do."

"That trip up the Pillar was hard on you. You shouldn't have tried it."

Graves shrugged. "I made out all right." But he had not, and Bill could see that he had not. The old man was "poorly."

They slept and they ate and they talked and they slept again. The routine that Eisenberg had grown used to alone continued, save with company. But Graves grew no stronger.

✿ ✿ ✿ .

"Doc, it's up to us to do something about it."

"About what?"

"The whole situation. This thing that has happened to us is an intolerable menace to the whole human race. We don't know what may have happened down below—"

"Why do you say 'down below'?"

"Why, you came up the Pillar."

"Yes, true—but I don't know when or how I was taken out of the bathysphere, nor where they may have taken me. But go ahead. Let's have your idea."

"Well, but—OK—we don't know what may have happened to the rest of the human race. The fireballs may be picking them off one at a time, with no chance to fight back and no way of guessing what has been going on. We have some idea of the answer. It's up to us to escape and warn them. There may be some way of fighting back. It's our duty; the whole future of the human race may depend on it."

Graves was silent so long after Bill had finished his tocsin that Bill began to feel embarrassed, a bit foolish. But when he finally spoke it was to agree. "I think you are right, Bill. I think it quite possible that you are right. Not necessarily, but distinctly possible. And that possibility does place an obligation on us to all mankind. I've known it. I knew it before we got into this mess, but I did not have enough data to justify shouting, 'Wolf!'"

"The question is," he went on, "how can we give such a warning—now?"

"We've got to escape!"

"Ah."

"There *must* be some way."

"Can you suggest one?"

"Maybe. We haven't been able to find any way in or out of this place, but there must be a way—has to be; we were brought in. Furthermore, our rations are put inside every day—somehow. I tried once to stay awake long enough to see how it was done, but I fell asleep—"

"So did I."

"Uh-huh. I'm not surprised. But there are two of us now; we could take turns, watch on and watch off, until something happened."

Graves nodded. "It's worth trying."

Since they had no way of measuring the watches, each kept the vigil until sleepiness became intolerable, then awakened the other. But nothing happened. Their food ran out, was not replaced. They conserved their water balls with care, were finally reduced to one, which was not drunk because each insisted on being noble about it—the other must drink it! But still no manifestation of any sort from their unseen captors.

After an unmeasured and unestimated length of time—but certainly long, almost intolerably long—at a time when Eisenberg was in a light, troubled sleep, he was suddenly awakened by a touch and the sound of his name. He sat up, blinking, disoriented. "Who? What? Wha'sa matter?"

"I must have dozed off," Graves said miserably. "I'm sorry, Bill." Eisenberg looked where Graves pointed. Their food and water had been renewed.

Eisenberg did not suggest a renewal of the experiment. In the first place, it seemed evident that their keepers did not intend for them to learn the combination to their cell and were quite intelligent enough to outmaneuver their necessarily feeble attempts. In the second place, Graves was an obviously sick man; Eisenberg did not have the heart to suggest another long, grueling, half-starved vigil.

But, lacking knowledge of the combination, it appeared impossible to break jail. A naked man is a particularly helpless creature; lacking materials wherewith to fashion tools, he can do little. Eisenberg would have swapped his chances for eternal bliss for a diamond drill, an acetylene torch, or even a rusty, secondhand chisel. Without tools of some sort it was impressed on him that he stood about as much chance of breaking out of his cage as his goldfish, Cleo and Patra, had of chewing their way out of a glass bowl.

"Doc?"

"Yes, son."

"We've tackled this the wrong way. We know that X is intelligent; instead of trying to escape, we should be trying to establish communication."

"How?"

"I don't know. But there must be *some* way."

But if there was, he could never conjure it up. Even if he assumed that his captors could see and hear him, how was he to convey intelligence to them by word or gesture? Was it theoretically possible for any nonhuman being, no matter how intelligent, to find a pattern of meaning in human speech symbols, if he encountered them without context, without background, without pictures, without *pointing?* It is certainly true that the human race, working under much more favorable circumstances, has failed almost utterly to learn the languages of the other races of animals.

What should he do to attract their attention, stimulate their interest? Recite the "Gettysburg Address"? Or the multiplication table? Or, if he used gestures, would deaf-and-dumb language mean any more, or any less, to his captors than the sailor's hornpipe?

"Doc?"

"What is it, Bill?" Graves was sinking; he rarely initiated a conversation these "days."

"Why are we here? I've had it in the back of my mind that *eventually* they would take us out and do something with us. Try to question us, maybe. But it doesn't look like they meant to."

"No, it doesn't."

"Then why are we here? Why do they take care of us?"

Graves paused quite a long time before answering: "I think that they are expecting us to reproduce."

"What!"

Graves shrugged.

"But that's ridiculous."

"Surely. But would they know it?"

"But they are intelligent."

Graves chuckled, the first time he had done so in many sleeps. "Do you know Roland Young's little verse about the flea:

"'*A funny creature is the Flea*
You cannot tell the She from He.
But He can tell—and so can She.'

✿ ✿ ✿

"After all, the visible differences between men and women are quite superficial and almost negligible—except to men and women!"

Eisenberg found the suggestion repugnant, almost revolting; he struggled against it. "But look, Doc—even a little study would show them that the human race is divided up into sexes. After all, we aren't the first specimens they've studied."

"Maybe they don't study us."

"Huh?"

"Maybe we are just—pets."

Pets! Bill Eisenberg's morale had stood up well in the face of danger and uncertainty. This attack on it was more subtle. Pets! He had thought of Graves and himself as prisoners of war, or, possibly, objects of scientific research. But pets!

"I know how you feel," Graves went on, watching his face, "It's . . . it's *humiliating* from an anthropocentric viewpoint. But I think it may be true. I may as well tell you my own private theory as to the possible nature of X, and the relation of X to the human race. I haven't up to now, as it is almost sheer conjecture, based on very little data. But it does cover the known facts.

"I conceive of the X creatures as being just barely aware of the existence of men, unconcerned by them, and almost completely uninterested in them."

"But they hunt us!"

"Maybe. Or maybe they just pick us up occasionally by accident. A lot of men have dreamed about an impingement of nonhuman intelligences on the human race.

Almost without exception the dream has taken one of two forms, invasion and war, or exploration and mutual social intercourse. Both concepts postulate that nonhumans are enough like us either to fight with us or talk to us—treat us as equals, one way or the other.

"I don't believe that X is sufficiently interested in human beings to want to enslave them, or even exterminate them. They may not even study us, even when we come under their notice. They may lack the scientific spirit in the sense of having a monkeylike curiosity about everything that moves. For that matter, how thoroughly do *we* study other life forms? Did you ever ask your goldfish for their views on goldfish poetry or politics? Does a termite think that a woman's place is in the home? Do beavers prefer blondes or brunettes?"

"You are joking."

"No, I'm not! Maybe the life forms I mentioned don't have such involved ideas. My point is: if they did, or do, we'd never guess it. I don't think X conceives of the human race as intelligent."

Bill chewed this for a while, then added: "Where do you think they came from, Doc? Mars, maybe? Or clear out of the Solar System?"

"Not necessarily. Not even probably. It's my guess that they came from the same place we did—*from up out of the slime of this planet.*"

"Really, Doc—"

"I mean it. And don't give me that funny look. I may be sick, but I'm not balmy. *Creation took eight days!*"

"Huh?"

"I'm using biblical language. 'And God blessed them,

and God said unto them, Be fruitful and multiply, and replenish the earth, and subdue it: and have dominion over the fish of the sea, and over the fowl of the air, and over every living thing that moveth upon the earth.' And so it came to pass. But nobody mentioned the stratosphere."

"Doc—are you sure you feel all right?"

"Dammit—quit trying to psychoanalyze me! I'll drop the allegory. What I mean is: We aren't the latest nor the highest stage in evolution. First the oceans were populated. Then lungfish to amphibian, and so on up, until the continents were populated, and, in time, man ruled the surface of the Earth—or thought he did. But did evolution stop there? I think not. Consider—from a fish's point of view air is a hard vacuum. From our point of view the upper reaches of the atmosphere, sixty, seventy, maybe a hundred thousand feet up seem like a vacuum and unfit to sustain life. But it's not vacuum. It's thin, yes, but there is matter there and radiant energy. Why not life, intelligent life, highly evolved as it would have to be—but evolved from the same ancestry as ourselves and fish? We wouldn't see it happen; man hasn't been aware, in a scientific sense, that long. When our granddaddies were swinging in the trees, it had already happened."

Eisenberg took a deep breath. "Just wait a minute, Doc. I'm not disputing the theoretical possibility of your thesis, but it seems to me it is out on direct evidence alone. We've never seen them, had no direct evidence of them. At least, not until lately. And we *should* have seen them."

"Not necessarily. Do ants see men? I doubt it."

"Yes—but, consarn it, a man has better eyes than an ant."

"Better eyes for what? For his own needs. Suppose the X-creatures are too high up, or too tenuous, or too fast-moving for us to notice them. Even a thing as big and as solid and as slow as an airplane can pass up high enough to go out of sight, even on a clear day. If X is tenuous and even semitransparent, we never *would* see them—not even as occultations of stars, or shadows against the Moon—though as a matter of fact there have been some very strange stories of just that sort of thing."

Eisenberg got up and stomped up and down. "Do you mean to suggest," he demanded, "that creatures so insubstantial they can float in a soft vacuum built the Pillars?"

"Why not? Try explaining how a half-finished, naked embryo like *homo sapiens* built the Empire State Building."

Bill shook his head. "I don't get it."

"You don't try. Where do you think *this* came from?" Graves held up one of the miraculous little water spheres. "My guess is that life on this planet is split three ways, with almost no intercourse between the three. Ocean culture, land culture, and another—call it stratoculture. Maybe a fourth down under the crust—but we don't know. We know a little about life under the sea, because we are curious. But how much do they know of us? Do a few dozen bathysphere descents constitute an invasion? A fish that sees our bathysphere might go home and take to his bed with a sick headache, but he wouldn't talk about it, and he wouldn't be believed if he did. If a lot of fish see us and swear out affidavits, along comes a fish-psychologist and explains it as mass hallucination.

"No, it takes something at least as large and solid and permanent as the Pillars to have any effect on orthodox conceptions. Casual visitations have no real effect."

Eisenberg let his thoughts simmer for some time before commenting further. When he did, it was half to himself. "I don't believe it. I won't believe it!"

"Believe what?"

"Your theory. Look, Doc—if you are right, don't you see what it means? We're helpless, we're outclassed."

"I don't think they will bother much with human beings. They haven't, up till now."

"But that isn't it. Don't you see? We've had some dignity as a race. We've striven and accomplished things. Even when we failed, we had the tragic satisfaction of knowing that we were, nevertheless, superior and more able than the other animals. We've had faith in the race— we would accomplish great things yet. But if we are just one of the lower animals ourselves, what does our great work amount to? Me, I couldn't go on pretending to be a 'scientist' if I thought I was just a fish, mucking around in the bottom of a pool. My work wouldn't *signify* anything."

"Maybe it doesn't."

"No, maybe it doesn't." Eisenberg got up and paced the constricted area of their prison. "Maybe not. But I won't surrender to it. I *won't!* Maybe you're right. Maybe you're wrong. It doesn't seem to matter very much *where* the X people came from. One way or the other, they are a threat to our own kind. Doc, we've got to get out of here and warn them!"

"How?"

Graves was comatose a large part of the time before he died. Bill maintained an almost continuous watch over him, catching only occasional cat naps. There was little he could do for his friend, even though he did watch over him, but the spirit behind it was comfort to them both.

But he was dozing when Graves called his name. He woke at once, though the sound was a bare whisper. "Yes, Doc?"

"I can't talk much more, son. Thanks for taking care of me."

"Shucks, Doc."

"Don't forget what you're here for. Some day you'll get a break. Be ready for it and don't muff it. People have to be warned."

"I'll do it, Doc. I swear it."

"Good boy." And then, almost inaudibly, "G'night, son."

Eisenberg watched over the body until it was quite cold and had begun to stiffen. Then, exhausted by his long vigil and emotionally drained, he collapsed into a deep sleep. When he woke up the body was gone.

It was hard to maintain his morale, after Graves was gone. It was all very well to resolve to warn the rest of mankind at the first possible chance, but there was the endless monotony to contend with. He had not even the relief from boredom afforded the condemned prisoner— the checking off of limited days. Even his "calendar" was nothing but a counting of his sleeps.

He was not quite sane much of the time, and it was the twice-tragic insanity of intelligence, aware of its own instability. He cycled between periods of elation and periods of extreme depression, in which he would have destroyed himself, had he the means.

During the periods of elation he made great plans for fighting against the X creatures—after he escaped. He was not sure how or when, but, momentarily, he was sure. He would lead the crusade himself; rockets could withstand the dead zone of the Pillars and the cloud; atomic bombs could destroy the dynamic balance of the Pillars. They would harry them and hunt them down; the globe would once again be the kingdom of man, to whom it belonged.

During the bitter periods of relapse he would realize clearly that the puny engineering of mankind would be of no force against the powers and knowledge of the creatures who built the Pillars, who kidnapped himself and Graves in such a casual and mysterious a fashion. They were outclassed. Could codfish plan a sortie against the city of Boston? Would it matter if the chattering monkeys in Guatemala passed a resolution to destroy the navy?

They were outclassed. The human race had reached its highest point—the point at which it began to be aware that it was not the highest race, and the knowledge was death to it, one way or the other—the mere knowledge alone, even as the knowledge was now destroying him, Bill Eisenberg, himself. Eisenberg—*homo piscis*. Poor fish!

His overstrained mind conceived a means by which he might possibly warn his fellow beings. He could not escape as long as his surroundings remained unchanged.

That was established and he accepted it; he no longer paced his cage. But certain things *did* leave his cage: left-over food, refuse—and Graves' body. If he died, his own body would be removed, he felt sure. Some, at least, of the things which had gone up the Pillars had come down again—he knew that. Was it not likely that the X creatures disposed of any heavy mass for which they had no further use by dumping it down the Wahini Pillar? He convinced himself that it was so.

Very well, his body would be returned to the surface, eventually. How could he use it to give a message to his fellow men, if it were found? He had no writing materials, nothing but his own body.

But the same make-do means which served him as a calendar gave him a way to write a message. He could make welts on his skin with a shred of thumbnail. If the same spot were irritated over and over again, not permitted to heal, scar tissue would form. By such means he was able to create permanent tattooing.

The letters had to be large; he was limited in space to the fore part of his body; involved argument was impossible. He was limited to a fairly simple warning. If he had been quite right in his mind, perhaps be would have been able to devise a more cleverly worded warning—but then he was not.

In time, he had covered his chest and belly with cicatrix tattooing worthy of a bushman chief. He was thin by then and of an unhealthy color; the welts stood out plainly.

His body was found floating in the Pacific, by

Portuguese fishermen who could not read the message, but who turned it in to the harbor police of Honolulu. They, in turn, photographed the body, fingerprinted it, and disposed of it. The fingerprints were checked in Washington, and William Eisenberg, scientist, fellow of many distinguished societies, and high type of *homo sapiens*, was officially dead for the second time, with a new mystery attached to his name.

The cumbersome course of official correspondence unwound itself and the record of his reappearance reached the desk of Captain Blake, at a port in the South Atlantic. Photographs of the body were attached to the record, along with a short official letter telling the captain that, in view of his connection with the case, it was being provided for his information and recommendation.

Captain Blake looked at the photographs for the dozenth time. The message told in scar tissue was plain enough: "BEWARE—CREATION TOOK EIGHT DAYS." But what did it mean?

Of one thing he was sure—Eisenberg had not had those scars on his body when he disappeared from the *Mahan*.

The man had lived for a considerable period after he was grabbed up by the fireball—that was certain. And he had learned something. What? The reference to the first chapter of Genesis did not escape him; it was not such as to be useful.

He turned to his desk and resumed making a draft in painful longhand of his report to the bureau. "—the message in scar tissue adds to the mystery, rather than clarifying it. I am now forced to the opinion that the

Pillars and the LaGrange fireballs are connected in some way. The patrol around the Pillars should not be relaxed. If new opportunities or methods for investigating the nature of the Pillars should develop, they should be pursued thoroughly. I regret to say that I have nothing of the sort to suggest—"

He got up from his desk and walked to a small aquarium supported by gimbals from the inboard bulkhead, and stirred up the two goldfish therein with a forefinger. Noticing the level of the water, he turned to the pantry door. "Johnson, you've filled this bowl too full again. Pat's trying to jump out again!"

"I'll fix it, captain." The steward came out of the pantry with a small pan. ("Don't know why the Old Man keeps these tarnation fish. He ain't interested in 'em—*that's certain*.") Aloud he added: "That Pat fish don't want to stay in there, captain. Always trying to jump out. And he don't *like* me, captain."

"What's that?" Captain Blake's thoughts had already left the fish; he was worrying over the mystery again.

"I say that fish don't *like* me, captain. Tries to bite my finger every time I clean out the bowl."

"Don't be silly, Johnson."

Project Nightmare

"Four's your point. Roll 'em!"

"Anybody want a side bet on double deuces?"

No one answered; the old soldier rattled dice in a glass, pitched them against the washroom wall. One turned up a deuce; the other spun. Somebody yelled, "It's going to five! Come, Phoebe!"

It stopped—a two. The old soldier said, "I told you not to play with me. Anybody want cigarette money?"

"Pick it up, Pop. We don't—oh, oh! *Tenshun!*"

In the door stood a civilian, a colonel, and a captain. The civilian said, "Give the money back, Two-Gun."

"Okay, Prof." The old soldier extracted two singles. "That much is mine."

"Stop!" objected the captain. "I'll impound that for evidence. Now, you men—"

The colonel stopped him. "Mick. Forget that you're adjutant. Private Andrews, come along." He went out; the others followed. They hurried through the enlisted men's club, out into desert sunshine and across the quadrangle.

The civilian said, "Two-Gun, what the deuce!"

"Shucks, Prof, I was just practicing."

"Why don't you practice against Grandma Wilkins?"

The soldier snorted. "Do I look silly?"

The colonel put in, "You're keeping a crowd of generals and V.I.P.s waiting. That isn't bright."

"Colonel Hammond, I was told to wait in the club."

"But not in its washroom. Step it up!"

They went inside headquarters to a hall where guards checked their passes before letting them in. A civilian was speaking: "—and that's the story of the history-making experiments at Duke University. Doctor Reynolds is back; he will conduct the demonstrations."

The officers sat down in the rear; Dr. Reynolds went to the speaker's table. Private Andrews sat down with a group set apart from the high brass and distinguished civilians of the audience. A character who looked like a professional gambler—and was—sat next to two beautiful redheads, identical twins. A fourteen-year-old Negro boy slumped in the next chair; he seemed asleep. Beyond him a most wide awake person, Mrs. Anna Wilkins, tatted and looked around. In the second row were college students and a drab middle-aged man.

The table held a chuck-a-luck cage, packs of cards, scratch pads, a Geiger counter, a lead carrying case. Reynolds leaned on it and said, "Extra-Sensory Perception, or E.S.P., is a tag for little-known phenomena—telepathy, clairvoyance, clairaudience, precognition, telekinesis. They exist; we can measure them; we know that some people are thus gifted. But we don't know how they work. The British, in India during World War One, found that secrets were being stolen by telepathy." Seeing doubt in their faces Reynolds added, "It is conceivable that a spy five hundred miles away is now 'listening in'—and picking your brains of top-secret data."

Doubt was more evident. A four-star Air Force general said, "One moment, Doctor—if true, what can we do to stop it?"

"Nothing."

"That's no answer. A lead-lined room?"

"We've tried that, General. No effect."

"Jamming with high frequencies? Or whatever 'brain waves' are?"

"Possibly, though I doubt it. If E.S.P. becomes militarily important you may have to operate with all facts known. Back to our program: These ladies and gentlemen are powerfully gifted in telekinesis, the ability to control matter at a distance. Tomorrow's experiment may not succeed, but we hope to convince the doubting Thomases"—he smiled at a man in the rear—"that it is worth trying."

The man he looked at stood up. "General Hanby!"

An Army major general looked around. "Yes, Doctor Withers?"

"I asked to be excused. My desk is loaded with urgent work—and these games have nothing to do with me."

The commanding general started to assert himself; the four-star visitor put a hand on his sleeve. "Doctor Withers, my desk in Washington is piled high, but I am here because the President sent me. Will you please stay? I want a skeptical check on my judgment."

Withers sat down, still angry. Reynolds continued: "We will start with E.S.P. rather than telekinesis—which is a bit different, anyhow." He turned to one of the redheads. "Jane, will you come here?"

The girl answered, "I'm Joan. Sure."

"All right—Joan. General LaMott, will you draw something on this scratch pad?"

The four-star flyer cocked an eyebrow. "Anything?"

"Not too complicated."

"Right, Doctor." He thought, then began a cartoon of a girl, grinned and added a pop-eyed wolf. Shortly he looked up. "Okay?"

Joan had kept busy with another pad; Reynolds took hers to the general. The sketches were alike—except that Joan had added four stars to the wolf's shoulders. The general looked at her; she looked demure. "I'm convinced," he said drily. "What next?"

"That could be clairvoyance or telepathy," Reynolds lectured. "We will now show direct telepathy." He called the second twin to him, then said, "Doctor Withers, will you help us?"

Withers still looked surly. "With what?"

"The same thing—but Jane will watch over your shoulder while Joan tries to reproduce what you draw. Make it something harder."

"Well . . . okay." He took the pad, began sketching a radio circuit, while Jane watched. He signed it with a "Clem," the radioman's cartoon of the little fellow peering over a fence.

"That's fine!" said Reynolds. "Finished, Joan?"

"Yes, Doctor." He fetched her pad; the diagram was correct—but Joan had added to "Clem" a wink.

✳ ✳ ✳

Reynolds interrupted awed comment with, "I will skip card demonstrations and turn to telekinesis. Has anyone a pair of dice?" No one volunteered; he went on, "We have some supplied by your physics department. This chuck-a-luck cage is signed and sealed by them and so is this package." He broke it open, spilled out a dozen dice. "Two-Gun, how about some naturals?"

"I'll try, Prof."

"General LaMott, please select a pair and put them in this cup."

The general complied and handed the cup to Andrews. "What are you going to roll, soldier?"

"Would a sixty-five suit the General?"

"If you can."

"Would the General care to put up a five spot, to make it interesting?" He waited, wide-eyed and innocent.

LaMott grinned. "You're faded, soldier." He peeled out a five; Andrews covered it, rattled the cup and rolled. One die stopped on the bills—a five. The other bounced against a chair—a six.

"Let it ride, sir?"

"I'm not a sucker twice. Show us some naturals."

"As you say, sir." Two-Gun picked up the money, then rolled 6-1, 5-2, 4-3, and back again. He rolled several 6-1s, then got snake eyes. He tried again, got acey-deucey. He faced the little old lady. "Ma'am," he said, "if you want to roll, why don't you get down here and do the work?"

"Why, Mr. Andrews!"

Reynolds said hastily, "You'll get your turn, Mrs. Wilkins."

"I don't know what you gentlemen are talking about." She resumed tatting.

Colonel Hammond sat down by the redheads. "You're the January Twins—aren't you?"

"Our public!" one answered delightedly.

"The name is 'Brown,'" said the other.

"'Brown,'" he agreed, "but how about a show for the boys?"

"Dr. Reynolds wouldn't like it," the first said dutifully.

"I'll handle him. We don't get USO; security regulations are too strict. How about it, Joan?"

"I'm Jane. Okay, if you fix it with Prof."

"Good girls!" He went back to where Grandma Wilkins was demonstrating selection—showers of sixes in the chuck-a-luck cage. She was still tatting. Dr. Withers watched glumly. Hammond said, "Well, Doc?"

"These things are disturbing," Withers admitted, "but it's on the molar level—nothing affecting the elementary particles."

"How about those sketches?"

"I'm a physicist, not a psychologist. But the basic particles—electrons, neutrons, protons—can't be affected except with apparatus designed in accordance with the laws of radioactivity!"

Dr. Reynolds was in earshot; at Withers' remark he said, "Thank you, Mrs. Wilkins. Now, ladies and gentlemen, another experiment. Norman!"

The colored boy opened his eyes. "Yeah, Prof?"

"Up here. And the team from your physics laboratory, please. Has anyone a radium-dial watch?"

Staff technicians hooked the Geiger counter through

an amplifier so that normal background radioactivity was heard as occasional clicks, then placed a radium-dial watch close to the counter tube; the clicks changed to hail-storm volume. "Lights out, please," directed Reynolds.

The boy said, "Now, Prof?"

"Wait, Norman. Can everyone see the watch?" The silence was broken only by the rattle of the amplifier, counting radioactivity of the glowing figures. "Now, Norman!"

The shining figures quenched out; the noise died to sparse clicks.

The same group was in a blockhouse miles out in the desert; more miles beyond was the bomb proving site; facing it was a periscope window set in concrete and glazed with solid feet of laminated filter glass. Dr. Reynolds was talking with Major General Hanby. A naval captain took reports via earphones and speaker horn; he turned to the C.O. "Planes on station, sir."

"Thanks, Dick."

The horn growled, "Station Charlie to Control; we fixed it."

The navy man said to Hanby, "All stations ready, range clear."

"Pick up the count."

"All stations, stand by to resume count at minus seventeen minutes. Time station, pick up the count. This is a live run. Repeat, this is a live run."

Hanby said to Reynolds, "Distance makes no difference?"

"We could work from Salt Lake City once my colleagues knew the setup." He glanced down. "My watch must have stopped."

"Always feels that way. Remember the metronome on the first Bikini test? It nearly drove me nuts."

"I can imagine. Um, General, some of my people are high-strung. Suppose I *ad lib*?"

Hanby smiled grimly. "We always have a pacifier for visitors. Doctor Withers, ready with your curtain raiser?"

The chief physicist was bending over a group of instruments; he looked tired. "Not today," he answered in a flat voice. "Satterlee will make it."

Satterlee came forward and grinned at the brass and V.I.P.s and at Reynolds' operators. "I've been saving a joke for an audience that can't walk out. But first—" He picked up a polished metal sphere and looked at the E.S.P. adepts. "You saw a ball like this on your tour this morning. That one was plutonium; it's still out there waiting to go *bang!* in about . . . eleven minutes. This is merely steel— unless someone has made a mistake. That would be a joke—we'd laugh ourselves to bits!"

He got no laughs, went on: "But it doesn't weigh enough; we're safe. This dummy has been prepared so that Dr. Reynolds' people will have an image to help them concentrate. It looks no more like an atom bomb than I look like Stalin, but it represents—if it were plutonium— what we atom tinkerers call a 'subcritical mass.' Since the spy trials everybody knows how an atom bomb works. Plutonium gives off neutrons at a constant rate. If the mass is small, most of them escape to the outside. But if it is large enough, or a critical mass, enough are absorbed by other nuclei to start a chain reaction. The trick is to assemble a critical mass quickly—then run for your life! This happens in microseconds; I can't be specific without upsetting the security officer.

"Today we will find out if the mind can change the rate of neutron emission in plutonium. By theories sound enough to have destroyed two Japanese cities, the emission of any particular neutron is pure chance, but the total emission is as invariable as the stars in their courses. Otherwise it would be impossible to make atom bombs.

"By standard theory, theory that works, that subcritical mass out there is no more likely to explode than a pumpkin. Our test group will try to change that. They will concentrate, try to increase the probability of neutrons' escaping, and thus set off that sphere as an atom bomb."

"Doctor Satterlee?" asked a vice admiral with wings. "Do you think it can be done?"

"Absolutely not!" Satterlee turned to the adepts. "No offense intended, folks."

"Five minutes!" announced the navy captain.

Satterlee nodded to Reynolds. "Take over. And good luck."

Mrs. Wilkins spoke up. "Just a moment, young man. These 'neuter' things. I—"

"Neutrons, madam."

"That's what I said. I don't quite understand. I suppose that sort of thing comes in high school, but I only finished eighth grade. I'm sorry."

Satterlee looked sorry, too, but he tried. "—and each of these nuclei is potentially able to spit out one of these little neutrons. In that sphere out there"—he held up the dummy—"There are, say, five thousand billion trillion nuclei, each one—"

"My, that's quite a lot, isn't it?"

"Madam, it certainly is. Now—"

"Two minutes!"

Reynolds interrupted. "Mrs. Wilkins, don't worry. Concentrate on that metal ball out there and think about those neutrons, each one ready to come out. When I give the word, I want you all—you especially, Norman—to think about that ball, spitting sparks like a watch dial. Try for more sparks. Simply try. If you fail, no one will blame you. Don't get tense."

Mrs. Wilkins nodded. "I'll try." She put her tatting down and got a faraway look.

At once they were blinded by unbelievable radiance bursting through the massive filter. It beat on them, then died away.

The naval captain said, "What the hell!" Someone screamed, "It's gone, it's gone!"

The speaker brayed: "Fission at minus one minute thirty-seven seconds. Control, what went wrong. It looks like a hydrogen—"

The concussion wave hit and all sounds were smothered. Lights went out, emergency lighting clicked on. The blockhouse heaved like a boat in a heavy sea. Their eyes were still dazzled, their ears assaulted by cannonading afternoise, and physicists were elbowing flag officers at the port, when an anguished soprano cut through the din. "Oh, *dear!*"

Reynolds snapped, "What's the matter, Grandma? You all right?"

"Me? Oh, yes, yes—but I'm so sorry. I didn't mean to do it."

"Do what?"

"I was just feeling it out, thinking about all those little bitty neuters, ready to spit. But I didn't mean to make it go off—not till you told us to."

"Oh." Reynolds turned to the rest. "Anyone else jump the gun?"

No one admitted it. Mrs. Wilkins said timidly, "I'm sorry, Doctor. Have they got another one? I'll be more careful."

Reynolds and Withers were seated in the officers' mess with coffee in front of them; the physicist paid no attention to his. His eyes glittered and his face twitched. "No limits! Calculations show over *ninety per cent* conversion of mass to energy. You know what that *means?* If we assume—no, never mind. Just say that we could make every bomb the size of a pea. No tamper. No control circuits. Nothing but . . . " He paused. "Delivery would be fast, small jets—just a pilot, a weaponeer, and one of your 'operators.' No limit to the number of bombs. No nation on Earth could—"

"Take it easy," said Reynolds. "We've got only a few telekinesis operators. You wouldn't risk them in a plane."

"But—"

"You don't need to. Show them the bombs, give them photos of the targets, hook them by radio to the weaponeer. That spreads them thin. And we'll test for more sensitive people. My figures show about one in eighteen hundred."

"'Spread them thin,'" repeated Withers. "Mrs. Wilkins could handle dozens of bombs, one after another—couldn't she?"

"I suppose so. We'll test."

"We will indeed!" Withers noticed his coffee, gulped it. "Forgive me, Doctor; I'm punchy. I've had to revise too many opinions."

"I know. I was a behaviorist."

Captain Mikeler came in, looked around and came over. "The General wants you both," he said softly. "Hurry."

They were ushered into a guarded office. Major General Hanby was with General LaMott and Vice Admiral Keithley; they looked grim. Hanby handed them message flimsies. Reynolds saw the stamp TOP SECRET and handed his back. "General, I'm not cleared for this."

"Shut up and read it."

Reynolds skipped the number groups: "—(PARA-PHRASED) RUSSIAN EMBASSY TODAY HANDED STATE ULTIMATUM: DEMANDS USA CONVERT TO 'PEOPLE'S REPUBLIC' UNDER POLITICAL COMMISSARS TO BE ASSIGNED BY USSR. MILITARY ASSURANCES DEMANDED. NOTE CLAIMS MAJOR US CITIES (LIST SEPARATE) ARE MINED WITH ATOMIC BOMBS WHICH THEY THREATEN TO SET OFF BY RADIO IF TERMS ARE NOT MET BY SIXTEEN HUNDRED FRIDAY EST."

Reynolds reread it—"SIXTEEN HUNDRED FRIDAY"—Two P.M. day after tomorrow, local time. Our cities booby-trapped with A-bombs? Could they do that? He realized that LaMott was speaking. "We must assume that the threat is real. Our free organization makes it an obvious line of attack."

The admiral said, "They may be bluffing."

The air general shook his head. "They know the President won't surrender. We can't assume that Ivan is stupid."

Reynolds wondered why he was being allowed to hear this. LaMott looked at him. "Admiral Keithley and I leave for Washington at once. I have delayed to ask you this: your people set off an atom bomb. *Can they keep bombs from going off?*"

Reynolds felt his time sense stretch as if he had all year to think about Grandma Wilkins, Norman, his other paranormals. "Yes," he answered.

LaMott stood up. "Your job, Hanby. Coming, Admiral?"

"Wait!" protested Reynolds. "Give me one bomb and Mrs. Wilkins—and I'll sit on it. But how many cities? Twenty? Thirty?"

"Thirty-eight."

"Thirty-eight bombs—or more. Where are they? What do they look like? How long will this go on? It's impossible."

"Of course—but do it anyhow. Or try. Hanby, tell them we're on our way, will you?"

"Certainly, General."

"Good-bye, Doctor. Or so long, rather."

Reynolds suddenly realized that these two were going back to "sit" on one of the bombs, to continue their duties until it killed them. He said quickly, "We'll try. We'll certainly try."

✲✲✲

Thirty-eight cities . . . forty-three hours . . . and seventeen adepts. Others were listed in years of research, but they were scattered through forty-one states. In a dictatorship secret police would locate them at once, deliver them at supersonic speeds. But this was America.

Find them! Get them here! *Fast!* Hanby assigned Colonel Hammond to turn Reynolds' wishes into orders and directed his security officer to delegate his duties, get on the phone and use his acquaintance with the F.B.I., and other security officers, and through them with local police, to cut red tape and *find those paranormals.* Find them, convince them, bring pressure, start them winging toward the proving ground. By sundown, twenty-three had been found, eleven had been convinced or coerced, two had arrived. Hanby phoned Reynolds, caught him eating a sandwich standing up. "Hanby speaking. The President just phoned."

"The President?"

"LaMott got in to see him. He's dubious, but he's authorized an all-out try, short of slowing down conventional defense. One of his assistants left National Airport by jet plane half an hour ago to come here and help. Things will move faster."

But it did not speed things up, as the Russian broadcast was even then being beamed, making the crisis public; the President went on the air thirty minutes later. Reynolds did not hear him; he was busy. Twenty people to save twenty cities—and a world. But how? He was sure that Mrs. Wilkins could smother any A-bomb she had seen; he hoped the others could. But a hidden bomb in a far-off city—find it mentally, think about it, quench it, not for the microsecond it took to set one off, but for the billions of microseconds it might take to uncover it—was it possible?

What would help? Certain drugs—caffeine, benzedrine. They must have quiet, too. He turned to Hammond. "I want a room and bath for each one."

"You've got that."

"No, we're doubled up, with semi-private baths."

Hammond shrugged. "Can do. It means booting out some brass."

"Keep the kitchen manned. They must not sleep, but they'll have to eat. Fresh coffee all the time and cokes and tea—anything they want. Can you put the room phones through a private switchboard?"

"Okay. What else?"

"I don't know. We'll talk to them."

They all knew of the Russian broadcast, but not what was being planned; they met his words with uneasy silence. Reynolds turned to Andrews. "Well, Two-Gun?"

"Big bite to chew, Prof."

"Yes. Can you chew it?"

"Have to, I reckon."

"Norman?"

"Gee, Boss! How can I when I can't see 'em?"

"Mrs. Wilkins couldn't see that bomb this morning. You can't see radioactivity on a watch dial; it's too small. You just see the dial and think about it. Well?"

The Negro lad scowled. "Think of a shiny ball in a city somewhere?"

"Yes. No, wait—Colonel Hammond, they need a visual image and it won't be that. There are atom bombs here— they must *see* one."

Hammond frowned. "An American bomb meant for dropping or firing won't look like a Russian bomb rigged for placement and radio triggering."

"What will they look like?"

"G-2 ought to know. I hope. We'll get some sort of picture. A three-dimensional mock-up, too. I'd better find Withers and the General." He left.

Mrs. Wilkins said briskly, "Doctor, I'll watch Washington, D.C."

"Yes, Mrs. Wilkins. You're the only one who has been tested, even in reverse. So you guard Washington; it's of prime importance."

"No, no, that's not why. It's the city I can *see* best."

Andrews said, "She's got something, Prof. I pick Seattle."

By midnight Reynolds had his charges, twenty-six by now, tucked away in the officers' club. Hammond and he took turns at a switchboard rigged in the upper hall. The watch would not start until shortly before deadline. Fatigue reduced paranormal powers, sometimes to zero; Reynolds hoped that they were getting one last night of sleep.

A microphone had been installed in each room; a selector switch let them listen in. Reynolds disliked this but Hammond argued, "Sure, it's an invasion of privacy. So is being blown up by an A-bomb." He dialed the switch. "Hear that? Our boy Norman is sawing wood." He moved it again. "Private 'Two-Gun' is still stirring. We can't let them sleep, once it starts, so we have to spy on them."

"I suppose so."

Withers came upstairs. "Anything more you need?"

"I guess not," answered Reynolds. "How about the bomb mock-up?"

"Before morning."

"How authentic is it?"

"Hard to say. Their agents probably rigged firing circuits from radio parts bought right here; the circuits could vary a lot. But the business part—well, we're using real plutonium."

"Good. We'll show it to them after breakfast."

Two-Gun's door opened. "Howdy, Colonel. Prof—it's there."

"What is?"

"The bomb. Under Seattle. I can feel it."

"*Where is it?*"

"It's down—it *feels* down. And it feels wet, somehow. Would they put it in the Sound?"

Hammond jumped up. "In the harbor—and shower the city with radioactive water!" He was ringing as he spoke. "Get me General Hanby!"

"Morrison here," a voice answered. "What is it, Hammond?"

"The Seattle bomb—have them dredge for it. It's in the Sound, or somewhere under water."

"Eh? How do you know?"

"One of Reynolds' magicians. Do it!" He cut off.

Andrews said worriedly, "Prof, I can't *see* it—I'm not a 'seeing-eye.' Why don't you get one? Say that little Mrs. Brentano?"

"Oh, my God! Clairvoyants—we need them, too."

Withers said, "Eh, Doctor? Do you think—"

"No, I don't, or I would have thought of it. How do they search for bombs? What instruments?"

"Instruments? A bomb in its shielding doesn't even affect a Geiger counter. You have to open things and look."

"How long will that take? Say for New York!"

Hammond said, "Shut up! Reynolds, where are these clairvoyants?"

Reynolds chewed his lip. "They're scarce."

"Scarcer than us dice rollers," added Two-Gun. "But get that Brentano kid. She found keys I had lost digging a ditch. Buried three feet deep—and me searching my quarters."

"Yes, yes, Mrs. Brentano." Reynolds pulled out a notebook.

Hammond reached for the switchboard. "Morrison? Stand by for more names—and even more urgent than the others."

More urgent but harder to find; the Panic was on. The President urged everyone to keep cool and stay home, whereupon thirty million people stampeded. The ticker in the P.I.O. office typed the story: "NEW YORK NY—TO CLEAR JAM CAUSED BY WRECKS IN OUTBOUND TUBE THE INBOUND TUBE OF HOLLAND TUNNEL HAS BEEN REVERSED. POLICE HAVE STOPPED TRYING TO PREVENT EVACUATION. BULLDOZERS WORKING TO REOPEN TRIBOROUGH BRIDGE, BLADES SHOVING WRECKED CARS AND HUMAN HAMBURGER. WEEHAWKEN FERRY DISASTER CONFIRMED: NO PASSENGER

LIST YET—FLASH—GEORGE WASHINGTON BRIDGE GAVE WAY AT 0353 EST, WHETHER FROM OVERLOAD OR SABOTAGE NOT KNOWN, MORE MORE MORE—FLASH—"

It was repeated everywhere. The Denver-Colorado Springs highway had one hundred thirty-five deaths by midnight, then reports stopped. A DC-7 at Burbank ploughed into a mob which had broken through the barrier. The Baltimore-Washington highway was clogged both ways; Memorial Bridge was out of service. The five outlets from Los Angeles were solid with creeping cars. At four A.M. EST the President declared martial law; the order had no immediate effect.

By morning Reynolds had thirty-one adepts assigned to twenty-four cities. He had a stomach-churning ordeal before deciding to let them work only cities known to them. The gambler, Even-Money Karsch, had settled it: "Doc, I know when I'm hot. Minneapolis *has* to be mine." Reynolds gave in, even though one of his students had just arrived from there; he put them both on it and prayed that at least one would be "hot." Two clairvoyants arrived; one, a blind newsdealer from Chicago, was put to searching there; the other, a carnie mentalist, was given the list and told to find bombs wherever she could. Mrs. Brentano had remarried and moved; Norfolk was being combed for her.

At one fifteen P.M., forty-five minutes before deadline, they were in their rooms, each with maps and aerial views of his city, each with photos of the mocked-up bomb. The club was clear of residents; the few normals needed to coddle the paranormals kept carefully quiet. Roads nearby were blocked; air traffic was warned away. Everything was turned toward providing an atmosphere in which forty-two people could sit still and *think*.

At the switchboard were Hammond, Reynolds, and Gordon McClintock, the President's assistant. Reynolds glanced up. "What time is it?"

"One thirty-seven," rasped Hammond. "Twenty-three minutes."

"One thirty-eight," disagreed McClintock. "Reynolds, how about Detroit? You *can't* leave it unguarded."

"Whom can I use? Each is guarding the city he knows best."

"Those twin girls—I heard them mention Detroit."

"They've played everywhere. But Pittsburgh is their home."

"Switch one of them to Detroit."

Reynolds thought of telling him to go to Detroit himself. "They work together. You want to get them upset and lose both cities?"

Instead of answering McClintock said, "And who's watching Cleveland?"

"Norman Johnson. He lives there and he's our second strongest operator."

They were interrupted by voices downstairs. A man came up, carrying a bag, and spotted Reynolds. "Oh, hello, Doctor. What is this? I'm on top priority work—tank production—when the F.B.I. grabs me. You are responsible?"

"Yes. Come with me." McClintock started to speak, but Reynolds led the man away. "Mr. Nelson, did you bring your family?"

"No, they're still in Detroit. Had I known—"

"Please! Listen carefully." He explained, pointed out a map of Detroit in the room to which they went, showed him pictures of the simulated bomb. "You understand?"

Nelson's jaw muscles were jumping. "It seems impossible."

"It *is* possible. You've got to think about that bomb—or bombs. Get in touch, squeeze them, keep them from going off. You'll have to stay awake."

Nelson breathed gustily. "I'll stay awake."

"That phone will get you anything you want. Good luck."

He passed the room occupied by the blind clairvoyant; the door was open. "Harry, it's Prof. Getting anything?"

The man turned to the voice. "It's in the Loop. I could walk to it if I were there. A six-story building."

"That's the best you can do?"

"Tell them to try the attic. I get warm when I go up."

"Right away!" He rushed back, saw that Hanby had arrived. Swiftly he keyed the communications office. "Reynolds speaking. The Chicago bomb is in a six-story building in the Loop area, probably in the attic. No—that's all. G'bye!"

Hanby started to speak; Reynolds shook his head and looked at his watch. Silently the General picked up the phone. "This is the commanding officer. Have any flash sent here." He put the phone down and stared at his watch.

For fifteen endless minutes they stood silent. The General broke it by taking the phone and saying, "Hanby. Anything?"

"No, General. Washington is on the wire."

"Eh? You say Washington?"

"Yes, sir. Here's the General, Mr. Secretary."

Hanby sighed. "Hanby speaking, Mr. Secretary. You're all right? Washington . . . is all right?"

They could hear the relayed voice. "Certainly, certainly. We're past the deadline. But I wanted to tell you: Radio Moscow is telling the world that our cities are in flames."

Hanby hesitated. "None of them are?"

"Certainly not. I've a talker hooked in to GHQ, which has an open line to every city listed. All safe. I don't know whether your freak people did any good but, one way or another, it was a false—" The line went dead.

Hanby's face went dead with it. He jiggled the phone. "I've been cut off!"

"Not here, General—at the other end. Just a moment."

They waited. Presently the operator said, "Sorry, sir. I can't get them to answer."

"Keep trying!"

It was slightly over a minute—it merely seemed longer—when the operator said, "Here's your party, sir."

"That you, Hanby?" came the voice. "I suppose we'll have phone trouble just as we had last time. Now, about these ESP people: while we are grateful and all that, nevertheless I suggest that nothing be released to the papers. Might be misinterpreted."

"Oh. Is that an order, Mr. Secretary?"

"Oh, no, no! But have such things routed through my office."

"Yes, sir." He cradled the phone.

McClintock said, "You shouldn't have rung off,

General. I'd like to know whether the Chief wants this business continued."

"Suppose we talk about it on the way back to my office." The General urged him away, turned and gave Reynolds a solemn wink.

Trays were placed outside the doors at six o'clock; most of them sent for coffee during the evening. Mrs. Wilkins ordered tea; she kept her door open and chatted with anyone who passed. Harry the newsboy was searching Milwaukee; no answer had been received from his tip about Chicago. Mrs. Ekstein, or "Princess Cathay" as she was billed, had reported a "feeling" about a house trailer in Denver and was now poring over a map of New Orleans. With the passing of the deadline panic abated, communications were improving. The American people were telling each other that they had known that those damned commies were bluffing.

Hammond and Reynolds sent for more coffee at three A.M.; Reynolds' hand trembled as he poured. Hammond said, "You haven't slept for two nights. Get over on that divan."

"Neither have you."

"I'll sleep when you wake up."

"I *can't* sleep. I'm worrying about what'll happen when *they* get sleepy." He gestured at the line of doors.

"So am I."

At seven A.M. Two-Gun came out. "Prof, they got it. The bomb. It's gone. Like closing your hand on nothing."

Hammond grabbed the phone. "Get me Seattle—the F.B.I. office."

While they waited, Two-Gun said, "What now, Prof?"

Reynolds tried to think. "Maybe you should rest."

"Not until this is over. Who's got Toledo? I know that burg."

"Uh . . . young Barnes."

Hammond was connected; he identified himself, asked the question. He put the phone down gently. "They *did* get it," he whispered. "It was in the lake."

"I told you it was wet," agreed Two-Gun. "Now, about Toledo—"

"Well . . . tell me when you've got it and we'll let Barnes rest."

McClintock rushed in at seven thirty-five, followed by Hanby. "Doctor Reynolds! Colonel Hammond!"

"*Sh!* Quiet! You'll disturb them."

McClintock said in a lower voice, "Yes, surely—I was excited. This is important. They located a bomb in Seattle and—"

"Yes. Private Andrews told us."

"Huh? How did *he* know?"

"Never mind," Hanby intervened. "The point is, they found the bomb already triggered. Now we *know* that your people are protecting the cities."

"Was there any doubt?"

"Well . . . yes."

"But there isn't now," McClintock added. "I must take over." He bent over the board. "Communications? Put that White House line through here."

"Just what," Reynolds said slowly, "do you mean by 'take over?'"

"Eh? Why, take charge on behalf of the President. Make sure these people don't let down an instant!"

"But what do you propose to *do?*"

Hanby said hastily, "Nothing, Doctor. We'll just keep in touch with Washington from here."

They continued the vigil together; Reynolds spent the time hating McClintock's guts. He started to take coffee, then decided on another benzedrine tablet instead. He hoped his people were taking enough of it—and not too much. They all had it, except Grandma Wilkins, who wouldn't touch it. He wanted to check with them but knew that he could not—each bomb was bound only by a thread of thought; a split-split second of diversion might be enough.

The outside light flashed; Hanby took the call. "Congress has recessed," he announced, "and the President is handing the Soviet Union a counter ultimatum; locate and disarm any bombs or be bombed in return." The light flashed again; Hanby answered. His face lit up. "Two more found," he told them. "One in Chicago, right where your man said; the other in Camden."

"Camden? How?"

"They rounded up the known Communists, of course. This laddie was brought back there for questioning. He didn't like that; he knew that he was being held less than a mile from the bomb. Who is on Camden?"

"Mr. Dimwiddy."

"The elderly man with the bunions?"

"That's right—retired postman. General, do we assume that there is only one bomb per city?"

McClintock answered, "Of course not! These people must—"

Hanby cut in, "Central Intelligence is assuming so, except for New York and Washington. If they had more bombs here, they would have added more cities."

Reynolds left to take Dimwiddy off watch. McClintock, he fumed, did not realize that people were flesh and blood.

Dimwiddy was unsurprised. "A while ago the pressure let up, then—well, I'm afraid I dozed. I had a terrible feeling that I had let it go off, then I knew it hadn't." Reynolds told him to rest, then be ready to help out elsewhere. They settled on Philadelphia; Dimwiddy had once lived there.

The watch continued. Mrs. Ekstein came up with three hits, but no answers came back; Reynolds still had to keep those cities covered. She then complained that her "sight" had gone; Reynolds went to her room and told her to nap, not wishing to consult McClintock.

Luncheon trays came and went. Reynolds continued worrying over how to arrange his operators to let them rest. Forty-three people and thirty-five cities—if only he had two for every city! Maybe any of them could watch any city? No, he could not chance it.

Barnes woke up and took back Toledo; that left Two-Gun free. Should he let him take Cleveland? Norman had had no relief and Two-Gun had once been through it, on a train. The colored boy was amazing but rather hysterical, whereas Two-Gun—well, Reynolds felt that Two-Gun would last, even through a week of no sleep.

No! He couldn't trust Cleveland to a man who had merely passed through it. But with Dimwiddy on Philadelphia, when Mary Gifford woke he could put her on Houston and that would let Hank sleep before shifting him to Indianapolis and that would let him—

A chess game, with all pawns, queens and no mistakes allowed.

McClintock was twiddling the selector switch, listening in. Suddenly he snapped, "Someone is asleep!"

Reynolds checked the number.

"Of course, that's the twins' room; they take turns. You may hear snores in 21 and 30 and 8 and 19. It's okay; they're off watch."

"Well, all right." McClintock seemed annoyed.

Reynolds bent back to his list. Shortly McClintock snorted, "Who's in room 12?"

"Uh? Wait—that's Norman Johnson, Cleveland."

"*You mean he's on watch?*"

"Yes." Reynolds could hear the boy's asthmatic breathing, felt relieved.

"He's asleep!"

"No, he's not."

But McClintock was rushing down the corridor. Reynolds took after him; Hammond and Hanby followed. Reynolds caught up as McClintock burst into room 12. Norman was sprawled in a chair, eyes closed in his habitual attitude. McClintock rushed up, slapped him. "Wake up!"

Reynolds grabbed McClintock. "You bloody fool!"

Norman opened his eyes, then burst into tears. "It's *gone!*"

"Steady, Norman. It's all right."

"No, no! It's gone—and my mammy's gone with it!"

McClintock snapped, "Concentrate, boy! Get back on it!"

Reynolds turned on him. "Get out. Get out before I punch you."

Hanby and Hammond were in the door; the General cut in with a hoarse whisper, "Pipe down, Doctor, bring the boy."

Back at the board the outside light was flashing. Hanby took the call while Reynolds tried to quiet the boy. Hanby listened gravely, then said, "He's right. Cleveland just got it."

McClintock snapped, "He went to sleep. He ought to be shot."

"Shut up," said Hanby.

"But—"

Reynolds said, "Any others, General?"

"Why would there be?"

"All this racket. It may have disturbed a dozen of them."

"Oh, we'll see." He called Washington again. Presently he sighed. "No, just Cleveland. We were . . . lucky."

"General," McClintock insisted, "he was asleep."

Hanby looked at him. "Sir, you may be the President's deputy but you yourself have no military authority. Off my post."

"But I am directed by the President to—"

"Off my post, sir! Go back to Washington. *Or to Cleveland.*"

McClintock looked dumbfounded. Hanby added, "You're worse than bad—you're a fool."

"The President will hear of this."

"Blunder again and the President won't live that long. Get out."

By nightfall the situation was rapidly getting worse. Twenty-seven cities were still threatened and Reynolds was losing operators faster than bombs were being found. Even-Money Karsch would not relieve when awakened. "See that?" he said, rolling dice. "Cold as a well-digger's feet. I'm through." After that Reynolds tested each one who was about to relieve, found that some were tired beyond the power of short sleep to restore them—they were "cold."

By midnight there were eighteen operators for nineteen cities. The twins had fearfully split up; it had worked. Mrs. Wilkins was holding both Washington and Baltimore; she had taken Baltimore when he had no one to relieve there.

But now he had no one for relief anywhere and three operators—Nelson, Two-Gun and Grandma Wilkins— had had no rest. He was too fagged to worry; he simply knew that whenever one of them reached his limit, the United States would lose a city. The panic had resumed after the bombing of Cleveland; roads again were choked. The disorder made harder the search for bombs. But there was nothing he could do.

Mrs. Ekstein still complained about her sight but kept at it. Harry the newsboy had had no luck with Milwaukee, but there was no use shifting him; other cities were "dark" to him. During the night Mrs. Ekstein pointed to the bomb in Houston. It was, she said, in a box underground. A coffin? Yes, there was a headstone; she was unable to read the name.

Thus, many recent dead in Houston were disturbed. But it was nine Sunday morning before Reynolds went to tell Mary Gifford that she could rest—or relieve for Wilmington, if she felt up to it. He found her collapsed and lifted her onto the bed, wondering if she had known the Houston bomb was found.

Eleven cities now and eight people. Grandma Wilkins held four cities. No one else had been able to double up. Reynolds thought dully that it was a miracle that they had been able to last at all; it surpassed enormously the best test performance.

Hammond looked up as he returned. "Make any changes?"

"No. The Gifford kid is through. We'll lose half a dozen cities before this is over."

"Some of them must be damn near empty by now."

"I hope so. Any more bombs found?"

"Not yet. How do you feel, Doc?"

"Three weeks dead." Reynolds sat down wearily. He was wondering if he should wake some of those sleeping and test them again when he heard a noise below; he went to the stairwell. Up came an M.P. captain. "They said to bring her here."

Reynolds looked at the woman with him. "Dorothy Brentano!"

"Dorothy Smith now."

He controlled his trembling and explained what was required. She nodded. "I figured that out on the plane. Got a pencil? Take this: St. Louis—a river warehouse with a sign reading 'Bartlett & Sons, Jobbers.' Look in the loft. And Houston—no, they got that one. Baltimore—it's in a ship at the docks, the S.S. *Gold Coast*. What other cities? I've wasted time feeling around where there was nothing to find."

Reynolds was already shouting for Washington to answer.

Grandma Wilkins was last to be relieved; Dorothy located one in the Potomac—and Mrs. Wilkins told her sharply to keep trying. There were four bombs in Washington, which Mrs. Wilkins had known all along. Dorothy found them in eleven minutes.

Three hours later Reynolds showed up in the club messroom, not having been able to sleep. Several of his people were eating and listening to the radio blast about our raid on Russia. He gave it a wide berth; they could blast Omsk and Tomsk and Minsk and Pinsk; today he didn't care. He was sipping milk and thinking that he would never drink coffee again when Captain Mikeler bent over his table.

"The General wants you. Hurry!"

"Why?"

"I said, Hurry! Where's Grandma Wilkins—oh—I see her. Who is Mrs. Dorothy Smith?"

Reynolds looked around. "She's with Mrs. Wilkins."

Mikeler rushed them to Hanby's office. Hanby merely said, "Sit over there. And you ladies, too. Stay in focus."

Reynolds found himself looking into a television screen at the President of the United States. He looked as weary as Reynolds felt, but he turned on his smile. "You are Doctor Reynolds?"

"Yes, Mr. President!"

"These ladies are Mrs. Wilkins and Mrs. Smith?"

"Yes, sir."

The President said quietly, "You three and your colleagues will be thanked by the Republic. And by me, for myself. But that must wait. Mrs. Smith, there are more bombs—in Russia. Could your strange gift find them there?"

"Why, I don't—I can try!"

"Mrs. Wilkins, could you set off those Russian bombs while they are still far away?"

Incredibly, she was still bright-eyed and chipper. "Why, Mr. President!"

"Can you?"

She got a far-away look. "Dorothy and I had better have a quiet room somewhere. And I'd like a pot of tea. A large pot."

Water is for Washing

He judged that the Valley was hotter than usual—but, then, it usually was. Imperial Valley was a natural hothouse, two hundred and fifty feet below sea level, diked from the Pacific Ocean by the mountains back of San Diego, protected from the Gulf of Baja California by high ground on the south. On the east, the Chocolate Mountains walled off the rushing Colorado River.

He parked his car outside the Barbara Worth Hotel in El Centro and went into the bar. "Scotch."

The bartender filled a shot glass, then set a glass of ice water beside it. "Thanks. Have one?"

"Don't mind if I do."

The customer sipped his drink, then picked up the chaser. "That's just the right amount of water in the right place. I've got hydrophobia."

"Huh?"

"I hate water. Darn near drowned when I was a kid. Afraid of it ever since."

"Water ain't fit to drink," the bartender agreed, "but I do like to swim."

"Not for me. That's why I like the Valley. They restrict the stuff to irrigation ditches, washbowls, bathtubs, and glasses. I always hate to go back to Los Angeles."

"If you're afraid of drowning," the barkeep answered, "you're better off in L.A. than in the Valley. We're below sea level here. Water all around us, higher than our heads. Suppose somebody pulled out the cork?"

"Go frighten your grandmother. The Coast Range is no cork."

"Earthquake."

"That's crazy. Earthquakes don't move mountain ranges."

"Well, it wouldn't necessarily take a quake. You've heard about the 1905 flood, when the Colorado River spilled over and formed the Salton Sea? But don't be too sure about quakes; valleys below sea level don't just grow—*something* has to cause them. The San Andreas Fault curls around this valley like a question mark. Just imagine the shake-up it must have taken to drop thousands of square miles below the level of the Pacific."

"Quit trying to get my goat. That happened thousands of years ago. Here." He laid a bill on the bar and left. Joykiller! A man like that shouldn't be tending bar.

The thermometer in the shaded doorway showed 118 degrees. The solid heat beat against him, smarting his eyes and drying his lungs, even while he remained on the covered sidewalk. His car, he knew, would be too hot to touch; he should have garaged it. He walked around the end of it and saw someone bending over the left hand door. He stopped. "What the hell do you think you're doing?"

The figure turned suddenly, showing pale, shifty eyes

He was dressed in a business suit, dirty and unpressed. He was tieless. His hands and nails were dirty, but not with the dirt of work; the palms were uncalloused. A weak mouth spoiled features otherwise satisfactory. "No harm intended," he apologized. "I just wanted to read your registration slip. You're from Los Angeles. Give me a lift back to the city, pal."

The car owner ignored him and glanced around inside the automobile. "Just wanted to see where I was from, eh? Then why did you open the glove compartment? I ought to run you in." He looked past the vagrant at two uniformed deputy sheriffs sauntering down the other side of the street. "On your way, bum."

The man followed the glance, then faded swiftly away in the other direction. The car's owner climbed in, swearing at the heat, then checked the glove compartment. The flashlight was missing.

Checking it off to profit-and-loss, he headed for Brawley, fifteen miles north. The heat was oppressive, even for Imperial Valley. Earthquake weather, he said to himself, giving vent to the Californian's favorite superstition, then sternly denied it—that dumb fool gin peddler had put the idea in his mind. Just an ordinary Valley day, a little hotter, maybe.

His business took him to several outlying ranchos between Brawley and the Salton Sea. He was heading back toward the main highway on a worn gravel mat when the car began to waltz around as if he were driving over corduroy. He stopped the car, but the shaking continued, accompanied by a bass grumble.

Earthquake! He burst out of the car possessed only by the primal urge to get out in the open, to escape the swaying towers, the falling bricks. But there were no buildings here—nothing but open desert and irrigated fields.

He went back to the car, his stomach lurching to every following temblor. The right front tire was flat. Stone-punctured, he decided, when the car was bounced around by the first big shock.

Changing that tire almost broke his heart. He was faint from heat and exertion when he straightened up from it.

Another shock, not as heavy as the first, but heavy, panicked him again and he began to run, but he fell, tripped by the crazy galloping of the ground. He got up and went back to the car.

It had slumped drunkenly, the jack knocked over by the quake.

He wanted to abandon it, but the dust from the shocks had closed in around him like fog, without fog's blessed coolness. He knew he was several miles from town and doubted his ability to make it on foot.

He got to work, sweating and gasping. One hour and thirteen minutes after the initial shock the spare tire was in place. The ground still grumbled and shook from time to time. He resolved to drive slowly and thereby keep the car in control if another bad shock came along. The dust forced him to drive slowly, anyhow.

Moseying back toward the main highway, he was regaining his calm, when he became aware of a train in the distance. The roar increased, over the noise of the car—an express train, he decided, plunging down the valley. The thought niggled at the back of his mind for a moment, until he realized why the sound seemed wrong: Trains should not race after a quake; they should creep along, the crew alert for spread rails.

The sound was recast in his mind. *Water!*

Out of the nightmare depths of his subconscious, out of the fright of his childhood, he placed it. This was the sound after the dam broke, when, as a kid, he had been so nearly drowned. Water! A great wall of water, somewhere in the dust, hunting for him, hunting for *him!*

His foot jammed the accelerator down to the floorboards; the car bucked and promptly stalled. He started it again and strove to keep himself calm. With no spare tire and a bumpy road he could not afford the risk of too much speed. He held himself down to a crawling thirty-five miles an hour, tried to estimate the distance and direction of the water, and prayed.

The main highway jumped at him in the dust and he was almost run down by a big car roaring past to the north. A second followed it, then a vegetable truck, then the tractor unit of a semi-trailer freighter.

It was all he needed to know. He turned north.

He passed the vegetable truck and a jalopy-load of Okiestyle workers, a family. They shouted at him, but he kept going. Several cars more powerful than his passed him and he passed in turn several of the heaps used by the itinerant farm workers. After that he had the road to himself. Nothing came from the north.

The trainlike rumble behind him increased.

He peered into the rear-view mirror but could see nothing through the dusty haze.

There was a child sitting beside the road and crying— a little girl about eight. He drove on past, hardly aware of her, then braked to a stop. He told himself that she must have folks around somewhere, that it was no business of his. Cursing himself, he backed and turned, almost drove past her in the dust, then managed to turn around without backing and pulled up beside her. "Get in!"

She turned a dirty, wet, tragic face, but remained seated. "I can't. My foot hurts."

He jumped out, scooped her up and dumped her in the right-hand seat, noting as he did so that her right foot was swollen. "How did you do it?" he demanded, as he threw in the clutch.

"When the *thing* happened. Is it broke?" She was not crying now. "Are you going to take me home?"

"I—I'll take care of you. Don't ask questions."

"All right," she said doubtfully. The roar behind them was increasing. He wanted to speed up but the haze and the need to nurse his unreliable spare tire held him back. He had to swerve suddenly when a figure loomed up in the dust—a Nisei boy, hurrying toward them.

The child beside him leaned out. "That's Tommy!"

"Huh? Never mind. Just a goddam Jap."

"That's Tommy Hayakawa. He's in my class." She added. "Maybe he's looking for me."

He cursed again, under his breath, and threw the car into a turn that almost toppled it. Then he was heading back, into that awful sound.

"There he is," the child shrieked. "Tommy! Oh, Tommy!"

"Get in," he commanded, when he had stopped the car by the boy.

"Get in, Tommy," his passenger added.

The boy hesitated; the driver reached past the little girl, grabbed the boy by his shirt and dragged him in. "Want to be drowned, you fool?"

He had just shifted into second, and was still accelerating, when another figure sprang up almost in front of the car—a man, waving his arms. He caught a glimpse of the face as the car gained speed. It was the sneak thief.

His conscience was easy about that one, he thought as he drove on. Good riddance! Let the water get him.

Then the horror out of his own childhood welled up in him and he saw the face of the tramp again, in a horrible fantasy. He was struggling in the water, his bloodshot eyes bulging with terror, his gasping mouth crying wordlessly for help.

The driver was stopping the car. He did not dare turn; he backed the car, at the highest speed he could manage. It was no great distance, or else the vagrant had run after them.

The door was jerked open and the tramp lurched in. "Thanks, pal," he gasped. "Let's get out of here!"

"Right!" He glanced into the mirror, then stuck his head out and looked behind. Through the haze he saw it, a lead black wall, thirty—or was it a hundred?—feet high, rushing down on them, overwhelming them. The noise of it pounded his skull.

He gunned the car in second, then slid into high and

gave it all he had, careless of the tires. "How we doing?" he yelled.

The tramp looked out the rear window. "We're gaining. Keep it up."

He skidded around a wreck on the highway, then slowed a trifle, aware that the breakneck flight would surely lose them the questionable safety of the car if he kept it up. The little girl started to cry.

"Shut up!" he snapped.

The Nisei boy twisted around and looked behind. "What is it?" he asked in an awed voice.

The tramp answered him. "The Pacific Ocean has broken through."

"It can't be!" cried the driver. "It must be the Colorado River."

"That's no river, Mac. That's the Gulf. I was in a cantina in Centro when it came over the radio from Calexico. Warned us that the ground had dropped away to the south. Tidal wave coming. Then the station went dead." He moistened his lips. "That's why I'm here."

The driver did not answer. The vagrant went on nervously, "Guy I hitched with went on without me, when he stopped for gas in Brawley." He looked back again. "I can't see it any more."

"We've gotten away from it?"

"Hell, no. It's just as loud. I just can't see it through the murk."

They drove on. The road curved a little to the right and dropped away almost imperceptibly.

The bum looked ahead. Suddenly he yelled. "Hey! Where you going?"

"Huh?"

"You got to get off the highway, man! We're dropping back toward the Salton Sea—the lowest place in the Valley."

"There's no other place to go. We *can't* turn around."

"You can't go ahead. It's suicide!"

"We'll outrun it. North of the Salton, it's high ground again."

"Not a chance. Look at your gas gauge."

The gauge was fluttering around the left side of the dial. Two gallons, maybe less. Enough to strand them by the sunken shores of the Salton Sea. He stared at it in an agony of indecision.

"Gotta cut off to the left," his passenger was saying. "Side road. Follow it up toward the hills."

"Where?"

"Coming up. I know this road. I'll watch for it."

When he turned into the side road, he realized sickly that his course was now nearly parallel to the hungry flood south of them. But the road climbed.

He looked to the left and tried to see the black wall of water, the noise of which beat loud in his ears, but the road demanded his attention. "Can you see it?" he yelled to the tramp.

"Yes! Keep trying, pal!"

He nodded and concentrated on the hills ahead. The hills must surely be above sea level, he told himself. On and on he drove, through a timeless waste of dust and heat and roar. The grade increased, then suddenly the car broke over a rise and headed down into a wash—a shallow arroyo that should have been dry, but was not.

He was into water before he knew it, hub high and higher. He braked and tried to back. The engine coughed and stalled.

The tramp jerked open the door, dragged the two children out, and, with one under each arm, splashed his way back to higher ground. The driver tried to start the car, then saw frantically that the rising water was up above the floorboards.

He jumped out, stumbled to his knees in water waist-deep, got to his feet, and struggled after them.

The tramp had set the children down on a little rise and was looking around. "We got to get out of here," the car owner gasped.

The tramp shook his head. "No good. Look around you."

To the south, the wall of water had broken around the rise on which they stood. A branch had sluiced between them and the hills, filling the wash in which the car lay stalled. The main body of the rushing waters had passed east of them, covering the highway they had left, and sweeping on toward the Salton Sea.

Even as he watched, the secondary flood down the wash returned to the parent body. They were cut off, surrounded by the waters.

He wanted to scream, to throw himself into the opaque turbulence and get it over. Perhaps he did scream. He realized that the tramp was shaking him by the shoulder.

"Take it easy, pal. We've got a couple of throws left."

"Huh?" He wiped his eyes. "What do we do?"

"I want my mother," the little girl said decisively.

The tramp reached down and patted her absent-mindedly.

Tommy Hayakawa put his arm around her. "I'll take care of you, Laura," he said gravely.

The water was already over the top of the car and rising. The boiling head of the flood was well past them; its thunder was lessening; the waters rose quietly—but they rose.

"We can't stay here," he persisted.

"We'll have to," the tramp answered . . .

Their living space grew smaller, hardly thirty feet by fifty. They were not alone now. A coyote, jack rabbits, creepers, crawlers, and gnawers, all the poor relations of the desert, were forced equally back into the narrowing circle of dry land. The coyote ignored the rabbits; they ignored the coyote. The highest point of their island was surmounted by a rough concrete post about four feet high, an obelisk with a brass plate set in its side. He read it twice before the meaning of the words came to him.

It was a bench mark, stating, as well as latitude and longitude, that this spot, this line engraved in brass, was "sea level." When it soaked into his confused brain he pointed it out to his companion. "Hey! Hey, look! We're going to make it! The water won't come any higher!"

The tramp looked. "Yes, I know. I read it. But it doesn't mean anything. That's the level it used to be before the earthquake."

"But—"

"It may be higher—or lower. We'll find out."

The waters still came up. They were ankle-deep at

sundown. The rabbits and the other small things were gradually giving up. They were in an unbroken waste of water, stretching from the Chocolate Mountains beyond where the Salton Sea had been, to the nearer hills on the west. The coyote slunk up against their knees, dog fashion, then appeared to make up its mind, for it slipped into the water and struck out toward the hills. They could see its out-thrust head for a long time, until it was just a dot on the water in the gathering darkness.

When the water was knee-deep, each man took one of the children in his arms. They braced themselves against the stability of the concrete post, and waited, too tired for panic. They did not talk. Even the children had not talked much since abandoning the car.

It was getting dark. The tramp spoke up suddenly. "Can you pray?"

"Uh—not very well."

"Okay. I'll try, then." He took a deep breath. "Merciful Father, Whose all-seeing eye notes even the sparrow in its flight, have mercy on these Thy unworthy servants. Deliver them from this peril, if it be Thy will." He paused, and then added, "And make it as fast as You can, please. Amen."

The darkness closed in, complete and starless. They could not see the water, but they could feel it and hear it. It was warm—it felt no worse when it soaked their armpits than it had around their ankles. They had the kids on their shoulders now, with their backs braced against the submerged post. There was little current.

Once something bumped against them in the darkness—

a dead steer, driftwood, a corpse—they had no way of knowing. It nudged them and was gone. Once he thought he saw a light, and said suddenly to the tramp, "Have you still got that flashlight you swiped from me?"

There was a long silence and a strained voice answered, "You recognized me."

"Of course. Where's the flashlight?"

"I traded it for a drink in Centro.

"But, look, Mac," the voice went on reasonably, "if I hadn't borrowed it, it would be in your car. It wouldn't be here. And if I *did* have it in my pocket, it'd be soaked and wouldn't work."

"Oh, forget it!"

"Okay." There was silence for a while, then the voice went on, "Pal, could you hold both the kids a while?"

"I guess so. Why?"

"This water is still coming up. It'll be over our heads, maybe. You hang onto the kids; I'll boost myself up on the post. I'll sit on it and wrap my legs around it. Then you hand me the kids. That way we gain maybe eighteen inches or two feet."

"And what happens to me?"

"You hang onto my shoulders and float with your head out of the water."

"Well—we'll try it."

It worked. The kids clung to the tramp's sides, supported by water and by his arms. The driver hung onto the tramp where he could, first to his belt, then, as the waters rose and his toes no longer touched bottom, to the collar of his coat.

They were still alive.

"I wish it would get light. It's worse in the darkness."

"Yeah," said the tramp. "If it was light, maybe somebody 'ud see us."

"How?"

"Airplane, maybe. They always send out airplanes, in floods."

He suddenly began to shake violently, as the horror came over him, and the memory of another flood when there had been no rescuing airplanes.

The tramp said sharply, "What's the matter, Mac? Are you cracking up?"

"No, I'm all right. I just hate water."

"Want to swap around? You hold the kids for a while and I'll hang on and float."

"Uh . . . No, we might drop one. Stay where you are."

"We can make it. The change'll do you good." The tramp shook the children. "Hey, wake up! Wake up, honey—and hold tight."

The kids were transferred to his shoulders while he gripped the post with his knees and the tramp steadied him with an arm. Then he eased himself cautiously onto the top of the post, as the tramp got off and floated free, save for one anchoring hand. "You all right?" he said to the tramp.

The hand squeezed his shoulder in the darkness. "Sure. Got a snootful of water."

"Hang on."

"Don't worry—I will!"

He was shorter than the tramp; he had to sit erect to keep his head out of water. The children clung tightly. He kept them boosted high.

Presently the tramp spoke. "You wearing a belt?"

"Yes. Why?"

"Hold still." He felt a second hand fumbling at his waist, then his trousers loosened as the belt came away. "I'm going to strap your legs to the post. That's the bad part about it; your legs cramp. Hold tight now. I'm going under."

He felt hands under water, fumbling at his legs. Then there was the tension of the belt being tightened around his knees. He relaxed to the pressure. It *was* a help; he found he could hold his position without muscular effort.

The tramp broke water near him. "Where are you?" the voice was panicky.

"Here! Over here!" he tried to peer into the inky darkness; it was hopeless. "Over this way!" The splashing seemed to come closer. He shouted again, but no hand reached out of the darkness. He continued to shout, then shouted and listened intermittently. It seemed to him that he heard splashing long after the sound had actually ceased.

He stopped shouting only when his voice gave out. Little Laura was sobbing on his shoulder. Tommy was trying to get her to stop. He could tell from their words that they had not understood what had happened and he did not try to explain.

When the water dropped down to his waist, he moved the kids so that they sat on his lap. This let him rest his arms, which had grown almost unbearably tired as the receding water ceased to support the weight of the children. The water dropped still more, and the half dawn showed him that the ground beneath him was, if not dry, at least free from flood.

He shook Tommy awake. "I can't get down, kid. Can you unstrap me?"

The boy blinked and rubbed his eyes. He looked around and seemed to recall his circumstances without dismay. "Sure. Put me down."

The boy loosened the buckle after some difficulty and the man cautiously unwound himself from his perch. His legs refused him when he tried to stand; they let him and the girl sprawl in the mud.

"Are you hurt?" he asked her as he sat up.

"No," she answered soberly.

He looked around. It was getting steadily lighter and he could see the hills to the west; it now appeared that the water no longer extended between the hills and themselves. To the east was another story; the Salton Sea no longer existed as such. An unbroken sheet of water stretched from miles to the north clear to the southern horizon.

His car was in sight; the wash was free of water except for casual pools. He walked down toward the automobile, partly to take the knots out of his legs, partly to see if the car could ever be salvaged. It was there that he found the tramp.

The body lay wedged against the right rear wheel, as if carried down there by undertow.

He walked back toward the kids. "Stay away from the car," he ordered. "Wait here. I've got something to do." He went back to the car and found the keys still in the ignition lock. He opened the trunk with some difficulty and got out a short spade he kept for desert mishaps.

It was not much of a grave, just a shallow trench in the

wet sand, deep enough to receive and cover a man, but he promised himself that he would come back and do better. He had no time now. The waters, he thought, would be back with high tide. He must get himself and the children to the hills.

Once the body was out of sight, he called out to the boy and the girl, "You can come here now." He had one more chore. There was drift about, yucca stalks, bits of wood. He selected two pieces of unequal length, then dug around in his tool chest for bits of wire. He wired the short piece across the longer, in a rough cross, then planted the cross in the sand near the head of the grave.

He stepped back and looked at it, the kids at his side.

His lips moved silently for a moment, then he said, "Come on, kids. We got to get out of here." He picked up the little girl, took the boy by the hand, and they walked away to the west, the Sun shining on their backs.

Afterword

by Robert Buettner

Robert Buettner's first novel, *Orphanage*, nominated for the Quill Award as best Science Fiction, Fantasy and Horror novel of 2004, was compared favorably to Robert Heinlein's *Starship Troopers* by the *Washington Post, Denver Post, Sci-Fi Channel's Science Fiction Weekly*, and others. His sixth novel, and first in his *Orphan's Legacy* series, will be published by Baen Books in 2011.

Today a wooden chair sits on the second floor of Thomas Edison's laboratory, nailed to the floor. The chair is pushed back from a tool-strewn table, as though someone had stepped away from his work momentarily. Minutes earlier, Edison had, in fact, put down those tools and stepped away. Henry Ford, who had rebuilt Edison's lab outside Detroit, then ordered the chair nailed down. Edison had just reenacted the moment half a century earlier when he invented the electric light.

They say that, while the electric light's inventor was a genius, all who thereafter strove to improve it were mere electricians. Similarly, Robert Heinlein's art and craft did for speculative fiction what Edison's electric light did for midnight. So reading this Heinlein collection is, for me as a speculative fiction writer, like running my fingers across the wood of Edison's chair, and finding it still warm.

I don't mean Heinlein's predictive genius about science or about social change. Others have chronicled how much Heinlein got right (in 1939 he postulated that in 2001 third-world terrorists would attack New York with two aircraft) and wrong (how was your vacation on the Moon?)

I mean Heinlein's genius at what Stephen King calls "the art and craft of telling stories on paper," which, King laments, "Nobody ever asks [us] about."

Of course not, you say. Don't stories, like the eighteen 1941 through 1957 Heinleins collected here, speak for themselves? Sure. So, why do you care about this Afterword?

Well, this Afterword presumes to reverse-engineer some of Heinlein's contributions to the nuts and bolts of speculative fiction writing. You care about that if you're a closet author. And based on my fan mail, lots of you, especially the ones enthusiastic enough to read afterwords, are.

Even if you don't aspire to publish this generation's *Stranger in a Strange Land*, you may also itch to learn how deliberately all those writers you've been reading since kindergarten have been manipulating you.

More importantly, this Afterword reveals the one story in this collection that exposes the core of what

evergreens Heinlein's work even against the libraries full
of speculative fiction that have followed it. I'll bet (no
peeking) it's the last story you would have guessed.

First, my ground rules; so you can read ahead without
stopping to type me grumpy email.

1. I interchangeably call what Heinlein wrote both
"speculative fiction" and "science fiction." But *you* know
that Heinlein owned the authorial patent on keeping his
science accurate. He wrote to his agent, Lurton
Blassingame, in 1948:

> I know what I am talking about—I am a
> mechanical engineer, a ballistician, a student of
> reaction engines, and an amateur astronomer . . .
> I won't give an editor any Buck Rogers nonsense.

So, I must be an idiot. Okay. But Heinlein elaborated
in 1949:

> Speculative fiction (I prefer that term to
> science fiction) is also concerned with sociology,
> psychology, esoteric aspects of biology, impact of
> terrestrial culture on the other cultures we may
> encounter when we conquer space, etc., without
> end. However, speculative fiction is *not* fantasy
> fiction, as it rules out the use of anything as
> material which violates established scientific fact,
> laws of nature, call it what you will . . .

2. *You* know that I have miscredited Heinlein with a
literary invention that somebody else did earlier. So, I
must be an idiot. Okay.

But most editors and authors agree that there arc no
new stories and no new techniques. Not since the first
hunters whoppered up their campfire retellings of the

first mammoth hunts, anyway. I am simply cataloguing here things that Heinlein did earlier, and/or better, and/or more influentially, than anybody else in this genre.

3. *Your* favorite Heinlein brilliantly illustrates a point I make. But I haven't even mentioned it. So, I must be an idiot. Again, okay.

But this Afterword covers only, well, the words it comes after. Some of my favorite Heinlein is missing, too.

4. I sometimes pigeonhole Heinlein's writing into classroom techniques. Yet *you* know that Heinlein was a self-taught genius, not a formulaic technician! In 1947 he wrote to his agent:

> I'm afraid of coaching, of writers' classes, of writers' magazines, of books on how to write. They give me centipede trouble—you know the yarn about the centipede who was asked how he managed all his feet? He tried to answer, stopped to think about it, and was never able to walk another step.

So, . . . sigh.

But Heinlein was nothing at his typewriter if not a student of his craft. He continued in the same letter to his agent:

> I do get a great deal of help from studying other writers' stories . . . I find such study of what they have *done* more use to me than their discussions of how they do it.

So, without further ado, let's see what Heinlein did, and thereby understand how—and even why—he did it.

Let Us Begin With Beginnings

Every successful writer has learned, by instinct plus practice, like Heinlein, or otherwise, that first words matter most. Why? Because the crystal insight of Chapter Eight is lost to readers who quit after Chapter One, or paragraph one, or even line one, because it bored or confused them.

The ultimate test of a successful beginning is whether the reader keeps reading. Heinlein wrote in 1972, "[I]f a writer does not entertain his readers, all he is producing is paper dirty on one side." But other tests and yardsticks against which to test a story abound, and Heinlein mastered most of those that he didn't invent.

A beginning recipe suggested often to new writers is: "Begin by answering three questions, that orient the reader, then compel reading forward: Where am I? Whose head am I in? What has changed or is about to change?" Bonus points for doing so with brevity and style.

Heinlein may never have articulated the recipe, or read it, but he demonstrated it brilliantly in 1952's "The Year of the Jackpot":

> At first, Potiphar Breen did not notice the girl who was undressing.
>
> She was standing at a bus stop only ten feet away. He was indoors . . .

Can any reader stop after that? And bonus points for brevity, as well as for the protagonist's name.

Heinlein may have mistrusted writing coaches' calculations, but if you think that "Jackpot"'s beginning was uncalculated, read "Sky Lift," published a year later, in 1953:

"All torch pilots! Report to the Commodore!"
The call echoed through Earth Satellite Station.

Joe Appleby flipped off the shower to listen.
"You don't mean me," he said happily, "I'm on
leave—but . . ."

Those examples suggest that Heinlein had the "three
question" beginning down pat from his first try. However,
consider his earlier (1942) "Goldfish Bowl," when
neophyte Heinlein had been published for barely two
years:

On the horizon lay the immobile cloud which
capped the incredible waterspouts known as the
Pillars of Hawaii.

Captain Blake lowered his binoculars. "There
they stand, gentlemen."

In addition to the naval personnel of the
watch, the bridge of the hydrographic survey ship
U.S.S. *Mahan* held two civilians; the captain's
words were addressed to them.

Heinlein's beginning narrative ambles on from there
for a full page. Finally, we learn that a ship's boat is about
to be launched to approach the waterspouts, which are
newly-appeared and apparently dangerous. We have been
introduced to several characters, but we still don't know
which one we're supposed to feel for (it isn't Captain
Blake). Also, compared to the two later examples, this
beginning earns no brevity bonus points.

In other words, in 1942, Heinlein was feeling his way
into the "three questions" beginning technique. By 1952
he mastered it. By 1953 he executed the technique as
casually as his space pilots punched out their course tapes

(Heinlein anticipated plenty, but he muffed the paradigm shift from analog to digital information transfer).

If you still doubt that Heinlein consciously practiced now-standard fiction techniques like the "three questions" beginning, reread the beginnings of "By His Bootstraps," "Space Jockey," "Logic of Empire," "'It's Great to Be Back!,'" and "'We Also Walk Dogs.'"

But there's more than one way to hook readers, and in the other stories in this collection Heinlein demonstrated how easily he could reel us in with other baits.

"Once upon a time, an unhappy princess . . ." is a technique successful writers have been using since the brothers Grimm. It works when the person and story promised embody majesty and an unanswered question. Thus begins 1947's "The Green Hills of Earth":

> This is the story of Rhysling, the Blind Singer of the Spaceways—but not the official version. You sang his words in school . . .

"The Long Watch" (1949) hooks us in the same way:

> Nine ships blasted off from Moon Base. Once in space, eight of them formed a globe around the smallest . . . [that] displayed the insignia of an admiral—yet . . . she carried nothing but a lead coffin . . .

Sometimes the technique that hooks us isn't the story, but the storyteller's distinctive voice. Especially if it's a young voice. A young viewpoint captivates us because we've all been of that certain age when the commonplace can be exciting—while our parental units can be so obtuse.

Heinlein used the technique as early as 1948, in "The Black Pits of Luna."

The morning after we got to the Moon we went over to Rutherford . . . it looked like just about my only chance to get out on the surface of the Moon. Luna City is all right, I guess . . .

By 1957, Heinlein had published ten of his so-called "juvenile" novels, and had adolescent voice (at least within the censored parameters of the fifties) down cold. "The Menace From Earth" begins:

My name is Holly Jones and I'm fifteen. I'm very intelligent but it doesn't show, because I look like an underdone angel. Insipid.

In sum, Heinlein chose and executed those most important first words with the skill and flare that a chess master applies to standard openings.

But well begun is, at most, half done.

Heinlein—Master of the Middle

The middle game in chess, or mid story in fiction, is where options multiply, variables explode, and where rote chess players and average writers founder. Conversely, the innovative middle is where Heinlein shone like the grand master he was.

Perhaps Heinlein's greatest innovation in speculative fiction affects the middles of his stories. But you won't find it in any one of them. Heinlein's Future History chart prefaces the collection assembled under the title *The Green Hills of Earth*. As Bill Patterson explains in his introduction to this collection, the chart first appeared back in 1941, in *Astounding Science Fiction*.

But the chart became more widely known much later, when Heinlein's subsequent stories and novels populated updated versions of the Chart during the near-decade bookended by his *The Green Hills of Earth* collection in 1951 and by his *The Menace From Earth* collection in 1959.

The chart was "history," but the interwoven story-to-story references often added color and texture to individual stories, rather than substance. In 1941's "Logic of Empire," Heinlein's protagonist, enslaved on Venus during the early 2000s (Heinlein also whiffed on the Solar-System-Turns-Out-to-Be-Dead-Rocks future), finds his fellow slave's chorus of a "a ditty entitled 'That Redheaded Venusburg Gal' . . . inexcusably vulgar." Six years later, in 1946's "The Green Hills of Earth," Heinlein finally gave us the backstory that "Hills'" protagonist, Rhysling, the late and famous Blind Singer of the Spaceways, wrote the unpublished "That Redheaded Venusburg Gal." But again, the ditty can't be quoted "in a family magazine."

Heinlein spent years as a young sailor, no doubt exposed to, well, all that implies. His later work embraces all manner of sexual liaison. Yet he was described as so formal that he would dress for dinner in the jungle. Wouldn't you love to read the lyrics to "That Redheaded Venusburg Gal"? But I digress.

Beyond bawdy lyrics and recurring locales like Venusburg, broad social and technologic changes animated Heinlein's future history stories. Venus was rebelling against an Earth in the thrall of a religious dictator. Rocket travel became commonplace, then was suspended for a time, for reasons not disclosed on the chart. It all subtly, often in ways explained only in later works, fit together.

Good heavens! This simply wasn't how American short stories were written in the fifties. The short story was bite-sized popular entertainment, not so different from the doughnut-holed pop-single forty-five rpm records of the time.

The stories in this collection originally appeared not just in science fiction pulps, but in the mass-circulated *Saturday Evening Post*, *Town and Country*, *Blue Book* (a monthly of short fiction by the likes of Edgar Rice Burroughs, Agatha Christie, and Philip Wylie, as well as Heinlein), *American Legion Magazine*, and *Argosy* (the most literary of a pulpy, pre-Playboy pin-up magazine category called "Men's Adventure").

Like those forty-five rpm records, Fifties science fiction short stories enjoyed the wide consumption and ephemeral shelf life of glazed doughnuts, and were as unrelated one to another. When Heinlein wove his discrete short stories into an organic—albeit ambiguous—whole, his little chart upended the way the institution of science fiction thought about itself.

To find an analogous impact in another field, say, popular music, one must look ahead a decade, to 1967. Songs that would have been released as unrelated forty five rpm single "cuts" were for the first time woven into an organic—albeit ambiguous—whole by the Beatles' *Sergeant Pepper* album. What a concept! *Rolling Stone* magazine later named *Sergeant Pepper* the greatest record album of all time. That's not to say that the Beatles copied Heinlein. Nor do I suggest that the Future History sold, or should have sold, like the Beatles. But it all validates the maxim that great minds think alike. Then others follow.

Today, books, stories and series written in a "common universe," where history and physical rules remain constant, permeate speculative fiction. Shelvesful of *Star Wars* sequels, prequels and parallel-quels flood space opera. More fantasy worlds than you can shake an orb at have swollen into never-ending sagas. Ditto all those post-apocalyptic, dystopian futures. Nowadays everybody has a chart.

But Heinlein's innovations in the middles weren't all global strokes. Space prevents discussing them all, but I can't leave middles without discussing at least one of Heinlein's subtle little strokes.

Many critics credit Heinlein with a device now so common to the speculative fiction landscape that it seems no more "inventable" than the sky. It is the device of addressing the reader as though the reader and the narrator were conversing as contemporaries in a future time.

For example, "Ordeal in Space" was published during 1948, but was set, according to the Future History chart, a half century later in the early 2000s. In passing, the narrator reminds the reader, "Only a small part of Great New York was roofed over in those days." No long description. No footnote backstory to slow pace. The future landscape is painted in, but it flashes past like the blur outside a monorail train window.

The technique is a Heinlein trademark, but you won't find many more examples in this collection. Why not?

First, five of the eight stories in the *Menace* collection are set in the time in which Heinlein wrote them. No future, no history to hearken back to. Those non-future stories are "The Year of the Jackpot," "By His Bootstraps,"

"Goldfish Bowl," "Project Nightmare," and "Water Is for Washing." Therefore, of course, those five stories didn't make the Future History chart, either.

Second, of the eleven stories in this collection that *did* make the Future History chart, ten were published before 1950. Remember that it wasn't until nearly 1940 that Heinlein's first stories were published. From 1943 through 1946, Heinlein was preoccupied with his World War II defense production job, and published nothing. So these ten stories were written while Heinlein was still a relative neophyte, still developing and perfecting the techniques we came to regard as his trademarks.

So. What else?

Endings, and More Importantly, Ends

I mean here not the clever twist or the lump-in-the-throat finale. Reread "Columbus Was a Dope" for an example of the former sort of ending, and "Sky Lift" for an example of the latter sort. Heinlein ended his stories as well as any producer of shorts, but that wasn't what made his best stories special.

I mean the ends that animated Heinlein's imagination. He repeatedly and famously claimed that he wrote merely "to entertain and to buy groceries." But he also noted that "a writer can indulge in [something more] if he clears the first two hurdles." It is that indulgence, that *end*, that separates a good Heinlein story from a NASA-produced cartoon that shows us how a Mars landing would look.

I don't mean Heinlein advocating sex among pretty

much everybody, nor his belief that society should consist of each Libertarian Everyman defending his homestead with his personal minefield and razor wire. Heinlein *did* stump for such causes in his later novel-length fiction. But he didn't in these stories, and I promised you earlier that I wouldn't stray far beyond these stories. He acknowledged that he never could have sold those later novels if he had not, over a career, "developed . . . a solid enough commercial market to risk taking a flyer."

Heinlein developed that commercial market because in the Fifties he produced fiction the ends of which honored two maxims that many successful writers live by: First, "commercial fiction is what characters will do next, and why." Second, "we read fiction for assurance that people like us, in circumstances we will never endure, will do the right thing."

I don't know whether Heinlein ever heard those maxims. But I know his best Fifties fiction met those ends. That fiction opened doors that let him publish his socially adventurous Sixties and Seventies novels.

"The Green Hills of Earth" is likely the best-known, perhaps the most representative, and arguably the best-loved Fifties-vintage story in this collection. I don't believe that is so because the story is set within Heinlein's elaborately crafted future history. I don't believe that is so because Heinlein's underlying math and radiation-science conformed rigorously to the science of the time of writing.

I believe "The Green Hills of Earth" earned its collection-title podium spot because in it Heinlein palpably expressed his conviction that a hero lives in everyone.

"The Green Hills of Earth" tells the story of Rhysling,

a reprobate slacker, a bawdy balladeer, who, when the chips are down (for Heinlein's heroes, the chips are always down, eventually) makes the ultimate sacrifice for the greater good. Readers bought that idea in the fifties, and they buy it today.

A similar tale, and one perhaps closer to the heart of former junior naval officer Heinlein, is "The Long Watch." Johnny Dahlquist is no reprobate, but he is just a wet-behind-the-ears kid officer. Nonetheless, he stands up to a nuke-brandishing junta of senior officers, and dies foiling them.

Heinlein's unlikely heroes always lay it on the line, but they don't always pay the ultimate price.

In "Gentlemen, Be Seated," sandhog laborer Fatso Konski interposes himself between tragedy and the Moon's vacuum, his considerable backside filling the role of the little Dutch boy's finger in the dike. Fatso and the narrator live to tell the tale. So does young Dickie Logan, when he rescues his runt little brother from a hole out on the surface of the Moon, in "The Black Pits of Luna." We wanted to know what each of those people, like us but in situations we would never endure, would do next, and why. Heinlein reassured us that they would do the right thing.

By contrast, Heinlein could and did write merely-clever stories without heroes. His shortest, a virtual *haiku* at less than 2,500 words, "Columbus Was a Dope," is everyday banter in a bar about how stupid and risky space exploration is—but the bar turns out to be on the Moon. It's sly. It's crisp. It's succinct. But it is never so compelling as his stories of characters under stress.

And that's all I have to say.

Oh, that's right. I promised to tell you which story in this collection reveals the most about what mattered to Heinlein, what mattered in his work, and why that work still matters to us, today.

That story is "Water Is for Washing."

I'm kidding, right? It's not in Heinlein's future history. It wasn't published in the *Saturday Evening Post*, or even in a self-respecting science fiction pulp. It ran in *Argosy*, amid illustrated stories about Nazis torturing damsels in distress, damsels drawn as naked as the law allowed in 1947. "Water Is for Washing" is tacked on to the end of *The Menace From Earth* collection like a leftover Post-It note. It's not science fiction, or even speculative fiction, for crying out loud. And yet . . .

The story starts with bar banter about hydrophobia. A flashlight goes missing from the viewpoint character's glove compartment. Then an earthquake floods California's Imperial Valley, with a rumble like an onrushing train. The tramp (PC translation: itinerant homeless person) who stole the flashlight sacrifices his life, and saves two children he has never seen before from the rising waters. The end.

Not exactly. In April, 1978, Midshipman Heinlein returned to the U.S. Naval Academy and addressed its cadets. His always-fragile health had failed. His career had foundered, as he had produced no fiction for five years. Heinlein had a reputation for saying exactly what he believed. But, under the circumstances, one suspects he never spoke truer than on that day in Annapolis. He told the Midshipmen:

> In my home town sixty years ago when I was

a child, my mother and father used to take me and my brothers and sisters out to Swope Park on Sunday afternoons. It was a wonderful place for kids, with picnic grounds and lakes and a zoo. But a railroad line cut right through it.

One Sunday afternoon a young married couple were crossing these tracks. She apparently did not watch her step, for she managed to catch her foot in the frog of a switch to a siding and could not pull it free. Her husband stopped to help her.

But try as they might they could not get her foot loose. While they were working at it, a tramp showed up, walking the ties. He joined the husband in trying to pull the young woman's foot loose. No luck—

Out of sight around the curve a train whistled. Perhaps there would have been time to run and flag it down, perhaps not. In any case, both men went right ahead trying to pull her free . . . and the train hit them.

The wife was killed, the husband was mortally injured and died later, the tramp was killed—and testimony showed that neither man made the slightest effort to save himself.

The husband's behavior was heroic . . . but what we expect of a husband toward his wife: his right, and his proud privilege, to die for his woman. But what of the nameless stranger? Up to the very last second he could have jumped clear. He did not. He was still trying to save this woman he had never seen before in his life, right up to the very instant the train killed him. And that's all we'll ever know about him.

This is how a man dies. This is how a man . . . lives!

—Robert Buettner
Woodstock, Georgia
October 15, 2009

Epic Urban Adventure by a New Star of Fantasy

DRAW ONE IN THE DARK

by Sarah A. Hoyt

Every one of us has a beast inside. But for Kyrie Smith, the beast is no metaphor. Thrust into an ever-changing world of shifters, where shape-shifting dragons, giant cats and other beasts wage a secret war behind humanity's back, Kyrie tries to control her inner animal and remain human as best she can....

"Analytically, it's a tour de force: logical, built from assumptions, with no contradictions, which is astonishing given the subject matter. It's also gripping enough that I finished it in one day."
—Jerry Pournelle

1-4165-2092-9 • $25.00

WEBSCRIPTIONS:
The Last Word in EBOOKS

FREE EBOOKS FOR YOU!

Just type in the first word from page 224 of the volume now in your hands and email it to: ebooks@baen.com and you will receive immediate, no-strings access to a full month of publications from your favorite publisher.

(Ahem, "favorite publisher": that's us, Baen Books. ;)